Dennis K. Hausker is a retired financial consultant and Vietnam war veteran who graduated from Michigan State University in 1969. He is an avid fan of Spartan sports and enjoys traveling, attending family events, and savoring good food. Dennis met his wife, who hails from Maine and was a warm and nurturing teacher, while they were both in college. They have been happily married ever since. Dennis is known for his positive attitude, which he believes is the key to a fulfilling life.

I always dedicate to my wife.

Dennis K. Hausker

ANYA

AUSTIN MACAULEY PUBLISHERS™

LONDON • CAMBRIDGE • NEW YORK • SHARJAH

Copyright © Dennis K. Hausker 2023

All rights reserved. No part of this publication may be reproduced, distributed, or transmitted in any form or by any means, including photocopying, recording, or other electronic or mechanical methods, without the prior written permission of the publisher, except in the case of brief quotations embodied in critical reviews and certain other non-commercial uses permitted by copyright law. For permission requests, write to the publisher.

Any person who commits any unauthorized act in relation to this publication may be liable to criminal prosecution and civil claims for damages.

This is a work of fiction. Names, characters, businesses, places, events, locales, and incidents are either the products of the author's imagination or used in a fictitious manner. Any resemblance to actual persons, living or dead, or actual events is purely coincidental.

Ordering Information
Quantity sales: Special discounts are available on quantity purchases by corporations, associations, and others. For details, contact the publisher at the address below.

Publisher's Cataloging-in-Publication data
Hausker, Dennis K.
Anya

ISBN 9781685623265 (Paperback)
ISBN 9781685623272 (ePub e-book)

Library of Congress Control Number: 2023902218

www.austinmacauley.com/us

First Published 2023
Austin Macauley Publishers LLC
40 Wall Street, 33rd Floor, Suite 3302
New York, NY 10005
USA

mail-usa@austinmacauley.com
+1 (646) 5125767

Chapter One

Taking a deep breath, he stepped out of the classroom building and walked briskly toward the student union. Peter glanced up at the overcast sky. There was no sign the drizzle would stop any time soon, as the fast-moving cloud bank stretched across the entire horizon. The smell of water was heavy in the air.

It wasn't a drenching downpour, but a strong enough rainfall to be annoying, since he'd forgotten his umbrella that morning when he'd left the dorm. It was one of those steady, all-day occurrences, with no relief.

His pace increased in direct proportion to the amount of water rolling down his neck and under his shirt collar.

"Damn," he muttered, hunching his neck in a futile attempt to prevent the drips from rolling down his back. The ball cap he wore could only protect his head.

Arriving at the student union and hustling in the front door, he went up the steps, headed past the lobby filled with sofas, decorative paintings, and numerous students lounging around, and went up another set of stairs to the food court. The joint seating area was already bustling with noisy fellow students claiming open tables for a lunchtime snack between classes.

Viewing the array of various food types, he pondered for only a short time.

Opting for a slice of pizza and a cola, he purchased his meal and went to find a seat. By now, the large room was mostly full. Glancing around, toward the back, he noticed a coed he recognized sitting alone. On impulse, he weaved his way through the mass of bodies and approached her table.

"Hi, Anya. Can I join you?"

She eyed him cautiously. Finally, she shrugged her shoulders. Unbeknownst to Peter, from her background and experiences, she had little trust in strangers. For her, nothing was different here, even though he was a classmate.

Peter sat down. "This kind of rain seems to find every possible opening to get in. I hate to sit through classes in wet clothes."

Anya looked up from her meal with a dour expression. "I'm not a blonde."

"Correct. You're not a blonde." Peter eyed her quizzically. An obvious statement, it made no sense without a context.

They stared for a moment before Peter smiled.

She added, "I'm not a twig."

"You're not a twig. That's also true." He gave her an amused look, curious as to where this was going.

"What do you want?"

Peter chuckled. "Right now, to eat my lunch, just like you. Am I missing something here?"

"I don't understand American boys, sometimes. I've learned English, but you people can have subtle meanings that elude me in what you say and do."

Frowning, he replied, "Eh...that's not a problem for me. Is that an issue for you, right now this minute? We're just sharing a table, eating lunch. There's nothing subtle about that."

"Do you understand I'm not from here?"

"I do."

"I'm Anya Seminova, from Russia." She eyed him for a reaction.

"I realize that, Anya. Do you imagine that fact is problematic for me?"

"Many Americans don't like Russia, or Russians." Eyeing him closely to gauge his reaction, she waited.

"You're probably right about some, but I'm not one of them. Have you had some troubles with this? You're acting defensive."

She shrugged. "I've learned to be cautious with strangers. What's in their minds, well, I don't take chances."

"Okay...by the way, my name is Peter Brown." Uncertain with how to react, verbally he stumbled forward awkwardly.

"I know who you are."

"Is that good or bad?"

"I haven't decided."

"Wow, I wasn't expecting this verbal sword fight, although I should have probably known. In class, you seem to delight in challenging whatever I say."

"That's because you're wrong in class."

Peter laughed. "I'm wrong? I'm never right?"

"Yes, that's true." Anya smirked.

"Right, Anya. For the record, I beg to differ."

She chuckled, smirking again.

"You laughed…so is this some level of rapport, ma'am?"

"What do you think?"

"I believe you think you can toy with me. Do you honestly feel I'm stupid or something?"

"I didn't say you're stupid; you're just wrong."

"So…apparently, I follow this trail of bread crumbs of yours, is that it? What would be waiting for me at the end of that trail?" It was his attempt to sound cool to a coed he instantly liked.

"I guess you'd find out, if you got there."

"If? Wow, you see me pretty low in the food chain, eh?"

"I repeat. What do you want from me?"

"Other than the enjoyment of this verbal evisceration, I guess I'd like to see if I can get out of your mind's lower-life-form category and into the mammal class. Does that seem like a reasonable goal?"

She laughed. "You are a silly man."

"Thank you, I think. Was that a compliment, of sorts?"

"What do you think?"

"Answer a question with a question, very shrewd. Listen, if I'd come on to you, like, 'What's your sign?' what would you have said?"

"My sign…it's a fist."

They both laughed.

"Anya, you're a trip."

For the first time, her cautious facial expression softened. The guarded hostility finally melted away as he saw the slightest hint of a smile. He decided to let her initiate any conversation until the meal was finished. She said nothing.

"I must go to my next class, Peter."

"Likewise; it was nice sharing lunch. Have you decided if you'll allow me to live?"

"Perhaps, we'll see."

"I guess I'll see you in class tomorrow."

"You will."

Peter walked with her out of the union building, where they turned in opposite directions to head to their next classes.

He smiled, replaying the encounter in his mind. His interest had been piqued.

#

The steady rain continued for the entire afternoon. Going back to the dorm after his last class was no less unpleasant, as the rain had increased slightly. Walking into the dorm, he glanced down the hallway, noticing Allison Smithson walking with a guy. Peter's high school sweetheart, she always stirred his emotions. Unfortunately, in his mind, that was still a one-way street.

The guy walking with her was the type who would be walking with her: athletic body, alpha male, brash, cocky—the whole mantra Peter wasn't.

"Forget it, Peter," he muttered, self-consciously. "That's a lost cause."

His mind could grasp the concept, but his emotions seemed eternally stuck in neutral about her.

As if she sensed him, Allison suddenly looked back. Her smug smile was annoying. Peter turned away and went to the stairs to walk up to his second-floor dorm room.

"Hey, Bob."

"Come on, Peter. I'm hungry."

"When are you not hungry?"

"I love food. I'm a 'fleshy' person. What can I say, so sue me."

"I can't afford a lawyer for a frivolous lawsuit. Give me a moment to get a towel to dry off."

Shortly, they went down to the cafeteria and sat down with some friends from their floor.

Bob eyed Peter. "What's up? You seem distracted. Is it that girl from your high school again?"

"Not totally. I did see her smirk at me, but I ate lunch today with Anya. It was sort of invigorating."

"Anya?"

"She's in my political science class. She's from Russia."

"And…"

"And, she's smart. She's very pretty, but I really like smart."

Allison walked past, walking with the same guy. She glanced at Peter, like she was counting coup. He glowered for a moment at her but looked away when the guy looked at him.

Bob spoke up. "What did you ever see in her, Peter?"

Peter chuckled. "Other than the fact that she is drop-dead gorgeous, captain of the high school cheerleaders, sassy, sexy…"

"Yeah, exactly, what's the lure? I don't get it?"

"Bob, you're such an idiot. You're worse than me."

They snickered together. The other guys at the table turned their heads to look at Allison as she walked away. Their neighbor from the floor opined, "Peter, she is really hot, but I've got to say, I don't like your chances going down that road."

"Thanks for your valuable insight, Bud. I could have never figured that out on my own."

"This Anya, is she a sophomore also?" Bob piped in.

"I think so, but I'm not sure. I guess I need to check into her a little more now."

"Nowadays, you can't be too careful. What if she's a KGB plant?"

All the guys laughed.

"Bob, the KGB doesn't exist any longer," Peter replied. "There's a new Russia, for a couple of decades, actually. Nowadays it's the FSB, or GRU, something like that."

"Yeah, yeah, yeah…you mark my words. She may have computer-hacker pals back in the motherland, in some basement, waiting to steal your identity or something."

"Hey, if they want to steal my identity, God help them. I'm a nothing, but, Bob, I think you might have a future in conspiracy theories. Maybe you should start a blog."

"Go ahead and scoff, dude. You can't be too careful."

"Duly noted."

Peter looked at Allison one last time. She was surrounded by her type: the socially relevant, stuck-up, and disdainful of any life form not themselves. Their preening and contrived displays no longer interested him. Coping with the out-of-my-league concept had finally taken root, and in watching their behaviors, he was comfortable with his step forward.

"I'm heading up."

Peter stood, along with Bob.

"See you guys later."

Returning to their room, Peter completed his homework right away. Classwork wasn't a problem for him. Rather, he very much enjoyed learning, and he was an excellent student. As an accounting major, his courses were finally in his area of interest, with the freshmen year behind him.

Afterward, he went outside to take a walk. The rain had finally died away, though the ground was still saturated with water. Pooling puddles were everywhere after the nonstop rain. The clean smell in the air invigorated him. It was like the world had been washed clean and all of the grime was gone.

Going first to stare at the massive football stadium, he smiled. Their team was very good, so game day was usually a very happy experience. Looping around the far end of the structure, Peter took his time at a steady but not demanding pace.

I should have looked up Anya's dorm, he mused.

"Oh well," he muttered, continuing until he arrived back at his dorm just at dusk. The sky to the west was a gorgeous sight with brilliant red and gold hues following the sinking sun as it disappeared below the horizon.

In a first, he went to bed that evening not with Allison in his head. Instead, he thought about Anya.

#

The following day, he looked forward to political science class. Arriving before Anya did, he sat down glancing frequently at the door. When she came in, he didn't get as much as a sideways glance. As always, she sat on the opposite side of the room. His warm glow faded quickly.

After class, he edged toward her, but she was too many students away and left before he could speak to her in the hallway. Walking away briskly, she never looked back. He shook his head in disappointment, dismayed by the unanticipated turn.

Oh, well. I guess you can close the book on Anya. He knew how to feel sorry for himself; Allison had trained him well in that department.

However, the funk he felt for the rest of the day surprised him. He mused, *Why go through this? Who is Anya to warrant such attention?* However, his disciplined mind couldn't manage to rationalize away the emotional impact of her snub.

Returning to his dorm, sitting in his room, Peter stared at the wall in a funk. Bob asked, "Are you ready to eat?"

"I'm going to do my homework first tonight. You go ahead."

"Something must have happened," Bob asked with a look of concern.

"Bob, I don't really want to talk about it. I just need a little alone time, okay? It has nothing to do with you." Peter looked out the window to hide his distress.

Bob hesitated before continuing, "Okay, but I'm here if you need anything."

"Thank you. Go ahead to dinner."

The homework went rapidly, after which Peter walked to the union for exercise and to grab a quick meal, away from Bob's piercing questions and the embarrassment of having to admit to the snub from Anya.

As he took his tuna sub, cola, and chips and a macadamia nut cookie from the Subway vendor, he noticed Anya sitting alone, again in the back, this time staring out the window. He debated whether to approach her. Seeing her always evoked his feelings.

Although deciding against it in his mind, his feet wouldn't cooperate, and in a moment he eased up to her table. It took a minute before she turned to look at him. Her face was wet, her cheeks tear-stained.

"Anya?" he said with concern. "What is it?"

The tears began to stream from her eyes, and she sobbed softly.

"Anya, please tell me what's wrong."

He handed her his handkerchief.

Anya dabbed her eyes. "Thank you," she answered in barely a whisper.

Peter sat down and waited.

She looked at him in misery. "I called home. It's my mother. She was diagnosed with cancer. It's a tumor in her brain. She waited too long, so it's advanced. They told her she has only a few months left, at most."

"My God, Anya, I'm so sorry."

Impulsively, he took her hand. "What can I do for you? I want to help."

"What can you do? There is nothing. It's out of the hands of men."

"Are you going back?"

"I can't. I have no money for that. I can only go to school here because of scholarships."

"Anya, that's terrible. I wish I had an answer."

She didn't reply.

"Can I sit to eat with you?"

Anya shrugged her shoulders, turned her head, and looked back out the window.

Gobbling down his food, he remained seated at the table. Finally, she looked at him again.

He explained. "Can you at least understand I'm not looking for anything? I don't want to take advantage, or whatever you think. Is it possible maybe I just want to be your friend?"

"Don't misunderstand when I say, no offense intended, but I judge people by their actions rather than their words. I'm a stranger in this country, alone in trying to make my way."

"That doesn't need to be the case. I'm right here, if you'll give me a chance."

She eyed him thoughtfully.

"Do you want for me to leave? Should I say *do svidaniya?*"

Anya smiled. "Your accent is terrible."

He smiled, ruefully. "Okay, well then, let's stick with talking English. I just used up the only Russian words I know."

"Peter, thank you for showing me genuine concern, but I just need to be alone right now to digest the shock. I'm going to lose my mother, and there's nothing I can do about it. Do you understand? She's my mom."

The thick tears started again, splashing on her blouse, leaving wet spots the size of quarters. It resonated in Peter, evoking both his compassion and his own deep sadness at her emotional pain. "I know you want to grieve, but I don't want to leave you like this. You barely touched your food."

She looked at him again, this time looking deep into his eyes. "I think maybe you are a good person, Peter Brown."

"I hope I am. I try."

They eyed each other for another moment.

"How about your roommate, she can provide some emotional support, right?"

"I think she does not like Russian peoples."

"That's terrible. I got lucky that I got a good guy for a roommate. He's a friend, a little demented, but a friend nonetheless."

"That's good for you."

"Will you walk with me? The exercise will help you feel better. However, you're required to eat your food first, ma'am. You need to keep your strength up."

Anya looked at her sandwich and took a bite. After that, she finished it off and drank her cola.

"That's better. You don't need to starve."

Peter took the trash from both meals to the waste barrel and dropped off the trays before walking her out of the building.

"When I first talked to you, what was that about 'blonde' and 'twig'?"

"American men love blondes, skinny models from magazines."

"Well, I'm not sure where you're getting your information, but I prefer long dark hair, like yours, and I like my women to have some meat on their bones. You look just fine as you are, Anya."

She looked straight ahead, but Peter saw the hint of her smile.

"What does your father say?"

"My father was not a nice man. My mother divorced him when I was young. We heard he died later, in a car accident. He was driving drunk. It was always just her and me. We had too little money, even with her working multiple jobs. My grades were at the top of the class, so I got this chance for college in America. I wanted to stay home, but Mama forced me to come to America. She said I needed to get out of that terrible place where we lived to have a chance at a better life."

"I had no idea."

"What about you?"

"My folks had me later in life. They're already retired now. My father sold his business for a big number, and my mother retired from teaching. They're set financially. My tragedies were losing my grandparents on both sides. I remember every one of those funerals like it was yesterday. Otherwise, my childhood was pretty boring, really."

"You had a father, and you were loved."

"That's true. I guess I need to do a better job of counting my blessings. So tell me more about this thing with your roommate?"

"She is…how you say…'hotty'? She has her own world. There's no place for Anya there. Her friends are…not so nice either. I don't mind being away."

"By away, you mean…"

"I spend my time out of the room. I go to library to study. I only sleep in my room."

"The more I hear, the less I like it."

"It's fine. I don't mind."

"Anya, this isn't acceptable. I need to do an intervention."

"What is that?"

"I start to right all of your wrongs."

She looked amused, but confused. "I think you talk crazy to pull a joke on me."

"No joke. I go after your demons, full bore."

"What does that mean?"

"It means you're no longer alone. I know it was me picking you, and I didn't give you a chance to say no, but I want to start spending time with you. Maybe we can think about having a date…at some point?" He eyed her hopefully.

Anya didn't reply, walking in silence for a while. Finally, she turned her head to him. "Okay, Peter."

"Thank you. I'm officially a happy man." Thrusting his fist into the air, he let out a loud whoop.

Anya chuckled, looking around. "Please stop. People will think I'm crazy too."

"Crazy isn't so bad, really. It works for me and my friends."

"I don't think so. I think you; how you say…jerk me around?"

Peter laughed heartily. "Anya, if I jerk you around, you won't have any trouble understanding it."

Glancing at her, Peter recognized that the sadness had returned to her face. "I'm sorry. I know you're hurting. My flippancy is not what you want right now."

"I hate to feel helpless. I can't bear the thought of losing her. She's all that I have."

"I hear what you're saying. Can you at least accept me as a friend?"

"Yes, I said that already, Peter."

"Good. Can our walk end at your dorm? I'd like to get your phone number and room number."

"I…eh…" She got a vacant look for a moment.

"Anya, there's no obligation on your part."

Shrugging, she replied softly, "Okay."

"If I start sitting beside you in class, are you okay with it?"

"Okay. I guess it would be fine."

"Good. We're making progress."

Passing other students on the sidewalk, Peter felt pleased to be seen walking with an attractive girl.

"I'll try to refrain from embarrassing you with any further foolish gestures."

Anya snickered.

"However, if you want any foolishness at any time, just let me know, ma'am."

"Thank you. I'll keep that in mind."

Her dorm was across campus from Peter's. They walked into the downstairs lobby, where Peter produced a pen and paper, though he had to borrow them from the front desk. He looked at Anya, who paused.

Peter waited patiently. Finally, she shared them, the room and phone numbers.

"Thank you, Anya. I'll see you in class tomorrow."

"Yes, Peter. Thank you again."

The brisk walk back to his dorm was buoyed with the return of hope.

"Yes," he muttered, with a clap of his hands.

As they walked into his room, Bob didn't fail to notice he was happy. "Apparently, you had a big turnaround. It's good to see you smiling."

"It's bittersweet. I ran into Anya at the union. We ate together, but she was devastated emotionally. Back in Russia, her mother was diagnosed with brain cancer, terminal brain cancer."

Bob was distressed, and it showed on his face. "That's terrible. What did you say?"

"I just offered to be there for her. What can you say to a person at a time like this? Her pain really got to me. As bad as that is, though, she's got a terrible roommate, so she feels totally alone."

"I assume that's the bad. So, what's the good?"

"Well, she gave me her phone number and agreed to consider having a date. Maybe I just got her at a weak moment. I guess I'll find out. She's definitely out of my league, if I have a league."

"You seem to have a fatal view of things in your life. Why is that?"

"I wouldn't say fatal."

"I would, and I did. So, what's the answer?"

"Well, maybe I started out aiming too high."

"You mean in romance."

"Yeah, you've seen Allison. Obviously, she too is well out of my league."

"Is that right? Is it possible that maybe you're looking at this wrong? If you got her, are you sure it would make you happy? I've never met Anya, but I'd bet she's the better choice. Get a clue, dude. Girls like Allison are a pain. You'd be putting out fires with her forever. She wants the eternal chase, for her ego. You wouldn't exist except to serve her in some menial way. She's one of those people who should marry themselves, the person they most love in the world."

"Perhaps you're right, Bob."

"There's no perhaps about it. I am right; you're wrong."

Peter snickered.

"What?"

"It's funny. Anya started out telling me the same thing…that I'm wrong."

"Then that's proof you were right: she is smart."

"Okay, it's time for you to shut your pie hole. I can only take so much criticism on any given day. Let's go eat."

"Mark my words."

Peter talked little at the meal; instead, he thought about Anya's major challenges. It irked him to the point that he called her number later, back in his room.

"Hello?"

"Eh…yes, this is Peter Brown."

"Do I know you?"

"No, I'm calling for Anya."

"Anya? You're calling for Anya?"

"That is what I said."

"She's not here. I'm her roommate, Megan. Is there a message?"

"No message. I'll talk to her in class."

He smiled at his plan. Knowing Anya wasn't in her room, he'd put Megan on notice that there was a guy interested in Anya.

"Take that," he muttered, in satisfaction.

"What was that?" Bob asked.

"Were you eavesdropping?"

"Of course. I have no life, so I live vicariously through yours."

"You have a life."

"Not a romantic life, I don't. Roly-poly isn't a body type that lures women."

"You're being unrealistic."

"Am I? You've never walked in my shoes. You're an emotional basket case, but I'm that plus a physical basket case. When you walk into a room, you get some smiles from girls. I walk into a room and get disdain, or outright aversion. It is what it is. I've coped with it all of my life."

"I never realized you have such a terrible self-concept. You're wrong. I'm not saying you should go for a Miss America, but there are plenty of girls you can connect with. We have something like twenty-five thousand girls on this campus. Having a better outlook would help. Women can sense if you're fragile about relationships. That's not a good approach. They'll mash you like a potato."

"So, what should be my approach? Selection of the fittest is an undeniable truism of nature."

"Think of those coeds as a garden of flowers to harvest. They want to be harvested."

The boys laughed.

"That's a good one, Peter. I doubt they'd agree with you on the harvesting idea."

"Hey, I never said my humor is good. If I got a comedy gene at birth, it's malfunctioning."

"I'll second that."

"Anyway, we start going to the dorm mixers. Girls go there to meet guys."

"That's a good idea. It's loud and dark, so maybe I look less offensive in the dark."

"Good plan, dummy. By the way, I was told by an expert to work on my dancing skills. Girls equate how good you are in bed with how well you dance."

"Really? It makes sense, now that you mention it. My dancing has a long ways to go. You know a lot about mating rituals."

"Yeah, I'm a real hoot. Knowing about it doesn't translate into being competent. There's a quantum leap necessary for both of us. Also, don't drown yourself in aftershave lotion. Girls don't mind a nice scent, but not overpowering."

"Do you think girls sit around and worry like we do?"

"They've got one big edge. Usually it's the guy making the first move, putting himself out there, and taking the risk. They can sit back to pick and choose. I realize some girls chase guys these days, but we're not in that class of guys. The alphas own that privilege."

"I can't disagree. I've been discouraged for so long; I wonder if I'm capable of optimism."

"Where there's life, there's hope."

"Did you just invent that saying? Wow, I'm dazzled."

"Okay, smartass, give me a break. The point is, we get out of neutral and get into the game."

"Sure, whatever. I've got nothing else going."

"Friday, I'm going to invite Anya."

"So, I'm a third wheel, right out of the chute?"

"We'll get you fixed up, Bobster. Having a pretty girl sitting with us will lend us credibility, like we must be cool if she hangs with us."

"I'll believe it when it happens."

"You'll see—she makes me smile, and she'll make you smile too."

"I'll try to have some hope, and I'll try not to put my foot in my mouth. Usually, girls blow my mind, and my usual stupid remarks get stupider."

Peter snickered. "Stupider? You're such a scholar."

"It's who I am. I didn't get to this sorry state by accident."

"Well, things are going to change, my friend."

Chapter Two

When Anya came to class the following day, she looked at Peter curiously. He got up and went over to sit down beside her.

"Hi, Anya."

"Hi." She acted cautious.

"Are you okay with this?" Reading her mood was tough for him.

"My roommate said you called last night."

"I did. I knew you wouldn't be home, but I wanted to stir the pot."

"What? I don't understand."

"It's a figure of speech for stirring her up. If she's going to act mean toward you, there will be a price to pay."

"I don't want to have trouble."

"No trouble, just giving her something to think about. Did she act differently?"

"She asked me about you."

"See, that's a good thing. What did you say?"

"I told her you're a classmate."

"Oh." He frowned.

"This makes you unhappy?"

"Well, I'm not unhappy. I guess I'm thinking about being more…with you."

"More?"

"Maybe you'll describe me differently if we have a date. How about coming with me to the football game on Saturday?"

"I don't know football."

In spite of her look of concern, he pressed ahead anyway. "That's an excellent reason to come with me—to learn about the game."

"I don't know."

Peter tried to interpret the uncertain look on her face, without success. It could mean many different things. "You came to America to get an education. This is a part of an American education."

"I do not think that's true, but…"

"Good, I'll come by your dorm and get you in the morning. The game starts at noon. Wear a school sweatshirt."

"I don't have a school sweatshirt."

"What? Everybody wears their school colors."

Anya's face reddened.

"I'm sorry. I didn't mean to embarrass you. Is there a reason you don't want to wear school clothes?"

"I have no money for such things."

"I didn't think about that. I apologize again, Anya. Will you allow me to buy a couple of things for you?"

"No, I can't accept…"

"Listen, Anya, it's not a big thing. I told you my folks are pretty flush with money. They built up a big college fund for me, but when I got scholarships, most of that money was left just sitting there. I want to do this for you, please?"

"It doesn't seem right, Peter. I don't want charity." She eyed him and his determined look.

"Don't look at it that way because this isn't charity. Bringing you up to speed with the other girls at this school is, well, I don't have the word. In the meantime, walk with me later to the bookstore and let's do this thing?"

She gave him a meek smile.

"I'll meet you after class this afternoon and we'll go shopping," he continued.

#

Later, going into the crowded bookstore, he led Anya to the apparel section. She looked around in awe at the huge array of clothing.

"Does anything stand out to you?"

"Will you pick for me? There's just so much here, I can't choose."

"Okay, I'll make clothing choices, but you can't complain."

Anya chuckled.

Peter opted for more than just a sweatshirt. He selected a skirt, blouse, and also a sweater.

"This is too much."

"No, it's not. I said no complaining."

"Yes, sir." His warm smile, unassuming nature, and honest concern for her had a positive effect.

"Go into the fitting room to try them on."

He waited patiently until she came out.

"They're fine, but this is too expensive." Her long hair always looked good; seemingly nothing could leave it askew.

"Leave that to me. This isn't too expensive."

"I have no way to repay you."

"Anya, you owe me nothing, other than to be happy."

"Thank you for these clothes."

"Let's go upstairs to get some food, so we don't starve."

"I can't…"

"This is my treat."

"You do too much."

"I'm happy to do it. It gives me a chance to be with you." He smiled at her again.

Anya shrugged and glanced away, suddenly shy acting.

They ate and chatted about their courses before getting up to leave. In tiny increments, she was gradually relaxing with him. During their lively chat, Anya clarified, again, Peter's various "wrong ideas," to which he objected, but also laughed. Her attempts at a joke encouraged him.

"Let's go back to your dorm to drop off the bags, and then maybe we can have a study date back at my dorm? You bring some books and then we study together. I'm sure you've had enough of going alone to the library."

"Okay, but I've not done this before, this study date."

"Neither have I."

#

On the walk to Anya's dorm, it felt different for Peter. The wary edge was gone in Anya, like she finally felt trust enough to let her guard down.

Peter smiled. "Anya, this is nice, being with you."

"It's nice being with you also. Thanks again for the gifts."

It felt good to him to see her smile. "My pleasure. I can't wait to see you dressed up on Saturday morning."

It was a pleasant fall day. The prior storm front had moved out of the area to leave a clear azure sky over the sprawling campus. Autumn in the Midwest is idyllic, and this day was another in a long line of pleasant experiences. The great bell tower chimed six times, echoing across campus.

"Anya, I want to say one other thing. Any time you want to call home, I'll pay for those calls."

"Peter, they're very expensive." She turned her head in amazement.

"It doesn't matter. These are precious moments and, as you said, she's your mom."

Her face suddenly clouded.

"Anya, I didn't mean to upset you."

"You're too kind to me. I feel…" She looked away.

"I can't imagine being where you are. I'm blessed to have both my parents. I wish I could do more for you."

"I believe you."

"I hope you can start to understand I care about you, a lot."

She turned her head to look at him, but said nothing.

"I really do prefer dark-haired women, with meat on their bones."

Anya laughed heartily.

"Admittedly, I'm brain-damaged, but I think I grow on you with time."

"You are a silly man, and you're still wrong."

Now it was Peter who laughed heartily. "We'll just see about that, madam."

#

Arriving at her dorm, Anya went upstairs to drop off the clothes. It took a little time before she came back down. Her facial expression was troubled.

"Did something happen?"

"Megan and her friends questioned me."

"About…?" His scowl spoke volumes to her about how he felt.

"Because you buy my clothes, they ask if, eh, they think I…it's not nice."

Peter bristled. "Why don't you invite her down for a little chat with me."

"No, Peter, please. I'm fine. They don't matter to me." Her worried expression caught his attention.

"Okay, but I'm not going to let this go on." He shrugged but still smoldered with ire.

She took his hand to quickly lead him out of her dorm for the walk back to his dorm.

Peter simmered with outrage the entire way. "I can't believe them. With what you're facing, to be cruel like that—I can't believe how people act."

"It's okay. It's over. I've dealt with it before. Let me say, you make me feel better about many things."

He turned his head. "I hope I do. You deserve better treatment from those snarky, smug little bitches."

"About your offer to call my mother…it means more to me than you could ever know." With a look of gratefulness, she touched his hand.

"It's the least I could do. Is it okay if I think of you as my girlfriend? I know we haven't even had a date yet, but, well, there it is."

"This is important to you, this having-a-girlfriend thing?"

"Yeah, I felt drawn to you right away, and it keeps growing stronger by the minute."

"By the minute," Anya laughed. "That's amazing, by the minute."

"Well, I'm just being honest. With me, what you see is what you get."

"Is that another American adage?"

"It is."

Arriving at his dorm, they headed for the lounge and claimed a sofa.

"Before I forget, I'd like to invite you here for the Friday-night mixer."

"What is that?"

"It's like a dance, a chance for students to mix and mingle. You can meet my roommate."

"I don't know American dances."

"That's fine. I'll teach you. What dances do you know?"

"Back in Russia, I didn't really dance either. It could draw attention on me, in a bad way. There were people there I needed to avoid. I know you don't understand, being from America. You see things through your experiences. You must simply accept what I'm saying. We didn't live in a nice area."

"Thankfully, that's behind you now."

She looked away, pondering her life and her mother left behind.

Peter didn't say anything. He simply started to study.

Anya took out a textbook and started reading. After a moment, he slid over, pressing his body against hers.

"I don't want for you to get cold," he whispered.

Shaking her head, she chuckled, "You are…I can't think of right word."

"I defy description. That's why you can't come up with the word."

Spending several hours together, Peter felt spiritual closeness with a girl beyond anything in his life up to that point.

Anya smiled at his fumbling attempts at humor. Walking her back to her dorm, on impulse, at the front door, he hugged her. "I'll see you tomorrow. Sleep well, and dream about me."

Anya laughed heartily. "You're still a silly man."

"I am. No doubt about it."

For Peter, it was another lively walk back to his dorm. "Life is good," he muttered cheerily.

When he walked into his room, Bob smirked. "Wow, Peter, you're beaming. Did you tickle her tonsils?"

"No, you moron. You say the most insane things I've ever heard."

"It's a gift."

"Some gift."

"I have many more."

"A chilling thought. I shudder to think. By the way, we're all set with Anya for Friday."

"Good. I guess I need to come up with some skinny clothes to make me look passable."

"Somehow, I suspect that's a sight the world isn't ready for. I hope you're not planning on something weird."

"*Moi?*"

"Uh-oh."

Highly entertained with himself, Bob laughed, clapping his hands.

"You better not! I'm trying to win over Anya."

"No worries, bro."

"We'll see. I've given you fair warning. If you screw up…you're going down the toilet."

"Ooh, I'm trembling."

Peter brandished his fist, making Bob laugh all the more.

#

On Friday in class, Anya seemed a little nervous. She fidgeted noticeably. Peter asked her afterward, "Is something wrong?"

"About tonight, I feel anxious in crowds sometimes."

"There's nothing to worry about. You'll be there with me and Bob. This will be fun."

"I'll try, but this is a risk I'd never take back home in Russia. Bad people are in crowds."

"You're not in Russia."

"I know, but you need to understand my feelings. I had a big scare in a crowd. I've never forgotten that fright."

"I'm sorry that happened to you. If you want to talk, I'm all ears."

"I'm just saying, I don't like to draw attention."

"I know. You've told me that already. I'll take care of you." He smiled and patted her shoulder.

"I know this seems silly to you."

"Not really. Your experiences shape your point of view. However, you're living here, and things aren't like where you came from. It's okay to trust."

"You're right, it is much different here, but there are still dangers."

"Are you talking about the mean girls?"

"That's one of them. I understand if they don't like me, but why can't they just leave me alone?"

"That's a difficult question. I don't know what makes some people tick."

"Some things they do are evil."

"If you run into any of that bad in the future, the evil you're talking about, you call me immediately. There's no reason for you to put up with anything. As I said, I'll be there for you."

Her smile warmed Peter.

"Thank you," she whispered.

"Good. Now, moving right along, are you looking forward to this weekend?"

"Possibly."

Peter chuckled. "You don't want to concede anything. Is that your plan, to provoke me into acting like a love-starved puppy?"

"No." She snickered.

"You're sneaky smart, ma'am. I know what you're doing, and I've got my eye on you."

She laughed.

"At any rate, after dinner tonight, I'll walk to your dorm to get you, and then we can walk back here. We can talk with Bob down in the lounge until the party starts, okay?"

"Okay."

#

When Peter went to her dorm later, Anya came down to the lobby, but she was accompanied by Megan. It was clear, from watching Anya's unease, that this wasn't her choice.

Megan was exactly what he'd imagined: a girl who would fit in with Allison's crowd, the bevy of smug beauties. Her sneer irked him, although that sneer transformed into surprise when she saw him.

"You're Peter?"

"I am."

"You're with Anya now?"

"You'd have to ask Anya, but from my perspective we are. Did you have a point to make?"

"There are American girls all over this campus, a lot of us."

"I choose Anya."

Megan shrugged her shoulders. "Whatever. That's your loss."

Peter was about to lash out at her snarky remark, but Anya took him by the arm, eyeing him in alarm, before he could speak. Megan had already turned and walked away, having successfully cast her aspersion.

"Peter, please don't. I have trouble enough."

"I see what you mean. What a bitch. You realize you can change rooms and get a different roommate."

"I have no guarantee it would be an improvement. The next girl might hate Russians too."

"I'll think about that. This is a solvable problem, honey."

"Honey?"

"It's a term of endearment. You're dear to me now."

"I see." His remark didn't fully land, as she was lost in her thoughts.

"By the way, you look really nice."

"You look nice too." Still distracted, she answered like a reflex.

"One other thing, Anya; how she said that about American girls, that is her flaw, not yours. She can't arbitrarily exclude you from the other coeds on this campus because you have an accent."

"I know what you say, but she has the power, do you see?"

"I don't buy it. I really think we need to look into moving you out of her room. Probably you should relocate to my dorm."

"Maybe."

"You could crash with Bob and me."

Anya laughed. "You're talking foolish."

"Seriously, we can get you on the girls' side and find a nice girl to be a friend."

"Okay."

"There's no reason to put up with that crap from Megan any longer."

"I don't know how to do that."

"I'll talk to people at the dorm here to find out the process."

"Thank you."

"So, tonight we party, and tomorrow we've got the game. Believe me, it will be an awesome experience. Our football team is really good." He took her hand as they walked. His warm inner glow resumed. "Also, I'm going to learn some Russian."

"Are you?" She smirked.

"I am. We're going to have a conversation in the future."

"Well in the future." Anya laughed heartily.

"Real funny, Anya. You're a real comedian. You might be surprised at what I can do. I am capable of learning things."

"I think you rub off on me."

"Well, then you're in big trouble. By the way, we can go shopping on Sunday to buy a few more clothes for you. I know your wardrobe is limited. I want to help. We can chip away a little at a time."

"I feel badly. I know you mean well, but you do too much for me."

"I don't see it that way. Maybe I didn't explain it clearly enough. If I couldn't afford it, that would be one thing, but, as I explained, my family is flush. I mean, they are really set, and I have more money available than I can spend, so why not?"

She glanced at him.

He spoke before she could answer: "Okay, so it's settled: we shop on Sunday."

"I didn't agree."

"You did, without realizing it. The matter is settled. It's time to start helping you be part of the *bourgeoisie*."

"I'm not Communist."

"That was a joke, honey. I warned you about my low level of humor. *Мы вас похороним.*"

Anya laughed. "We will bury you? Where did you learn that?"

"I looked it up on the Internet: that old Khrushchev speech from the sixties."

"I think maybe you were dropped on your head as a baby."

"That's a strong possibility."

"Oh my, maybe I teach you some Russian. You're not doing so well on your own."

"I'm in."

Her gentle squeeze of his hand was gratifying nonverbal communication that spoke volumes, just like her warm smile.

"We will bury you." She snickered again, shaking her head in amusement. "That's idiotic. What have I done?"

"You've decided to join the American peoples, of which I'm the prime representative. I will teach you everything you need to know."

"I see."

Arriving at the dorm, Peter led Anya up the stairs to go to his room. Bob was waiting excitedly. He sprang out of his chair.

"Bob, this is Anya."

"Hi, Anya, it's nice to meet you."

"Hello, Bob."

"You look really pretty."

She blushed, glancing shyly at Peter. "Thank you."

Suddenly Bob stepped over to embrace her, firmly. In an extended hug, she got a look of alarm.

Peter spoke. "Okay, Bob, she's already got a date tonight."

Bob laughed. "So, are you ready to cut some rug?"

Anya eyed him in confusion. "What?"

Peter chuckled. "It's slang for dancing."

"Oh. I don't know American dances."

"We'll teach you, honey."

Bob added. "Let's go. We can get a table before the room fills up."

They made their way down the stairs, up the hallway into the grill, where there was already considerable student traffic. Peter sat down at a table with Anya, while Bob went to order colas.

Anya looked around nervously.

"Don't worry. These people aren't a threat to you. They're just other students looking to have a good time."

She didn't reply. Her mind whirred with her past, and those terrifying emotions, and it showed in her facial expressions.

Bob came back with three drinks. With a young man sitting on each side of her, this seemed to calm Anya only slightly. The increasing noise level of more students arriving affected her. She glanced around frequently, almost furtively.

Conversing turned into shouting to be heard.

Bob touched Anya's arm to get her attention. "So, do you like America?"

"There are some things I like."

"What don't you like?"

"Being an eternal foreigner, I feel I must be guarded always. After time, it gets burdensome."

"I'm sorry. I didn't think of it that way. Saying the right thing is one of my opportunity areas."

At that moment, Allison arrived with her entourage. She looked directly at Peter and then at Anya. Peter looked at Anya, feeling instantly protective of her. To their chagrin, Allison came over.

"Peter, what a nice surprise to see you; and out socially. Who is this?"

"This is Anya, my girlfriend."

"Girlfriend? Really."

"Yes, ma'am."

"Hello, Anya." Coolly, Allison eyed her up and down with a calculating glance. Anya didn't sense friendship in her visit.

"Hello," she answered in a low voice.

"How did you meet Peter?" Her tone was pointed, a little too sharp.

He answered. "We have class together."

At that moment, the music started, along with the dancing.

"Do you mind if I dance with your boyfriend?" Allison didn't wait for a reply. She grabbed a reluctant Peter by the hand and dragged him bodily out into the middle of the swirling bodies.

Allison was particularly sensual in how she danced, violating his personal space frequently, swaying and swirling in rhythm with the music. Bumping against him often, it was just the encounter he would have prayed for not so long ago. However, this was the time of Anya, and seeing the discomfort on her face while watching Allison rubbing her nose in it, Peter nearly walked off the floor.

Once the song ended, Allison grabbed his hand before he could leave. "We've known each other a long time, Peter. What's with hooking up with her?"

"Hooking up? Anya and I have just met, and are very early in a relationship. I like her because she's a nice person."

"And I'm not?"

He eyed her, curious. "Allison, what are you saying? You and I have never been together."

"Is that my fault? You were always so passive. Do you think I liked that?"

"I never thought about it. Of course, you know I liked you, but you had your options, elsewhere."

"I'm a social person. There's nothing wrong with having a lot of friends."

"I don't know what you want. I'm here tonight with Anya."

"That's your choice. Perhaps you have options, too. Did you ever think of that?"

Turning and walking away, she stirred him up, but toward confusion. Although provoked, his focus remained with Anya. Sitting back down at the table, he scooted his chair close to her.

"I'm sorry, honey. I have no idea what that was about."

"She likes you. That's easy to see." She eyed him with a neutral expression.

"I knew her from high school, but we didn't date."

"I think she would like to date."

"I doubt that. I think she was just twisting my tail. I'm not sure why, though. Women are mystifying creatures that can't be understood."

Bob spoke. "Do you want for me to take her off your hands?" He laughed hysterically.

"I'd appreciate it, but even if it was doable, I'd warn you to give her a wide berth. I don't think I could ever trust her. She's more the type to leave a trail littered with the bodies of her romantic discards."

"She is like my roommate."

"You might be right, Anya. So, do you want to try our first dance?"

"No, but you'll make me do it." She paused and took a deep breath before she stood up.

They rose and went to the edge of the dancers, Peter leading her by the hand. Anya was tentative, mimicking Peter's steps. Starting to gain a little confidence, she duplicated the moves of the other girls around her and relaxed into the dancing. Even with her first dance, she was better than passable; she was decent.

Peter noticed Allison not far away, dancing with a stud, but she was watching Anya. Her expression was less than friendly, eyeing her grimly.

Again, Peter felt protective of his new "girlfriend." Taking her into an embrace as they danced, he eyed Allison harshly. She smirked in return, like Peter had fallen for a ploy. Anya was focused on mastering the dance and missed the entire exchange.

Staying on the floor for the start of the next song with Anya, to his shock, they were joined by Bob, with an actual girl.

"Hey, Bob," he spoke with surprise, but in a pleasant way.

"This is Christy. She agreed to allow me to trample her toes."

The four of them laughed. Peter bumped fists with Bob. Anya smiled at Christy.

When the music started, Bob proved to be a better dancer than Peter would have thought. Christy seemed to enjoy being with him. Not only did they dance together but she chatted the whole time.

They stayed through a succession of tunes before finally sitting back down at the table for a breather.

"Hi, I'm Christy." She smiled at Anya. Christy had a lively manner. She came across as genuinely friendly and fun to be with.

"I'm Anya."

"What's your major, Christy?" Peter asked.

"Marketing. I've got a big mouth, so I figured it's the right choice for me. I'm not Miss America, so I've got to use what assets I have."

"You look fine to me," Bob said. "I'm not Mr. America."

"How are things with your roommate?" Peter continued.

"My roommate? Why do you ask?"

"I'm looking for someone as an option for Anya, my girlfriend. She drew a short straw over at her dorm. I want her out of that hostile environment as soon as possible."

"Oh. Eh, I can certainly inquire. I'm not sure if it could be done mid-semester, but I'll ask. What do you say, Anya? Could you live with me?"

Anya smiled. "I think it's more if you could live with me. I'm the foreigner."

"Foreigner has nothing to do with it. I gather it's pretty bad over there at your dorm?"

Peter answered. "You have no idea."

To break a momentary awkward silence, Peter continued.

"Listen, we're going to the game tomorrow. Will you join us?"

"My ticket isn't beside you."

"We can trade around to get four together. I'll handle it. Don't worry about that."

She looked at Bob, who replied, "Is that okay...hanging out with me, Christy?"

"Sure, why not?"

"I'm sorry to put all of this on you. I know we're strangers, but we're good people." Peter added.

Bob smiled hopefully.

"That's okay, Peter. If I can help out, I'm happy to do it. My roommate and I aren't particularly close. I can certainly live with Anya."

The music resumed, along with their dancing. Smiling, Anya looked to be enjoying herself. Peter was happy to have Anya violating his personal space, following Allison's lead with how to dance. From her first dance to her final one, it was remarkable to him not only the transformation in her grasp of the moment, but also the blossoming of her spirit. Her dancing was very good at the end, comparable to the girls around her.

Afterward, Peter walked her out of the event with an arm around her waist.

"I told you this would be fun."

"I'm surprised. It isn't something I would seek to do. I concede that for once, you weren't wrong."

"Oh, come on, Anya. Give me a break with the 'wrong' thing."

They both chuckled, and she put her arm around his waist. As they walked into the night air, it was cool after leaving the hot dance floor. The clear sky shimmered with the Milky Way arrayed in splendor over their heads.

"It's so peaceful," she whispered. "I like this very much."

"Don't forget, tomorrow it's a noon start for the game, and Sunday we shop for clothes."

"Peter…"

"Don't even say it. The matter is closed. Maybe after we get back to your dorm, we'll call your mother?"

"There is time difference. Day here is night there."

"Well, tomorrow night then. I'll stay up with you if you'd like. I've got a phone card with plenty of credit."

"She will be surprised to hear from me."

"I've got some other ideas, but I'll tell you later. First, I've got to figure some things out."

Suddenly stopping him, turning her body, Anya put her hands to his face for their first kiss, gentle and soft. It was immensely provocative for Peter.

"Wow, that was nice, Anya."

"I like you, Peter. I want you to know that."

"Thank you, darling. I was hoping you would come around. I didn't want you to feel beholden."

They continued their gradual stroll. Neither of them was anxious for the evening to end.

At the door of her dorm, they kissed again, this time with more passion. Peter was in awe; grateful she hadn't rejected him.

"Was my kiss okay? I really want to be sure I don't screw up with you."

She chuckled. "Peter, you're fine. You don't need to worry about silly things."

"I guess I'll see you tomorrow in the new clothes."

"You will. I look forward to it."

"I'll get with Christy about changing rooms to see what she finds out."

"Thank you."

Chapter Three

The boys were up early, the first in the weekend breakfast line at the cafeteria. Christy found them at their table a little later when she came for her breakfast.

"Christy, I'm glad to see you," Bob said.

"Having a date to the game has me pumped."

"Me too."

Peter spoke. "Call me as soon as you know something about rooming with Anya. She's got it bad over there. I can't understate that fact."

"I will."

"What do you say about maybe doing something together this evening, like a double date?"

"I'm fine with it, Peter. I gather you haven't asked Anya yet?"

"I'm pretty sure that won't be an issue. She doesn't stay in her room except to sleep. I'll ask her when we pick her up to go to the game."

"Okay, but be careful about making assumptions."

"Huh? Is there something you're trying to tell me?"

"I'm speaking in general. Sometimes girls can have other plans."

"You mean like dates?"

"That would be one example."

"She never mentioned any other guys."

"I'm not saying there are any; I'm just saying you need to approach it without assuming it is a sure thing she can go with you. Do you understand the distinction? I'm not saying anything is wrong, but things can change over time."

"Wow, are you saying I'm coming on too strong with Anya?"

"I'm not trying to make any judgment. I just met you, so I have no basis for giving advice. Maybe I shouldn't have said anything."

"No, don't apologize. I'd rather get an impartial observation. Trying to understand her perspective and her thoughts is definitely something I need to do."

They sat for an awkward moment while Peter stared away, pondering the possible issue.

Bob spoke to break the impasse. "So, Christy, you look good in the school colors."

"Thank you," she replied to Bob but continued to look at Peter.

"Peter, are you okay?"

"I am." He smiled. "This should be a good game today."

Bob answered. "It should. I agree."

"Are you guys ready to go?" Peter asked, his impatience to go pick up Anya showing.

"Sure, let's go." Bob shrugged. He recognized Peter's moods and temperament.

"Did you have any problems getting tickets together?" Christy asked.

"No. There are always people going out of town, and they don't come to the game for other reasons, like they need cash. We're all sitting together. I told you I would handle it."

Walking outside moments later, it was a perfect fall day in the Midwest. The air was crisp, though the sun lent enough warmth they didn't feel cold. They did wear sweatshirts over their shirts, however, as there was a breeze.

All of them walked to Anya's dorm. When she came down to the lobby, she was dazzling in her new clothes, wearing the school colors for the first time in her life.

"Wow, Anya, you look astounding."

She smiled demurely. Looking at Christy, she asked, "Do I look okay?"

"You look beautiful."

Peter smiled, but Christy's prior comments stuck with him.

Leaving her dorm, they headed for the stadium. Walking on the sidewalk, Peter and Anya were in front of Bob and Christy. Already, there was considerable traffic all over campus. Cars arrived from all over the state, alums returning to the site of their college joys. The air was filled with the smells of food cooking at numerous tailgates. Burgers, hot dogs, chicken, ribs: the variety of offerings was as diverse as the people cooking the meals. In the distance, they could hear the thump of the drums of the university marching band coming to the stadium.

The crowd was like a vast river of humanity flowing inexorably to its destination. The school colors dominated the crowd, with occasional clashes with people wearing the colors of the opponent.

This wasn't a school with empty seats at football games. For that matter, the crowds were excellent at all of its sports. Winning is always a great reinforcement for maximizing attendance.

As they walked, it was Anya who took Peter's hand, like she needed his touch to feel secure in the midst of the mob.

"This will be fun," he said reassuringly, realizing her fear of crowds. Still, she looked around furtively at the mass of humanity on the move, like there were still hidden threats.

Meanwhile, Bob and Christy enjoyed a lively chat. Christy laughed at Bob's jokes, which emboldened him. Peter appreciated her easygoing manner, which also helped Anya feel at ease.

Approaching the gates, Peter pulled out the four tickets from his pocket.

Christy turned to Anya. "Come with me to the restroom?"

"Yes. Thank you."

The guys walked to the vendor station to buy colas, regular for them and diet for the girls.

Walking to the correct section, they waited for the girls. When Christy appeared, chatting with Anya as they walked, she smiled at the guys. "Here we are."

"Finally," Bob said.

Christy gave him a playful punch to the arm. "Brat."

Out of the corner of his eye, Peter happened to notice Allison wasn't far away. She was eyeing them while she stood with some handsome guys. He was mildly curious at her continuing attention to him, but they turned and walked up the ramp into the stadium to find their seats in the student section.

Their seats were in the middle of a row. Placing the girls between the guys, Christy talked to Bob but talked equally with Anya. Peter was content initially to sit in silence other than when on occasion Anya turned her head to speak to him. Mostly, she spoke to Christy.

Anya was greatly taken with the pregame band performance. She perked up and paid attention, smiling with excitement. The cheers of the crowd and singing the fight song aroused her spirits.

Peter asked, "How did you like that?"

"I've never seen such a thing. I like it very much. It's very exciting."

When the game started, she had no clue what was happening. Whenever the home crowd cheered, she cheered, but far less boisterously.

Late in the game, at a critical point, the home team quarterback threw an interception. The crowd groaned. When the noise quieted, she touched Peter's arm. "Why did he throw the ball to the other team? I don't understand?"

Peter chuckled. "It wasn't intentional. The other team tries to stop us from moving the ball to score. Their player just made a great play."

"Oh." Anya still looked confused.

The home-team defense made a stand and the game ended with a narrow victory, to the delight of the throng.

Easing their way through the crowd moving out of the stadium, Anya talked with Christy.

"Did you like it?" Christy asked.

"I liked the band. Football confuses me. Perhaps I'll be better if I see another game."

"It will grow on you, believe me. I love the games."

"I will try."

"Anya, just relax and enjoy. It's the same thing with the dancing. Once you got into it, I think you'd agree you had fun."

"Yes, I did. You're right, Christy."

Bob said, "Anya, we talked about maybe doing something, like a double date. What do you think?"

"What do I do?"

"We go together, the four of us, to a movie, or something. We grab some food somewhere. Does that sound good to you?"

"I guess I could. Is that what you want, Peter?"

"Sure. Of course."

She glanced at him.

He added, "But only if you want to go."

Glancing at him again, she replied. "I will go."

"Then it's a date. We'll walk you back to your dorm. I'd say we reconvene around four to go out to eat dinner."

"I'll be ready."

Arriving at her dorm, Peter pondered a kiss but hesitated.

Anya turned to him. "Thank you for the enjoyable time. Goodbye until later."

She made no move toward romance, so he left it at that. There was no hug coming from her, and certainly no kiss.

The three walked back to their own dorms with Peter deep in thought while Christy and Bob talked virtually nonstop.

Leaving Christy at the elevator on the girl's side, Bob gave her a hug, and the boys walked back to their room.

"That was so great being with Christy. Peter, you were so right to get me out there. I know she isn't a beauty queen, but I really like her. She's my kind of girl in virtually every possible way."

"I'm glad, partner."

"Why are you quiet?"

"I was just thinking."

"About what?"

"What Christy said, it makes sense. I can see how maybe I was getting carried away and overwhelming Anya. As I look at today more impartially, I can see she doesn't necessarily share my exuberance of expression."

"Are you inventing a boogeyman? I didn't see any problems."

"If there were problems, you have to admit you only saw Christy. That's fine, but I'm going to try to find an even keel. I don't want to blow it with Anya."

"Well, my advice is just be yourself. You're a good guy, and that comes through."

"We'll see about that. I'm going to do a little studying for a minute before it's time to go."

"Do you mind driving?"

"Bob, I'm the only one with a car. Of course I'll drive." He laughed, along with his roommate.

"I'll pay you for gas, if I ever get any money."

"Will you shut up, moron."

"Anyway, this will be fun tonight, Peter. I think Anya feels out of her element with American ways of doing things. She'll adjust. Be patient with her. You're the one who has to decide if she's worth the effort."

"Of course she's worth it. That isn't what I'm worrying about. I'm looking at the other side of it: her view of me. I can't seem to get a feel for what she really thinks. Do you understand?"

"Well, maybe look at it as an evolving situation. That doesn't have to be a bad thing."

"I've got all the patience of Job, but whether it will ultimately make a difference, I wonder about."

"Put your worries on the shelf for the time being, and let's just enjoy this evening."

Peter shrugged. "Whatever. I guess you're right."

"Life is tough enough without you being your own worst enemy. Whatever is supposed to happen will happen anyway. Don't sweat the small stuff."

"If you say so."

#

Shortly, Peter walked with Bob to the parking lot to get his car. They drove back to the dorm to pick up Christy before driving over to get Anya.

Glancing in the rearview mirror, Peter saw Christy slide over to sit against Bob. Anya, however, did not move to the center of the seat when she got in. She stayed beside the car door.

"Ladies, Bob and I picked a restaurant for dinner, family style. Is that good for you?"

"Sure," Christy replied, happily. Anya merely nodded.

Peter's concerns simmered to life.

The restaurant proved a good choice, with good food and plenty of families and children. With the resulting din, there was no danger of tenuous romantic ambience. Anya talked with Christy a great deal. Christy's bubbly nature was contagious, brightening the mood at the table.

The difference in how warmly Christy acted toward Bob versus the cautious way Anya responded to Peter was a stark contrast for a somewhat insecure young man. Anya paid far more attention to Christy than Peter, which didn't help his fragile confidence.

"What would you girls like to see at the show, romance or action-adventure?"

"Is that a trick question?" Christy asked.

They all laughed.

She continued: "Do I need to answer your question?"

Bob replied, "I thought I'd give it a shot. What could be better than mindless nonstop action, blowing up stuff?"

"Duh," Christy replied.

Everybody looked at Anya. "I will see whatever you want."

"Anya, you're supposed to side with me," Christy said jokingly.

"You lose," Bob piped in.

"Hey, are you sure, Bob? I think you'd be the one who loses."

"Low blow, Christy, but I change my vote. A nice romance would be perfect."

"All's fair in love and war." Christy smirked at Bob.

He smiled warmly at her before replying, "Apparently. I give up. You girls win. Peter, can you stomach a romance?"

"Sure."

"Well, a romance it is."

The boys paid the dinner bill and then they went to the car. The seating on the drive remained the same, with Anya sitting apart against the door, again.

#

In the movie theatre, they selected seats in the center of a row, halfway down. Those student couples more romantically inclined took seats in the back. Bob and Peter sat with the two girls between them. Anya was able to talk to Christy and Bob. Again, Peter was relatively passive. He didn't initiate conversation, opting to respond only if Anya spoke to him.

This didn't seem to bother her. She acted content with conversing mostly in the other direction.

Christy and Bob were close, mutually deciding on holding hands. Peter never attempted the risk of that move, especially with Anya's hands clasped on her lap.

Mercifully, the movie began, though it was arduous for Peter, running for over two hours. Peter fidgeted, which was out of character for him.

Afterward, the two couples arose. Bob led the way toward the aisle. Peter glanced at Anya's attractive female form as they walked. She never looked back at him.

Reaching the aisle, Bob took Christy's hand. Anya waited for Peter to step beside her to walk out together.

Walking out to the parking lot to the car, Peter never considered going somewhere to "park."

That didn't stop Christy and Bob from sharing some *amore* in the backseat on the short drive back to campus. As they arrived first at Anya's dorm, Peter got out, walking her to the door.

Pausing for an awkward moment, Peter spoke. "Well, thank you for coming with me for the day. It was nice spending time with you."

"Peter, are we still shopping tomorrow? That isn't necessary."

"We are. As I said, supplementing your wardrobe will help you in many ways."

"I feel badly you do so many things—too many."

"I've already explained it isn't a problem. Let's leave it at that." Peter eyed her with chagrin.

They eyed each other for another awkward moment. Her arms were crossed, and she wasn't looking in his eyes. Peter had no trouble understanding her closed body language.

"Good night," he said meekly, turning away, walking briskly and sadly back to his car.

Bob and Christy said nothing when he got back in. Peter felt embarrassed, like he was incompetent and had just publicly displayed it for them to see.

"Listen, I'll drop you guys off on the girls' side and go to park the car. I'll see you back in the room, Bob."

"Okay."

It was a quiet ride, though Peter heard them whisper briefly.

Once they got out of the car, Peter spoke. "Good night, Christy."

"Good night."

He took his time driving to the lot and then ambled at a crawl back to the dorm, deep in thought.

Expecting a critique from Bob, he was surprised when Bob said nothing. They merely got ready and went to bed.

#

On Sunday morning after breakfast, he drove back over to her dorm to pick up Anya.

"Good morning, Peter," she remarked, as she got off the elevator.

"Good morning." His tone was subdued.

He walked her out to his car in silence, opening the passenger door for her, and then walking around to the driver's side.

After a moment, he asked, "Rather than try to park in the city, I'm going to the outskirts, to the big shopping mall. Is that okay?"

"Yes."

They rode in relative silence. The small distance between them, with Anya sitting by the car door, felt like a vast chasm to Peter.

Parking in the massive mall lot, Anya got out before he could walk around to open her door.

"Do you regret this?" she asked, eyeing him directly.

"No, of course not. I've told you I've got plenty of money."

"I wasn't talking about the money."

"I guess I don't understand then."

"You're acting differently. Did I do or say something to offend you?"

"No."

They stared for a moment.

Shaking her head, she turned and they walked into the mall, heading for a clothing store. Going to the women's clothing department, she tried to pick only a few clothes, but Peter picked other clothes to add to the stack. Her modest tastes and demure style choices clashed with the sexy clothes he selected. Her slacks and bulky blouses varied from his choices of tight short dresses and short skirts with tight blouses. Displaying cleavage or plenty of leg wasn't her norm.

He gave her no real option to reject them, since he was paying. "You'll get more comfortable having wider options, Anya. There will be times and places you'll be glad to have the clothes I picked."

"Thank you for these gifts. I can't believe the size of the bill."

"It's my free gift. Now we can head back to your dorm. I'm giving you this phone card so you can call your mother tonight. Talk as long as you want."

Her face turned sad, but she took the card. "Peter, this is over fifteen hundred, just for the clothes. Calling Russia too is so expensive."

"I've got it covered, Anya."

Back on campus, Peter carried most of the packages to the women's side, following Anya, who carried a lesser amount of the bags.

"I'll come up to your room to drop them off to save you multiple trips."

"Okay," she replied softly.

Two girls got on the elevator with them, a blonde and a brunette.

"Wow, somebody is having a good day," said the blonde.

Anya smiled and chuckled.

The girls looked at Peter, who smiled at them. "I'm just the beast of burden, ladies."

The girls snickered.

Arriving on her floor, Peter and Anya walked to her room.

"Check to see if Megan is decent before I go in. I'll wait here in the hallway."

Anya came out a few minutes later. "Come in."

"What's this?" Megan asked, in surprise.

"I'm helping Anya carry the heavy bags. She needed to expand her wardrobe."

"Did you pay for these clothes?"

"I did. Why do you ask? I would think it's my business what I do."

Megan was taken aback at the terse tone, the hostility in his eyes, and the grim stare. She wasn't accustomed to being challenged, living as the darling in the room. She glared. "Whatever, dude."

"Goodbye, Anya." He turned abruptly and exited quickly.

Walking back outside, he exhaled and relaxed before getting into his car to drive back to the parking lot for his dorm. Rather than return to the room, he decided to take a walk around campus for exercise, but mostly to calm his troubled spirit.

Moving briskly, he brought up his breathing and cardiovascular work to the level he intended. The short walk developed into a very long trek. However, pondering his situation as he walked brought no solutions to imagined problems.

When he finally returned to his dorm, Bob was out with Christy. It suited him in his current funk. Turning to his standby, his college studies, he immersed himself in reading accounting textbooks for hours. Answering the chapter questions correctly in every case gave him satisfaction. It was comforting to know his romantic angst didn't damage his intellectual prowess.

Bob spent the day away, returning at bedtime.

"Hey, Peter."

"Bob."

"I…"

"Let's agree to let it rest. I don't really want to talk now—maybe later."

"Sure."

#

When Peter and Bob went to breakfast the next morning, it was the new normal Christy joined them.

"Peter, I checked and it's not going to work out, Anya moving here now. The first possible chance is semester break. I'm sorry."

"That's okay. Thanks for looking into it."

"Are you okay? It seems like you're really provoked about something."

"It's nothing I won't handle. Thanks for asking."

Christy glanced at Bob, who was eyeing Peter sadly.

Peter spoke. "Listen, guys, I've got something to do. I'll see you later."

Peter went to his room to get his notebook and then headed for the classroom building.

In political science, Anya came in wearing new clothes. On this day, she'd picked one of Peter's sexy choices. A dress, white with a floral pattern, it was form-fitting.

"Do you like it?"

"I do. It makes you look really nice."

"It makes me feel differently, dressed like this. Being a spectacle, it's an adjustment for me."

"Believe me, it's no adjustment for people looking at you. It's a good change."

"Thank you for the phone card. I talked to my mother a good length of time last night."

"No problem. If the balance gets down, just let me know and I'll replenish the card."

"You're too good to me."

"Not really. You've had too much bad in your life. Now it's time for the good."

"I will repay you, Peter."

"No. A gift is a gift. These aren't just words. I really mean what I say. You're not obliged to me in any way."

Realizing it was the size of the clothing bill that still bothered Anya, regardless, Peter was still determined. With only his own opinions to guide him, his generous acts had the feel of points of contention for Anya. Although her wardrobe was greatly increased both in number of outfits and variety of styles, she acted less than satisfied.

"This should give you a good start, Anya." He no longer used terms of endearment in addressing her.

She didn't reply.

#

The prompt ride back to campus, in lieu of spending any time together at the mall, was one of awkward silence. His optimism about a romantic future dimmed markedly with his brief roller-coaster relationship ride with Anya. That glum opinion carried over into the subsequent days.

Again, he'd helped carry the purchases up to her room. This time, Megan merely eyed the numerous packages, opting to make no comments. Still, Peter eyed her frostily before another prompt departure. His dire feelings percolated on a number of levels.

The considerable use of his phone card and the shopping sprees on his credit card drew the notice of his parents. He got a call from his mother later.

"Hi, Mom. What's up?"

"Dad and I were talking. We noticed a bunch of recent purchases."

"Yeah, I was going to call to tell you. I met this girl from class, Anya. She's a Russian coed studying here. Anyway, we talked and she's got some really bad situations she's coping with. Her roommate here is a bitch, who's giving her a real hard time, and on top of that, her mom back in Russia was diagnosed with terminal brain cancer. She is devastated. It broke my heart, so I decided to help her. I let her use the phone card to call her mom. Maybe you don't understand, but for them the clock is running out. Also, they're very poor, so I helped her get clothes so she can fit in with the rest of the girls on campus."

"That's very noble, son, but you need to use great caution about that. I don't know this girl, but sometimes our generous acts don't have the effect we wish. People respond to acts of kindness in different ways. Our well-intentioned gifts can make them feel beholden."

"I realize that, Mom. She acts kind of embarrassed about it, but it's done now. I'm not sorry that I helped her."

"I would guess you like her. I suspect your interest is more than just Christian compassion."

"I…well, probably in the beginning, you're right, but I'm starting to think I'm barking up the wrong tree. She's very pretty, and she has a lot of other options farther up the food chain."

"Peter, stop that. Don't say demeaning things about yourself."

"Girls are an area I haven't gotten a good handle on in the past, and nothing is different this time."

"Stop moping and get your head up. You have nothing to feel badly about."

"Sure, Mom."

"You listen to what I'm saying, Peter Brown. As far as this girl, maybe you should think about using better restraint. Let her figure out things in her life at her own pace."

"I'm going to do that very thing. However, I will continue funding her phone calls. If her Mom only has a few months left…well, I try to imagine such a horror and I can't. I never call anybody to use up that money anyway, other than to call you guys."

"Okay, Peter. Are you coming home for a visit?"

"I might just do that. Getting away sounds like a great idea. Am I on Dad's hit list?"

She laughed. "Of course not. Let us know when you're coming. We've been doing some traveling lately."

"I will, and thank you for calling, Mom. I feel much better after talking to you."

"We love you, son."

"I love you guys too. Tell Dad we'll play golf. Maybe I'll let him win." She laughed heartily at his joke. "Speaking of that, he just got back from a round with his friends. He's pretty happy, so I think he did well. The four of them are pretty loud in the den. You know what I'm talking about: a pack of old fools, with their boasting and banter, surely exaggerating their exploits."

Peter laughed. "I know exactly what you're saying. I wish I was there with them."

"Well, I'm going to arrange a meal, so I'll let you go, son. Goodbye, Peter."

"Bye, Mom."

Peter sat for a moment, struggling with the sudden onset of a strong pang of homesickness. The idea of walking straight to his car to drive home forever suddenly had great appeal.

The moment of angst passed when Bob returned to the room. "Hey, Peter."

"Bob."

"Is something wrong?"

"It's just me being my usual stupid self. I talked to Mom, and like a little baby I get crushed by homesickness."

"We all feel that. There's nothing stupid about missing your parents. Is this still about Anya?"

"There is that possibility."

"Did she do, or say, something troublesome?"

"It's just…I'm not getting a good vibe. Maybe it's just me, but…"

"I'm sorry. I really am. Because I've finally gotten a girl, and things are going so well with Christy, I don't want to seem like I don't care about your troubles."

"Bob, I'm happy you got Christy. She's a neat girl and the best thing for you. I'll deal with my situation, one way or another."

"Just be sure there even is a situation to deal with. I worry you read too much into things. In reality, there may be no problem at all, other than in your mind."

"There's an equal possibility there is a problem. In my life, I prepare for the worst possible outcomes, so that way whatever actually happens can't be worse than I'd anticipated."

"Can I say be careful about that? Your own moods and actions can make your fears self-fulfilling prophecies."

Peter frowned. "Wow. I never thought of it that way."

"It's just a word of warning."

"Just as an example, when we rode in the car, Christy slides over to sit by you. Anya is welded to my car door like I'm poison."

"What if it's part of the cultural differences? She didn't see what Christy did, and maybe they do things differently back in Russia."

Peter shrugged. "Maybe, but there are a lot of things that…"

"Or not. I'm not going to join your pity party."

"Okay, Bob. I'll give it another try."

"It's like I said before, you need to decide if she's worth the effort. You can't just say the expedient thing to me. You've got to feel it in your heart."

"Bob, I know everything you're saying, but I don't think you understand. You've got a girl where you know how she feels. There are no questions. With Anya, I don't know. Whether that's some cultural thing, or whether she doesn't like me, I haven't figured out. If I go into this thing thinking I'm on the right path and…I'm not…Do you see?"

"I understand, but let me say if there's a bad ending there, remember what you told me. There are twenty-five thousand coeds on this campus. There are other girls to choose from."

"That first time with Anya, she just grabbed me, for whatever the reason. I don't know if I'd call it love at first sight, but I haven't felt this way about any other girl. Allison was an interest, but mostly in my dreams. I never thought there was a realistic chance at her. Also, I think Anya is a much better person than Allison. I don't want to waste my time dating a bunch of girls I don't care about."

"I know what you're saying. First, I didn't think I could get a girl, and then once Christy came into my life, I'm shocked at how quickly our bond grew. You're right; I don't have any problem knowing where I stand with her."

"I envy you that. This has got me stirred up all the time with no rest, so I'm going to go for a run. I know the truth of my feelings for Anya, but what does she truly feel about me, if anything?"

After changing into his sweats, Peter headed for the outdoor track. He was a decent-enough athlete that he could pass for a runner on the school team. This session was particularly grueling, as he tried to purge his troubling emotions with grit and physical effort. Though he felt somewhat better afterward, he didn't fully succeed in his goal.

He did see Allison walking toward him on the sidewalk, heading for the dorm. As always, a handsome guy was with her.

"Peter. Trying out for varsity?"

"Hardly, I'm just trying to stay in shape."

"This is Derek."

"Hello, Derek, nice to meet you."

"Hey."

"Well, Allison, it was nice seeing you again. I'll let you go. I'm going to take a walk for my cool down."

That statement turned Derek's sneer into a smile of contempt.

Peter fought down his ire. He had no patience for games. Turning in the other direction to begin a brisk walk, unfortunately, he carried his angst, reignited at full force. Though Allison had been a trigger, it was Anya who was in his mind.

His feet carried him toward her dorm, though he had no plans to stop in and see her. It was like fate had intended this walk because as he approached the dorm, he happened to see Anya. Smiling, she was walking with a very handsome guy. They were having an animated conversation and she seemed to be very much taken with him, laughing at his jokes and, to Peter's horror, they were holding hands.

It was a shock to his system, an unanticipated plot twist that jolted him to his core. Stopping in his tracks, he felt like screaming. Anya had her back to him, so she never saw him when he turned around and jogged back to his dorm, shattered.

His demons had come home to roost. There was no innocent way to rationalize what he'd seen. Anya was, in fact, capable of the warm actions he saw in Christy—apparently, if she was with the right guy. At that point, it was easy for him to take a fatal view, and he did.

Walking up the stairs in a daze, Peter went into his room in stunned silence.

Bob looked up from studying. "How was your run?"

Peter couldn't manage a reply.

"Peter, what's wrong?"

"I'm going to take a shower. Give me a minute and then we'll talk."

It was a long shower as he burned with shame, like he deserved disdain from Anya.

Walking out later, he sat down on his bunk. "I saw Anya walking with this studly guy."

"What exactly does that mean?"

"Eh…walking hand-in-hand, lovey-dovey, like Christy does with you. Clearly, I'm toast."

"Eh…"

"Don't bother with some spin; I'm not in the mood."

"Did she see you?"

"No. Listen, I'm going to crash early. I've had enough of today. I don't want to talk about this."

Chapter Four

Going back to class, he debated where to sit in political science class. The idea of moving back to the other side of the room was tempting.

Anya came in later, smiling. "Hello, Peter."

"Hello, Anya. I'm glad to see you're happy." She seemed preoccupied and missed his pinched tone. In light of what he'd seen, Peter had his opinion as to why.

"Thank you. I feel very happy."

Peter grimaced. Holding it back proved impossible. "Eh...I'm going to be honest. I saw you when I was out walking after my workout...you were with a guy. You guys seemed to have really hit it off because you were clearly happy to be there...with him."

Her face clouded. "I'm sorry, but I felt like I needed to date some other people too. You were my first date in my life."

"Well, I don't own you. You're free to date elsewhere. There's no disputing that fact." He stared ahead, struggling to resist an angry outburst.

"Peter, can't we be friends?"

"Friends..." he muttered, shaking his head in dismay. The word every guy dreads hearing, the kiss-of-death word for a relationship. "Sure, Anya, we're pals now. You've got your wish."

Unable to handle his feelings of shame, he stood up to walk to the other side of the room, to his old seat.

#

After class, she looked over at him, but he wouldn't make eye contact. Finally, she got up and left.

Again, Peter muttered, "So much for Anya."

He stood feeling utterly defeated and went through the remainder of his day in an emotional stupor. Rather than return to the dorm cafeteria for supper, he ate at the student union, alone. After lengthy consideration, he decided his usual self-flagellation would not be the path he'd follow out of this particular dilemma. "So be it. If she wants out, *vaya con Dios, señorita,*" he said to himself.

When he finally did go to his room, Bob spoke. "Anya left a message for you. She wants you to call her to talk about…well, you know. She's sorry it made you feel badly."

"Although she wasn't sorry she was with him." He turned his face away, so Bob wouldn't see his painful expression from the emotional blow.

"Peter, c'mon. Give her a break."

"Sure, I'll call back. What the heck?"

With his ire greatly evoked, he dialed the number.

Megan answered the phone.

"This is Peter. I got a message Anya asked for me to call her."

"Oh, I'm so sorry, Peter. She's out on a study date now, with Steve."

Her sickly sarcastic tone jumped through the phone at him. He said nothing for a moment as he simmered with rage.

Megan continued to gloat. "What did you expect: that she'd settle for a head case like you? Coming into my room and acting like an ass to me, there had to be consequences. How could you not know that? Not to worry: we've got her covered now. I know plenty of cool guys. You can take your song and dance and…"

Peter hung up on her.

Bob looked on in alarm.

Peter stood for a time in a daze before turning to face Bob. Mounting low blows were having an effect. "That was Megan. Seemingly, Anya has moved out of their bull's-eye of abuse and into acceptance in their clique. I think Megan supplied that guy I saw. She certainly relished piling it on me just now, twisting the knife. Wow…I thought I'd seen the worst, but I guess there's no bottom to how far I can fall. I'm definitely going home this weekend. I've got to get away to clear my head and purge Anya from my memory banks. I definitely need to look in other directions."

"Peter, I'm so sorry."

"I'll cope—what other choice do I have? I'm tougher than you might think."

He didn't believe his own statement.

#

The following class day, he went straight to the other side of the room.

After class, Anya walked over to him. He spoke before she did, cutting her off. "I got your phone message and returned your call. Didn't Megan tell you she got in her slams? Trust me, I won't bother you again. Megan made it crystal clear she has your life well in hand, and she's got plenty of dudes to keep you busy."

Anya's face flushed with embarrassment. "Peter, please. I didn't reject you. I wanted to meet other guys, but I still want to see you. I'm sorry Megan said mean things to you. She did introduce me to Steve. He's a nice boy, and we have fun together."

"That's so nice, Anya." He couldn't manage to keep snarky out of his tone.

Anya bristled. "If that's the way you feel, I'm sorry. It isn't what I want, but it's your choice. I hope we can still…"

"Under the circumstances, I can't say I'm optimistic about that. I'm going home this weekend to think this through."

"Do you want your gifts back?" She eyed him sadly.

"Of course not—what would I do with women's clothes?"

"I meant I would return them to the stores and give you the refunds."

"No, Anya, they were gifts with no strings attached, and the same with the phone card. You may not see much merit in me as a boyfriend, but I'm not a vengeful person. You still need to talk to your mother, and I'll still pay that bill."

Tears formed in her eyes.

It bothered him a great deal. Hurting her was never a goal. "I hope you have a good life with your new boyfriends. I've got to go."

He left swiftly. It was the most difficult walk he'd ever taken; feeling like this was the actual end with Anya. If he'd walked straight into a blast furnace, it couldn't have hurt more. Ending his pain in an instant of searing flame played through his wounded mind and spirit. At that point, he felt hope was gone from his life.

#

Returning to his room at the end of the day, he went to dinner in the cafeteria with Bob.

As always, Christy joined them at the table. Uncharacteristically quiet, finally she spoke. "Peter, I'm so sorry. I still talk to Anya and she's so upset about how things have worked out; it's got her constantly on pins and needles. She can't sleep from the worry."

"That makes two of us." He stared at the wall, sullen and hurt.

"I'm not trying to make excuses, but I think you need to understand her situation. She's never dated before you. Bringing her out of her bubble, she was curious to try life. Dating some other people, I know how it tears you up, but girls understand it. She knew you wanted a serious relationship right away, but she had to figure out what she wants. She never said you're the wrong guy. It's just…well, she wanted to try others too."

"Why do you think I don't understand, Christy? I saw her with Steve, and he was definitely much further along than I ever got with her. So be it."

"Anya doesn't want that reaction from you. She still wants to date you also."

"After the verbal abuse I got from Megan, I don't like my chances. She's vicious and vindictive. She'd be a constant viper in Anya's ear. I have no doubts about that. I don't need that aggravation."

"Anya can think for herself. Megan's sudden reversal to accept her into the group doesn't fool Anya. She knows Megan has a grudge against you, and she hates that." She eyed Peter closely, trying to decide if he was getting it.

"It doesn't change the facts. Anya's going to be dating these hunk guys Megan supplies. I got the clear impression Steve's a user. He'll get around to his ultimate goal with Anya, and probably sooner than later."

"She's a big girl, Peter. She's not stupid about guys."

"Let me ask you this: Would you have done this to Bob?"

Surprised, she paused before answering. "It's not apples to apples. I'm not the stunner Anya is. I wouldn't have those options she has."

"You know what I'm saying."

"Okay, no, *I* wouldn't, but I haven't lived Anya's life. In her shoes, I can't say I'd do any better."

"Hmph," Peter muttered. "Diplomatic answer, but at this point I feel I need to protect myself. I don't know about any future with Anya. I'll think long and hard this weekend, at home."

Christy scowled. "You can draw a line in the sand, but is that the best course of action? I happen to think Anya is a good person. Maybe you should think about putting your bruised ego on the shelf."

Peter grimaced. "That's easy for you to say, Christy. You're not the one in Megan's gun sights."

"Granted, but I care about both you and Anya. This can be resolved, but not if you get mean."

"Me? Of course, I should have figured that in there somewhere…I'm the one at fault."

"That attitude is not going to win you too many friends. I hope you know that. Are you more interested in winning or getting Anya?"

"Okay, you win: I'm a bad boy."

"Peter, don't act childish. You're a better person than that. I know you feel like she's cheated on you. There was no mutual agreement. You only dated a couple of times. Toughen up. If you want Anya, you're going to need to go get her. If there's other competition along the way, that's life. Getting a girl isn't like picking low-hanging fruit."

"You've got my stomach tied up in knots, but thanks for your perspective. Let's take a rest."

"Sure, but remember Bob and I are here for you."

"Thank you. I do appreciate that."

#

After classes on Friday, Peter packed his bag and headed for his car, for the three-hour drive home. He expected it would give him plenty of time to ponder his troubles. Yet, with his painful ruminations—he'd stayed seated across the classroom from Anya for the balance of the week—it seemed like no time at all before he was pulling into the family driveway and into the garage.

His mother came out to greet him. "Oh, Peter, it's so good you're home."

Here he could feel at peace. He felt much-needed inner warmth as she hugged him firmly. Home was always a safe haven, no matter what issues he wrestled with. "Mom," he whispered.

"Do you have any clothes to be washed?"

"No, I do them at school."

"Come in. Dad's in the den, watching ESPN."

Peter chuckled. "It's funny. I find myself doing so many things just like him."

"That's not a bad thing. He is your father."

"He is that, and I'm certainly his son."

They walked into the den, where his father was intently watching football highlights in preparation for the weekend games.

"Hi, Dad."

"Oh, Peter, sit down. They're about to talk about the Big Ten games. I know we're on the road tomorrow."

Peter sought out his usual easy-boy chair, a place he'd logged many hours watching games. "I like our chances. I know things can happen, but we've built a tradition of winning for a while now, so I'm not worried."

"I agree. People can rise up and pull off upsets, but I think we're in pretty good shape."

"I'll get some cola for you boys."

"Thanks, Mom."

She'd stood by her son's chair. As she started to walk away, her husband spoke. "Honey, would you bring a bag of Cheetos also?"

"When you start on those things, you can't stop."

"I promise I'll be good."

"The doctor wants you to watch your eating."

"Okay. I'll watch every single one of those suckers as they go into my mouth."

Peter laughed loudly.

His mother grimaced. "Don't encourage him, son. This is important."

"Sorry, Mom, I'll shut up, but it was funny."

"We'll see how funny it is if he ends up in the hospital. His blood pressure has been worrisome lately."

"Dad, is that true?" Peter mirth turned to concern.

"Don't worry, Peter. I've got a handle on it." His dismissive tone didn't mollify Peter or his mother.

"Some handle," she replied, perturbed. "Forget the snacks."

Riled, she left them to their program.

"Dad, are you upset about what I did for Anya?" Peter asked.

"It caught me by surprise. We hadn't heard about a girl beforehand, and suddenly you're spending big money on her? It's not the money; you know that. You haven't been impulsive in the past. Acting out of character made us wonder what was going on."

"I made a snap decision, that's true. I can't say I could defend it other than I felt for this girl. She has it rough here and at home in her country, so I tried to help. I think it will end up being a non-issue before long. I would have liked to date her, but she's going in another direction with that. I saw her cozy up to some buff guy. The writing's on the wall."

"I'm sorry, Peter. I think you can see that in a world in turmoil, you can't single-handedly save everybody. It's fine you did this noble thing for her, but I wouldn't make it a habit."

"I know. Partly why I came home this weekend is to think about things. She told me she wants to see other guys. I was her first date."

His mother returned with the colas. She joined the discussion. "What else did she say?"

"She tried to be gentle with me, I believe. Like, 'Peter, I still want us to date.' Things like that. I wasn't buying it. She doesn't need to *settle* for me when she's got plenty of options higher up the food chain."

His mother scowled. "I told you I don't want to hear those kinds of remarks. They're not true, and bashing yourself is never a good idea."

"Sure, although I want to say, ironically, I think part of the dynamic is her mean roommate got her nose out of joint when I stood up for Anya. She completely changed her approach. All of a sudden, Anya is no longer poison and is accepted into the bitch clique. Megan told me she's got plenty of hot guys to keep Anya busy."

"I hope you're misinterpreting the situation, but if it's true, that's terrible. I do understand there are people out there who have real problems. Sometimes children of privilege can think they have no rules. It's an ugly side of our society."

His dad added, "Peter, you don't need to sink down into the muck with those types of people. That's a huge school you attend. There are plenty of other options."

"I realize that, but something about Anya just struck me. I've liked girls before, but this was so different, how I felt. Actually, how I still feel. When I saw her with that other guy, I was crushed."

"Romance has many perils, son. When I went after your mother, we had our share of misunderstandings."

"Like what?"

"She was always swishing her bottom at the boys." He smirked.

His mother laughed and then objected. "I was not. Stop lying, you old fool. You dated other girls too."

"Not after you showed up."

"Well...that was a long time ago. You got me, so what's the difference now?"

"It did have a happy ending. I'm just making a point to Peter. The girl of your dreams isn't just going to just fall in your lap. You're going to need to work to get her. She gets to make decisions too."

"That's what I'm afraid of. I watched how we were together compared to my roommate and his new girlfriend. It was the difference between night and day."

"It's not necessarily the same," his mother replied. "She comes from a much different culture, and honestly, I can understand why she wants to meet other boys. My suspicion is you came on very strong. That can be intimidating, in spite of your good intentions."

"Lately I've given her plenty of leeway, but I know what you're saying, Mom."

"What I want you to understand is...Dad and I aren't saying you should or shouldn't pursue this girl. Maybe you should take a more relaxed approach. Accept what she says at face value, and don't let your hurt and jealous feelings cloud your judgment."

"I know you don't want to hear this, but facts are facts. She has options with higher-profile guys. If I'm thrown into open competition, I don't like my chances."

"Peter, let her make those decisions. Don't prejudge anything. What you think appeals to girls may not be right. Some of those supposed *hunks* are not men women want to make a life with. Do you understand?"

"Yes and no, Mom, I can only judge by what I see. Really pretty girls don't seem to pick average guys very often."

"That's your hurt feelings talking. Because you see two people together, you have no idea of their feelings for each other. I repeat, go by what she says. Don't be fragile. You've got so much to offer, and at your age you've got plenty of time. Concentrate on the important things, like your classes and future career."

"I wish I could just dismiss the whole thing, but my feelings for Anya are really stubborn and won't go away. Maybe I need to get a clue."

"Well, then talk to her. Don't act hurt, or threatening—just let her talk honestly and go from there."

"Okay, Mom, I'll try, but it's easy to get discouraged."

"I know. You can handle this, son." She leaned over to kiss the top of his head.

"You know?" his father asked, skeptically. "You bulldozed me. I was a living speed bump in your path."

"Will you stop with the 'poor me' crap, George?"

"My point is you can only see things through female eyes. I understand what Peter is saying; I lived it. This isn't easy for him to go through."

"You don't think I know that?" She eyed her husband grimly.

"Listen, Mom and Dad, I didn't mean to cause an argument. It seems you guys have some old wounds, and the last thing I want to do is drag you down into my misery. Can we let it go and change the subject?"

"Good idea. We'll watch football tomorrow and maybe go to dinner and a movie after church on Sunday, before you drive back to school."

His father was eyeing his mother. Each had a determined look.

"I like it, Dad. We can play golf another time."

"You're on."

"Are you good with our weekend itinerary, honey?"

She continued to eye him coolly. "It's fine."

Peter eyed them both with concern. Whatever their issues over the years, his parents seldom showed them in front of him. Apparently, his troubles had hit a nerve with them. This departure from routine was concerning. They were normally pleasant and calm; an underlying issue had never surfaced in front of Peter.

His mother turned to him. "Let me say one last thing. They're young women, so, by definition, mostly they're not fully matured. Even so, ultimately, they judge boys by their character. Looks can draw initial attention, I'll grant you that, but if they're jerks, girls will drop them in a hurry. In the end, it's quality young men, like you, who are left standing. You don't have to believe me now, but you will."

"We'll see, Mom." His smile was a weak one.

She left the room. She was still irked; neither husband nor son had any problem grasping that dismal fact.

"Dad, what was that?"

"We have a past too, son. That isn't something I need to get into. Suffice it to say, I understand completely where you're at right now, trying to figure things out about a woman. They're a different animal, beyond our reckoning. Sometimes you've just got to jump down into the trenches to slug it out."

"That's encouraging."

"We all go through it. Also, I don't hold it against you, the generous things you did for Anya. In your shoes, I might have done the same thing. I certainly extended myself to chase down your mother. I was not alone in that pursuit. She had plenty of other options."

"I understand, Dad. I think you know how painful these setbacks are. The hard knocks leave a mark."

"They do. There's no way around it."

"Anyway, enough talk. Let's watch sports."

"Good choice."

#

Christy talked at length with Anya, who had called for the latest on Peter.

"He went home to clear his head, Anya."

"What does that mean? Does he no longer like me? Does he think I only wanted those gifts?"

"I don't believe so. My opinion: when a guy makes a play for a girl, and then she goes out with somebody else, it hits him straight to the core. You understand how jealous girls can be. It's no different for guys. You and I know what you were doing—harmless testing of the waters with different guys—but Peter couldn't see it that way. He read it as him coming up short, like you rejected him."

"That's wrong. I didn't intend that. He is…should I say, friend? He didn't like when I said that to him."

"Reverse the roles. If you caught him with some other girl and he told you he wanted to be friends, well…"

"Yes, I see it now. I was stupid about this. What should I do?"

"What do you want to do? From what you've said, you're having fun and enjoying these dates with other guys."

"Yes."

"Are you ready to shut that down?"

"I don't know. Does Peter want…"

"A wife? Possibly he does."

"We're too young for that. With my mother dying, I can't I consider such things. I never even thought about a husband."

"Is Peter somebody you'd consider in that role?"

"Of course."

"I don't think he knows that."

"I'm not an expressive person. Maybe I'm shy? What must I tell him?"

"I suspect you need to have a serious talk, in depth. If there's a communication gap, you guys need to resolve it. He's thinking things, you're thinking things, and you never tell each other those thoughts. That's where the train goes off the rails."

"What do I tell the other guys? Megan keeps them calling me."

"I go back to my first question: Are you ready to shut that down?"

"I must think about that. I do like it. The first boy, he was so nice at first, but then he wanted me to…I said no. I'm not ready. Why would he think I would do such things with somebody I just met?"

"It's just my opinion, but I'd be very cautious dealing with Megan and the boys she sends your way. I don't have a good feeling about her. From what Peter told me, I think her sudden reversal in how she's treating you might be nothing more than getting revenge on Peter for defending you."

"Is it possible she could be so cruel?"

"You remember how cruel she was before. I still think we can get you moved over here after the semester break. I'd be happy to be your roommate."

"That is so kind of you. Perhaps I will reconsider these dates she sends me on. I do sense an insincere feeling from many of the guys. They think they fool me, but they do not."

"It's just a word to the wise."

"Thank you. I trust you, Christy. I can't say that about too many Americans I've met so far."

"Meanwhile, keep your guard up and play the game with Megan. We don't want to set her off again."

"I will talk to Peter when he comes back."

"Be honest. Tell him the truth, so he understands. If you want to keep dating other guys, make him understand why. Definitely make sure he knows to keep dating you, or he'll face the music from me, and Bob will help me with the beat down."

The girls chuckled.

"What is that Americans say? You're a good egg."

"That's right, Anya." Christy laughed heartily. "Seriously, we're on your side."

"I appreciate your kind words, Christy. *Ya lyublyu tebya.*"

"What is that?"

"I love you, in Russian."

"Oh, that is so sweet. I love you too, as does Bob. You already know Peter loves you."

"I understand that more and more. It is overwhelming. He's never even tasted my cooking."

Christy laughed. "Wow, Anya. I didn't see that coming. So, are you suddenly on board with going in that direction with Peter?"

"I think I must be ready for anything. You opened my eyes. I must stop thinking like a little girl."

"Well, I've got news for you, Anya. You're definitely a woman—time to put on your big-girl pants."

"Big-girl pants?"

"It's just a joke, of sorts. Don't worry about it."

"Okay."

"I'll have Bob call me when Peter gets in on Sunday evening. If you want to call him, at least you'll know when he is there."

"Thank you, and thank Bob for me. You're dear friends."

#

Peter felt better when he got into his car to drive back to school Sunday evening. Although the issue of Anya remained up in the air, being with his parents had helped.

Turning on the radio, he played music loudly to keep him alert. Leaving much later than usual, he drove in the dark right from the start of the trip. His mind was busy in problem-solving mode. Solving this particular problem wasn't easy, no matter how he looked at it. There was another person involved he couldn't control. She also had choices, and what she chose to do could go in many different directions. The one thing he did decide is he wouldn't go on this way, in constant turmoil.

Arriving back at school, it was after eleven when he walked into his room.

Bob looked at him. "I was getting a little worried. You normally don't travel this late."

"I got a late start, but I really needed to be at home. My mom has always been a calming influence. She makes me think things can work out okay."

"They can work out, Peter. While you were gone, Christy has been talking to Anya. It isn't what you think with her. I don't want to try to speak for her, but suffice it to say, she meant nothing bad toward you. She'd never dated before, so she was curious. I'm sure you can understand that."

"I can understand, but I can't say I like it. Everybody is telling me the same thing, but put yourself in my shoes. You see Christy with some other guy, all smiley-faced and enamored: how do you think you'd react?"

"Eh…not well."

"There it is. I rest my case. Everybody wants me to look at it through her eyes. Doesn't it work the other way too? What about looking through my eyes?"

"I…eh…"

"You can't truly understand. You haven't seen your girl smile at another guy, hold hands, act all lovey-dovey. If that happens, you'll know where I am with this, believe me. It's a burning coal in your gut. I can't get past it."

Bob eyed him sadly. "She still wants you."

"We'll see about that."

"Don't give up on her. It would be a huge mistake."

Peter frowned but didn't reply.

The guys went to bed. Bob didn't call Christy because it was so late.

#

On Monday in class, when Peter went to the opposite side of the classroom, Anya got up and walked over to sit beside him there.

"Peter, we must talk."

"Okay," he replied in a neutral tone, looking straight ahead.

"Will you talk with me?"

"Sure."

"After classes, will you meet me at the student union? We'll eat supper there."

"Okay." This time he shrugged, acting nonchalant.

"Please don't be angry with me."

"We'll talk later, Anya." He still refused to look at her directly.

#

His mind was astir for the rest of the day, until later when he bought his food and walked over to her table. She had no food as she sat waiting for him.

"Aren't you hungry?"

"I…eh…"

"Anya, you've got to eat. I'll be right back."

Walking to a vendor, he ordered what he'd seen her eat before, healthy choices of salads and vegetables.

"Peter, you don't need to buy this food."

"Anya, this is fine. Eat your dinner and then we can talk." It was a quiet meal.

After finishing their meals, they walked to the lounge, claiming seats on a sofa together.

When she didn't speak immediately, he did. "I went home, like I said. Being with my folks is a tonic for me. It's safe, they don't judge, and they're on my side. It was a good choice."

Anya suddenly looked sad.

"Oh, I'm sorry. I wasn't thinking. My saying that, it made you think about your mom."

"I know what you mean, Peter. It is fine. My mom's situation is a part of my life. I don't want to get distracted from the situation between you and me. Before you say anything, please listen to what I have to say."

"Okay."

"I've been talking with Christy, and she's helped me understand better about this trouble. I want to say I'm sorry I hurt your feelings. It wasn't my intention. Perhaps I got carried away when guys started asking me for dates. I never fully realized how it affected you. I should have been better with thinking about you. If I say I care about you, does that matter?"

"Of course it matters. I don't want to seem like a petulant child. You don't need that."

"All of the gifts, the kind things you do, it isn't why I'm interested. I hope you understand that."

"I do."

"Good. Christy asked me if I was ready to stop dating…those other boys."

"And…"

"I liked having fun, but honestly, after a few dates, things started turning in directions I didn't want to go. She also said maybe Megan doesn't have good intentions. I knew that. These boys are her friends and possibly, how do you say it, she pulls strings?"

"I'd say that's a very strong possibility."

"The idea of us, that's not a problem for me—it never has been. I just didn't know if I was ready to…become close, like I think you want."

"Anya, I would never try to force anything, and certainly not about doing those things. I guess I thought you knew me better than that."

"I know, Peter, and I do trust you. What I was talking about is…well…"

"Being a couple, thinking about getting serious? I started thinking about you in that way right from the start. I understand I came on too strong. That's what I was going to say to you. I'm willing to step back and give you some space."

"I don't want space. I'm ready to take some steps, if that's what you want. Can we be honest? Are you saying you'd want a Russian girl as…"

"A wife? Sure, why not? That wasn't the problem for me. We aren't ready to get married while we're in school, but I wouldn't be afraid of it. The honesty I need from you is in how you really feel. If this is too much, or if you have reservations about us, now is the time to say it. Can you live with an American, in America?"

"Some people think Russian girls only come here to dupe American boys to get US citizenship. That isn't my intention. Honestly, I have nothing back home other than my mother."

"Does that mean you could be on board with an *us*, down the road?"

"Do you want for me to be a girlfriend only to you?"

"That would be nice."

"You don't want to date other girls? There are so many pretty ones here."

"There are many nice girls, but for me, all I need is you. Is that clear enough?"

She smiled. "It's a nice thing for you to say."

"What *I'm* still unclear about are your deeper feelings. I can't make it any clearer how I feel, but I truly want to know how you feel. If we considered getting really close with a future *us* in mind, if you have reservations, sooner or later it would become an issue. Maybe you do need time to think about this. Do you agree?"

"I…eh…can we get back to where we were? I like being with you. I think maybe I don't feel the way you feel, but I'm moving in that direction. I hated this bad between us."

"Okay, fair enough. Are you okay with coming home with me to meet my parents?"

"What if they don't like me?"

"Anya, that won't happen."

Chapter Five

That night's "talk" helped both of them. Anya's request was easy enough for Peter. Dating her again was a good thing. However, his underlying angst was stubborn and not so easily vanquished. He chose not to share that fact with Anya, still unable to manage feeling he'd turned the corner with her. Down deep it still felt to him that their connection was flawed, or missing altogether.

Smiling blithely when he walked into his dorm room, to a battery of Bob's questions, he merely shrugged his shoulders. "We're in a better place now than yesterday at this time."

Bob eyed him closely, unconvinced. Peter didn't act like he was in a better place. "Are you sure everything is okay? Something seems funny. You're not acting normal."

"Well, I guess we'll see how things go. Anya is still living with Megan, and I suspect Megan is nowhere near finished with me. She can still go to the 'aces-up-her-sleeve' hunks to mess up Anya and me."

"True, but Anya has a say in things. I really think you need to trust what she says. The fact you think she can't resist the guys Megan keeps sending her way doesn't mean that she can't do it. Christy has taught me a lot about girls. I wouldn't have thought I could get a cool girl like her, but she's convinced me they don't look at us the way we think. They really do want good character, humor, decency, and other things we wouldn't think would matter to them."

"Christy is a gem; no disputing that, Bob."

"I've been around Anya enough to know she's a good girl, and Christy's talked in depth with her, so I'm confident you're in a good place. I can't say she'll never date another guy, but Christy said Anya holds you up as the standard to measure other guys she meets."

"Really? That's surprising."

"Don't look a gift horse in the mouth. Let's pick up where we left off and get you back in the game. You turned my world around when you convinced me to go to that first mixer, where I met Christy. I would never have done that on my own. Now I'm returning the favor. You can't seem to look at your situation as it really is. You automatically build in negativity, and it's not helping you."

"Whatever. I'm going to do a little studying. I've got some exams coming up soon."

"Okay, but you heed my words, or else…"

Peter chuckled. "I've got it, moron."

Again, hearing the encouraging words wasn't the same as believing the worst was over. Peter was still a cautious person and, thus far in romance, the worst had never been over.

#

Anya did act differently all week in class. She looked at him, smiled, and made her way over to wherever he was sitting. With the classroom seating, he made her do the work.

"I want to tell you; Megan has noticed I'm not dating these guys of hers. When I say I can't, she doesn't believe the reasons I give."

"Just be careful with her. The end of the semester isn't far away. By the way, I think our football team will get a really nice bowl game. Would you consider going with me?"

"Bowl game?"

"It's like a reward for the team having an excellent season. Probably it would be in some nice warm-weather site. I'd pay your way, of course."

"I guess that would be fine." She looked away.

"You can say no."

"Would you allow Bob and Christy to come along too? It would be more fun with the four of us."

"They could come, but I couldn't afford to pay for four trips. I'm not sure if they can swing it."

"Will you ask them?"

"Sure. I'll talk to Bob tonight."

"Good. I would like that."

"Has Christy said if she's made any progress with the relocation piece?"

"She says things are looking up. I think that means a good thing for the future."

"It does. Perhaps we can close the book on Megan, once and for all."

"I would like that. She doesn't fool me."

"I didn't think so, but you're the one living under stress. People can react in a lot of different ways under trying circumstances."

"I do much better now that I have friends." Smiling at his insightful words, she turned her face to him.

"I'm glad we can help." He'd almost added "honey," but was cautious about using terms of endearment again. "The final home game is this Saturday. Do you want to go?"

"Yes."

"It could be a cold one, so wear your woolies."

She snickered. "What are woolies?"

"You know, your muck-a-lucks, your tundra gear."

Anya laughed. "You are still a silly man."

"I am that. You won't need them in the sunny South. What do you say to a study date tonight? We've both got finals coming up."

"Yes, I would like that."

"I can come down to your dorm this time."

"Thank you, Peter. I still think you yank my chain with the words that you use."

"Hey, those are actual documented terms! Like I said, if I ever yank your chain, you won't have any problem knowing it."

"I don't think so, but I look forward to tonight." She chuckled.

#

Back at his dorm, Bob and Christy were pleased when Peter explained his evening study plans with Anya.

"See, things are fine with her. You got all crazy over nothing. All of us have dated other people. It's no big deal."

"If you say so, Christy."

"No more moodiness, dude."

"Yes, ma'am."

Bob asked, "You dated other guys?" He had a facetious forlorn-puppy look.

"Shut up. Don't you start, or I'll clean your clock too."

They both laughed. Peter admired that Bob could dismiss any potential feelings of jealousy so easily. He made a mental note to work on that trait himself. "Folks, I'm going to split, so I have plenty of study time."

"See ya." Christy smiled.

"Oh, by the way, have you guys thought about the bowl-trip idea?"

"We like it. Christy can come up with the money and I'm still working some things around. I think it's doable. My dad understands the lure, thank God."

Peter added, "By the way, we put on our game faces this Saturday. We don't need any upsets to mess up this excellent season."

"Agreed." Bob nodded.

"Take care, guys."

#

Peter donned his coat to walk to Anya's dorm. Going into the lobby, he called her room and got no answer, which made no sense. Walking down the hallway to the lounge area, he saw Anya sitting on a sofa; she looked concerned. Megan was talking to her, or, more accurately, haranguing her, and was accompanied by the same stud guy. He was an intimidating presence, hulking over Anya.

Peter walked over. "Is everything okay, Anya?"

Megan glared at him. She and the guy sneered, like Peter was less than a person.

"Peter, I..." Anya started.

"We can study at my dorm," he said. "It seems the atmosphere here isn't conducive for preparing for exams."

"Yes." She stood up quickly, easing behind Peter, who felt strongly protective, even in the face of this physical specimen Megan had conjured up. For a tense moment, he wasn't sure what they would do.

Megan huffed. "If that's the way you want it, Anya, so be it. You'll regret this." Megan turned abruptly and led her tempter away.

"I was frightened," Anya whispered. "She has never been so threatening before. She is angry that I still see you."

"I understand. If she tries to start something, we'll take it to the school officials. People can't get away with that type of behavior. I won't stand for it. Let's go."

"I must go up to get my coat."

"I'm going to walk up there with you, just in case. I'm tempted to have you crash in Christy's room tonight."

"Is that allowed?"

"We just do it. Nobody will care. It's preferable to putting up with Megan's…"

"I will get my things."

Megan hadn't returned to the room yet, so Anya gathered her overnight items for a prompt departure. Once they arrived back at Peter's dorm, he took her up to his room to call Christy. After explaining, Christy agreed immediately to an overnight for Anya.

Bob and Christy came down to join them for a joint study date. Peter was happy to see Anya relax noticeably.

Looking gratefully at Christy, Anya spoke. "Thank you for doing this, Christy."

Smiling warmly, Christie replied. "My pleasure, sweetie pie, I'm glad I can help."

"This will not be a problem for your roommate?"

"No. I told her what happened. It's fine. I can't believe people can act as evil as Megan. I've met vindictive people before, but she takes it to a new level."

"She's some piece of work," Peter muttered, shaking his head in dismay. "I was a little worried that guy would try to throw down. He was one of those bodybuilder types that stand in front of the mirror all day admiring themselves."

"I know the type," Christy replied. "They can't believe all people aren't equally in love with their muscles. Most of them can't even finish a sentence, or put down their muscle magazines."

"Apparently you've dated some of them?" Bob said.

"Rarely, and those were short dates."

Bob smiled. "I understand. After all, when you've got the best, who needs the rest?"

They all laughed heartily.

"Bob, you are so lame. I don't know why I'm with you." Christy gave him a warm hug.

Anya put a hand on Peter's hand, smiling appreciatively. "I feel safe here."

"You are safe; you're among friends."

They opened their textbooks and began their studies. Four excellent students were quickly immersed in their course materials.

Much later, when they parted ways, Anya looked at Christy. "Are you sure this isn't a problem?"

"I'm sure. This will give you a taste of what it would be like to live with me."

"I know I will like it. You're a good person, Christy."

"You're a good person too, Anya. Good night, boys—dream about us." She gave them a playful smirk.

The guys snickered before leaving to go up to their room. Bob looked at Peter as they walked. "All's well that ends well."

"I wish Anya never had to go back to Megan's room. I hope she won't do some other mean thing we're not anticipating."

"If she does, she'll have a price to pay."

"I think she's a child of privilege, so if she involves her rich parents, who knows where it goes? If she's like this, they must be that way also. They probably have resources, if they want to wreak havoc."

"We cross that bridge if we get to it."

Bob opened their room door and they got ready to sleep.

"Okay, good night, Bob." Even with his mind busy sorting through the events of the day, Peter fell asleep fairly rapidly.

#

It was gratifying for Peter to go to breakfast the following morning with Bob, to be joined by both girlfriends. Sitting beside Anya warmed his heart, and to see her relaxed manner bolstered his hopes he was making progress.

"Good morning, Anya. You look really good."

She smiled demurely, though his effusive affections always seemed to overwhelm her. "Thank you, Peter."

She glanced at Christy, who was also smiling at Peter.

"What?" he asked.

"Nothing," Christy replied.

"Somehow, I think it's not 'nothing'."

"Was that a double negative I just heard?"

"I don't use double negatives—not never."

They all laughed at his semi-joke.

"Hey, comedy is not my strong suit."

"Agreed," Christy replied.

"'I am what I am, and that's all that I am.' *Circa* Popeye, if memory serves me."

"Duh."

Anya smiled, but she had no clue. Peter tried to explain. "Popeye was a cartoon character. That was his big saying."

"Oh. There is much in this country I don't understand."

Christy interjected, "Don't worry, Anya. I'll keep the boys from causing you brain damage with their lame attempts at banter."

Anya laughed at that.

"So, Anya, have you thought about coming home to meet my parents?" Peter said without warning.

Anya got a glazed-eye look.

Christy started to speak. "Peter. Maybe…"

"Christy, it's not a proposal; just a trip to meet my folks. That's not obliging Anya to anything. They're actually very nice people."

"I wasn't saying they weren't," Christy replied.

"Anya, you can say no." He tried not to sound defensive, but only with partial success.

She turned her head to him and replied softly, "Okay, I will go with you."

"Good. I'll call my mom and see when they're free."

Christy eyed him critically. However, before she could state her obvious question, he spoke again. "I've got this. Do you think I'm not a gentleman or something?" Instantly, he regretted it.

"Oh, Peter," she replied, shaking her head.

He stood up. "Well, ladies, it's off to classes. Have a great day."

"Likewise."

He walked away, embarrassed at his awkward and needless defensive *faux pas*. "Damn, you're such an idiot," he muttered. "They're just girls. Why do you let them blow your mind?"

He already knew the answer. He cared about Anya.

#

Between classes, sitting in an empty classroom, he called home.

"Hi, Mom. Did I interrupt anything?"

"No, son, I always like to hear from you. What is it?"

"I was thinking…maybe I bring Anya home to meet you guys? Would that be okay?"

"What does she say about that idea?"

"Well, she said okay."

"I assume that means you…"

"Forced it on her? I probably didn't handle it the best. You know me."

"It isn't a problem on our end. Do I need to tell you to be careful? There is a lot she's coping with. Beyond the obvious problem of her mother's disease, the cultural differences are probably daunting."

"She has Christy, Bob's girlfriend, looking out for her now."

"I see. My point is you still need to temper your desires and maybe ease her along. This is very early in a relationship to bring her here. If the die is cast, I understand, but try to be a little more forward-thinking of her feelings."

"The die is cast, as you say."

"We're free anytime."

"I'll see if she'll come this next weekend. Okay?"

"Okay, son. Let us know."

"Thank you, Mom. I love you."

"I love you too."

"Can I talk to Dad a moment? I've got an idea."

"I'll get him."

#

When he called Anya's room that night, Megan answered the phone.

"Anya, please."

"She's not here."

"Do you know where she is?"

"Aren't you supposed to be her boyfriend now? You should know where she is."

Peter's ire simmered at the snarky tone. Even with anticipating she would bait him into an argument, he wasn't fully prepared for it.

"Okay, goodbye, ma'am."

He hung up and headed for the library. Anya was sitting at a full table. A handsome guy was chatting with her. She was smiling, seemingly enjoying the attention.

Her expression changed when she got a glimpse of Peter approaching. So as not to turn the awkward moment into a dismal one, he tried to smile. "Hi, Anya. I'm sorry to bother you. I called your room, but Megan was less than helpful."

"Hi." She eyed him for a moment. "Oh, this is Ron, a classmate."

Peter glanced at Ron, who frowned slightly.

"Hi, Ron, it's nice to meet you. Can I borrow you for one second, Anya?"

"Eh…yes."

She stood and followed him over to the stacks and into an aisle.

"Listen, I talked to Mom and they'd love to have you visit. I set it up for next weekend."

Again, she got the deer-in-headlights look. "I…well…"

"If you're not comfortable coming with me, just say so. I don't want to force you. I think you'd enjoy the visit. You'd have your own bedroom, but I assumed you knew that."

She smiled. "I know that, Peter. I guess I could go. I just don't want to impose on your family."

"Impose? You've got to be kidding. Anyway, we leave that Friday afternoon, right after dinner. As a matter of fact, it's something of a long drive, so maybe we start right away and pick up something to eat on the road. Don't say it. The food is my treat, okay?"

"Okay. I will pack my things, then."

"This will be a fun trip—you'll see. I'll let you get back to your studying now."

"Are you upset I'm here with Ron?"

"No. I'm sorry if you feel I'm all crazy about you being with other guys. That was a sorry episode with those dudes before. You enjoy your time with your friends. I'm okay with it."

He walked her back to her table. "Sorry for the interruption. Take care, Ron. Nice meeting you."

Ron smiled, nodding like he'd won a contest over Peter.

"Bye, Anya."

"Goodbye, Peter."

His verbal assurances to Anya didn't reflect his real truth. It bothered him, seeing her with other guys. However, he managed to refrain from looking back at her until he got to the door. Glancing back to see her snickering at whatever Ron had just said, his emotions punished him as his jealousy kicked in. At that point, getting out the door was the only rational choice, and he succeeded in leaving without fumbling the awkward situation.

Anya was going home with him; that's what mattered—or so he told himself.

#

The few remaining days and subsequent week passed without further issues. Although Peter wondered whether Ron was a new threat for Anya's affections, wisely he kept it to himself.

Leaving to get his car after classes that Friday, he picked up his suitcase in his room.

"Take care, Peter. Enjoy your visit home, and remember, calm your fertile mind. Anya isn't up to any mischief, okay?"

"I know, Bob. I'm an idiot. I'll act like a human, not a lunatic. I promise."

"See that you do."

He walked to his car as his excitement built. After driving to Anya's dorm, he walked up to her room. Anya opened the door and smiled as she let him in.

"Have a nice weekend, Megan," he said.

"Whatever." She flipped him a hand gesture.

Peter ignored her and picked up Anya's suitcase. They walked out to the car and departed. Finally, he felt some measure of confidence with having her in his car, safe from the ravages of Megan's plots.

She didn't sit in the center beside him, but she wasn't acting guarded. That was definite progress in his book.

"Are you happy about this?" he asked.

"Yes. I haven't seen many places since I've come to America."

"Maybe while we're home, I'll take you to some of the local attractions."

"I would like that. Thank you, Peter."

Glancing over, Peter saw her looking at scenery, smiling, but still she seemed guarded to him.

"My parents are looking forward to meeting you."

When she glanced at him, Peter noted the stoic expression on her face.

"Don't worry: they'll love you." He tried for reassuring in his tone.

"I don't think you understand. In my country, many believe Americans look at Russians as backwards, illiterate, unwashed peasants. We're a lower life form compared to your rich people. Don't say it's wrong because I've seen it for myself. Because there are some women who look to take advantage of unwary men to get into this country; every Russian woman is seen that way."

"Anya, I know what you're talking about. Can I say that attitude doesn't represent everybody, or even most people? When I first saw you, I didn't think any of those things. All I knew was that I saw a girl who interested me. Our little verbal contests piqued that interest. I've told you I like smart girls because I actually do."

"Thank you. I don't always feel like I'm smart. Being here is very challenging. It's amazing, hearing other students talk about how smart they are. You pick up on underlying subtleties you know from living here. Too many things go right over my head."

"That's not a problem. Your friends help you with that issue. I'm glad you've got Christy now."

"Yes, it's good. I had a few girlfriends back home. It's nice with Christy. I now have it in America. She makes me believe she honestly cares and even understands some things I explain to her."

"Christy is genuine. That's a rare gift."

"You're a rare gift. I owe you so much."

"Whatever I do, it's just my nature. That works both ways, good and bad. I can be pretty stupid."

Anya chuckled.

"Hey, you're not supposed to agree and pile on."

"I was just thinking about some things Christy told me about American boys."

"What?"

"She said it's girl talk, not meant for male ears."

"Okay. Be that way."

She laughed and touched his arm. At that point, he felt as happy as at any other time in his life up to that point. "I'm so glad you're coming home with me."

"I feel safe with you."

"Good to know, you realize I'll always take care of you. I mean that."

"I know you do. I also know that many times I don't act as you would like. I'm sorry that I'm still trying to find my way. There are so many new things to figure out."

"A lot of it is me. I know I'm too pushy about wanting you all for myself. I hope you can realize you still have all of your options. There are a lot of cool guys out there, and you're too pretty for them not to notice."

Anya chuckled. "You think I'm pretty?"

"Duh."

She laughed fully. "You are always a silly man."

"Guilty, but someday I hope you'll feel I'm *your* silly man. I don't know how you feel about me…well, feeling like I do about you. If you have reservations, I think that can change…for the better." He looked to see her reaction.

"Peter, I do like you, very much. If I seem cautious, it isn't anything against you. Putting trust in people is difficult with my past. I'm working on it. Am I not going alone with you now? It's a big step for me, putting myself in your control."

"I never thought of it that way. I appreciate your trusting me. I'd never take advantage of you."

"I do know that, or I wouldn't have come."

"Can I ask: do you understand how I feel about you?"

"It's very obvious. No girl would miss it."

"Are you okay with…well, my love?" It felt like walking the plank, taking such a chance.

Again, she got a glazed-eyed, distressed look.

"I'm sorry, Anya. I don't mean to swamp you with my drivel. I apologize. Let's change the subject."

"To answer you: I'm adjusting to your strong feelings. I like you very much."

"Thank you. My mom will have a late dinner waiting for us. We'll be dining fashionably late. I hope you won't get too hungry."

"No, that's fine. I hope I'm not putting them to inconvenience."

"Anya, you're the first girl I've brought home to meet them. That should tell you something. Oh, I'm sorry…I'm doing it again."

"It's not a problem. I do understand all of that." Anya glanced out the window.

Again, she put a hand to his arm, for a brief touch. That made him smile broadly. "It's the first time I'm going to meet somebody's parents. We both have a first."

Peter chuckled. "*Touché.*"

Their conversation shifted to talking at length about their shared political science course before they approached the outskirts of his hometown.

"There's my high school."

Anya perked up, paying close attention. "Wow, it's gigantic. We don't have such lavish schools in Russia."

"This is a well-to-do area. As I said, my folks are pretty flush. That store is where I had my first job. My dad wanted me to understand working. I'm glad I did it. I learned a lot."

"My mother wouldn't let me work. Where we lived, it was too dangerous."

"This is my street."

"You have gates?"

"It's a gated community."

Pulling ahead, they approached his parents' home. Anya eyed it in awe. "This is like a palace."

Peter chuckled. "It's just a house."

"I don't think so."

Pulling into the driveway and opening a garage door, one of four, he pulled in. The door into the house opened and his parents came out to meet them. Anya sat for a moment to collect herself before getting out of the car.

"Hello." His mother came over to embrace Anya. "We're so glad you came for a visit. Welcome to our house."

"Thank you, ma'am."

"You're such a lovely girl. I'm Edith, and this is my husband, George."

"It's very nice to meet you. Thank you for inviting me."

"Please come in. The men will get the luggage."

Edith took her by the arm to lead her into the house. Again, Anya was agog at the opulent surroundings. The hand-crafted Italian tile custom lain in the foyer, the massive chandelier hanging overhead, the pricey art pieces—it was just the start of the splendor of the five-thousand-square-foot multistory home. Sitting on a sizable wooded lot, it had more the feel of an estate than a simple residence. Domestic employees were another first in her experience. A maid peeked around a corner at her.

"We've probably indulged ourselves too much," Edith explained. "We feel that a person only lives their life once, so what the heck, do it right. We had a great deal of success in our working years. George got much more from selling his business than we could ever have hoped for. We're quite comfortable."

"Comfortable?" Anya hadn't meant it as a joke, but the family took it that way and they all laughed.

"I told you, Mom. She's a gem."

"Come, children. Dinner is ready."

Sitting down in the formal dining room, being served the multicourse meal, Anya had no words for life at this level. A step in their dining process she liked very much was the habit of saying grace before the meal began.

"It's our religious practice. Is that okay, Anya?"

"Yes, Mrs. Brown. This is a good thing."

During the meal, Peter turned to his dad. "Did you get an answer about what I asked?"

"I just did, son."

"And…"

"I have some friends in high places and called in some favors." He gave a thumbs-up signal.

Peter turned to Anya. "Eh…my folks and I have talked about some things. I hope you don't think we're butting into your business, but we're really bothered by your family situation. We've checked into the background facts and…I'll just say it: we'd like to invite you to travel with us during the Christmas holiday over to Russia, to your hometown, to see your mother."

"What? You'd do that for me?" Tears formed in her eyes.

"That's not all. We checked into your mother's medical situation, and it seems she could use a second opinion. What my dad checked was if we could clear having her come to America for medical treatment with American doctors. My opinion, I think maybe she didn't tell you everything. She couldn't afford treatment, so she just told you she was terminal."

Thick tears in Anya's eyes rolled down her cheeks. She sobbed fitfully.

"Oh…my dear." Mrs. Brown got up to go over and hug her. "It's okay. This will be fine. Don't worry, honey. We've got good doctors who can help her."

"I don't know what to say. You're all so generous with me. There are no words to express how grateful I am. Giving me back my mother…"

"We care about you," Peter said.

#

After dinner, they went outside for a walk around the grounds.

Anya was ebullient. "You've made me so happy. I can't believe people can be so caring about a stranger."

"If you feel like a stranger, that's wrong. We don't see you that way, darling."

"You're good people. It's nice to know there are good people in the world, Mrs. Brown."

It was chilly with a brisk wind that limited their leisurely walk outside. Dark clouds on the horizon foreshadowed the approach of the first snowfall of the season. Anya looked up at the sound of Canadian geese squawking, flying in their V formation, heading south. This flock was late to begin their trek. The smell of wood fires from chimneys in the neighborhood wafted through the air.

Heading back, going into the house, Anya then looked out the door wall later from the downstairs great room. It was a modest accumulation of snowfall, but a scenic sight nonetheless. Mr. Brown ignited the great fireplace, the first fire for the season. The family sat down to sip hot cocoa and chat.

This time, Anya sat beside Peter on the couch. This gratifying moment *felt* to Peter like she was a girlfriend for the first time.

"We're sorry to spring this on you, but having you live under this belief you were going to lose your mother shortly, we couldn't abide that. Our doctors have reviewed some of the medical workups and there appears to be an operative alternative."

"Thank you, Mr. Brown. This is the greatest gift there could ever be. I must repay you, somehow."

"Have you ever heard the term 'pay it forward'?"

"No."

"It means if we do a kindness for you, your repayment is someday doing a kindness for someone else. It starts an ongoing movement of people taking care of one another."

"I like that. I will do it someday, when I am able. I can't believe we're going to Russia. I thought I would never see Mama again."

"We're happy to help. We've never been to Russia, so it will be a mini-vacation of sorts."

"Where we live, it isn't a place to vacation. I'm sorry."

"We have a local agency making the arrangements for a hotel and transportation. We're going to pick up your mom to come back home with us on a temporary visa."

Again, tears formed in Anya's eyes. Peter hugged her this time. "Don't say it, Anya. We're happy to be here for you. I've always tried to be a glass-half-full guy. I think you've been a half-empty girl. Maybe we can bring you over to our side, and you can look at things more optimistically."

"That would be nice. I feel truly blessed. I will do this pay-forward thing."

Chapter Six

When Anya went into the guest bedroom that evening, it was an adventure in discovery. The bedroom was huge and had a gigantic walk-in closet. Chairs and a table, expensive art, paintings on the wall, and vases on the furniture pieces, and there was also a huge television. It was like a self-contained room she could live in. On the table was a plate of large strawberries, dipped in thick chocolate. Anya couldn't resist trying one. Like most women, she very much loved chocolate.

The massive trundle bed had a custom comforter and pillow shams that perfectly matched the wallpaper in color and design. Pulling back the covers, Anya slid her hand along the silky high-thread-count sheets, experiencing such luxury for the first time in her life.

She dove onto the bed, like falling into a soft cloud, with a laugh. Rolling around like a little girl, she savored with great relish this taste of the high life. With the possibility her mother could now be saved, suddenly her world seemed radically different. Adding hope into her life was a powerful tonic for her spirit.

"Oh, Mama, I will see you soon," she whispered. "This is like a dream come true."

Sleep came quickly and easily. The ultra-luxurious bed kept her asleep late the following morning. Awakening finally, it took a moment for her to realize the time. Jumping out of bed in a panic, Anya hustled into the bathroom to shower and dress for the day. Making her way down the stairs, she eased into the kitchen meekly. The family was sitting at the table, talking and drinking coffee. They smiled at her.

"I'm so sorry I overslept. I hope I didn't inconvenience you."

"Of course not, dear," Mrs. Brown replied. "We waited to have breakfast with you."

"I must seem so rude." The maid handed Anya a cup of coffee, and she went to sit down with the family.

The family laughed. Mr. Brown spoke. "It's quite the opposite, Anya. You seem delightful to us."

Peter added, "Once we eat, we're going out for the day. We'll see the sights and have some fun. We've got a nice museum in town and later we're going to a symphony concert."

"I'd like music very much."

"You'll like this. They're playing *Russian Christmas Music*."

"Christmas songs?"

"Actually, it's the title of the piece. It was composed in 1944 by Alfred Reed. It's a masterpiece, in my opinion. For this rendition, they're including a full choir along with the orchestra. It will be a sumptuous sound I'm sure you'll enjoy."

"I look forward to it, Peter."

"They're playing other great pieces too. Another Russian masterpiece is *Pictures at an Exhibition*, one of the great compositions of all time. It will be a really nice event. It's so fortunate the concert coincides with our being home this weekend."

"Indeed it is."

"Did you get enough to eat, Anya?" Mrs. Brown asked. "You eat like a bird. We've got plenty of food."

"Yes, thank you. I don't eat big meals, normally."

"We can leave any time you're ready."

"I'm ready now. Can you give me a moment to brush my teeth? Am I dressed properly?" She looked at Edith.

"You look beautiful, dear. You look just fine. We'll go brush also." Edith smiled warmly.

After a short time, the family walked into the garage, climbing into the black Mercedes sedan. Mr. Brown's 'fleet' included a red Corvette for his vanity and a blue BMW that Mrs. Brown drove, in addition to Peter's green Ford Mustang.

The day 'out and about' was eye-opening for Anya. At each stop, the Browns were known and treated like royalty.

When they stopped for lunch at a swanky eatery, the hostess moved them to the head of the line. "Hello, Mr. Brown. We have your table ready. Please come this way."

Peter noticed Anya's reaction and the look on her face. "Is this too much?"

"It's not, but I'm dazzled. How could I not like this magical life you live?"

"I didn't want to tell you before. I want to be judged on who I am as a person, not on all of this sideline stuff."

Anya smirked. "The sideline stuff isn't so bad."

They chuckled and he hugged her. "I know you realize I'm the same idiot I was before."

"Yes, I know."

"Hey, you're not supposed to agree."

She laughed again. Turning her head, she eyed him. "Peter, I feel so welcomed. Your parents are wonderful people. I wish my father had been such a man as your dad."

"Do you feel better about all of this now?"

"I was worried, but I always worry about everything. Yes, I feel comfortable. Your mom reminds me of my mom: a person full of love."

"I look forward to meeting your mom."

Anya looked embarrassed at the prospect. "I must warn you, where we are going is a corrupt and difficult place. We live very modestly. Things in your life you take for granted are mere dreams for us."

"Don't worry. I suspect my dad will have made necessary provisions for our safety. I wish we could go right now to get your mom and take her out of danger."

"I still can't believe your family is willing to spend so much on us. With doctors, if there's an operation, the huge travel costs, it's mind-boggling."

"Anya, when I said they're flush, that's probably an understatement. Not only did my dad get a huge number for his business sale, Mom was well-compensated and saved a large amount, and their investing has gone incredibly well. Yes, there will be big expenditures, but the money won't put a dent in what they've got. This chance to potentially save a life, this is what they live for. When you see how they're treated around town, it isn't because of the pile of money. It's because of what they do with it. They do benevolent things as a matter of their routine."

"That's so nice to hear." Anya smiled thoughtfully.

"We're stopping at a great restaurant for a great dinner before we head for the auditorium. That's what will be nice for you to hear. Trust me, it will be spectacular."

"I do trust you, about everything now. I'm sorry if I seemed to waffle in my feelings. It's my insecurity and fear, not anything you did wrong. Right now, I feel happier than at any time in my life. With what you and your family are doing for Mama and me...I must find a way to repay this incredible gesture."

"Anya, you're going to make me say something stupid. I'm trying to restrain my penchant for putting my foot in my mouth."

"What do you mean?" She eyed him, truly curious. "What is it you would say?"

"Don't ask. I'd think you could sense it."

"I'm sorry. I have no idea what you're thinking." She eyed him guardedly.

"Let's leave it at that for now."

"Okay, Peter. If that's how you want it to be." Her expression turned to a look of relief.

However, in a surprise, she warmed his heart by taking his arm as they walked.

Spending a magical day with the Brown family culminated with entering the great auditorium to enjoy the musical performance. Anya felt excited, invigorated; there were many words to describe her happy mood. For her, it was like coming into a hallowed hall for a solemn rite.

The conductor came out and the lights went low. As he moved his baton, the concert began and Anya understood what Peter had told her. She was captivated instantly, and the music swept her away in awe. It was every bit the masterpiece Peter had promised and more. The blend of the choir with the orchestra, the superbly written phrasing, and the stirring finale of *Russian Christmas Music* left her moved deep in her spirit. The finale of the concert was "*The Great Gate of Kiev*," the last movement of *Pictures at an Exhibition*. The feelings it evoked in her, the magnificent strains of the arrival moment, brought tears of joy to her eyes. It was like she'd been pulled into a cathedral and cleansed in her spirit of all the bad from her entire life.

They stood up from their seats and Peter saw her emotional response. He hugged her briefly. Following his parents down the row toward the aisle to exit the auditorium, he felt close to her. "Did you like it?" he asked.

"It was…" She couldn't finish the sentence.

As she wiped tears from her eyes, he eyed her with concern. "Anya?"

"These are good tears, Peter. I feel…well, I can't think of a strong-enough American word."

"I was worried."

They all stayed up late at home, sitting together in the downstairs great room. Anya felt at peace with them, and with her life. Her issues, the heartbreak and fear, seemed distant.

#

In the morning, she truly regretted having to return to school. The Anya who had arrived on Friday wasn't the same Anya who departed on Sunday.

Leaving after lunch, she gave Peter's parents warm hugs. "You've given me back my life."

"Anya, don't…" Mrs. Brown was touched by Anya's deep emotions. "We'll just keep looking forward. Soon it will be time to depart for the airport to go get your mother."

Anya hugged Mrs. Brown again.

This time in Peter's car, Anya did slide over to the center beside him. For Peter, it was the miracle he'd hoped for. He reached out to take her hand. "Anya, is your sign still a fist?"

She laughed. "No. I'm a Virgo, if that matters."

"Everything about you matters to me. I want to learn everything, good and bad. I'll tell you whatever you want to know about me, as long as you realize I'm a dolt."

"Peter, you don't need to say those mean things about yourself to me. I know you try to joke, but the deep feelings, the insecurity, I know about that. Let us put that aside between us. It serves no good purpose."

"Agreed, I'll try to watch myself in the future."

"With this Christmas trip, I'm afraid I'll get too excited and do poorly in my classes," she said.

"You know better than that. You can't help but be the scholar you are. I do want to point out, though, I'm not always wrong."

Anya laughed. "You'll never let me forget that. I didn't know you then."

Peter smirked. "I know that. I just think I can still get a little mileage out of it."

"Oh my—what have I done?" Anya smirked also.

"You jumped into the deep end of the pool, madam."

"I'm sure that's some American adage, but I don't know what you mean."

"I'm saying I think I'm…" He started to laugh.

"You will always be a silly man. That's obvious to me."

"I can't argue with that. It's part of what makes me endearing."

"This is endearing?"

"Yes, ma'am. It's a documented fact."

"I don't think so. Always I believe you 'pull my leg,' as you say."

He chuckled. "I can pull your leg any time you want it."

"You know what I say."

"I do. Seriously, though, it's so good to feel close to you. I hope I grow on you with time."

"You know I like you. It isn't just gratefulness for your kindnesses. Perhaps it takes longer for me to reach where you are in your feelings. Do you understand? What I do each day in my life, I don't want to worry it offends you. When I happen to be with another boy, I know it hurts you, and I don't want that."

"About that—it's all on me. I need to grow up and show trust in you."

"How you act in those situations, it makes it difficult for me." She turned her face toward him to see his reaction.

"Again, it's all on me making you feel uncomfortable. When I see how other guys act, making moves on you, I've got to get to the point of realizing it doesn't necessarily mean you're interested. I know it with my head, but still I can't help feeling protective over you."

"That's nice of you to say. I'm trying to change, but I have…a ways to go. Did I say that right?"

"Anya, don't waste any time on what you think I want you to do. Just be yourself. Mostly, it's up to me to do the heavy lifting. You know the happy ending I want."

Glancing over and seeing her sudden troubled look, he spoke quickly. "I'm sorry. No pressure; I'm just thinking out loud. You still have all of your choices. If ultimately you feel I'm not the right one for you, I'll cope."

"I don't know what to say."

"You don't need to say anything. We simply go about our business and let the chips fall where they may."

She shrugged her shoulders but turned her head to look at him closely. "You're very driven about this. I…eh…"

"Let's change the subject. I want for you to be happy. This is a good time of life. We need to enjoy it. Each day that goes by, we never get back, so we need to do it right the first time."

#

Time passed rapidly for the rest of the semester. Finals week proved a non-issue for the two brilliant students, and soon they were packing the car for the trip home to Peter's house.

"We sleep at home tonight and then head for the airport tomorrow morning, early, for the flight to Europe."

"I can't wait to see Mama again."

"I'm looking forward to meeting her too. How do you say hello in Russian?"

Anya smiled. "Привет."

Peter tried the word.

Anya snickered. "Your accent is still terrible."

"Sorry."

"No, I'm happy you try. I was making my own joke. My humor is not so good either."

"I guess that makes us a good pair."

Suddenly, Anya took his hand. "Thank you for this, Peter."

"You're welcome, Anya."

This drive home was pleasant. Each day with her, Peter felt like he was making progress, although they remained baby steps. All of his sense of resistance in her seemed to be gone, though it was clear she wasn't at the same emotional place he was. It was still possible she was a long way from it.

Pulling into the driveway at his home, it was still a pleasing wonder for Anya. She hugged Mrs. Brown tightly.

"My dear, it's so good to see you again. I feel like I've known you for years."

"I feel very good when I'm here."

"I'm sure you're excited about tomorrow. We've got an early flight, so it will be an early morning. Do you need a wake-up call?"

"That's a good idea. Your bed makes me sleep too long."

"I'll have a talk with the bed to straighten it out."

Everybody chuckled.

"Well, come in, children. Dinner is ready."

They chatted amicably at the meal and afterward. Everybody was in bed by nine for the early departure, factoring in the long drive and getting through security in the international terminal at the airport.

"Anya, I'm sure you remembered to bring your passport."

"Yes, ma'am. I keep it in my purse at all times."

Again, climbing into that bed was an experience for Anya. "Mama, I'm coming home," she whispered with great satisfaction. "Ummm," she purred, savoring the luxury.

Rather than fall asleep immediately, she pondered the staggering ramifications of her future. Peter's hopes, a blind person couldn't miss. In her mind, she wrestled with troubling realities. Was it a path she wanted to follow? He was a good person, being nice, affectionate, polite, and generous beyond belief. He had about every positive quality she could ask for, yet why did she hesitate? Being brutally honest, was it that this relationship lacked the thrill, not having her bell rung, setting off emotional explosions? Was he the person she couldn't get out of her mind? It was an uncomfortable moment, discordant thoughts on the verge of her momentous trip home.

She rolled over, but the mental distress continued, keeping her from falling asleep immediately. There had been dates with guys that evoked her in that way, and one guy in particular. Was a relationship with Peter a compromise of her true desires? She could arrive at no viable answers, and eventually dozed off.

#

Morning came very early and Anya ate her breakfast like in a trance. Once into the Mercedes, both females leaned over onto the men and slept for the entire trip to the airport.

The nap refreshed and revived Anya. Her excitement resurfaced and she approached the airport security line relaxed and anxious to start the long journey.

Peter, of course, had no inkling of her prior night's emotional angst. He was simply his normal self, grateful to be in her presence. At these times, she could tolerate his feelings of "ownership" better than on campus, when other handsome guys hit on her. Feeling guilty, like she was 'stealing candy from a baby', she wrestled a great deal with the idea she should tell Peter the truth. However, the strong possibility of hurting him deeply was a major deterrent to her coming clean.

When the TSA agent saw her Russian passport, she eyed Anya closely and paused. It was an indignity she was accustomed to, but it always irked her, being treated like she was a criminal.

Standing directly behind Anya, Mrs. Brown spoke. "We're all going to Russia to see her family."

The TSA shrugged and let them pass.

Once into the main terminal, they went to a restaurant to get coffee and muffins.

Peter touched Anya's arm, misunderstanding her distant look. "I'm excited too."

She smiled. "I hope you find some things to like in my country. Compared to your world…"

"Anya, everything will be fine," Mrs. Brown responded.

Mr. Brown spoke. "It will be our first time on a Russian airliner."

"The attendants speak English."

"Regardless, we'll let you take the lead once we're in the air and after we've landed. We don't want to miss something inadvertently."

"I'll take care of you."

Soon they walked to the departure gate. Anya smiled at the Russian girls at the gate and spoke with them in her native tongue. For her it felt good, like they were long-lost friends.

Peter tried out his Russian "hello," causing the attendants and Anya to chuckle.

"Did I screw up?"

"No. We know what you were trying to say."

Boarding the plane, Anya sat beside Peter, one row ahead of his parents. She asked for the window seat. Peter quickly ceded the seat, not being a person who liked heights.

"We fly to New York before changing planes for the flight to Europe."

"That's good, Peter. Having a chance to stretch our legs will be a good thing."

"How far is it from St. Petersburg to your hometown?"

"About three hours, by car."

"I think my dad arranged for us to be driven."

"That's good. Renting a car for us to drive isn't the same as in America."

"I think he hired some protection over there. I hope that doesn't bother you."

"Hardly, it's dangerous where Mama lives. Going there alone wouldn't be wise. I don't think you understand when I say we live in modest circumstances."

"I think her life is about to take a turn for the better, in a lot of ways."

Anya smiled.

"I'm not sure where we're staying, where the hotel is located."

"It doesn't matter. I'm happy anywhere."

"I think Dad is having your mom come to stay in your room with you. I assume that's okay."

"It's like I'm living this miracle dream. Of course, it's okay with me. Getting her out of that hovel will be such a blessing."

Peter spoke. "We do what we can, honey. Oh, I'm sorry. I was going to stop using those terms of endearment."

Anya stared ahead a moment before saying, "It's fine, Peter." She didn't look at him.

"Dad said they got papers worked out for your mom to come to America for medical treatment. She'll be flying home with us after our visit."

Anya shook her head in amazement but then looked away. Of all possible things to feel at that moment, the memories from her prior night's ruminations and angst simmered to life. Again, the question, was it right for her to take advantage of Peter's infatuation? Her mind tried to cope by thinking, *I didn't ask for any of this.*

However, the rationalization didn't fully assuage her feelings of guilt. He was out-of-control in love with her and seemingly incapable of logical thinking. It was charming and distressing all at once.

"Anya, are you happy?"

"I am, Peter."

She pondered again, was a life with him so bad? Her every need would be met, wouldn't it? However, a memory of a particular date flashed through her mind. That date had inflamed her unlike any other, and now it punished her like a sudden hot flash. That date hadn't been with Peter. It had been with one of Megan's friends, a dazzling guy named Jeff Bond. If he called her again, would she say no—could she? Did she even want to say no to him? In truth, he was the one in her mind whom she couldn't get out. She dreamed about him, whether she wanted to or not.

Shifting in her seat to try to fight off the stubborn thought, it wasn't easy, and the memory continued to linger.

"I will take a nap," she whispered.

"Okay," Peter replied. "It's a long day of flying, and we started very early. Maybe I'll nap also."

She closed her eyes, but her mind remained active. Peter laid his head against her shoulder and hugged her arm. It didn't help or hinder her musings. Another guy still floated her boat in the secrecy of her dreams, and those thoughts were compelling.

They slept through the passing of the refreshment cart. When they landed in New York, it was a rapid turnaround to board the next flight and depart for Paris, the next leg of the journey.

On that flight, they were awake later for the in-flight meal.

Their delay in Paris was longer before they boarded the Russia-bound flight to St. Petersburg. Here their fellow passengers included mostly Russians returning home. Peter got a taste of Russian being the predominant language spoken around him. It was slightly unsettling; not knowing what was being said.

Anya noticed. "Is something wrong?"

"I wouldn't say something is wrong. I understand what it's like for you having to speak a second language in America is all."

"You become accustomed to it. It isn't a problem. There are enough good things to cancel out the bad."

"If somebody says something concerning, please let us know."

"There are good and bad people everywhere. I don't think you'll need to worry. As you say, your father arranged for our safety. Those people who have bad opinions about Americans, we just ignore them."

"Okay. It's in your hands."

After the meal, they dozed off to sleep for the balance of the flight, awakening to the bounce of the wheels touching down on the landing strip. It was a rough landing.

For them, to walk into the airport and see the signs in Russian was eye-opening. Compared to the airports they just passed through, it was a much different scene. Anya took the lead, guiding them through customs and then to baggage claim. There they saw the security detail Mr. Brown had hired, four fierce-looking burly men, no-nonsense types.

"I wonder if they're former Russian soldiers?" Peter whispered.

"Perhaps," Anya replied.

"They look like they could do some damage."

"Yes, but I'm glad we have them. You'll understand soon enough."

"You're kind of scaring me."

"I want to prepare you."

"What is that name for your special forces: *Spetsnaz*?"

Anya smiled. "Yes, and I suppose they could have been."

"Our special forces are called special forces."

Anya laughed.

Their "guardians" guided them out of the terminal to waiting cars. The family climbed into a limo, where four more guards were waiting. The remainder of the guards got into a second car to follow the limo.

They departed immediately to drive toward Anya's home village.

As Peter looked out the window, it was far different than scenes in America, like they'd traveled to a different planet. Modern areas tended to end abruptly rather than blending into rural undeveloped places.

Anya chatted with the guards. They relaxed only slightly in their grim stares. She managed to get them to smile once with whatever she said.

Peter whispered to her, "I wouldn't want to have these guys angry at me."

Anya snickered and told the guards, causing them to smile at Peter.

"They're our friends, Peter," she explained.

"Somehow, I don't think 'friends' is an accurate description. I think we're more like raw meat in their eyes."

Anya laughed again, as did the guards. It helped ease the tense mood in the car. Mr. and Mrs. Brown started to speak with the guards, through Anya.

By the time they got to the hotel, the social atmosphere in the car was far more pleasant. However, when they pulled into the town, immediately the guards became attentive, scanning all around outside of the cars for threats.

"Is this your home?" Peter asked.

"No, this is where they got a hotel. My village is elsewhere."

Mr. Brown spoke. "Anya, we're going to check in to get our rooms before we drive over to get your mother."

"Yes, I understand. She isn't far away from here."

Again, Anya did the talking, although the desk clerk spoke passable English. Like Anya, she was young and pretty.

After depositing the luggage in the rooms, they went back to the vehicles for the final leg of the journey.

#

It was half an hour before they pulled into Anya's home village. When she said it was modest, it was an understatement, looking like a scene from the fifteenth century. There was no new building anywhere in sight. Everything was run down.

"Home" was a ramshackle apartment building that looked to be in need of demolishment. Old USSR-era 'hammer and sickle' signs caught Peter's attention. They were badly faded but still there. The guards preceded them in entering the building, AK-47s at the ready. Their arrival drew considerable notice. Suddenly, numerous rough-looking thugs appeared streaming out of the building. Peter worried there would be trouble, seeing bellicose stares on both sides, but they chose not to test the guards. What they did was serenade Anya with plenty of jeers. She bristled angrily, so Peter assumed whatever they said was not nice, nor was it hard to figure out.

Her mother's place was on the third floor. When Anya knocked on the door; they heard footsteps and then the sound of numerous locks and deadbolts unfastened. When her mother opened the door, Anya cried out and grabbed her. Looking like an older version of Anya, but one prematurely aged, her mom didn't look healthy. Pale, emaciated, frail looking to the point of feeble, she clearly needed an intervention.

The two women blubbered and whispered in Russian. Peter didn't know the words, but the emotions were easily understandable. Even the rugged guards appeared to be moved. That didn't mean they relaxed their vigilance. Softened facial expressions didn't stop them from looking about for threats.

"Please come in," Anya said.

It seemed impossible two people could live in such a tiny space. There was only one main room, with two single beds, and a small bathroom.

"This is where I grew up, Peter." She looked at him, embarrassed.

"Anya, we didn't come here to judge. Your mom did the best she could."

"Thank you for understanding."

Anya spoke at length with her mother, explaining the arrangements Mr. Brown had made and their plans for her.

Mr. Brown spoke up. "We've arranged for your travel visa. You'll come with us back to the hotel to stay with Anya until we go back to the airport to fly to America. Do you understand?"

"*Da.*"

"Are you ready now?"

"*Da.*"

Anya continued to hug her mother.

The guards gathered up her things, which consisted of a suitcase and a satchel. Returning back down the stairs to leave the building, again they were serenaded with verbal abuse from the local gang. Whatever the leader said to Anya provoked her. She turned and replied in an angry hiss. The leader grimaced and took a step toward her. The guards reacted instantly, pulling out weapons and training them on the entire gang. For a tense moment, two groups of armed men stood in a confrontation.

Stepping close to their leader, the grim-faced Russian commander spoke in terse tones, and suddenly the gang backed down. Quickly loading into the cars while their guardians kept automatic weapons trained on those thugs, the family held their breath until the vehicles pulled away, leaving Anya's home village behind forever.

"I see what you mean, Anya. That was scary. I can't imagine living in constant fear like that."

"The most difficult thing for me was when I left, leaving Mama behind and alone."

"Well…it's all over now."

"Peter, my mother's name is Mariska."

"Hello." He smiled at her. She returned the smile and spoke to her daughter.

"Mama says it's very nice to meet you, and your family. She's very grateful for what you're doing for us."

"We're happy to do it. Have you told her about…us?"

"I said you're my dear friend."

"Okay. If you think that's the best way to approach it."

Mrs. Brown spoke and Anya translated a conversation of the two mothers. Soon they arrived back at the hotel. Anya and her mother went into their room to talk and spend time together.

"We'll all gather later for a meal," Mrs. Brown said. "Take all the time you need together. I know it's been a long time apart."

Anya hugged her mother as they went into the room and closed the door.

Peter and his folks went into their room.

"What I want to tell you guys is how much I appreciate what you're doing for me, and for them."

"No problem, son," his father replied. "We've been blessed in our lives, and having this chance to help other people in distress is very gratifying."

"I really like Anya. Actually, more than just like. I've never been in love to know, but maybe it's that for me. I think about her all the time."

He looked at his mother. She had a contemplative look. "Does that bother you, Mom?"

"It's not that, son. Anya is a fine young woman, and I believe she's genuine. I'd just caution you again about trying to move too fast. Some women need time to figure things out. Also, I think you have too thin a skin when it comes to her. Don't make every happening into a life crisis. Concentrate on having enjoyable times with her. The rest will come along in due time."

"Do you think I could be in love?"

"Peter, you're our son. We'll always think of you as that little baby boy we brought home from the hospital after you were born. Thinking of you as a grown-up, facing grown-up emotions, it's just an adjustment for us to make. To answer your question, you'll answer that matter all on your own."

"I know I'm young, but my opinion is I'm not that young. After meeting her, all the other girls don't seem to matter to me any longer."

"Just be careful. It doesn't make Anya a bad person if she feels persuaded to move in other directions. I know that's not what you want to hear, but you can't force people to go where you want them to go."

"So, I might be her Plan-B guy, or worse."

"Peter, that's an example of what I'm saying. Don't interpret everything as trouble. I've picked up on nothing concerning in the time I've been around Anya. Let's change the subject."

"Okay, Mom. That's probably a good idea." He smiled weakly.

#

Later, they all gathered to go to a local restaurant. Sitting down at the table and eyeing the Russian-language menu, Peter had no clue. Anya snickered. "Peter, I'll help you pick. What would you like to eat?"

"I always wanted to try *borscht*."

"Do you know what it is?"

"I think it's soup?"

"It's beet soup, cold beet soup."

"Okay. I'll still give it a try. You only live once."

"What else would you like?"

"Possibly meat and potatoes, maybe roast beef or something. They do use cows, right?"

Anya laughed and told her mother. She laughed also. "Yes, Peter. We don't eat horses, or other exotic things, in restaurants here."

"Good. I was just checking."

The food was better than he expected.

Anya's mother spoke. "My mother says thank you for this sumptuous meal. She's not accustomed to high living. It's a rare luxury in her life."

Mrs. Brown answered. "Tell her we're happy to be here with her."

"I think she'll be stunned by America. She has no basis of experiences for such a place. You saw our humble home."

"Anya, it makes us happy to give her a new beginning. She's suffered enough in her life."

After dinner, they went to the cars for a quick trip to a local museum. It was fairly small, but an interesting diversion. The indelible stamp of their Communist past was everywhere. The old symbols of the USSR appeared in many photos, and red was the predominant color. In one photo, Peter was amazed to see a Russian hockey star surrounded by smiling locals. He was wearing his Detroit Red Wings jersey, his NHL team.

Anya explained, "He was from a town not far from here. When he got big money in America, he came back to help out his town. He was a generous man, like your father."

Chapter Seven

They stayed one more day before returning to the airport. With the medical condition of Anya's mother, they didn't want to delay getting her into the hands of an American medical team. Before parting from their protection squad, Anya spoke to each and every one of them, hugged them, and kissed their cheeks. The men were all surprised and moved by the gesture. Anya affected people, even the most hardened types.

On the return flights, Peter's seat at Anya's side was replaced by her mother. He sat a row behind next to a matronly Russian woman for the flight to London. Unable to communicate with her, he dozed off and slept for the entire flight.

Walking off the plane and into the terminal at Heathrow was a wonder for Mariska. Not only was it the first time she'd left Russia, it was the first time she'd left her home village. Anya kept her arm interlocked with her mother's. Mariska looked about with uncertainty.

"Mama, it's okay. Everything will be fine. We're all here with you. There's nothing to fear."

"It's very different."

"It is. The rest of the world is a wonder."

Peter watched, making assumptions, since they spoke in Russian. He noted the frightened look on Mariska's face. "Tell her we have a fairly long layover in London, so we'll stop, get food and relax."

Anya spoke in Russian, and her mother replied. Still, with her look of concern, Peter didn't need a translation. "Tell her also this is a gift to her. We can afford this trip, and the food."

Mariska answered him directly: "*Spasibo*."

"She said, 'Thank you'."

"I got that, Anya. I think every American has heard that word."

"Okay, I wasn't sure you knew."

"Thank you, though."

She eyed him mirthfully. Her mother made a quiet comment, causing Anya to snicker. Anya replied to her, also in a low voice.

"Am I the butt of some Russian joke, Anya?"

"It's mother-daughter talk, and none of your business." She smirked playfully.

"Okay, ladies, have it your way. I'll rise above it because I'm the bigger person here."

Anya translated and both women laughed. Mariska spoke again to her daughter.

"Mama says she likes you, Peter."

"Thanks. I take that as a very good sign?" He was only partially successful suppressing a smile.

"You should. She doesn't give out compliments."

It made him feel good. He tried not to spoil the positive step with a foolish comment, concentrating on keeping his mouth closed.

The group wandered throughout the airport, eyeing storefront displays and searching for a suitable restaurant. Mariska was dazzled by the variety of wares and the volume of items in stock. She talked frequently with Anya. Eventually they went into an eatery.

Sitting down at the table, Peter longed to claim a seat beside Anya, but that didn't happen. She was flanked by Mrs. Brown and Mariska, while Peter was relegated to sit beside his father. In her mother's presence, Anya was far more relaxed than Peter had ever seen her. The women started a lively conversation.

His father glanced at Peter, like he recognized his disappointment. Peter looked back and shrugged his shoulders. "Well, Dad, so we have Christmas at the house. I wish we could go to the bowl game, but I realize with her mom's medical situation, that's out of the picture."

"We make do, son. There will be other years and other bowl games."

"Do I understand she's moving into our house after surgery for her post-op convalescence and rehab?"

"Mom and I made that decision from the start. We've got plenty of space, extra bedrooms, and she'll be in no condition to be alone. She doesn't speak English, she knows nobody, has no job or source of income, and no place to stay. We'll keep her with us as long as she wants to stay. If she gets to the point in the future she wants a separate residence, we'll help her with that. I doubt working is in her future. She's sort of near retirement age anyway, I think. It's not a problem for us. I've got them working on permanent US residency."

"She may be younger than you think, but just looks older because of this medical crisis."

"You're probably right. She's had a hard life."

"I'm so proud of you guys. Not many people in this world would take in a total stranger and absorb these kinds of costs."

"We go to church to live our lives this way, not just pay lip service. We've got more money than we could spend, so for us, doing this, it's a logical choice. I hope Anya and Mariska don't feel obligated, though. We don't intend they feel like charity cases. Also, we both know your ultimate desires for Anya. That being said, giving her the leeway, she needs to figure out what she wants may be the hardest thing you'll ever need to do in your life. If she married you out of gratitude but wasn't in love, if you get the distinction, it could lead to a disastrous ending for you both. I was in that situation, having to wait it out for your mother. I know how hard it is, but there's no way around it."

Peter got a pensive look. "I know, Dad. I've been thinking about that a lot lately. I tend to overreact, so I've tried to rein in my mistakes. I also understand why I may not seem like the best option out there from her point of view. You should see the guys at school. Believe me, I'm a pale shade compared to the long shadows they cast."

"That's something every guy faces. There will always be competition for quality women. What you can't do is get down on yourself. Don't beat yourself up. Dwell on the positives, and you do have a lot to offer. It strikes me how similar this is to my life."

"Getting the girl you wanted and your happy ending is what keeps me in there, plugging away."

"That's the spirit, son."

Anya glanced at them. "What are you saying?"

"It's father-son talk, and none of your business. Sound familiar?"

Anya laughed. "Ah yes, Peter, *touché.*"

"Gotcha, Anya."

"You did."

After the meal, they wandered around in the terminal before going to the gate to board for the flight to the USA. Gradually, Mariska acted less intimidated and more excited.

Peter smiled at Anya, specifically her being aglow at being with her mother.

She noticed and smiled back. "I think Mama is finally accepting that the bad of the past is over. It's so great to see her happy. She hasn't had much happiness in her life."

"I'm glad too."

Anya hugged him before they walked onto the plane for the final leg of the journey. On this flight it was a larger plane, so fortuitously there were three seats in a row. Peter took the window seat so Anya could sit beside him, with her mother on the aisle. Mother and daughter spoke a great deal, so Peter said little, allowing them their interaction. He was content just to be at Anya's side.

Mariska was dazzled by having so much food coming her way after a lifetime of privation. She muttered to her daughter.

Anya chuckled and turned to Peter. "Mama says she's going to get fat from all of this food."

"Tell her if she does, we don't judge."

Anya laughed, as did her mother. "Peter, she's never felt overstuffed with food before. It makes her feel guilty, with all the starvation in the world."

"She shouldn't feel guilty. She has no fault about that, having spent more than her share of time in that unfortunate state. Getting some good fortune now isn't a bad thing."

"We're just talking about our feelings. It's somewhat of the same way I feel about all of your gifts and kindnesses."

"It's my family's hope both you and your mother can get past those feelings. Let's all just live our lives in peace and get whatever enjoyment we can. Deal?"

"Deal."

After being fed, both Seminova women dozed off for the balance of the long flight. Peter followed their lead and nodded off too.

Eventually arriving back at their home airport, they made their way through baggage claim and went to the Mercedes parked in the long-term lot. The drive back home was eye-opening for Mariska, but truly she wasn't prepared for the gated community and the posh Brown residence.

She muttered to Anya in Russian. Anya chuckled and hugged her mother.

"She feels she should be one of the servants, not a guest."

"Welcome to the first day of the rest of her life," Mr. Brown said.

Mariska was equally agog as Anya had been when they showed her the opulence of the bedroom where she'd be staying. This bedroom was bigger than her entire apartment. She had no idea how to operate the television. Anya took great delight in carefully explaining the operation of the remote-control device. Her mother acted like a giddy school girl at Christmas with each new wonder.

Being served dinner was another luxury beyond her ability to relate to. Anya spoke in Russian a great deal with her mother.

"Mama says she's sorry to seem like a helpless infant."

Mrs. Brown replied, "Tell her the feeling of being lost at being exposed to so many new things is not a problem for anybody. We'd have trouble coping in her world too. Just relax and settle in here. We want her to feel welcome; this is her home now."

"She understands, and she's trying."

"Is the food acceptable?"

"She says it's very good."

"Good. She has a doctor's appointment on Monday morning. Other than that, we can go shopping to get her a new wardrobe."

"*Spasibo*," she answered.

"She thanks you," Anya explained.

"She's very welcome, dear," Mrs. Brown said.

#

They spent the balance of the day at home, first taking a leisurely walk outside to enjoy the pastoral scene of the wooded lot. It was a perfect sunny day, but one that required heavy winter coats. It had yet to snow heavily for the season, as fall hung on longer than usual. They did see their breath though as they walked.

Anya walked arm in arm with her mother and they chatted continuously. Turning her head to look at Peter, she explained, "Mama is dazzled. I'm so happy for her. This is a dream come true for us. Thank you, Peter, for the good you do."

"You're very welcome."

"I say 'thank you' to you a great deal."

"I'm glad we can give you something to be grateful about."

The chilly temperature drove them back inside the house. Mariska enjoyed her first experience sitting around the fireplace with a cup of hot cocoa. She stared in awe at the massive fieldstone fireplace. Life on this scale was idyllic.

She spoke and Anya translated. "It's a strange feeling being here, being safe. I've lived in peril nearly my entire life, never knowing if gangs would break down my door and come for me. I want to say I will learn English, so we can talk; Anya will teach me."

Mrs. Brown answered warmly, "That will be a wonderful day. Would you like more drink, Mariska?"

"I'm fine. Thank you."

"Maybe the Brown family will learn Russian. Anya can teach us."

Anya and her mother smiled.

"Is that too tall a task, Anya?"

"No, ma'am."

Where Anya had been dazzled by her first visit to the Brown estate and the luxury on display, her mother was stunned. Crawling into a large soft bed, onto high-thread-count sheets, she laughed, as her daughter had laughed. This taste of such a life was beyond her wildest dreams. Sinking into the plush bed was like lying on a cumulus cloud. She closed her eyes to savor the feeling.

"Ummm," she moaned softly.

At that point, it was easy to feel like all of her troubles were over.

#

The Monday-morning doctor's appointment involved considerable time with the tests they ran and the counseling session that followed.

Dr. Phil Strong was a college friend of the Browns, highly respected and renowned in his field, and regarded as the best surgeon at the hospital and in the region.

"Mariska, we've run a battery of tests and will need to wait on many of the results, but in viewing the brain MRI, I want to say I'm optimistic. This is definitely a situation where I feel we can attempt to rectify the problem surgically. I don't agree with the prior terminal diagnosis."

Anya had taken the day off to go with her mother and Mrs. Brown to translate.

"Mama says the Russian doctor talked about surgery, but she had no money, and there was no insurance like you have in America. He told her she couldn't ignore the condition. That's why he gave a terminal diagnosis."

Dr. Strong glanced at Mrs. Brown. "We've got it covered," she replied.

"That being the case, I'd like to take care of the surgery as soon as possible. It serves no good purpose to leave that thing in your head."

"Mama says okay."

"Good. I'll check the hospital surgical schedule and get back with you as soon as I have a date for an opening."

Mrs. Brown hugged him. "Thank you, Philip. We really appreciate you fitting us in on short notice."

"My pleasure, I'm glad to be of help. It's good seeing you again, Edith. You look really good. You realize you broke my heart in college? I've never really gotten over it."

She smiled at him, staring deep into his eyes, but then glanced self-consciously at Anya. "That's nice of you to say, but that was a long time ago."

"It was, but some wounds don't heal."

"Eh…perhaps we should change the subject."

"You're right. I'm sorry. I'll call you folks about the surgery."

"Thank you again. We'll wait to hear from you."

Moving out of the unexpected awkward moment and walking to the car in the parking lot, Edith felt she needed to explain. "I'm sorry about that, ladies. Phil is the best doctor possible for this surgery. When I was in college, I did date him and, as you heard, he developed some strong feelings. Honestly, back then I struggled with the situation. He was a driven man in everything he did. That included wooing me. I believe he was about to propose when I backed away. It just didn't feel like the right decision for me. He was a wonderful man, but something about George drew me in the end, so I decided to go in that direction. Do you understand?"

"I understand very clearly," Anya replied, a pensive look on her face.

"Anya, I suspect you're going through similar feelings. There are so many nice young men vying for your attention, it can get bewildering. I was there, so I know what it's like for you."

"Thank you for saying that. I believe I know what they all want, but I'm just not ready to get serious yet."

"You're still young, darling. There's nothing wrong with taking your time. A serious romantic relationship can be consuming. You want a chance to live your life and experience your options. Freedom is something we all hate to give up. I know I left some emotional bruises on my poor husband before we took that step. It took me time before I came to peace with committing exclusively to him."

"I feel badly so often. Peter is such a good person. I just…eh…"

"You can be honest with me. I'm his mother, but I'm also your friend. I hope you know I'll honor your privacy and keep our conversations between us. I know you aren't a girl to set out to take advantage and hurt my son." Edith moved close to pat Anya's shoulder.

"If he sees me talking to other boys, he gets…"

"Jealous, crazy-acting…I know; I'm married to his father. The acorn doesn't fall far from the tree."

"If we could just be friends for a while, I would like that, but he doesn't see it that way."

"You don't need to tell me. It's an identical replay of my earlier life. When I dated other guys, it killed George, and that mattered to me. I just couldn't stop until later. Maybe it was some flaw in me, but it was fun with other guys."

"That's it exactly. I do have feelings for Peter. I don't mean anything against him by enjoying the company of other boys."

Turning her head to Mariska standing patiently, she said, "Your mother is curious what we're saying."

"Let me explain to her."

After Anya talked for a time, Mariska got a look of comprehension.

"Mother says she understands us. She had her share of romantic suitors, but in her case there were no good options. My father seemed like the best choice at the time, but it didn't work out well. His drinking eventually cost him his job and everything went bad after that. She was stuck with a baby girl, an abusive husband, and having to work to support the family. It was terrible. It was a blessing for us he just left on his own."

"That's so bad. Tell her I sympathize. At any rate, my point is there's no guarantee life will be easy or fair. We roll with the punches and try to make good choices."

"I'm so happy to have you. It's like I have…eh…"

"A second mother? That's fine, darling. I never had a daughter."

Anya glanced at Edith shyly. "I hope that isn't a problem."

"Of course not. It's nice to get a chance to 'mother' you some."

Anya smiled and told her own mother. Mariska chuckled.

"She said I was a handful growing up, and gave her gray hairs."

The women laughed and then hugged.

"So, ladies, let's go clothes shopping."

"We would like that very much," Anya said.

#

Peter talked at length with his father while the females were away. "Dad, how did you manage to keep a lid on your jealous feelings? It's really a challenge for me."

"It's a challenge for anybody, son. It's like the old saying: you chase a girl until she catches you. They're the ones with the power and it's up to them to decide when, or if, they want to pull the trigger. As much as we might want to speed up the process, we can't. It's out of our hands."

"That's kind of discouraging."

"Hanging in there, it's the difficult choice we have, other than ditching the headache. If the girl is worth it in our hearts, we pay the price. I don't think Anya is a girl to string you along, but just in case, remember there are a lot of other nice girls on that massive campus."

"I know, but for me maybe it was a case of love at first sight. Once there was Anya, the other girls didn't seem to matter. I realized it when suddenly Allison became irrelevant. I once thought she was it, but now I look at her as this showy pompous snob and wonder how I could have ever been interested in that. It's funny that once I stopped mooning over her, it drew her notice and she's actually started trying to lure me. I have zero interest."

"I know what that's like. I knew I wanted to marry your mother really quickly, but I couldn't corral her. Watching her date other guys was murder, but I had no choice. Honestly, I couldn't be sure she'd ever come around. I could only hope that waiting it out would lead to a happy ending. For me, it worked out and I got the girl."

Peter chuckled when his father put a fist in the air. "I don't feel like Anya is a sure thing at all. She can do a lot better than me, and she knows it. You should see the guys sniffing around her. I don't stand a chance, going on my merits alone. I'm worried what we're doing for her and her mom will make her think she's got to repay us, and you know what I'm alluding to. If she gets engaged to me, it's fulfilling some obligation."

"As hard as it is, you've got to give her some slack back at school. If she wants to…well, date elsewhere, you can't let it poison the well with you."

"I can think about doing that with my head, but my gut starts roiling. Imagining her with them…it's almost more than I can bear. For me, saying all the right things isn't the same as enduring it."

"I know, Peter. I know."

"How did I get myself into this pickle?"

"Welcome to the real world. It isn't easy."

They sat in silence for a few moments, pondering the difficult issue.

"Maybe I'll take a walk. I'm all stirred up."

"I'll come with you, son."

They were away, out walking the back-forty figuratively speaking, when the women arrived home. Anya was waiting and anxiously watching out the back door wall when she spotted the men approaching. Opening the door, she stepped out onto the patio. "Oh, Peter, you must come in to see my mother's new clothes. They're so wonderful."

"Sure."

The entire family went to Mariska's bedroom, which now contained a walk-in closet full of new clothes. Mariska smiled proudly and went with her daughter into the closet to put on an outfit.

Anya translated. "Mama says she feels like a young girl again. This is such a special gift you've given, more than these items, but the return of possibilities in her life. Hope is so precious to anybody."

Her last sentence struck Peter, who thirsted for hope also. "That's good, Anya. Once the surgery is out of the way, we can move ahead toward those possibilities."

"Yes, Peter." She came over to give him a quick hug. He pondered what he took as a superficial gesture rather than a reflection of true affection. Suddenly, she looked back like something in his mannerism caught her notice. She eyed him questioningly, but said nothing.

Anya turned back to her mom and Edith. The women began a lively conversation. The men vacated the room.

The smell of a roast beef being cooked by the staff for dinner caught Peter's attention as they walked into the den.

"We know it's your favorite meal, son. It was your mother's idea."

"I do like roast beef; there's no denying that fact. I'm not sure if Anya is a carnivore."

"This meal is for you."

Peter smiled. "Are we talking about devil's food cake with white frosting for dessert?"

"We are. You can look forward to a great sugar buzz."

Peter laughed, along with his dad, and they did high fives.

His father turned on the massive sixty-inch HD television mounted on the wall. The inevitable channel came up: ESPN.

"Let's get caught up on events in the world of sports."

"Okay, Dad."

#

Later, at dinner, Mariska was stunned, eyeing the huge quantity of food on the table. Far more than five people could eat, it struck her as needless when so many in the world had so little.

Anya turned to Peter noting his curious stare. "She still feels guilty having so much food to eat when her acquaintances back home are still hungry."

"There's nothing for her to feel guilty about."

Anya shook her head as he seemed to miss the point. "It's her *feelings* I'm talking about. She knows the other, about being a gift. What I'm trying to explain is she feels, why her? That's how she feels; that she doesn't deserve this boon. Do you get the distinction?"

"I do, actually."

"I think the feelings of women don't always make sense to men. Your mother knows what I'm saying."

"Anya, I've got it."

They eyed each other for a moment, trying to read the other. Communicating even the simplest things always seemed difficult.

Anya broke the awkward impasse. "Your mother says this is your favorite meal?"

"It is. I like when the roast beef is cooked just right, tender, moist, and flakes apart with your fork. For me, it's like dessert. We always eat it with potatoes and carrots cooked in the pan with the meat. Do you like meat?"

"I don't dislike red meat; however, I tend to eat vegetables, with fish or chicken as the entrée."

"Good to know. What's your favorite meal?"

"I'm not sure I have a single favorite meal."

In the family tradition, George said grace before the meal began. Mariska commented to Anya.

"Mama likes the prayer before the meal."

"It's our habit. We've always been churchgoing folks. She's welcome to join us on Sundays."

"She said she'll give it a try. Not understanding English will make it confusing for her."

"It's a nice service I think she'll enjoy. We'll be right at her side. The music is great, and eventually she'll learn the language."

Anya and her mother chatted softly for a time. This time, Anya didn't translate whatever they were saying. Peter was curious, but didn't ask.

Over the course of the Christmas break, going into the New Year, Mariska ate ample food, slept late in comfort, feeling safe, and gradually her emaciated look and the pallor in her face disappeared. She felt better and looked much better. It was easy for Peter to see where Anya got her good looks. Mariska had been a beauty in her youth, and now she finally had reason to smile.

For the guys, it was the football bowl season, so they spent considerable time in the den watching games. On New Year's Day, when their school played, Peter thought about being in the stands to watch it live.

The women shopped, drove around town, and basically did their own thing for most of the time. They joined the men to watch the bowl game on New Year's Day. Anya spoke in Russian a great deal to her mother, explaining the game action as it occurred.

Again, Peter was curious what she was saying, and again he didn't ask.

The day had a happy ending, with their school pulling out a late victory over an excellent opponent.

Soon, it was time to climb back into the car for the drive back to school. Anya had a teary goodbye with her mother.

When they pulled away from the house, she was sad.

"Anya, she's in good hands. My folks will take care of her."

"I know, Peter. You need to understand women are emotional creatures. If I cry sometimes, it isn't always a bad thing. I love her and being apart is painful, especially until the medical crisis is resolved."

"I was just trying to be supportive."

"I wasn't complaining; just explaining. I think we don't always communicate well."

"I can't disagree. I'm probably trying too hard."

Anya got a pensive look.

He glanced at her. "No pressure, Anya. You're free to do, well, whatever. We go a step at a time."

She didn't reply.

Picking up his phone from the console, he handed it to her. "By the way, here's my cell phone. You can call Christy to see about the room situation…if she worked out the details for you to move in with her."

"Oh…yes. Thank you." Anya dialed the number.

"Hello, Christy? This is Anya. I'm riding with Peter back to school. He suggested I call about the room?"

Pause.

"Yes."

Pause.

"I see. I appreciate you trying to help. We'll see you soon."

Peter glanced at Anya. "What did she say?"

"She's still working on it. I'll be back with Megan for now, but Christy thinks I can make the move soon. Her current roommate is working out some details of her own."

"Hopefully it will be sooner rather than later. I hate to speak ill of anybody, but Megan is a real snake."

"I'll be fine. I'm accustomed to Megan, so I know what to expect. I'm not in that room a great deal, as you know."

"You're welcome to study with me at any time, at either dorm."

"I…eh…thank you for the invitation. I will have study dates with you, but not always. Sometimes I might need to…"

"Anya, there's no need to explain. I'm just putting it out there for you. You have no obligation to always be with me. It's your choice what you do, and with whom."

Anya looked at him directly. It dawned on her, his real concern: potential male competition. She started to speak, but he held up his hand.

After that, they rode in silence. Still sitting by the passenger door, Anya laid her head back to take a nap for the balance of the drive.

Peter dropped her off at her dorm and helped take her luggage upstairs to her room. Megan eyed him when he went into the room. He said nothing to her.

"Goodbye, Anya."

"Thank you, Peter."

Walking quickly out of the room, his emotions were astir, again. It seemed he was destined to be punished by his angst, without a means to eliminate it. The power was in Anya's hands, not his.

This time, he felt foreboding, like a giant shoe was going to drop and squash him like a bug. There was no actual event he could point to, but it had the feel of a dire premonition.

Returning to his room, Bob was all smiles. "Welcome back, bro."

"Thanks. It's great to be back."

"You must have had a heck of a semester break. How was the trip to Russia?"

"Scary. Anya didn't lie that her mom lived in a dangerous area. Dad hired some Russian bad-asses to protect us, thank God. There was a pack of criminals that insulted Anya, and I thought there would be trouble, the shooting kind. Our guys threatened them and they backed down. I never got the translation of what was said, but it was a situation I was glad to be away from. Both sides looked like they could, and would, do some real damage."

"Wow. I didn't think of that. As you say, thankfully you got out of there unscathed. I imagine Anya is ecstatic, having her mom over here."

"She is. It was a nice holiday. The women even came in to watch the bowl game with us. I'm sure her mom had no clue what was going on. Anya explained, but Anya has no clue either. Mariska did cheer when we cheered." The boys snickered.

"Before I forget, Christy told me she couldn't quite work it out for the room change for Anya yet. I think it's coming soon, though."

"I appreciate her efforts. Anya wasn't that upset. She still wants out of Megan's room, but I think she feels confident now that she can handle anything."

"If it gets bad with Megan, Anya can crash here, with us."

"Right, you idiot, like that is going to happen."

The boys laughed again.

"No girl in her right mind would choose to crash with us. Like the school would accept having a girl living in the same room with guys. Anya would never…"

"Peter, it was a joke. I was joking. Cool it, dude."

"Sorry. I'm not myself." Peter shrugged, nonchalant.

"I'm starting to think you're never yourself. What's got you stirred up this time?"

"The usual: I imagine the boogeyman in everything Anya."

"You're going to drive yourself crazy thinking like that. I'm no expert with girls, but in my experience with Christy, I just go with the flow. At some point, you're going to need to trust Anya. Otherwise, well, I think you know what I'm saying."

"I envy where you are with Christy. It's probably my fault I haven't been able to…"

"Win over Anya? Don't try so hard. Every girl is different. You can't treat Anya the same way I treat Christy. It's not apples to apples. That's not good or bad; it's just different."

Peter briefly considered calling Anya, but wisely opted against it. Bob was right with his warning about trying to push her.

#

Starting the new semester, Anya was in none of Peter's classes. The only time he would see her was after classes in the evening. She resumed studying elsewhere rather than staying in her room, exposed to Megan and her friends. Going to the library involved a familiar face: Ron.

She didn't tell Peter, who found this out when he went to the library for research on a class project of his own. Seeing them together roiled his gut, but rather than make an appearance, he chose to remain out of their sight. Anya acted as she always did, friendly, and seemingly romantically interested in Ron. He was all over her, figuratively speaking.

Peter went about his business, doing his work, and then he left the library, pained of spirit, plodding along, deep in thought, heading back to his room.

His boogeyman was alive and well.

Rather than go straight to his room, he decided to take a long walk in the dark. That involved heading toward Anya's dorm to see her being walked to the front door, and then inside by Ron. He had his hand to her back. This sign of affection, which she didn't resist, hammered at Peter. Rather than risk discovery, or the possibility they might share a kiss, he exited the area for a spirited walk around campus.

Peter's fatalistic thoughts tormented him until he finally returned to his room.

"That must have been some research," Bob said. "I expected you back long ago."

"I took a long walk. I needed to unwind."

"Unwind? What does that mean?"

"I don't really want to talk about it."

"Uh-oh."

"Bob, enough. Okay?"

"Sure."

Chapter Eight

Surprisingly, Peter fell asleep quickly. However, his fatalistic self-determined prognosis for a future with Anya, and the resultant emotional angst, accompanied him to breakfast.

Christy noticed. "Is something wrong, Peter? You're quiet, and you seem upset about something."

He replied tersely. "I'm fine. I'm dealing with some things. I've got it under control."

"Somehow, I don't think so. I've seen you in action enough to know when you're going off the rails."

"I tried to tell him," Bob piped in.

"You're worried about Anya. Why?" Christy eyed him harshly. This sudden critique of Peter was out of character for a mild-mannered, easygoing girl.

"Did I say I'm worried about Anya?"

"You didn't need to; you're easy to read."

He shrugged. His ire had simmered to life, and he didn't want to go down that road. "Listen, I know you guys are trying to be helpful, but I need to sort things out on my own. I appreciate your concern, but please give me some space about this."

"Okay, but I'm going to be watching. You realize I talk to Anya all of the time, and I can tell you there's nothing going on of concern. You remain your own worst enemy."

"Sure, and thanks for pointing that out."

Christy looked at Bob, who shrugged. She turned her head back to Peter. "Have it your way, Peter. Don't step in it." She shook her head in dismay.

#

Getting off on the wrong foot to start his day didn't help. Processing information from class lectures was problematic, possibly for the first time in his life. When he returned to his dorm that evening, he was angry, mostly at himself.

"What are you doing, Peter," he muttered. "This is not going to work."

As penance for his imagined shortcomings, he studied the chapter materials, rereading to get back into gear, scholastically speaking. Calling Anya was never a possibility in his current sour mood. Walking to the library to talk to her in person was doubly off the table.

"If she wants Ron, have at it," he muttered in a fit of childishness.

Bob had opted to spend the evening studying with Christy, giving Peter a chance to stew in his own juices, so to speak. Again, he went outside to walk around campus, his discordant feelings remaining a powerful negative stimulus.

When he finally returned, Bob was back in the room. "Your mom called for you."

"What's up?"

"They got a surgery date for Anya's mom in two weeks. She didn't have Anya's room phone number."

"Okay, I'll call over there."

Megan answered the phone.

"Could I speak to Anya, please?"

"She's out with some guy. I forget his name, there are so many."

"Would you tell her they have a surgery date for her mother?"

"Her mother, what's wrong with her?"

"Anya can explain, if she chooses to share private information. Please let her know the operation is in two weeks."

"This is Peter?"

"Of course it is. You know that, Megan."

"Sorry. She gets so many calls from different guys these days. I can't keep it straight who's who on her busy radar screen."

Peter debated whether to give a snarky reply, but thought better of it. "Goodbye, Megan."

She hung up without a reply.

"Bitch," he muttered.

#

He wasn't sure if Megan would deliver the message, so the following evening after supper, he made the trek to the library to seek out Anya. She was nowhere to be seen.

Grimacing, he walked to her dorm. Anya was studying with Ron in the lounge. Peter wanted very much to turn around and leave, but he made his way over to them.

Anya saw him coming and smiled. "Hello, Peter." She showed no sign of feeling guilt. For her, seemingly this was an innocent friendship with Ron.

"I'm sorry to bother you guys when you're studying. I just heard from my mom that they set a surgery date for your mother. I called Megan to pass on the information, but I'm never sure if she gives you the messages."

"She did tell me. Thank you. I assume we're going home then?"

He was caught off guard and stammered for a moment. "Eh…yes, of course. I guess I'll pick you up here that Friday evening."

"Peter, is something wrong? You haven't contacted me. I know you're busy with classes, but so are we."

"I was just getting my new routine down for the semester. As you know, I can't reach you in your room, and you don't have a cell phone."

"I'm sorry."

"Just showing up like this, I don't want to intrude on your prior plans, with other people."

Her eyes narrowed as she realized in spite of his words, Ron, or any other guy, was a problem for Peter. His version of "giving her space" was staying away, in a childish snit.

"So, I'll let you guys get back to your books. Nice seeing you again, Anya. Ron, take care, bud."

Ron replied, "Later."

Anya pondered the dismal plot twist but said nothing. She had no solution.

Stoically, Peter marched away, doing his own "pondering" as he walked. He mused; *You're an idiot, Peter.*

Conversing further with himself as he walked staring at the sidewalk, he muttered, "You're not on the same page with Anya."

"What?"

He hadn't noticed Allison walking toward him.

"I was talking to myself. Sorry."

"Do you answer yourself too?"

"I do when I want to have an intelligent conversation."

Allison laughed. "You're funny, Peter. So, what are you talking about?"

"My girl. I just have a knack for stupid when it comes to her."

"Your girl? Are you talking about that dark-haired girl?"

"Her name is Anya."

"I didn't know you'd gotten to the point of eliminating all other girls. So, what's the problem?"

"She's Russian, so sometimes I think things get lost in translation."

"Maybe there's a message in there, if you can figure it out. You realize you still have options elsewhere."

"Options—what are you talking about?"

"You can't figure it out? On this campus, don't you think there are other girls who would love to hear from you?"

"Me? You want to hear from *me*, Allison? You're swamped with guys chasing you around."

"It depends on your point of view. From where I stand, that chase, as you call it, can get old. Dealing with shallow people gets to be a waste of my time. In spite of your self-deprecating *persona,* it's easy to see through the smoke screen. You're a quality guy, and that means a lot to girls. We all look to leave this place with more than a college degree. We want a serious relationship that can lead to marriage. Is that so hard for you to understand?"

"Eh…"

"Very profound, Peter."

They chuckled.

"Thank you, Allison. That was a nice thing to say. By the way, what are you doing out here, walking alone in the dark?"

"I just needed to get away and get some exercise. You're welcome to escort me, if you feel I'm in danger."

"I wasn't saying you're in danger, but there are such things as crimes of opportunity. We don't want you to be seen as a target. I'll walk with you."

"Thank you, kind sir."

For a young man accustomed to confusion about romance, this was a most befuddling turn. Allison, interested in him? What an impossible idea.

As they walked and talked, she was surprisingly comfortable to be with. His angst about Anya momentarily went to the back burner.

"So, what are you thinking, Peter?"

"About?"

"About after graduation?"

"The usual: get a job and go from there. If you're talking about…that other stuff…"

Allison chuckled. "You can't say the word 'marriage.' That's funny."

"Marriage…is not something I dwell on."

"I very much doubt that. I think it's exactly what you think about with this Anya of yours. How's that working out? She must not be on board with the idea."

"Okay…it's true she may not be in a position of looking for a serious commitment like that."

"Is that what you want, to get engaged?"

"I don't know."

"Ah, but you do know. You need to grow a pair and go for it."

"That could be a mistake at this point."

"Sorry to burst your bubble, but risk is a part of life. Look at your options. You roll the dice and she says yes, or no. At that point, you know where you stand, and then maybe you see what I'm saying. There are other girls. Perhaps there are *yeses* out there, if you just ask."

"Allison, you've kind of knocked me off my pegs. I'm at a loss for words."

"That would be a first."

"I do have my share of opinions, I admit. However, using you as an example, you've got so many options, better options, much higher up the food chain. Why would I suddenly have any merit in your eyes?"

"I've already told you. Now you're coming across as fishing for compliments. Not a good move."

"You think I'm self-deprecating. It shows you why. I've earned that distinction with my litany of screw-ups and misdeeds. Perhaps I don't have any merits."

"For girls, you're kind of frustrating. Do you see why I feel like slugging you most of the time?"

"Go for it. I can take that kind of punishment."

Suddenly she stopped and turned to face him. Grasping his face in her hands, she kissed him deeply.

"Eh…" He gaped at Allison, befuddled to the extreme.

"Enough with the 'dull normal' act; put on your big-boy pants."

This time he laughed out, and soon she was laughing with him.

When they walked back to the dorm, Peter was in a much different mood. After walking up to his room in a stupor, Bob glanced over at him. "Did you get lost between Anya's dorm and ours?"

"You won't believe it. Anya was camped out in the lounge with that Ron guy again. I told her about the surgery, so we're going home next weekend. I was, well, stirred up, so walking back I'm thinking about the mess when Allison appears in front of me. She's out taking a walk and we strike up a conversation. Bob, she said some things I still can't process, about me having options…"

"What does that mean?"

"She implied she's interested."

"In you?"

"I know—it makes no sense. Anyway, she kisses me, and I mean a real kiss."

"I didn't know there were unreal kisses."

"Shut up. She kind of led me to believe she wants a date."

"Do you want my opinion?"

"Probably not, but I'll get it anyway."

"If you two-time Anya, you will regret it, guaranteed. Allison is really hot, but I never get a good feeling about her. If she has ulterior motives, like she knows your parents are rich, I would tread very lightly. If you upset her, she might react like another Megan. Beauty is no guarantee that a girl won't act crazy. They've all got it in them."

"I do understand, and thank you for ruining my momentary buzz. It was nice being kissed by a hot babe. She's a good kisser."

"That's because she gets plenty of practice. Of course she would know how to kiss. It isn't rocket science. Maybe her lips are experienced all over campus."

"Duh…anyway, back to reality." He took out a text.

"It's your choice, Peter. You're free to shoot yourself in the foot."

"Blah, blah, blah."

Bob shook his head. "I can see a big crash coming, my friend. It doesn't need to be this way."

"You're welcome to your opinion."

#

The following morning after breakfast, when Peter left for classes, he thought about Bob's warning. Although it was nice for his ego, Allison's sudden reversal, implying this was a new opportunity, just wouldn't take root. Peter was dubious for the very reasons he'd discussed with Bob.

Blotting out those thoughts and emotions to concentrate on his classes, he felt better at the end of the day. It was a brisk winter day, so there would be no dallying outside. As a matter of fact, a cloud bank rolled in quickly and flakes of snow started to filter down from above. Pulling the hood of his winter coat over his head, Peter hustled back to the dorm. On this evening, he had a number of pressing class assignments, including considerable research to write a paper, so after dinner he headed for the library. Deciding to combine reading his daily text assignments with the research he needed to do, he did both at the library.

Almost as a matter of habit, he looked around for Anya. Again, she wasn't present.

"Oh well," he muttered, and went into the stacks.

The research occupied his time and his mind, as he sifted through considerable documents to distill the data pertinent to his paper and his points. He had a theory to float and tended to cherry-pick data supporting his points. An impartial presentation was never his intention, and it posed no moral dilemma to him at that point. Rather, he was impressed with his own clever approach, perhaps more so than he should have been. As if a contrary theory had never been attempted before, Peter assumed his intellect would prevail.

Once he left the library, late, the accumulation of fallen snow crunched under his boots as he walked along the sidewalk, heading back to his dorm. There was a definite bite in the crisp air as a steady wind whipped at his winter garb. He smiled, self-satisfied with his mental prowess. A great intellectual coup was at hand, or so he told himself.

His face was red from the weather by the time he walked into his room.

"Nanook of the North," Bob said.

"It's a tester out there. I wouldn't want to be stranded and take a long walk, that's for sure. I might take a hot shower to warm up before I go to bed."

"Anya called and left a message. She wants to set up a study date."

"With whom?"

"Very funny, Peter."

"Okay. I'll call her."

He picked up the room phone and called. For once, Anya answered instead of Megan.

"Hello, Peter."

"It is. How are you? Bob said you called about a study date?"

"Yes. Is that okay with you?"

"Of course, why do you ask?"

"I sense you're not content about some things."

"You're wrong about that. I'm just peachy. When did you want to get together?"

"Is tomorrow evening okay?"

"Sure."

"I'll walk over to your dorm."

"That's not necessary. I can make the trek."

"I'll walk over, Peter. I can use the exercise."

"Then I guess I'll see you after dinner."

"We can talk, okay?"

"Sure, Anya. Bye."

Bob asked, "So, you're all set with Anya?"

"She's coming here to study tomorrow evening. I should put all of these calls on speaker, since you monitor everything we say."

"It's for your own good, Peter."

"Right."

"You've got to admit, you're kind of a loose cannon about relationships."

"Oh, thank you, wise one."

"Glad to be here in your time of need."

Bob laughed heartily. Peter shook his head. "Spare me."

#

The following day, Peter started to feel excited about being with Anya as he went through his classes.

When she came up to his room rather than call on the house phone, Bob opened the door and gave her a warm hug. "Anya, it's so good to see you. It's been too long."

"Hi, Bob. It's good to see you too."

They both looked at Peter.

"By the way, before you go down to study with Peter, Christy might have some good news for you very soon. I think her roommate finally has a landing place. We'll get you moved over here, so everyone has a happy ending."

Anya laughed, along with Bob.

Peter walked over and she embraced him. "Hello, Peter."

"Hi. Let me get my notebook and texts."

They went down the elevator to the lounge. It was fortunate there was still one open sofa, as other students had already claimed the other seats.

"Peter, I want to say again, I have some friends now. Maybe it strikes you wrong, but I've been alone in America for so long, it's nice to have friendships. I don't want to irk you. These other boys are just harmless friends. Is this something you can deal with? I don't get the sense you look at it that way." Anya sat closer than usual, but not very close.

"Anya, it's me. I'm the kind of person who can look at a situation the opposite of how I should. It's something I need to work on. I can only ask you to have patience with me."

"I must tell you, it gives me anxious feelings. Because I also like to share my time with others, now I must worry about how you will react. Do you see?"

"I do. I'm not saying you're doing anything wrong. I don't think you fully understand how you come across to others. You may mean for things to be innocent enough, but you're only half of the equation. You're beautiful, Anya, and that will lure these guys. They can have romantic aspirations too, just like me. I pick up on that, even if you don't."

Anya looked puzzled. "I don't intend anything romantic."

"I believe you, but the facts remain. When you choose to spend time alone with a guy, he thinks he's making progress. Don't be surprised if some of your so-called friends ask you out for dates."

"Oh…I didn't think of it that way."

"You have the right to do whatever you want—that will always be the case. You already know my feelings about you, but those are my feelings. When, or if, you get to where I am, you'll understand. Meanwhile, you hanging out with other guys, I'll cope as best I can, but I suspect I'll never do particularly well with it. I'm sorry."

"Peter, I'm sorry I'm such a problem for you."

"Anya, I'm my own biggest problem."

Anya shrugged and changed the subject. "I'll be glad to hear from Christy. Megan and I are in a place to tolerate each other. It isn't the warmth of being with Christy. I would like that."

"I'd love that too. By the way, did you want to call the house to talk to your mom? I've got my cell phone with me."

"Oh, yes I would, thank you."

Peter dialed home. "Hi, Mom. Anya and I are downstairs in the dorm studying. I thought I'd give her a chance to chat with her mother."

"Good, Peter, that's very thoughtful. Let me get Mariska. By the way, I've taught her a few words in English, and I've learned a few Russian words."

Soon Anya was chatting happily, in Russian. Seeing her genuine happiness warmed Peter's heart. At this moment, he felt his love for her ignite. She was so cute he nearly grabbed her in an embrace.

Once she finished her talk, she eyed him shyly. His strong affection was obvious for her to see, cow eyes and all. "Thank you for your phone," she whispered, but she didn't look him in the eyes.

"You're welcome. I gather your mom is doing well?"

"Yes. She's frightened of the surgery, but at the same time she's anxious to get it over with. She doesn't want that thing in her brain any longer than necessary."

"I understand. So, are you ready to study, or are there other things you wanted to say?"

"I'm done. Let's get to work."

She'd selected a cute dress to wear for the evening, which Peter admired a great deal. He tried to resist, but eventually he looked at her gorgeous legs.

She glanced up at him suddenly, a curious look on her face. "What is it, Peter? Is there a problem?"

"No problems. You're just really pretty."

She smiled, but straightened up her posture, straightened her dress downward. She also crossed her legs and began to stare intently at the textbook pages.

Noting her body language shift as signs and signals, she reflected closed rather than open feelings toward him. He could only conclude these were negative messages intended for him to pay attention to. These nonverbal means of communication were his signposts on his path toward making the difficult decisions.

Immediately, Peter responded, following her lead, immersing himself in his own studies, and the time passed without their speaking.

#

Hours later, Anya closed her book. "I must go back to my dorm."

"Would you like for me to walk you over there?"

"No, that's not necessary. It's late and you need your sleep."

Her denial didn't surprise him. "Okay then…well, I guess I'll see you when I see you."

She eyed him thoughtfully at his remark, unsure if there was an intended deeper meaning in his abrupt terse tone. Misunderstood signals were the norm between them.

"Good night, Anya. It was nice studying with you."

He went over to the elevator. She walked past him on the way out the door, into the night.

Glancing into the door glass as she walked, she could see Peter in the reflection behind her, staring at the elevator door. He never turned his head to look at her, and she took it as a troubling sign of her own. The easy rapport she experienced with the other guys on study dates, and real dates, always seemed difficult to find with Peter.

They had yet to have a social date in the new semester. For Anya, that was glaring.

Peter walked into his room. Again, Bob was out with Christy, though they weren't studying together in the lounge. Peter took the opportunity to crash early, in lieu of the third-degree from Bob when he got back.

#

The following day, while Peter went about his classes, Anya thought about him, and about them. She decided to call Christy.

"Hi, Anya, I've got some news. We should be able to get you moved over here in a couple of days. My roommate is going to move, finally. No offense to her, but I'm ready to move on to our next phase."

"Good. Thank you for doing this. Do you have a moment? Can we talk?"

"Sure. What's up?"

"It may just be me, but I don't think everything is right between Peter and me. We talk about solving issues, but the issues don't get solved. I listen to his words, but how he acts says something different to me. It makes me wonder if he's being honest with me. I try to ignore it, but should I? Does that make sense?"

"Unfortunately, it does."

"Because I'm not from here, I assumed it's the cultural differences. Now I don't think so. As I meet other boys, I don't seem to have the same problems as with Peter. I wonder, is it me?"

"Anya, this isn't a situation where there's just one answer. There's no right or wrong. We both know how much he loves you, but that's not the question, is it? He doesn't seem capable of coping with this relationship, and I gather he hasn't done well with any other girl either. That's not intended as a slam against him, but as much as we tell him about the same mistakes, he continues to fall back into the same rut. I understand completely where you're coming from."

"I feel terrible. We're driving home next weekend and as much as I love the fact I'll see my mother, and his parents, I feel uncomfortable with the never-ending issues. If he wants for me to be his wife, I try to think about that life. If I ever talk to a man, does that mean I face his jealousy forever? I understand what he says about how the other boys will woo me. Does it not matter when I tell him I'm not interested in them?"

"We've talked about that before. Guys can get crazy over their girls. Peter's not alone in that."

"I don't hide what I do if I study with other boys. I'm not dishonest. I tell him the truth: they're just friends."

"Anya, you call them *boy friends*: boys who are friends. From his viewpoint, there's no space between the words. They're boyfriends. It isn't fair, but it's something we all deal with."

"It makes me angry."

"You're not alone, babe."

"He hasn't taken me out on a date since we came back from Christmas. Why?"

Christy sighed. "Oh, darling, guys are like a bag of cats. You never know what's going to fly out when you open the bag."

Anya laughed. "That's very funny. Thank you—I needed a laugh."

"You're welcome. I have no answer for his behavior."

"I envy you with Bob—how he acts. You always have fun."

"Well, that's mostly true. I caution you, we all have our rough spots. It's no different for me. I choose to put up with…if you get my meaning."

"I believe I do. Either we accept a person or we don't."

"Nobody is perfect, me included. It's a matter of if the benefits are worth putting up with the aggravation. Am I helping?"

"Very much so. I feel I've started to realize being a Russian girl doesn't mean things are so different here with men. There are potential problems for men and women in every country."

"True. I'm glad you said that. I couldn't agree more. What I would choose doesn't mean that it is what you should choose."

"I want to choose, but…"

"You've still got questions. If it doesn't fit, I doubt you can force it. I love Peter too, but he just can't seem to get out of his own way when it comes to girls. We can tell him things, but in the end, if he's going to change, that must come from within him. The alternatives are to accept him how he is or to move on to look elsewhere. I hate to say that, but I suspect you've already figured that out."

"You see this clearly. With what he's done for me, and his family, with what they're doing for my mother, how could I hurt him by going back to dating other boys?"

"I say this with all honesty: I hope you guys end up together, but if this situation continues and you can't get past it, do you think a compromise marriage would last?"

"I…well, no."

"Whatever path you follow, I will always be your friend."

"I appreciate that. Let me know about the moving."

"I will, honey. I'm sorry for your predicament."

"I will think about it further, but lately I'm feeling discouraged about the prospects with Peter."

#

Peter didn't vary his routine. With the exception of seeing Anya at the library one evening the following week, they had no further contact until he drove over on Friday to pick her up for the drive home.

She eyed him questioningly when he came through the door to pick up her luggage. Every piece of it was brand new: recent gifts from Peter's parents.

Megan eyed him coolly. "Well, well, well, look who's here, Anya. It's your guardian angel and main benefactor. Got any new purchases to try to buy her off?"

"Hello, Megan. What a pleasure to see you again."

"My only pleasure is when you close the door on the way out."

"That can be arranged. Come along, Anya; let's go."

Preoccupied in thought, Anya said nothing about the confrontation. Her mind was occupied by her endless questions. Being at a major fork in her road, which way to go? Would she make the right choice—could she? What *was* the right choice?

Peter loaded the luggage into the car and they started the drive home. "How have you been, Anya? How are your classes?"

"Very well. I've been fine."

"How's Ron?"

Inwardly, she bristled, taking it as a barb. "I imagine he's fine. I don't see him often. I think perhaps I'll take a nap."

Taking the blanket, she covered up completely, turning away from Peter to face the door.

"Good night," Peter said. He felt embarrassed. Unable to rein in his jealous feelings, again, he'd done the last thing he wanted to do: upset Anya. The words couldn't be unsaid. In so many words, he'd come across as saying, *I don't trust you.* Peter shook his head in dismay, the recipient of another self-inflicted wound.

Driving for the balance of the trip in silence, he pulled up to the gate at his parents' community. Anya raised her head.

"We're almost there."

She sat up and fluffed her hair after pulling down the sun visor to look in the mirror.

"Anya, I'm sorry. I have a knack for saying the wrong things."

"Okay, Peter." Her curt tone cued him in to the fact she wasn't in the mood to be forgiving.

After he drove into the garage, Anya went straight into the house while Peter unloaded the luggage.

Mr. Brown came out to help his son. "Welcome home."

"Thanks, Dad. I'm glad to be here."

"The women went into the living room. Mariska has been a bundle of nerves, worrying about the surgery. That's understandable."

"I'd worry too. The thought somebody is going to cut my head open is really scary. I probably wouldn't do as well as her."

"We've tried to ease her mind."

"She knows her life is on the line."

"She does. Her motivation to fight through it is Anya. Being around to watch her daughter blossom into her life, being a grandmother…every mother wants that."

"That's understandable."

George noticed his son's reticent look. "Is something wrong?"

"The usual, I can't conquer my demons."

"Well, you're home now. Just relax. We can watch some basketball."

"That sounds good. So, the surgery is tomorrow morning?"

"Early tomorrow. She's the first surgery of the day for Phil—I mean Dr. Strong. He said the surgery won't be a short one. We'll camp out at the hospital until it's over."

"That makes sense."

"What are your plans afterward?"

"I guess the usual: drive back Sunday evening."

"What did Anya say?"

"We didn't talk about it."

"Peter, why not? You know she'll want to be with her mother."

"We don't communicate much lately."

"Is that by her choice, or yours?"

"Some of both, I'd say."

"Son, be very careful about this. Don't say things you can't take back. This may be uncomfortable to go through, but you need to suck it up and be a man here."

Peter frowned. There were many things he wanted to say, but they were defensive immature things that served no purpose. Feeling unfairly picked on was one of his issues. Wisely, he opted to remain silent.

Chapter Nine

It was a very early departure in the morning. Peter sat in the front seat with his father. The three women sat in the back for the long drive to the hospital. With snow flurries and slippery roads, the drive took much longer than usual. There was no conversation during the tense trip. Finally, Peter muttered, "Are you okay, Dad?"

"I've got it." Concentrating fully, he never glanced at his son.

Peter noticed his tight grip on the wheel.

It didn't help their worries, seeing several cars had slid off the slick road into the ditch.

Arriving safely at the hospital, but later than they wished, Mariska was hustled through the check-in and pre-op process. Later, as she lay on her bed waiting to be wheeled into surgery, Peter made a point of speaking to Mariska. "Everything is going to be fine."

She eyed him a moment. "Thank you. I do trust your doctors."

Anya still needed to translate. "We'll all be here waiting when you wake up."

She smiled, looked at her daughter, and squeezed her hand gently.

Anya smiled. "Good night, Mama. Have a nice sleep."

They spoke briefly in Russian before she was wheeled away.

The foursome turned and headed for the surgical waiting room, where the desk clerk gave them instructions. "If you leave the area, sign out on this sheet. You can check the monitor screen to get the details of the surgery, what stage they're at, and so forth. You can go eat your lunch because afterward she'll have a long time span in the post-op recovery room. With this kind of surgery, they may keep her under for another day, or maybe more. It depends."

Mr. Brown nodded. They went to claim seats in the mostly full waiting room. It happened there weren't four seats together.

"I'll sit over here," Peter said.

Anya sat next to Edith, while Peter sat next to an elderly woman. "Hello," he whispered, like he was in a library and needed to be quiet.

"Hello."

"Who's going into surgery?"

"My husband, it's his heart. I've told him he needed to eat right."

"I'm sorry."

"We've been married forty-five years."

"That's amazing, in this day and age."

"We've had our share of bumps in the road, but we decided to stick it out. Who are you waiting for?"

"That's my parents over there, sitting with Anya. It's her mom who's having brain surgery to take out a mass. We go to school together."

"It's nice that you're taking time to sit with her."

"She's here from Russia to go to college, so we're glad to help out."

Mable looked over at Anya. Talking with Edith, she didn't notice Mable's glance.

"She's a pretty young woman. Is she your girlfriend?"

"I'd like to think so. Whether she would agree, I'm not so sure about."

"Why do you say that?"

"I'm kind of a train wreck with girls."

She chuckled. "All young men are train wrecks with girls."

"I can't disagree."

"For me, that was so long ago I hardly remember it, but understand: girls have their issues too."

"I understand that, very clearly."

She patted his hand sympathetically.

"If I get on your nerves, ma'am, just tell me to shut up."

#

Meanwhile, Anya spoke continuously with Edith and never looked over at Peter. He continued to chat with the woman. Mr. Brown read a sports magazine.

Periodically, Peter got up to check the monitor. It was a while before Mariska made it into surgery and over an hour before they actually started the operation. At lunchtime, he stood when his parents stood. Turning to his new friend, he asked, "Would you like to join us?"

"I wouldn't want to intrude."

"That's not a problem. There's no reason for you to sit alone."

"Thank you."

The three came over and looked at Peter and then at the woman.

"This is Mable. Her husband is having heart surgery. I've invited her to join us in the cafeteria, so she doesn't have to sit alone."

Mrs. Brown responded. "That's fine, son. Hi, I'm Edith, and this is my husband, George. This is Anya."

"Hello, Edith. Thank you for showing kindness to an old woman."

Edith smiled. "Come along, Mable. Let's go eat."

Peter decided to walk on the other side of Mable, while Anya walked beside George, behind Peter and the other two women.

While Edith and Anya talked, George noticed his son's behavior. When he looked at Peter, he got a shrug.

Taking seats at the cafeteria table after buying meals, Peter sat beside Mable. Anya sat across the table, beside Edith. Peter sat across from his father.

While the three women conversed, he spoke with his dad.

George made a wisecrack. "Did you get enough food?"

Peter's tray was completely full. "I just couldn't choose, so I took them all. I think I covered all of the food groups."

"I wish I could still do that. Those days are over for me. If I overeat, it instantly goes to my belly. It's so much harder to burn it off than at your age. Enjoy it while you can because it doesn't last."

"I believe you, Dad. By the way, did I see on the weather they expect a big snowstorm tomorrow?"

"Yes. That's what they're predicting. If you're going back to school, drive very carefully."

"I will."

They took their time at the table, since neither surgery would resolve quickly. Ambling back later, they went to the monitor. Mable's husband was just out of surgery, but Mariska's procedure was still ongoing.

"Do you think that means there was a problem?" Anya asked.

"We can't assume that," Edith replied. "It's a complicated surgery. Let's assume the best."

They resumed sitting down to wait. This time, Mable and Peter were able to find seats closer to the others.

A nurse came out in surgical garb. "Mable Madison?"

"Here." She stood up and waved her hand.

"Please come into this conference room. The doctor will come out to speak with you."

Mable turned to them. "Thank you, again."

Peter spoke. "Good luck. It was nice to talk with you."

After her conference with the doctor, Mable was taken straight to her husband's room.

Peter wandered over to the monitor. "Hey, guys, she's out of surgery."

Anya stood up and came over to look at the screen.

A different nurse came out moments later. "Anya Seminova?"

"I'm here."

"Come into this conference room for the doctor to speak with you."

"May I bring my friends?"

"There's only a maximum of three."

"I can wait out here," Peter said.

"Thank you." Anya gave him a brief smile but turned away quickly to go into the room.

The conference took a while, between waiting for the doctor to arrive and the lengthy explanation. Peter waited patiently.

When they finally came out of the room, Edith came over. "Phil said it was a difficult surgery. There was more to it than they'd anticipated. They're going to keep her under for another day, minimum."

"Why is that, Mom?"

"They won't know until they wake her up if there are any cognitive deficits. Phil had to go into some areas that could be problematic."

"I can tell by looking at Anya's face. She looks worried."

"Mariska still has her life, in spite of any potential deficits. It isn't like she could have lived with that thing in her head."

They were led to Mariska's room. Edith walked beside Anya, while the men were a pace behind.

Mariska was heavily bandaged, still with a breathing tube. Her face was pallid, her skin slightly sunken over her cheekbones, an unhealthy skeletal look.

"Wow," Peter whispered to his dad.

The head nurse of the floor came into the room. "Listen, folks, I know it's hard to see her this way, but sitting here doesn't help her. We're going to be coming in frequently to check, but realize she'll be out for at least twenty-four hours, or maybe longer; it depends on the tests. It's best if you go home and get a good night's rest."

"Can I stay in the room with my mother?" Anya's face was pinched with a strained look.

"No."

Anya looked distressed, but didn't argue.

#

They drove home, sitting down to dinner later.

"Anya, it's supposed to snow tomorrow for our drive back to school. I think we should think about leaving earlier."

"No, Peter. I'm staying here. I'll just make up the class assignments another time. I'm not leaving with my mother like this."

The look on her face, like he was an idiot to suggest such a thing, floored him. "Okay," he whispered. He tried to act unfazed, but his face reddened nonetheless.

Anya turned her head to his father. "I hope this doesn't inconvenience you."

"Of course not, dear. You're welcome here, staying with us, for as long as you wish. You want to be sure your mother is out of the woods. That's understandable."

"Thank you, sir. Do you understand, Peter?"

"I do. I can see about getting your assignments from your professors and sending them here. Maybe I can email them to Dad's computer." Peter wanted to act and sound nonchalant. It didn't work.

"Thank you, but I don't have my books with me."

"That's true."

"I'll sort it out when I get back to school. I'm not worried about it. I can't leave Mama now."

"Okay, Anya."

She stared at him for his reaction. He tried his utmost to appear nonchalant. "Anya, it's fine."

She shrugged her shoulders, seemingly unconvinced by his façade.

"Peter, I think there are some ball games on," George said.

The men went to the den, while Anya stayed in the kitchen with Edith.

George glanced at his son, who was clearly distressed. "Peter, I know this is difficult, but Anya is picking up signals from you, ones that aren't helping."

"I don't know what to say. I feel like I need to be cautious around her. I'm not sure how it got to this point. Maybe I'm flawed worse than I thought."

"Maybe you should just relax. Just act normal rather than trying so hard."

"For me, it seems to be easier said than done."

"We'll watch sports and then join the ladies later. Your mom can talk to Anya and put her in a better mood. For her, worrying about her Mom, I'm sure that doesn't help."

"And I'm a stressor along the way."

"I didn't say that, but take a step back. Just be my son doing his usual thing at home. It's much better than walking around on eggshells."

"Okay, we can watch sports, no problem. I'll roll with the punches."

#

Rather than just talk in the kitchen, Anya decided to try her hand at making a cake. The cook smiled at her efforts and gave her plenty of suggestions. It helped to take Anya's mind off her mother lying unconscious in the hospital.

At dinner she smiled at Peter, which puzzled him.

"I have a surprise for you."

"What?"

"You've never tasted my cooking, so I made a cake for dessert."

"Thank you. I can hardly wait."

"And…thank you for putting up with me. I know it hasn't been easy."

"Anya, you're not a bother for me."

She shrugged, skeptical at his answer. His actions didn't support it.

The staff brought out the cake, devil's food with white frosting. It was moist and tasty; just perfect.

"Wow, this is really good, Anya."

She smiled at her first baking success. Even the cook came in to try a piece. She gave Anya a thumbs-up signal. "You did a nice job, dear. This is exactly how it should be."

"I had a great teacher. What you taught me; I'll remember."

"Anya, you have a knack for cooking. I gave you some pointers, but you would have figured them out on your own. Making things from scratch is very impressive, especially for a novice. I'm impressed and, believe me, that doesn't happen often."

Anya shrugged her shoulders, visibly pleased at the high compliment. She glanced at Edith.

"Yes, Anya. You certainly exceeded me. I wouldn't have even tried baking from scratch."

"Thank you. It does taste pretty nice."

Everybody chuckled.

#

Afterward, the men retired to the den, while the women returned to the kitchen to chat more.

Peter turned to his father. "Tomorrow I'm heading out early, before the snow accumulates. Since Anya is hanging back here, there's no reason to dally."

"I know what you're saying. This is a hard stage to get through, and I sympathize with you. I've been there."

"It seems to be my nature to feel pessimistic, no matter how much I try to fight it."

"In the end, things work out however they're supposed to. When I look back on my life, I can honestly say there were things I wanted that didn't work out. I didn't understand at the time, but later I could see it in a different light. It's like that old saying: be careful what you wish for because you just might get it."

"So, you're saying my fixation on Anya might not work out, and it might not be a bad thing?"

"Well, not exactly. What I'm saying is perhaps you should open your horizons again, in spite of your current feelings that she's the one. Since it's a two-way street…well…"

"You think she might decide to go with another guy. That's a feeling I've had for a long time I didn't want to accept. Maybe it's time I got a clue."

"Don't shoot yourself in the foot, but don't back yourself in a corner either."

"Thanks, Dad. That helps me a lot. I'm going to set a goal to do better rolling with the punches. This time not just words, but actions. If she wants to…well, I need to handle it."

"These things are fraught with peril, romantically speaking, but there is always an outcome. It's just that we can't assume it will be the happy ending we desire. Our imagination of a happy ending may not be their dream. Do you see what I'm trying to tell you?"

Shrugging, Peter answered. "I do. I really do. I suspect you also sense Anya and I just aren't clicking right now."

"With that being said, I want to assure you we'll handle Anya and Mariska as part of us, just like we promised. Edith and I have no problem with Mariska living here as long as she likes. She's a delightful woman. If she does have cognitive deficits, it's the only option anyway. I hope things clear up for you and Anya, but we will adjust, no matter which way things go."

"Agreed, I'm going to try to be a big boy from now on."

At that moment, the women walked in. Edith spoke. "What are you talking about?"

George replied, "We're just talking about getting Mariska healthy and back on her feet."

"I was telling Dad that with the big snowstorm moving in, I'm heading out early. I don't really like driving on bad roads."

Anya eyed him, trying to watch for any hidden meanings. He turned his head to her. "Anya, you'll be safe staying here. It's not necessary to get up early on my account. Feel free to sleep in."

She grimaced, but said nothing.

Glancing at each other, the women recessed to the formal living room to watch another television, as they weren't keen on watching sports.

#

Peter went to bed early, got up very early on Sunday, and went into the dark kitchen for a small glass of orange juice and a bowl of cereal he gobbled down before anybody got out of bed. The snowstorm was just starting, so for several hours of the trip the drive was tolerable, but the last hour was dicey. It slowed his progress considerably, but because it was Sunday, there was little traffic on the roads.

He played his radio loudly to keep him awake and alert, plowing his way through the hazardous road conditions. It was still a white-knuckler, tense and stressful.

Pulling into the parking lot at school, he felt great relief. Dragging his suitcase through accumulated snow was no easy task.

Bob was already returned from breakfast when Peter walked into the room.

"Hey, dude. You guys must have left really early. I didn't expect you until tonight."

"I left really early. Anya stayed back there with her mother still under. She wants to be sure her mom is okay. My dad will drive her back here when she's ready."

"Oh…are you okay with that?"

"Why wouldn't I be?"

"Because you're Peter. I'm not saying you object to her staying with her mom, under the circumstances. I'm talking about the casual tone I hear—like you don't care any longer."

"Bob, let's agree to let it go. I don't really need your opinions on the matter right now."

"Okay, Peter." Bob shrugged at the ongoing drama.

"If I ever want to talk, I'll let you know. By the way, Mom and Dad have decided to get Anya a cell phone. There's some sort of family-and-friends package. I don't know. I didn't get the details."

"You didn't care about the details," Bob muttered.

Peter glared at Bob, who put up his hands in surrender. "Sorry, but it's pretty obvious you're angry."

"I'm not mad, and it's a good idea for Anya to have her own phone to call her mom. I just want to get back into the school routine and put this out of my mind."

"Sure, Peter. My lips are sealed."

Peter chuckled. "Somehow, I doubt that. Your lips have never been sealed."

"By the way, Christy's roommate has moved out, so Anya can move in any time she's ready."

"That's a good thing for her."

Bob started a retort, but Peter held up his hand. "Enough, please."

Bob shrugged.

#

The next morning at breakfast, Christy joined them, as per usual.

"So, the operation is done?"

"It is."

They eyed each other a moment when Peter didn't elaborate.

"How is she?" Christy glowered at the surprise verbal swordfight. Peter's dour mood was unmistakable.

"Unknown. They kept her under for a day. I don't know if there was brain swelling or some other issues to deal with. Anya will ride back here with my dad…whenever."

"Of course she wants to stay with her mom, Peter."

"Of course."

Again they eyed each other, like in a standoff.

"Peter, I don't get you sometimes."

"I'm an enigma. What can I say?"

"An enigma that's going off the rails. There's a person in your life needing support and understanding right now."

"How am I not being understanding?"

"You're going through the motions, but…"

"But…but what?"

"Okay, Peter, I give up. Have it your way."

"On that happy note, I'm out of here. You guys have a great day."

He stood, turned, and walked away, stirred up again.

#

His classes only partially diverted his mind, so he went to the library to study. Ironically, he saw Ron studying with some other students. Peter decided to exchange pleasantries.

"Hey, Ron."

"Peter. What's up?" Ron had a wry smile.

"I was in the neighborhood."

Ron chuckled, along with the pretty coeds sitting with him. "Good one, Peter…so, no Anya?"

"She stayed back to keep tabs on her mom. It was a long and difficult brain surgery. They kept her under, so we still don't know if there are any residual cognitive problems. My dad will drive her back to school when she's ready."

"That's pretty nice how your family has taken on her problems."

"My folks are a rare breed. They're model citizens."

"Citizens with resources."

"They worked hard to get where they are. They started from scratch, coming out of college."

"Very commendable."

"I hope I can do even a fraction of what they've accomplished."

"I'm sure you'll do just fine."

"Thanks, Ron. I'll let you guys get back to work."

"Feel free to join us."

"Thank you, but I won't be here long. I've got some specific research to do, and then I'm off. Nice seeing you again, Ron, and ladies."

He went to a table as far away from them as he could find. His "research" was nothing more than going over his textbook assignments, which he quickly completed. Soon, he was up and heading outside into the snowy landscape. Walking along casually, even though it was brisk, with a steady wintry breeze, his boots crunched in the accumulated snow as he plodded along. Pulling his hood over his head, he tugged on the strings to tighten it to protect his face and neck. It was still a numbing breeze.

Bob nodded when he walked in the door. "All done with your research? Your face is red."

"I am done, and it's cold outside."

"Christy wants to know if you want to come with us to see a movie."

"I'll think about it. Third wheel doesn't usually work well for me."

"We're all friends. This isn't some dating referendum to judge you."

"I realize that. I didn't say no. I told you I'll think about it."

Later, when Bob asked again, Peter decided on a different choice for Friday evening. "You guys go ahead. I'm going to stay back. I might go down to the mixer to hang out."

"Do you want us to come with you?"

"No, I'm fine. You go and enjoy time with your girlfriend."

"Okay, but be careful." Bob had a rueful smile.

"Always."

#

On Friday, going down to the dorm party, Peter broke out of his usual shell and actually danced with various girls, and he approached them. Some were pretty girls, which gratified his bruised ego. Making a strategy decision for the evening, he'd made a point to talk a little with each girl before moving on to the next dance partner. There would be no verbal fumbling moves on his part to be misinterpreted, no awkward *faux pas* to haunt him. It generated curious looks among the girls when he *didn't* make a move. Seemingly, he was suddenly intriguing to them, a man of mystery, like he was a person of consequence worth noting.

Inevitably, like it was fate, toward the end of the evening suddenly Allison stepped in front of him. For the female bystanders, a very pretty girl successfully corralling him caught the notice of his prior partners, who hadn't.

"Do I get a dance?" she asked coyly.

"Sure. I can mash your toes too."

She laughed. "Peter, you seem more relaxed than usual. Apparently, you smoothed out the wrinkles with your girlfriend."

"I wouldn't say that. I'm evolving. I can't stay in the pupae stage forever."

"Ugh. What an image you just put in my mind. What a silver-tongued rogue you are."

"It's a gift."

"Some gift. You're a lunatic."

"I am. No doubt about it."

Again, dancing with Allison was evocative. Her dance skills were prodigious, and on this occasion, she provocatively bumped him frequently. Being a young man, he wasn't immune to her subtle ploys to stir him.

In her case when the music stopped, he couldn't just walk away—she wouldn't allow it. When he tried to turn, she grabbed his hand. "We're not done. Where do you think you're going? You're coming to the lounge for us to talk."

"About what?"

"About whatever I want to talk about."

"Okay."

When they found a sofa, she sat beside him, girlfriend close. It rattled Peter. That made her smile, seeing the unease she caused.

"You like yanking my chain, Allison. What's that about?"

She laughed heartily. "You're blunt, Peter. No beating around the bush. Is it so hard to sit beside me? Am I not pretty enough for you?"

"Your looks are not in question. You already know you're gorgeous. My question is how it relates to me. You've known me all through high school and now I'm suddenly interesting? I know who I am. I didn't just molt my exterior skin, like a snake."

"Give me a break with the disgusting images, Peter. You say the most idiotic things. I never have conversations with other guys like this. You're such a dolt, but, for whatever the reason, you seem to be the flame that draws me."

"And now you've put an image in my mind. If you're implying I have some subtle plan in play, you're wrong. I'm totally incapable of subtle, nor can I form romantic plans of any kind. I roll with the punches because that's all I can do. I'm reactive because I can't be proactive."

"I very much doubt that, Peter. You're as smart as anybody I know."

"Maybe I'm book smart, but in the ways of the world, and with romance in particular, I'll always go into gun fights unarmed. Maybe you haven't fully grasped the level of my incompetence."

Suddenly, she leaned over to kiss him. "Now what do you have to say, mister?"

"Eh…"

"Duh, Peter."

"I'm not sure what you want from me." He looked confused.

"Unless you're wearing a ring and are off the market, you're still fair game. I'm available for a date."

"You want a date—with me?"

"That is what I said." Pushing her body against his, she peered intently into his eyes.

"I would need to think about that." Peter stepped back.

"What is there to think about? Perhaps you might find a solution to your unending drama with your Russian girl."

"Anya."

"Whatever. So, what do you say?"

"I'm going to think about it, as I said."

"You're so damn frustrating, Peter. One of these days…"

She held up her fist.

Peter chuckled. "I'll keep your threat in mind."

She kissed him again, this time very passionately. "Just so you remember what you're missing."

"I've got it, Allison. Good night."

He left her sitting, walking briskly to his elevator.

"What is this?" he questioned. The door opened and he started his ascent. It made no sense to him, and instantly he remembered Bob's warning about her plotting for the riches in his family.

"You might be onto something, Bob," he muttered as he got off the elevator.

Bob wasn't back in the room yet from his evening with Christy, so Peter went to bed.

#

During the school week, he got a call one evening from Anya.

"Hello, Peter. Your parents got a cell phone for me. I wanted to give you my new number, so we can call each other."

"Oh…thank you, Anya. How's your mom?"

"She finally woke up, but speaking was a problem. The doctors are running tests, but they think because the growth went farther than anticipated, there were brain areas affected by the surgery. She may need therapy to relearn speech."

"I'm sorry to hear that."

"At least she's still alive. How do you say it: I want to count my blessings? Your parents say not to worry. They will bring her to the house and hire the best possible therapists to fix the problems."

"They'll do right by her, Anya."

"I know. I trust them completely. Your mother is so gracious. She's such a wonderful example for me to emulate."

"That's kind of you to say about her. Do you have a time frame in mind?"

"You mean before I come back to school?"

"Yes."

"Not exactly. Once Mama is alert, up and about, I think I'll feel safe to return."

"I would worry about getting too far behind, but really you're smart enough to catch up with no problems."

"Thank you. I hope you're right. It's still difficult for me to learn in English. For the longest time, I would read the English and then translate into Russian in my mind. Learning to think in English is maybe the hardest part of my learning process."

"I never thought of it that way. You're an exceptional person, and I'm truly amazed."

"I do look forward to getting back to school. There's much there that I enjoy."

"Did I tell you Christy's roommate finally moved out, so your way is clear to change rooms?"

"I did hear that. It will be fun to have Christy as my roommate. I look forward to it. Have you been going to games and things?"

"Yes. I like basketball. Actually, I like all sports. I even go to the other sports, like volleyball and so forth. Watching athletic girls cavorting about in shorts isn't hard on the eyes."

Anya laughed. "You are so silly."

Peter noted his comment about other girls evoked zero jealousy in Anya. He mused in his mind. *Is that because she doesn't care about me?*

He continued, "What have you been doing?"

"I spend what time I can with Mama. When we're at the house, I visit with your mom, watch television programs, read books, and I'm even trying your crossword puzzles. Coming up with the right English words is difficult for me.

Some questions with hidden meanings, I don't easily grasp. Your mother helps me to understand, though."

"Sounds like a blast."

"I know, Peter. It would be fun to be doing things at school, but I'm here, so I make the best of it."

"Okay. I'll program your number into my phone."

"You want to go, I know."

"Actually, it's not that. I have a big class assignment to knock out."

"Then I'll let you go."

"By the way, I saw Ron and friends at the library. He said to say hi."

"Goodbye, Peter," she replied curtly.

#

Peter pondered the call and his feelings about it. Allison's advances still affected him to an extent. Though it was nice Anya initiated the call, he still felt he was in the "pal" category rather than "significant other." Her coming back to school was no sure thing about their fragile relationship.

Bob had been strangely silent on the topic. Although Peter was happy to seemingly get out of his gun sights, it made him wonder why.

"Bob, so how is Christy lately? You haven't said much, and you're gone a lot."

"It's really good. We both agree we're in love and that's pretty nice. We're actually talking about after, if we want to make that type of commitment. By the way, Anya called to give Christy her new phone number. They talk all the time now."

"That's good. Christy is good for Anya."

"That's my thought too."

"Anya is considering coming back to school this weekend."

"Waiting around indefinitely on her mother is not a good choice. I suspect her progress will be slow, with the therapies and rehab. For as smart as Anya is, getting really far behind is an equally bad idea."

"I agree."

"I don't know if I told you, but Allison is back. She's sort of making some moves. I don't understand it, but I wonder if what you suggested is coming true. It's a fact she knows about the money in my family, and what if this is her new goal? It's perplexing for me. She's still really pretty and when a hot girl comes on to you, it can't help but affect you."

"You know me. If I were you, I'd set her straight right away. 'Get away from me, harpy.'"

"*Harpy?* You are so lame."

The boys laughed heartily.

Chapter Ten

Peter received a call from his father.

"I'm bringing Anya back to school on Saturday. We should arrive around noon or so."

"I'll be here, Dad. Thanks for doing this."

"I thought we'd get a bite to eat."

"I can eat. How about I get tickets to the basketball game in the evening? I assume Mom is coming?"

"Actually, Mariska is just out of the hospital and back in her bedroom at the house, so Mom is staying back with her. It will just be me and Anya."

"Okay. Then I can just get three tickets."

"I think I'll just have lunch, visit a bit, and then drive back home. Staying alone in a motel room doesn't appeal to me."

"Okay, Dad. I understand."

"Also, once Anya arrives, you'll need to help her move her things from her old room over to Christy's room."

"That will be a delight. It should be the last time I ever have to see Megan."

"Suck it up, son. It's one of the trials of life, dealing with unpleasant people. She won't be the last one you run into. None of us like that."

"I will. I'll plaster a phony smile on my face, keep my mouth shut, and take care of business."

"That's the spirit. I'll see you soon."

"Okay, Dad. Thanks for the heads up."

#

Peter stayed busy with schoolwork until the weekend, with the exception of another Friday-evening trip down to the mixer. Dancing with girls who were strangers had become an enjoyable diversion.

He mused, *is this my equivalent of life on the edge: running the chance of having more games with Allison? Boosting my ego during these little soirees with the opposite sex is preferable to living through more romantic uncertainty.*

On this evening, however, he had chaperones: Bob and Christy.

Christy spoke to him pointedly. "Hi, Peter. So, we can finally get Anya moved tomorrow."

He eyed her ruefully at her thinly veiled attempt to make him feel guilty, like he was cheating on Anya. "Yeah. Dad said they'll be in town around lunchtime. You guys are welcome to join us to break bread."

"Thank you. I think we will. After lunch, I get a chance to meet the infamous Megan. I've heard so much about her, I'm curious now."

"Believe me, she lives down to the low standard we've described. Do you mind if I go and dance? That *is* why I came tonight."

"Whatever, Peter." She eyed him reproachfully, but he simply got up and headed for the nearest collection of girls, to cut one of them out of the herd and begin his evening. It was a skill he'd mastered with practice.

Spinning, swaying, and twirling about, matching the moves of his female partners, Peter put all thought out of his mind, letting the hours roll past. When the music paused, he returned to the table. Christy and Bob had been dancing too, but only with each other.

Christy commented. "For as chilly as it is outside, you wouldn't know it in here. It's like a sauna."

"It doesn't bother me. I spent so much time on the sidelines, it's nice to get in the game and have some fun. Hanging with coeds is pretty cool."

"You've certainly made the rounds. Are there any girls you haven't danced with?" She eyed him critically.

"I'm not sure, but I think I got them all."

Bob laughed, but Christy did not. Again, she stared at Peter like he was in the midst of a great sin: cheating on Anya.

"Drinks, anybody?" he asked.

Bob replied, "I'll take a cola."

Christy frowned, but said, "Sure. Get me a diet."

Drinking the sodas cooled them down slightly, but Peter rejoined the fray the instant the music resumed. He remained dancing until the last song rather than sit through Christy's judgmental looks.

#

With the late hour, Peter slept in on Saturday morning, skipping breakfast. His Dad arrived just before noon. Bob called Christy and the group went out to lunch.

Anya hugged Christy warmly before turning to Peter. He waited for her to make the first move before he embraced her. Turning, she stepped toward him, opening her arms.

"Welcome back." Peter's embrace was cursory rather than extended. He stepped back quickly.

"I'll miss being with Mama, but I'm anxious to get back to classes." Anya tried to smooth yet another awkward moment.

"Did I hear she's having some troubles with speaking?"

"Yes, but they believe speech therapy can resolve the problem. They've located a Russian-speaking woman to come in and help. Your parents are too good to us."

"Good. With you having a cell phone now, you can call her once she's recovered enough to speak."

"Yes. I feel very good about her progress." She smiled warmly, but her glance switched over to Christy.

"We're going to go over right away to get your things moved out of Megan's room. There's no reason to delay."

"Eh...I didn't tell her I'm moving." A worried expression crossed her face.

"Uh-oh."

Christy spoke up. "That's not a problem. We'll all be there with you."

"I hope you're right. You haven't met Megan. She can be...difficult."

"We'll handle it. Don't worry."

Peter looked at Anya. Neither of them felt reassured by Christy's opinion because they knew Megan and the trouble she was capable of.

#

When Peter's dad left to go home, the group walked to the parking lot, to Peter's car. After driving to Megan's dorm, they walked up to the room. Anya opened the door. Megan was sitting with five of her friends. They eyed Peter sourly when he came in.

Christy took the lead. "Hello. You must be Megan. I've heard so much about you; it's a pleasure to put a face with a name. You're as lovely as Anya described you."

Megan was taken aback, and smiled, curious where this was going. She always loved compliments. "It's nice to meet you too. Who are you?"

"Oh, let me explain. Anya has decided to move over to my dorm to room with me. It's been a great learning experience for her, living with you, but now she's ready for new experiences, with me."

Megan's expression changed radically, from dismissive phony smile to a grim stare. "What? Anya, you're moving? After all I did for you? I let you in, with all that I taught you, the close things we shared? We never talked about this, and now you spring it on me, bringing these strangers into my room."

At that point, Peter expected Megan to launch into a blistering tirade, but suddenly she got a calculating look.

She glanced at her friends and then looked back at Peter rather than Anya. "Okay, so be it. Go ahead and move her. I'll survive just fine. Maybe you think you won, dude, but sometimes things don't work out the way you expect. Anya, I'm sure you understand to use great discretion when talking about the private things we shared. Saying nothing at all is the obvious best choice for you, and of course there is no coming back here."

Anya's face reddened.

Whatever Megan was talking about, Peter had no idea, but he took her words as a genuine threat.

They quickly packed up Anya's belongings and exited the room. Peter never replied to Megan. They were just thankful the uncomfortable scene was behind them.

#

Once they were all in the car, Bob spoke. "I see what you mean, Peter. What a bitch."

"Bob, please don't say that word," Christy said.

"Christy, he's right. I'd like to think we've closed the door on Megan forever, but somehow, I think there will be more to the story. I don't trust her as far as I could throw her," Peter said.

"Let's not be paranoid. She's just another college girl."

"I can't say I agree. She's a different breed of cat, and she has sharp claws. Revenge is well within her wheelhouse. I suspect she doesn't face much resistance in her life. Crossing her probably means a stiff price to pay. What in particular is going on in her head, I have no idea, but I got the clear impression she's not done. Whatever she can orchestrate from afar, I guess we'll find out."

"Wow. You make this whole thing seem pretty ominous, Peter."

"Sorry, Christy, but I call it like I see it. I hope I'm wrong."

Anya said nothing, staring glassy-eyed out the front windshield.

"Anya, are you okay?" Christy asked.

"Yes."

Peter glanced at her. The terse reply and worried expression spoke volumes to him: she shared his concerns.

Carrying her items into Christy's room, Anya was finally out of Megan's room. Whether she was free of Megan's influence was another matter. Peter very much doubted it.

He spoke. "I guess we'll go and let you girls get settled in. We'll talk to you later."

Both girls looked at him in surprise.

"Eh…you didn't want to go do something?" Christy asked.

"If you want to go out, we can do that. I've got a couple of things to do, but call us later when you're ready if that's what you want."

"Sure." Christy was irked. Anya turned her back as the boys walked away and closed the door.

"What was that, Peter?" Bob asked.

"As I said, I've got a couple of things to do. If you want to go back to their room to hang out, feel free."

Bob scowled but followed Peter back to their room.

Sitting down at his desk, Peter began to study a textbook. Grudgingly, Bob started his own studying, reading chapter assignments.

Hours later, Peter closed his book. "I feel better getting that out of the way."

"Are you talking about the class assignments, or moving Anya?"

"Both."

"So…what's next?"

"With Anya, I'll play it by ear. She's got a cell now, if she wants to talk to me."

"You're putting the onus on her? Is that wise? Girls don't normally want to be in the position of having to initiate contact. Christy and I have talked. We wonder if your ongoing adventures on the dance floor with those other girls are some kind of a danger sign."

"Anya was away, so I decided to dance rather than sit around bored. I don't see that as some great sin."

"This whole thing has a bad feel to it."

"Listen, Bob, Anya has made it abundantly clear she's not comfortable getting serious. Actually, I should qualify that by saying getting serious with *me*. Whether that applies to all the other guys, I don't know. I guess we'll find out."

"What was it Christy just said? Don't get paranoid?"

"Cool it, Bob."

Bob was perturbed. "I'm calling the girls."

"Go for it."

#

Shortly after, the guys headed back to the girls' side of the dorm. The four of them walked out to the lot, back to Peter's Mustang.

After driving to the cinema at the mall, they ate dinner at a restaurant inside the mall before walking to see the show. Bob and Christy were hand in hand. Anya took Peter's hand as they walked.

Ironically, they ran into Megan out on a double date. Peter noted Anya react, turning her head away. It dawned on him: she'd dated both of those guys in Megan's party.

Megan made a beeline to intersect their path. "Hi, Anya. Are you settled into your new room?"

"Yes, thank you," she replied in barely a whisper. Making no eye contact with Megan, nor the other girl and two guys, her face reddened.

"You remember Jeff." Megan smiled deviously.

"Hello, Anya. It's nice to see you again." Jeff spoke in a deep, resonant and sexy voice, and both Christy and Anya looked to be moved.

"Hello, Jeff," Anya replied.

Megan smirked. "It looks like we're all going to the same movie. We'll join you."

It wasn't a question.

Peter's group didn't get a vote. He and Bob eyed the strange encounter with curiosity and some concern.

Once in the theater, Megan led the group to seats in the center of a row, arranging it so her date, Jeff, was sitting beside Anya, on the other side from Peter. Anya acted like she was in shock. Jeff spoke with her a great deal, and she warmed to the conversation quickly. Peter felt his danger signals ignite, red flags waving wildly.

Peter couldn't hear what they were saying, but Anya was paying avid attention. The fact Jeff was a ruggedly handsome, chiseled physical specimen with a clear gift for charming the ladies played into Peter's insecurities. Additionally, the fact Anya was agog with the unplanned moment was obvious. It was like Peter was gradually eroding away as Anya shifted in increments, facing Jeff increasingly. She chuckled at his jokes or whatever he said. This bothered Megan not at all. She joined in the discussion wholeheartedly. Peter was left like a bystander, feeling irrelevant.

The movie was spellbinding for the group—all but Peter. He pondered the "date," but through his faulty perspective. At that point, he was a half-empty rather than a half-full young man, and he wasn't sure Anya even noticed. The movie ran for over two hours, after which the young students made their way out to the lobby.

Megan turned to Peter. "This was so much fun. We need to do it again, frequently. It was so nice running into you. Don't be a stranger."

Her smirk, the smug smile, like she'd scored a colossal triumph at his expense—he felt she was right. Anya smiled warmly at Jeff and continued to talk to him as they walked all the way out to the cars.

Peter replied ruefully to Megan's suggestion, "What an idea."

"I warned you," she whispered. "Be careful who you pick to fight. I can take you down."

They parted ways, leaving Peter shaken.

Anya finally turned her attention back to him. "This was so nice."

"Yeah, it was great."

She eyed him, his tone. However, she still didn't make the connection between his mood and her avid interest in Jeff.

Driving back to campus, going somewhere to "park" was never a consideration in Peter's mind. Christy and Bob whispered in the backseat, while Anya was quiet in the front. He drove straight to the girls' side of the dorm to drop off the girls.

"Bob, you don't need to ride with me to the parking lot. I'll see you back in the room, and Christy, Anya, good night, ladies."

"Good night," the three whispered in unison.

There was no kiss or any other exchange between Peter and Anya. They parted ways like mere acquaintances.

Peter didn't hurry back to the room, walking deep in thought.

Neither boy spoke; rather, they just went to bed.

In the morning, it seemed strange to have Anya join them for breakfast. She sat across from Peter, beside Christy. Bob also sat on the other side of the table, beside Christy. Two girls from their floor came around to sit beside Peter. Ironically, one of them had danced with him at mixers a number of times. She tried to engage him in conversation, with little success. Anya chatted with Christy and the other girls, seemingly oblivious to Peter's angst.

Peter was the first in the group to excuse himself from the table. "I'm heading to class, folks. Have a great day."

#

That evening at dinner, Peter had gone down early, so Bob and the girls had to join him later.

Bob asked, "In a hurry?"

"The usual, I've got class assignments to knock out."

"Of course you do."

The boys eyed each other darkly for a moment. It brought out simmering defensive feelings in Peter. He was incapable in that moment of seeing he was backing himself into a corner.

Anya suddenly piped in, "My mother said her first words today."

Peter looked at her. "That's good to hear. I'm sure she'll make a full recovery and regain everything."

"The therapist is optimistic. She's doing better than they thought so early in the process. Mama is fighting hard to get her life back."

"That's good; she is a fighter."

"Her life molded her into a person to overcome all barriers. I try to be like her in that way."

"Anya, I meant to tell you, I talked with my dad about getting you a used car, so you have transportation home any time you want to go. We may not always be on the same schedule to travel together. If I'm not available, you can make your own way. We've got plenty of extra bedrooms, so if you want to take a friend, or friends, on the trip so you're not driving alone, that option is there. He's looking into it."

"That's very thoughtful." Anya replied guardedly at his tone. Though it was a benevolent gesture, Peter had an odd expression on his face.

"You're welcome."

Christy glared at Peter. "Anya, if you need a passenger, I'll go with you."

"I appreciate that."

They ended up walking out together as a group. Christy sidled over to Peter. "I don't like you very much lately. Work on it. I don't like you acting like an ass to Anya."

"Sure thing, Christy, I'll get right on it."

The exchange bothered Peter, and he thought about it all day. His continuing defensive posture was having unanticipated consequences. Driving Anya away was never his intention.

#

On this evening, he waited to go to dinner with Bob, to be sure to see Anya. Anya noticed him eyeing her when they all sat down. She sat across from him, beside Christy again.

Christy saw it too, and spoke pointedly. "Hello, Peter."

"Hello, ladies. Did you have a good day?"

Anya replied. "Yes, it was good to be back in class. As you know, I have a great deal to do to catch up. I'm going to be busy in my room, or at the library, for a considerable time with the work, but I don't mind."

"Just keep chipping away. You'll catch up sooner than you think."

"I hope so. I feel a little anxious being behind. I want to close that gap."

"I'm sure a week from now you'll feel much differently. You'll knock this out just fine."

"I think I must pass on going to sports or any movies in the meantime." Anya eyed him for his reaction.

He didn't hesitate. "Understandable. We'll be here in the meantime."

"Thank you, Peter."

"You can always call me if you want a brief chat or something."

"Christy has been so nice to me. After living with Megan, it's a monumental change for the better."

"I can believe that."

Bob added, "She's a good egg."

Christy smiled warmly at Bob. "Thank you, dear."

Anya spoke. "Christy is going to teach me more 'American' things. I want to know everything over here. Peter, may I go with her to her parents' house for a visit?"

"Anya, you don't need my permission. You're a big girl and I'm just your friend, remember."

Both girls eyed him coolly, and then looked at each other.

"Is something wrong, ladies?"

"I guess not," Christy replied. She changed the subject and began a conversation with Bob. Anya joined that conversation. Neither girl spoke to Peter, although if he added anything, they merely answered him briefly and then went back to talking with Bob.

After eating, the girls left promptly, returning to their room. Bob didn't bother stating the obvious to Peter. Returning to their own room, wordlessly they started their homework.

Peter couldn't help feeling his deteriorating situation had gotten markedly worse.

#

The following day, he called home.

"Hi, Dad. I was curious if you have any news about the car for Anya?"

"I do. A friend of mine has a car. His wife only drove it around town, so it's got really low mileage. He's getting her a new car for her birthday. It's a Chevy, so it will be dependable. He's selling it to me for what they would have gotten as a trade-in. It's a really sweet deal for us."

"Great news, Dad. I appreciate all of the wonderful things you do for me."

"We feel like Anya is a part of the family now, so getting a car for her is no big deal. It was a good idea. I'll pick it up right away, and we'll bring it this weekend. Mom will follow me in her car, and if Mariska is up to it, she can ride with Mom."

"Perfect. That sounds like a plan. I'll let Anya know."

"Take care, Peter, and we'll see you soon."

"I will, Dad."

Immediately, he called Anya on her cell. "Hi, this is Peter. I'm sorry to disturb you, but I've got some news. Dad is coming this weekend to bring a car for you. Your mom will ride with my mom, so they'll all be traveling here for the weekend."

Clearing her throat, she spoke in something of a rasp. "I appreciate your call."

"Are you sick? You haven't been staying up too late trying to catch up on the work, have you?"

"I'll be fine by the weekend. I'll let you go so I can rest."

"Sure. Bye, Anya."

She'd already hung up. He was well aware Anya hadn't called him even once since she got her cell phone.

#

The following morning, when both girls arrived for breakfast, they looked very sleepy. Their usual bubbly personalities were muted.

"Ladies, you look trashed. What's up?" Peter asked.

Both girls eyed him ruefully.

Christy answered. "Peter, we're okay. We've been putting in work on Anya's backlog, but it takes a toll."

"How do you both 'work' on her assignments?"

"I help organize and sift through things so she can work efficiently. We've made up a lot of ground already."

"Oh."

"Any more questions?"

The terse tone and unfriendly expressions was very off-putting for Peter to see and hear. "Is there something else going on here? I'm picking up on some hostility."

"No, Peter. That would be your paranoia at work. We subscribe to live and let live."

"Really? You're doing a great job of mimicking bad moods."

"Assume whatever you want to. Not everybody in the world would arrive at your conclusions. I believe you already know you are your own worst enemy."

The dismal exchange early in the morning set the tone for his day. "I guess it's time I head for classes. Have a great day, everybody."

#

For the remainder of the school week, Peter got no calls from Anya, and of course he made no calls. Again, no study dates or social dates occurred. Their exchanges happened at mealtimes: brief, superficial, and stilted.

On Saturday morning, Peter tried to put on his best face for the occasion. He was not optimistic, however. He perceived severe decay in his relationship with Anya, and it haunted him. Seeing any light at the end of the tunnel seemed to have only the slightest possibilities.

Bob joined him to go down to the lobby to meet the parents when they arrived. Ironically, they'd gone to the girls' side.

Anya was ecstatic, seeing her car for the first time: the first thing of value she would own. Combined with seeing her mother, and Peter's parents, she was overjoyed. Anya drove her car with all of the females to the restaurant. Peter's dad drove his wife's car with the two boys, following the women.

Arriving at the restaurant, waiting briefly, Anya had yet to greet Peter, or even acknowledge him. When they went to the table, she sat between the two mothers. The women were all at one end of the table, the guys relegated to the other end. There were two separate conversations during the meal. The women were boisterous, amped up, and loud. The guys sat like spectators, conversing in normal tones, mostly about sports. For Peter, it was a familiar place: feeling on the outside, looking in.

"How's Mariska doing, Dad?"

"Physically, she seems to be fine. She moves around normally enough. The speech issues are going to be slow going. Her speech therapist is bringing her along in Russian, but she's trying to teach her English also. Although she's climbing a steep mountain back, she reminds me of what I've seen in Anya: determined to overcome her obstacles. She'll be fine in the end."

"Christy tells us Anya is working her butt off to get caught up. I think she's pretty much there, although with how busy they are, I haven't gotten a recent update."

Bob piped in. "Christy says Anya stays up too late too often, but they've turned the corner and she can finish the backlog very soon. She has one more major paper to write, if I understand them correctly."

George replied. "That's good. That poor child has faced too much adversity in her young life."

At the other end of the table, all the women laughed loudly.

"She looks happy now," Peter muttered.

Bob looked at him. "She is happy."

Peter shrugged and turned his face back to his father. "That's a newer car than I expected, Dad. It's really nice."

"My friend was very generous with us. I felt Anya needed a dependable car that doesn't present a hazard in any way. We all want her safe."

Bob spoke. "Mr. Brown, I know you don't like praise, but I've got to say I'm so moved by what you guys do. Generosity is one thing, but with you guys it's a statement about who you are as people. I'm awed. There are so many people with resources in the world who could care less about the peasants. We're just annoyances standing in their way, worthless lazy users. Nothing is more important to those types than adding to their obscene money piles."

"Well, thank you, Bob. Edith and I had humble beginnings and I think that helps in keeping us grounded. Those types of people you're talking about, we avoid them like the plague. We run into them, of course, but keep the exchanges brief and infrequent. You're right—there aren't many redeeming qualities among the self-centered pompous egotists. I prefer to feel good about what I do in my life."

"Well, you set a heck of an example for the rest of us to follow. It's an honor to know you."

"Hardly, Bob. I put my pants on one leg at a time, just like everybody else."

"I would quote some Bible verses, but I don't know any."

The men chuckled.

"It isn't necessary. The Bible verses I need I already know, like *a haughty spirit cometh before a fall*."

"Good one, Mr. Brown."

"They're words to live by, Bob; trust me. People should never become too full of themselves. It never works out well if they do."

"I believe you, sir."

"There's no need to be formal with me. I don't need any sirs."

"Force of habit, sir…I mean…"

Peter interjected: "Bob, you're just as much of a 'head case' as me."

"So true, bro."

The pleasant meal setting continued, although as a divided event. The women acted oblivious that they had any men in their midst. Anya seemed as happy as Peter had ever seen her. Of course, that was judging by what he'd seen personally. How she was away from him, with others, he had no idea. Mariska was ebullient, squarely in the midst of a life she could only have dreamed of not so long ago. Though she could say very little, it didn't stop her from enjoying the camaraderie and the joy around her. This new world was a wonder on a daily basis for her. Seeing her daughter blossom, prospering in this society, was all she could have hoped for in coming to America. That was validation for Mariska trusting there could be happy endings, no matter where you came from.

When the meal came to an end, they all arose to head back to campus. Again, the women rode together in Anya's car. George dropped off Peter and Bob and then drove around to pick up Edith and Mariska, driving away to head home. This time, it was Anya driving to the commuter lot to park her car rather than Peter.

The boys returned to their room, since the girls had said nothing about getting together. The basketball team was on the road for their game, so Peter decided to walk over to watch a volleyball game. Bob didn't go with him.

#

While he was attending the match, the first in a series of events occurred that would be major signposts. In a total surprise, Christy went to their door after hearing a knock. Opening it, she saw Allison standing there.

"Hello. You must be Christy."

"I am." She eyed Allison curiously.

"My name is Allison. I went to high school with Peter. May I come in?"

"Oh, yes, sorry."

Allison went straight over to Anya, who was sitting at her desk, studying. "Hello, Anya."

"Hello." Anya was equally puzzled at this stranger coming to their room.

"You don't know me, but I hope we can become close friends."

"You know me?"

"I've seen you with your boyfriend, Peter."

"My boyfriend?" Anya eyed her with a puzzled look. She glanced at Christy.

Christy replied. "Did you ask Peter if Anya is his girlfriend?"

"Why—is there a problem between you guys?"

It was Christy who spoke. "He's…well…difficult. It's very perplexing with the entanglements of his parents doing so much for Anya and her Mom. I mean, they've literally saved her life. I love them to pieces, and they're not even my parents. It makes it stupefying trying to figure out Peter and his odd behaviors. Anya has tried to cope, but honestly it's been tough sledding."

"Oh my. I had no idea. I guess I assumed everything is peachy between you two."

"Peachy would not be an accurate description of their situation." Christy continued to speak for Anya.

"Are you guys open to us being friends?" She smiled at Anya.

"Sure. Yes." Anya and Christy looked at each other.

Christy continued, "You can't have too many friends."

"You're wondering why I showed up suddenly, out of the blue."

"That thought has crossed our minds."

"Well, I agree you can't have too many friends, and in Anya's case being foreign, she's got challenges enough already. Having more people on her side to fight through the barriers is a good thing. Do you agree?"

Christy glanced at Anya. "I can't disagree. What do you say, Anya?"

"I would like to be her friend."

"Good. I think I have many things to offer you'll appreciate. I suspect you're already teaching her some things, Christy."

Christy didn't reply, instead showing an enigmatic smile.

"I thought so. I can teach her things also. We both have past experiences that can be enlightening for Anya. She'll be a far more rounded person, coming out the other end."

"Okay, so do you have something particular in mind?"

Allison had an amused expression. "Other than the obvious, I suggest a girls' night out with me and my friends. We all get dolled up and head for the club. It's a great way to get to know one another in a relaxed and fun atmosphere. You'll have a fantastic evening—trust me."

"Okay. I guess we can try it. We'll let you know when she's caught up on her backlog of work, but that will be very soon," Christy said.

"How about this Friday night I come by your room, and then we head out for the evening?"

"Deal."

Allison stayed, continuing to 'chat them up.' For a girl, a beauty on the scale of Megan, it made no sense to them.

#

Meanwhile, Peter went about his business. The following week, he tried a tentative tendril toward Anya. The status quo sitting on the sidelines with her was accomplishing nothing.

"Do you want to do something?"

"I'm sorry. I have plans Friday evening, Christy and I."

Bob looked up from his meal.

Christy spoke to Peter. "Actually, it's an old friend of yours: Allison. She stopped by our room to introduce herself. She said she wants to be friends, and offered us a night out with her crowd to break the ice. We said okay. Is that a problem?" Her eyes narrowed like she was looking for a fight.

"No, of course not; you're big girls. If you want to go and party with the elite, go for it. Anya, don't get drunk and then try to drive your car."

"Duh, do you think we're idiots?" Christy replied, with scorn.

"No, I don't think you're idiots."

"I don't drink, Peter," Anya whispered softly. "My dad was a drunk."

Christy turned to Bob. "I'm sorry I didn't tell you sooner. It's just a girls' night out, okay?"

"Sure, honey. No problem."

"We're both curious to hang out with them to see what it's like. They believe they're better than the rest of the world. We're going to find out. Maybe they *are* better."

The girls looked at each other and smirked.

"Good luck with that," Peter commented, tersely.

The revelation knocked him off his pegs, again. Allison initiating this "friendship"—it didn't feel right, although if there was an end-game scenario, he couldn't imagine it. Whatever Allison had to gain eluded him. So he made up his mind at that moment he would be attending the dorm mixer on Friday.

#

Friday arrived with the two girls looking forward to the adventure. When Allison arrived at their door, she was dressed to kill. Looking at them, she shook her head. "No, no, no, ladies; that won't do." She went to both their closets to pick out different choices: tighter, sexier garb.

"You always want to look 'hot.' That's what we do. Getting hot guys to admire us is not a bad thing. It can lead to fun nights and other possibilities."

Christy looked at Anya, who shrugged. "Okay, Allison. You're on."

Changing clothes, they walked out of their room feeling exposed, like they were only partially dressed. It was eye-opening, joining Allison's crowd, the socially relevant, for their typical social foray. For Anya, having all eyes on her was an experience. First feeling self-conscious in a tight short red dress, that feeling ebbed quickly. In this crowd, dressing this way was the norm. Gradually Anya relaxed, deciding to go with the flow. Christy was with her, and that was reassuring; she was having no problems being in that situation.

Going to a club for the first time, both girls were accosted immediately with male admirers, and they spent the entire evening on the dance floor. Anya found it stimulating, being with handsome guys, interested in her. Christy was on the dance floor an equal amount.

Anya had become a skillful dancer. She could dance sexily, if she chose. On this night, she made that choice often, as these guys evoked it in her, with their looks and skills.

At a break in the music, the girls sat down to cool off. Allison sat beside Anya. "Do you like it?"

"It's invigorating."

Allison laughed. "That's an interesting way of putting it. I feel invigorated too. Are you glad you came along?"

"I am. This is fun."

Allison smiled and patted Anya on the knee. "These nights can go in a lot of different directions. Some of these guys are driven. We each make our own individual choices about it."

"I understand what you're alluding to. I'm not of that frame of mind."

"I can respect that. Do you judge other girls about their choices?"

"No. If they feel differently, that's their choice. I have no problem with it. I'm not naïve about such things. It's just not my way."

"I like you, Anya. I really do."

"I like you too." Anya smiled warmly at Allison. Allison smiled back.

Chapter Eleven

Meanwhile, Peter had his own evening of dancing. Bob joined him, since Christy was also occupied elsewhere. Just like Anya, Bob had honed his dancing skills with plenty of practice and was now decent on the dance floor. During the entire evening, neither boy lacked for partners, as they shimmied and swayed to the loud and lively music.

They didn't face the choices of Anya's group: being hit on to go away afterward to do more. They were in the dark that their girls were facing guys of a caliber to make that dicey idea enticing.

#

Christy and Anya both managed to resist the strong temptations, making it back unscathed, but they were highly entertained by their first venture into the seductive world of the elite.

Back in their room, Christy turned to Anya. "I'd say we keep this evening to ourselves. We didn't do anything but flirt, but if we tell the guys it will definitely open a serious can of worms. Peter is jealous enough as is. Honestly, it was…well, pretty fun playing games with those hunky guys. They're definitely a cut way above anything I've ever dated. I think they figured we must have something, if we're hanging out with Allison's crew."

Anya laughed. "I think you're right."

Christy added, "You're pretty enough and you've got the body to be in Allison's gang. I'm happy with me, but from their point of view, I'm carrying too much weight."

"Christy, you're lovely." Anya stepped close, touching Christy's hand.

"That's not necessary, Anya, complimenting me. I'm just giving you a perspective on Allison's world. Did you listen to them talking about their exploits on the dance team, cheerleading, and that other stuff? I just smiled and ignored it. Some of them are pretty smug."

"Yes. I did hear it. That wasn't in my world back in Russia. It's much different there."

"I can't imagine. It's a miracle you got out of there, honey."

"My miracle is getting my mother out of harm's way."

The two girls hugged.

"Christy, for me, you're another of my miracles. Having a close girlfriend, I can't tell you how happy it makes me. Everybody needs a best friend. Now I finally have one."

"Likewise, my darling, you're dear to me also. After all of that dancing, I need a shower."

"You go first. Are you okay with being my best friend?"

"Thank you, Anya. I'm honored you feel that way. You're my best friend too. Frankly, I'm surprised this has worked out so well with Allison. I was suspicious of her motives, but so far so good."

"She seems very nice."

"I'm going to tell you something I'd like for us to keep secret, okay?" She spoke in a mock conspiratorial tone.

"What is it, Christy?" Anya snickered.

"Dancing with those guys tonight, I realized I really do like all of those muscles."

The girls laughed loudly, exchanging high fives.

"I like muscles too," Anya agreed.

#

At breakfast, Peter got a glimpse of the new landscape. The two girls came to join him and Bob, but this time they included Allison and some of her friends.

Allison eyed him directly. "Hello, Peter. May we join you?" She didn't wait for a reply. She smirked and sat down beside him.

"It's a free country," he replied.

"Hello, Bob. I'm Allison." She leaned around Peter to speak to Bob.

"Hello."

"How are your parents, Peter?"

"They're fine, and how about your folks?"

"It's the same old, same old. My younger sisters are a pain, although I'll admit they're just like me—because I'm a pain too, right?"

"Allison, there are a lot of things I could say to that."

She laughed heartily, drawing the notice of Anya and Christy.

"What are you laughing at?" Christy asked.

"Peter. He's a trip. He keeps me entertained, and that's not easy to do."

Peter looked at Anya and her cold expression at his 'rapport' with Allison. Seemingly he was guilty again, in spite of the fact he'd done nothing wrong.

"So, Allison, you took our ladies out for a night on the town. How was it?"

"We had a great time; thank you for asking. Would you agree, ladies?"

Anya replied quickly, and firmly, "Yes, we did."

It was like another body blow to Peter. "I'm glad it went well for you."

Allison snickered at the looks exchanged between Peter and Anya. "This is so great. I love it."

Peter grimaced at her.

Allison was undeterred. "By the way, sir, Christy and I are riding with Anya back home this weekend. She wants to see her mom, and it gives me a chance to see my family too."

Peter shrugged. "Have a safe trip."

"Is that okay, Bob?" Christy asked.

"Sure. You guys are close friends. That's no problem for me. I'll miss you."

"I'll miss you too."

"Oh, that is so sweet," Allison said. "What a nice relationship, caring and trusting like that."

She looked at Anya, who then looked at Peter like his flaws were on full display for the world to judge.

Peter attempted to stay silent, but he failed. "Yes, Allison, love is a many-splendored thing."

Allison laughed again. Peter did not laugh, nor did Anya.

"So, Anya, are you up for a study date this evening?"

It caught the girls by surprise, all of them.

"I guess that would be fine."

"Good. We can hit the lounge to get seats right after dinner."

"Okay. I'll meet you then."

"I look forward to it."

Allison scowled a moment, before getting a calculating look. She then gave Peter a passive smile, like there was now a plan in play.

#

After a routine day in classes, when Anya came down to meet Peter with her books, they selected seats in the back of the room.

"I gather you're caught up on the backlog?"

"I am now, finally. Thank you for being understanding and for being patient with me. I'm sorry…"

"No explanation necessary, ma'am. If you think your girls' night out was a problem for me, it isn't. Honestly, I don't get her, but I never did. In high school, I was lured by her good looks, but I feel there is another side to her."

"Thus far, she has been very nice to Christy and me."

"Well, remember, Megan started pretending to be nice too. Be careful."

"Peter, you see things so negatively. What if she's just being honest?"

"There is that possibility."

"You believe she has some dark motive."

"That is a strong possibility."

Anya shrugged. "I'm not sure what to say about that. I guess we'll agree to disagree about Allison."

Just as he was about to turn the conversation to their struggling relationship, Allison suddenly appeared, with her books. She wore a tight blouse and short sexy skirt.

"I hope you don't mind if I join you for the study date. Being around brains like you two might pull me up. I do okay in class, but I don't excel like you guys, especially at this level, where everybody around me is brilliant."

"Please sit down," Anya answered with a warm smile. "You look very nice."

"Thank you, Anya. You look nice too."

Peter glowered. For him, this had the feel of an Allison "intervention," and it annoyed the heck out of him.

"Is this okay with you, Peter?" Her smug smile, feigning innocence, added to his ire. Dressed in her very short tight skirt, Allison had a plan. Her sitting in such a way to draw his notice to her sexy outfit and legs, and sitting beside

Anya so Peter couldn't, this brought his anger simmering to life. Not sitting totally ladylike, Peter's face flushed and he glanced away.

He'd wanted to sit close to Anya, if their talk went well. Now the plan went into the dumpster, in flames, compliments of Allison.

Allison continued, "So, how does this work? Do we read in silence or do we talk with one another?"

"If you want help, I'm happy to do it," Anya replied.

Peter grimaced watching Allison skillfully maneuver the situation, like Peter and Anya were puppets on her strings, to be pulled about at her whim.

"Anya, you're so sweet. I appreciate any help you can give me." She turned her head to give Peter her best crocodile smile. "Isn't she sweet, Peter?"

"Sure." He scowled at Allison, who smirked in return. He felt helpless to do anything to avoid the train wreck Allison seemed to be engineering.

The plan well underway, Anya's attention successfully transferred off Peter and onto Allison, Peter noted the developing pattern. Irked that he could be pushed where Allison wanted him to go and seemingly helpless to stop it, his frustration grew. "Damn," he muttered.

The study session went much differently than he'd hoped for. Anya fell completely for Allison's ploys and launched into in-depth explanations of her course materials, and closely helped Allison with the chapter questions and fully understanding the materials. Peter was relegated to the back burner, studying in silence. Allison attempted to bring him into the discussions, without success.

He studied for a while, until he'd had enough. His 'talk' with Anya was not going to happen on this evening.

"Okay, ladies, I'm all set, so I'll bid you *adieu*."

Anya looked at him curiously. Allison's antics had gone over her head. Allison sat, smug at her success in breaking up any potential 'moment' for Peter and Anya.

She smirked at Peter. "Well, goodbye for now. We'll see you again."

"No doubt."

Resigned, he stood and went up to his room. Bob saw his distress, but these days he left it to Peter if he wanted to talk about it.

Peter looked at him. "I went down there intent on getting back in gear with Anya, but suddenly Allison shows up to announce she's joining us for the study date. I don't know what her ultimate game is, but in the short term it appears she's intent on breaking up Anya and me. You should have seen the looks on Allison's face. She definitely sent me a message. Anya had no clue, as Allison played her like a piano. As always, it doesn't make sense to me. I don't feel Allison is the right girl for me, but with this, what's in her mind, I can't even guess."

"That is strange."

"I don't want my paranoia to cloud my judgment, but Allison showing up at Anya's room, trying to buddy up with her and Christy, she's got some plan in play. To what end, I can't figure out. Even using your theory—she wants a crack at my parents' money—doesn't feel right. She'd be stuck with me as a husband for the rest of her life. I can't imagine that's the way she wants to go, with so many better options."

"Just to play the devil's advocate, don't be too sure about that idea. Gold diggers accept all kinds of compromises to get the treasure. Why you think it would be so abhorrent for a girl to marry you, I don't understand. For example, you're a heck of a lot better looking than me, and I got Christy. She's way out of my league. Do you see what I'm saying?"

"As I think about it, I was wrong when I said she'd be stuck with me for life. She'd only need to stick around until my folks passed away and I got their estate, and then she could divorce her way to a big payday and go her merry way."

"That's quite a theory. It sounds more like a movie than real life."

"Ascribing pure motives to any of the people around me is too far past what I honestly believe. I see the Megan's and Allison's of the world, the sneaky and nefarious things they do, and I wonder: Are there any good ones out there?"

"Christy and Anya are two good ones—don't you agree?"

Peter shrugged. "I'm of a mindset to stay on guard with all of them. I'll continue to plan for the worst in everything I do."

"Your mindset makes it difficult for any girl trying to deal with you, don't you see? Do you honestly feel you can go through life without extending any trust? Your point of view has a severe price tag."

"Whatever. How I got to this place is my real-life experiences."

"That's true for all of us—our experiences shape us—but remember, you have a hand in those experiences. Making it completely the fault of the girls you meet is a recipe for disaster. I don't agree with that logic. My life experiences haven't made me bitter like you."

"We're different people, Bob. You're a really good guy, and probably much better than me. At the very least, you cope better than I do."

"Hardly, you're well aware you pulled me out of my relationships funk. Don't canonize me; I don't deserve it. I'm as flawed as you are, and probably more so. It's a miracle I have Christy, but I think it's more I got her in a weak moment. With my relationship, it's more like I'm a fat bug squashed on the bottom of her shoe that she can't clean off."

Peter laughed with hilarity. "Bob, you will be an idiot to your dying day."

"No doubt, I can't argue with that."

"Anyway, I'm going to crash now. I'll see you in the morning. Tomorrow at breakfast you can judge for yourself. Did I tell you: Allison is going with Christy and Anya to my house, minus me? It's definitely a new paradigm. Buckle your seatbelt because they're dragging your girl into this *Kabuki* Theatre too."

"Peter, you're going to make me just as crazy as you are."

"Sorry. It is what it is."

#

Seeing Allison come to breakfast again with Christy and Anya was no surprise to Peter. For Bob, it was an unpleasant development: like Peter's skewed logic was coming to life. If Allison was a permanent new member of their group, it meant so was her entourage. Hanging out with stuck-up, snobbish people was the last thing either boy wanted.

Particularly distressing was neither Anya nor Christy seemed to be bothered by them.

Bob whispered to Peter, "Do you think Allison can actually remake our girls into them?"

"Welcome to my world."

"Oh my."

"What gets me is the feeling of helplessness, knowing there's nothing I can do about it. Girls run over me because they can."

"That's chilling. I'm surprised about them just accepting this farce."

"The Megan's and Allison's of the world are highly skilled manipulators. I think they probably came out of the womb that way."

Allison announced loudly, "Hello, boys. It's good to see you this fine day."

"Allison," Peter replied in a low tone.

The seating arrangements had become a fixture: Anya, Christy, and Allison sat side by side across the table from Peter and Bob. Nothing was different on this morning other than the number of Allison's "associates" who showed up. They were the ones who came around to sit beside Bob and Peter.

It was inevitable. The girls started up a boisterous discussion centering on makeup choices and, of course, boys. Shocking to the guys, Anya and Christy joined the inanity. Bored out of their minds, the two guys gobbled down their food and stood, unable to endure such drivel any longer.

Peter spoke before his brain was engaged. "Ladies, thank you for sharing this special moment—it's been fascinating—but we must go to classes."

His heavy sarcasm cast a momentary pall over the table, but suddenly Allison began to laugh heartily and the other girls joined in. "Oh, Peter, you're such a trip." She sounded affectionate, which further irked Peter.

"*Vaya con Dios, señorita.*" He made no attempt to hide a scowl.

After exiting the cafeteria, Peter glanced at Bob. "Do you see what I mean? You can think whatever you want, but that was flat-out blatant. Did you ever think you'd see Christy and Anya go off on an 'airhead' tangent? If Allison can make their brains stop functioning, what else can she do?"

"I don't want you to be right about this, but…"

"That girls' night out must have been some hot time. The girls are certainly on board now with Allison's 'dog and pony' show. I predict a train wreck in their future. It was as if we weren't sitting at the same table, how they talked about other hunk guys. What a crock!"

"I don't really know how to handle this with Christy. I suspect she'll watch me closely for my reaction the next time we're alone. Maybe they were toying with us?"

"More like taunting us."

"I'm upset too. I don't plan for the worst like you do. Maybe I need to start." Bob had an uncharacteristic frown.

"I don't want to drag you down with me. I still believe your romantic prospects are infinitely better than mine. Down deep, I think Christy truly loves you; however, I can't say that about Anya. There are a lot of different emotions she feels about me, but love among them, I doubt it."

"I've lost all of this weight to be better for Christy. Does it even matter?"

"I can say don't give up, if you like. Sound familiar?"

"If I turn into you, Peter…"

"We can drive off a bridge together."

"That's encouraging."

"Let's head out. Maybe things will change by tonight."

"Somehow, I seriously doubt that."

#

Each morning for the balance of the week, the girls seemed to be in their own realm, with the guys as an afterthought. Bob wasn't accustomed to these troublesome feelings Peter experienced routinely.

On Friday, the girls packed Anya's car for their trip back home for the weekend. Bob virtually dragged Peter downstairs for the obligatory goodbyes, taking Christy a few paces aside to talk softly with her. Allison stood close by Anya. While Anya watched Christy, Allison watched Peter. Finally, Anya looked at Peter.

"Drive safely, Anya. There's no rush, so take your time. Enjoy your visit and say hi to my folks for me."

"I will."

"Goodbye, Allison. I'm sure your family will be happy to see you."

Her condescending sneer disappeared, replaced by a sad look. Peter had no inkling what it meant, and Allison didn't explain.

When the girls climbed into the car, Peter was surprised it was Christy who climbed into the backseat, while Allison got in front with Anya. Anya pulled away quickly, never looking back.

The boys walked back to their room, deflated.

"I feel like there's impending doom out there about to bust out on us."

"I know the feeling, Bob. I have it nearly daily. I think it's a natural reaction when we sense things are amiss. Anxiety is like a warning bell for us to solve the problem or run away from it. Angst seems to be a permanent state for me. As I said before, I hate to drag you down into my misery. It's not a whole lot of fun."

"Have your feelings for Anya changed? You act so aloof around her."

"I wouldn't say that. It's just I get tired of the stress. Adding Allison into the mixture is a recipe for disaster. That doesn't even take into consideration Megan is still out there."

"Did you notice Allison's change of expression when you mentioned her parents?"

"I did. I never really knew them back at home. I think her dad worked as some sort of repairman and her mom worked in a small office. If there's some issue there, I have no way of knowing it."

"Maybe she doesn't get along with them. It might explain why she's so conniving. Did she have home troubles back in high school?"

"Not that I was aware of. That doesn't mean there weren't any. I tend to be out of the loop in most things."

"I can testify to that."

"I'd say we get cleaned up, go to the mixer, and dance the night away. It beats sitting in the room, sad and bored."

"You're on."

"Dancing the night away" eased the ruffled feathers for both boys. By the time they returned to the room, their roiled feelings about the girls had faded, momentarily out of mind.

#

Saturday was basketball-game day at the arena. After that, they went to a movie. On Sunday, they did their studying and each wrote a paper for class.

Peter looked at Bob. "I'm proud of us. Never once did I feel the urge to call Mom to check up on them. We got through this just fine."

"I thought about it, but when you didn't call, I figured I shouldn't either. Obviously, the girls didn't feel disposed to call us."

"I'm heeding the lessons they teach me. It's the world as they want it to be. For your sake, I hope Christy can shake off the bad influence, but be warned just in case. It seems they want this other life too, away from us. I'll take my share of the blame for Anya's hesitancy about us, but now they have a big hand in it too, compliments of Allison."

"Allison…" Bob muttered pensively.

"Maybe I'm making a mountain out of a mole hill, but I don't think so."

#

The drive home was wildly entertaining for the three girls, but for different reasons. For Anya, savoring companionship and acceptance with her gal pals was priceless. Christy enjoyed Anya, as always, but being treated like a friend by an elitist, Allison, gave her satisfied feelings and validation. For Allison, being able to put aside her perpetual *façade*, to let down her guard and trust, was rare and refreshing. Her inner pressure could finally be relieved. Laughing with Anya at Christy's silliness gave her a level of personal connection she'd never experienced before.

"Ladies, I want to tell you something. I feel like I can trust you to keep my secrets. My home life wasn't the best. My mother and father argued, a lot. I was a mere sidelight, as were my sisters. My parents worked a lot and frequently it fell on me to watch over my sisters. I sort of had to raise myself. Eh…I made some mistakes in those years, did some things I'm not proud of, but that was the past. Now my folks are separated because they can't work out their differences. I'm going to my mother's place. She lives in our old house with my sisters. I'll try to see my dad too. My dad accused my mom that I'm not his daughter. My mom hates me because I am his daughter, and I remind her of him. Isn't that screwed up?"

Christy answered. "Allison, we're so sorry to hear that. We're here for you."

"I know that; I truly do. I've never told another soul about this, and I don't regret telling you. I actually feel like a load has been lifted off my back. I am ashamed of the mess, though."

"It's not your fault."

"I know that with my head, but I feel like if I'd been a better child, a better big sister, maybe it wouldn't have come to this. I know that's irrational, but feelings are irrational sometimes. I caused my mom and dad a lot of grief with my childish antics. As I got older, some of those antics weren't so childish. I look back with plenty of regrets. I guess I wanted attention, even if it was bad."

"You know better than that. You were a child and they were the adults. They had an onus as your parents to keep you safe and guide you. Every child wants and needs the love of their parents."

Anya added, "I know about your pain. My father was not a good man. He drank and then became mean. He abused my mother when I was too little to do anything about it. When he left us, we were happy. I always wondered what it would have been like to have had a good man in my life. I see Peter's father and I am dazzled. He's an example of that 'good man' I missed out on."

"Peter was so fortunate. We don't have an option to select who our parents are going to be. He got the best ones I've ever met. They're truly decent and nowadays that's very rare."

Christy spoke. "I look forward to seeing them. What's the word on your mom, Anya?"

"She's making slow progress. Trying to regain her speech and learning English all at the same time is difficult."

"I know she's a good woman by how you came out as a person."

Anya chuckled. "I don't know how good I am, but you're right about my mother being good. You haven't seen me at my worst."

"Oh, Anya, you know you don't have a worst."

All the girls laughed.

Allison continued: "The one good thing my parents did do for me that I'm grateful for was they started when I was a baby and built up a college fund, or else I would have been stuck back home working as a waitress, or something like that. It isn't enough to pay my entire way and I will walk out the doors dragging a lot of student debt, not as bad as many but significant nonetheless."

"Without the scholarships, I would still be back in Russia, and my mother would be dying or already dead."

Christy piped in. "For me, it's a combination of both. My folks built a college fund, but I also got some scholarships. Thank God I'll be debt-free when I graduate."

"One other thing, ladies: I know when we met, you guys saw me as a bitch. Certainly Peter sees me that way. I can't say I'm the best person in the world, or even a particularly good one. I make plenty of mistakes; however, I'm trying to change my ways. Overcoming the wreckage in your life isn't so easy. I believe hanging out with quality girls like you is a big help in my efforts to change. Do you see? Maybe I really can turn over a new leaf."

Christy patted her on the shoulder. "It's funny—girls like me look at you and think, *She's got it made. She's beyond gorgeous, a social star, popular, a guaranteed hit in life.* To hear your perspective, I would never have thought that. It's mind-boggling you think Anya and me have anything to offer you."

"My so-called 'circles of friends' are filled with shallow, self-absorbed egotists, and I can't stand them. That's been my life forever. I draw them, so I've learned to tolerate their presence. If I could shut the door on them, once and for all, I wouldn't miss any of them."

"Wow. Shall wonders never cease?"

The girls laughed.

"My appearance I was born with; it isn't something I earned. Attractiveness in our society gives me a pass I don't deserve. It opens some doors for me, but it isn't a good thing."

Anya added, "This is so good, being with you both."

Allison turned her head. "Anya, I am curious about you and Peter. There seem to be big stumbling blocks."

"I don't know how to explain it. Obviously, I know how strongly he feels about me, and that's very compelling. Why I can't seem to reciprocate in kind, I honestly don't know. I have some reasons, but…"

"Talk to us. It may give you clarity to get it out in the open. We're not here to judge."

"Well…he says he loves me, and I don't doubt it at all. That's overwhelming, and I know where he wants us to go. I'm not ready for a life commitment yet, with anybody."

"And…?"

Christy added, "She doesn't like to admit she still wants to date. We've met intriguing guys. When you took us clubbing, being hit on by those studs was invigorating for both of us. Anya's beautiful, so it's no surprise they flock to her. I'm not your prototype beauty, but even in my case, I got plenty of traffic. That gets our attention."

"Listen, ladies, I've dated plenty of those hunks. They can get old in a hurry—believe me. Finding nice guys is much more of a challenge. It's funny to me how Peter can't see why he's alluring for girls, but we can all see it clearly. You can't fake decency and good character."

"I know, Allison. That's why I get so angry at myself. He wants to cherish me. What could be more compelling than that?"

"What's the real problem, Anya?"

Christy answered: "A guy…there was a guy she dated: one of those stud types who really made an impression she can't get out of her mind."

"Is that true?" Allison asked.

"Sadly, it is. I don't want it to be this way, but it is. I worry if he will call me again, and I worry he won't. Why he makes me so crazy stupid about this, I don't understand. Just seeing him makes me feel all funny."

"It sounds to me like something you need to work out, one way or another."

"I fight it every single day. How can I hurt Peter? For all the reasons you've given, I should treat him better, but I try to imagine putting on a wedding dress to walk down the aisle to him, and then my mind changes the groom to…"

"This other guy…"

"Yes. I imagine being his wife, not Peter's. I'm such a bad person."

"No, you're not. If your heart leads you in that direction, perhaps a marriage with Peter wouldn't work out."

"That's what I'm afraid of. I think Peter's mother knows this. She told me some things, conciliatory things, like she can see what's coming. She told me she went through similar issues."

"Amazing…so, what's stopped you from connecting with this other guy?"

"We explained to you how Megan has a grudge against Peter. She suddenly stopped treating me terribly and started including me in her circle, and then she started sending handsome boys to date me. One of those boys was Jeff Bond."

"I know of him. He does make girls go weak in the knees. I've never personally had any dealings with him, but he has a reputation. Do I need to explain?"

Christy piped in. "User, womanizer, cad, player—am I on the right track?"

"What's different with him is somehow he gets past the obvious revulsion for that type of man. Girls who date him will always date him again. I don't know if any girl can reel him in, though. He's a slippery *hombre*."

Anya answered, "I understand, so you can see why I get so mad at myself. You're right that I did date him and hope to date him again. Even though in a way it was frightening, I came close to some steps I shouldn't take. He's the only boy who ever got me to consider it. Do you understand? It was difficult to…say no."

"We understand completely, Anya. All of us come to that place where we have to decide difficult things. Not everybody chooses the best path."

Christy added, "Anya, you've made me curious to meet him."

Allison answered: "I can verify everything Anya has said, and feels. Jeff is a cut above even the best of them. He'll probably become a titan of industry. No one can say no to him."

\#

Arriving in town, they drove to Allison's mother's house. She wasn't home, so they drove to her father's place. He wasn't home either.

"Allison, you must come with us to Peter's house. They have enough bedrooms for all of us. We can't just leave you at one of these houses without knowing if anybody will come back. What if both your parents are gone away for the weekend? You'd be stranded." Anya touched Allison's knee with a pat.

"Do you think they'd mind, Peter's folks?"

"They're wonderful people. I'm sure it will be fine."

"Okay, ladies. Let's do it."

When they pulled into the driveway, Edith came out to greet them. Like every other visitor, Allison was awed at the sight of the mansion.

"Of course you can stay with us, Allison. Welcome to our house."

"Thank you so much, Mrs. Brown."

"Call me Edith. I'm sorry about your folks. We heard in church that they're having some issues."

"Thank you, ma'am. Honestly, they've had issues since I was a child. This isn't surprising to me."

First, they took their luggage up to the bedrooms. Christy and Allison were agog. Allison whispered, "I could get accustomed to this very easily."

The girls chuckled.

Anya muttered softly in response, "Each time I come here, it's as wondrous as the first. Come with me and let me introduce my mother."

Going into her bedroom, Anya hugged her mom and then said, "Ladies, this is my mother, Mariska Seminova."

"Hello."

Her speech was stilted and her English was still in the early stages, but Anya's mother was pleasant and welcoming.

"Mama, these are my friends from school. We've come to visit for the weekend."

"Hello. I'm Mariska," she was able to get out.

Switching to Russian, she did a little better talking with Anya.

Dinner at the house was a sumptuous feast. Outside, spring wasn't yet in full bloom, but it was warmer. With full bellies, the girls went outside to walk about the grounds. Birds were chirping and flitting around. Buds were visible on the trees, and the air had a sweeter smell. With a clear sky, the sun felt warm on their faces.

"This is incredible," Allison said. "What an estate."

"It is," Christy agreed.

Allison turned to Anya. "So…what are you going to do about Peter?"

Anya shrugged. "I don't know if that's completely in my hands. He's been hesitant for a long while now. We haven't had a social date in many months. I know he senses my dilemma and tries to be patient with me. He has his personal pride and doesn't deserve my intransigence. I certainly don't deserve him. I hope I can figure this out, somehow."

"How would you feel if he started dating other girls?"

"I…eh…it would be difficult. I know this is completely unfair to him, but Jeff Bond is a stubborn issue for me."

"Have you told him about your feelings for Jeff?"

"No, of course not, I don't want to risk losing Peter."

"That is a real predicament, honey. There's an old American adage about trying to have your cake and eating it too. It's one or the other."

"I'm going to talk to Mama and tell her everything."

"I envy that you can talk to your mother. If I went to my mother about any issues, I'd regret it. She would make me regret it. In the end, I'd come out the bad guy. She's really good at heaping on the guilt," Allison said.

"I'm sorry."

"I live with it. I've had plenty of practice being my own person."

They looked at Christy.

"I've got my own set of problems. They're different than yours, but no less troubling for me."

Allison took in a deep breath. "Umm, it's so peaceful and serene here."

"I first thought of this place as the Garden of Eden," Anya said. "It puts me at peace."

"This is a pretty nice life here."

"It is that," Christy added. "It would be really easy to settle in and get waited on for the rest of my life. Having available the financial wherewithal to do whatever I wanted, it's very alluring."

"It is that." Allison got a contemplative look in her eyes.

Anya spoke. "Let's go back in the house."

Chapter Twelve

Peter heard the phone ring in his room. Getting up, he walked over to answer it.

"Hi, Peter. Is Bob there? We're back."

"Hi Christy. He's downstairs. I can have him call you when he gets back. It should be very shortly. Did you girls have a good time?"

"Of course, you already know that, Peter! It was so great to meet your parents and Anya's mom. They're super people. For peasants like Allison and me, the house was absolutely dazzling. It was like we had been transported to a magical kingdom."

"Allison?"

"Yes. Her folks were gone, so she stayed at the house with us. It was a great time. Driving down with her, spending the weekend, and then driving back, we learned a lot about one another. My opinion of her has changed radically. I think your opinion of her would change, had you been there to listen in."

"Wow. I didn't see that coming."

"We feel like she's a friend now, Anya and me both. Before, I wouldn't have trusted her, but now I do. She let her guard down and told us private things. We all did. She's been through a lot."

"Letting your guard down—is that a good thing?"

"Of course, so did you want to speak to Anya?"

"Does she want to speak to me?"

"Duh. Stop being a dunce."

Anya came on the line. "Hello, Peter. Your mother says hi."

"I gather everything went well. I'm surprised Allison is now your close friend. That is quite a reversal."

"It was better than I could have anticipated. Christy and I feel she was being sincere, so we trust her. We all learned so much."

"Well, good for you. I'm glad it went smoothly."

"It's good to make new friends."

"That's true," he replied after a moment. This particular new friend concerned him but he didn't verbalize it.

"Do you want to have a study date?" Anya sounded slightly anxious.

"Sure. When?"

"Now."

"Now is fine. I'll get my books and meet you down in the lounge."

#

Although he continued to carry his usual angst, uncertainty, and caution, nonetheless it was always invigorating to be around Anya. If she was actually anxious to see him, that would be a bonus.

"Hi, Peter." She was already seated on a sofa, smiling warmly.

"Hi. Is this seat taken?"

She laughed. "You are a nut."

For this occasion, Anya wore a skirt, and Peter noticed. Anya was no less attractive, and dressing sexy for him was a departure from her norm.

"What brings you out of your cubbyhole?"

"I missed you. I don't like how distant we've become."

Peter shrugged his shoulders. Believing she'd suddenly changed her position; it was too hard to accept. Negativity was too familiar, and there were too many bruises.

"Okay, so do we study?"

"Yes, but I'd like to talk also. Is that okay with you?"

"Of course." He looked at Anya, feeling trepidation.

"Do you know how much I appreciate you? You're critical in my life, for so many reasons."

"I hope you're not going back down the 'I owe you' route. I thought we'd put that to rest."

"I do owe you, but that's not what I'm saying."

"What are you saying?"

"I, eh…need to be honest about my feelings, but it's a terrifying prospect. I don't know if you'll understand, and I certainly don't want to lose you."

"That sounds pretty ominous." He felt like standing, to flee before the shoe dropped on him.

"My feelings are…complicated. I can't understand them, so it's virtually impossible to explain them to you. Do you see?"

"No…but why don't you just spit it out, whatever this is."

Anya frowned before resuming. "You know I've been reluctant to make serious commitments. Regretfully, I can't say I've changed in terms of that. Asking for you to be eternally patient while waiting on me isn't fair to you. We talked on the trip, the three of us, and I want to say: if you want to date other girls in the meantime, I can't justify objecting to it."

"Why would you think I want your permission to date other girls? Is there anything in what I've said previously that's in any way unclear? Once you came into my life that was it for me. That was my choice back then and it's still true now. As I've said before, if you want to look elsewhere, I can't stop you. If you choose to go in another direction, I'll cope. What other choice do I have? There's something else you're not saying. Please give me the truth. I think I deserve it."

Anya's face reddened and she stammered a moment. "I've dated before…you know that. There was a boy…"

"He's the one you want." He said it neutrally, but also sadly.

"Don't say that. I don't know that, and I'm not saying that. He was…intriguing."

"Unlike myself."

"Peter, don't do this. It's the very reason I was afraid to have this talk."

"Well, Anya. My answer, if you're asking a question, is do your thing…go for it…however you want me to say it."

"Peter…"

"I've often pondered about us, what always breaks down, why we've never clicked. As you talk, I'm realizing I needed to get a clue, and I can say I get it at last. Don't worry about any fallout. This doesn't jeopardize your mother in any way, shape, or form. She will be taken care of, as we promised as a family."

Anya put her face in her hands.

"Listen, Anya, I really did want to know the truth. I'm not handling this well, but I'll get over it. I had a strong feeling I was your Plan B option. I just never wanted to admit it, but the time has come. It's clear to me you want to move on. I wish you well; I really do. I hope this other guy is all you hope he is."

She looked up suddenly. "This is not how I want it between us. You think I'm rejecting you. I'm not. I just feel I need time to sort this out. If we got together, seriously together, and I'm not right for you, I couldn't live with that failure."

At last, it dawned on him fully what was happening: a *de facto* breakup. "I think maybe I'll pass on the study date. I'm sure you understand."

"Peter, no. Please don't. Must we go back to the bad between us?"

"I can't really think of what to say to that."

Grimacing, Anya seemed to harden suddenly. "Okay, if that's how you want it. I tried."

With great difficulty and finality, he said it: "Goodbye, Anya."

His walk away from her was among the most difficult things he'd ever done. Feeling shattered was a vast understatement, as he truly pondered some terrible options. Color had faded from his life, leaving only pale shades, only shadows of living. Going straight to his car for a rapid drive into a tree crossed his mind.

He couldn't go to his room, so he went outside for a tormented walk, grappling with his roiling emotions and the overwhelming sense of loss. This time it was loss on a scale he'd never experienced before. He truly loved Anya, and seemingly it didn't matter to her. There were no answers to be found, only more pain. His mind further punished him, imagining Anya rushing eagerly into the arms of this other guy, freed at last from Peter.

At long last, as he walked, his feelings evolved, moving gradually from the shock and distress into escalating anger, and then into full-fledged rage.

"Okay, enough is enough, Peter. She made her choice."

Of all the things he could do at that point, he returned to the dorm and went downstairs to the basement, where there was a small exercise room. Taking some weights, he began to work out in a routine that quickly devolved into savage reps as he tried to exorcise his rage. By the time he completely exhausted his body, he was soaked in sweat. His muscles felt rubbery at the sudden extreme exertion.

When he made his way back to the room, Bob was on the phone with Christy. He looked at Peter in alarm. "Christy, I've got to go. I'll call you later. Peter, what happened?"

"You already know Anya kicked me to the curb. I took a walk, and then decided to go downstairs to work out."

"Christy said Anya's all broke up. It doesn't sound like she ditched you."

"You weren't there. She has some other guys on her wish list. Apparently one guy in particular."

"Who?"

"I have no idea, nor do I care at this point."

"What did you say?"

"I…wasn't happy, but I managed to keep my cool enough to say my family will still take care of her and her mom."

"That's a good thing. You did better than I could have in that situation."

"I was really…angry: case in point." He held out his arms to display his sweat-soaked body. "Obviously I need a shower."

#

Anya returned to her room, stirred up also. Christy looked at her. "Judging by that face, your talk with Peter didn't go well."

"I do understand how he feels. If the roles were reversed, I'd be upset too. I tried to tell him he could date other girls. He said it again: I'm his true love, and he doesn't want other girls."

"Wow, that's something. Most girls would pray to hear that from their guy, but you don't see Peter as your guy, do you?"

"I tried to say I'm not rejecting him." Anya was beside herself with worry.

"Think about it, Anya. If you heard that from him, what would you think and feel? In so many words, you admitted he doesn't float your boat, and that there is another guy who does. Can't you see how toxic that is? I'm not saying you're wrong because none of us can control our feelings. You feel how you feel; there's no right or wrong about it."

"He told me to 'do my thing.' What exactly does that mean?"

"He was hurt and feeling rejected. His telling you to go with other guys, that's not a magnanimous gesture—it's a statement of surrender. I think he feels it's over with you, by your choice. The battle is over and he lost."

"That's terrible. I need to get this straight." Pacing around, Anya was distraught.

"I suspect it's a little late. He's been on this downward spiral for a while. The truth is you have an inner fire burning for Jeff Bond, and it shows up in how you act around Peter."

"I…eh…"

"You need to do some hard thinking, all by yourself. That's your challenge. If you can get past your hurdle, that's when you could potentially try again with Peter. Where you are right now, maybe it means Jeff is your guy. Until you figure that out, you're going to be eternally treading water. I agree that Peter loves you. You can go either way, but eventually it will be too late with Peter. Maybe it's already too late."

Anya frowned in dismay. Her difficult dilemma had become more complicated.

#

The next day, not surprisingly, Peter didn't join the group at the breakfast table. Anya went through her classes feeling distressed, feeling like she'd made a huge mistake.

Instead of returning to her dorm after classes for dinner, she chose to walk to a different dorm. Eating was the last thing on her mind.

Going into the dorm lobby, she stared at the house phone, trying to get up her courage. By coincidence, her dilemma was solved when the elevator door opened and a group of guys got off. She looked over when she heard his voice.

"Anya?"

"Hello, Jeff."

"What a coincidence you'd be here in my lobby."

His smirking friends crowded around, eyeing her admiringly.

"You guys go ahead. I'm going to talk with Anya."

They snickered and whispered with one another as they walked away.

"Don't mind them, Anya. They're all idiots. So, it's nice to see you again. Why are you here?"

"Can we go down to your lounge to sit down and talk?" She felt like she was standing in a hot cauldron.

"Oh, yeah, sure we can."

Moments later, Anya was seated on a sofa, with Jeff close beside her. True to his nature, he glanced down at her legs and her sexy skirt.

"This is difficult…eh…I came to see you, Jeff. We've dated, but probably I wasn't a girl who stood out to you, but…"

"Anya, quite the contrary: you made a huge impression, but under those circumstances, where Megan put me onto you for her twisted reasons, I didn't think it was right. I could tell instantly you were a good girl. With what she wanted me to do, I was definitely the wrong guy for you."

"Are you talking about your reputation…with girls?"

"That reputation is well-deserved. I'm not much of a gentleman many times. You happened to catch me on my best behavior, but that's rare for me. If you saw me most other times, you'd have a much different opinion."

"I…eh…this is hard to say. There is a boy who wants me. He's everything a girl could desire—faithful, noble, upstanding, any good quality you could name."

"He sounds like a good choice for you."

"I went out with you once and it left me…dazzled. I had instant feelings about you, and I still do. They haven't gone away." Without realizing, she uncrossed her legs and turned her body toward Jeff.

He stared at what for him was a blatant signal. "Wow, Anya. You can't say things like that around a guy like me. It's like waving a red flag in front of a bull."

"I didn't come today so we would act badly. You know what I'm talking about. I came to understand these feelings, to see what they mean and what we should do."

"I can answer your questions about what you should do. Go back out that door, don't look back, and run as fast as you can back to your good boy. In a contest of who's best for you, the other guy wins, hands down."

"Jeff, I've tried that, and yet here I am." Suddenly, she took his face in her hands and kissed him tenderly. His hand, by reflex, went to her bare knee.

Jeff got a glazed-eyed look. "Wow, Anya. Let me try this one more time. Don't do this. I'm weak about women, so if you take this step with me, no matter how noble you want me to be, there will be a predictable outcome. It would be just a matter of time. Do you understand what I'm saying?"

"Will you go on another date with me?"

He shook his head in dismay. "Anya, if you ask me, there's no way I could say no to you. You do realize I'm a senior and will graduate soon to head out into the world. You're a sophomore, if memory serves me."

"I am."

"Think about this. Unless you just want to have some fun before graduation, what next? I'm going to be gone to my job, which could be anywhere. My kind of fun isn't what you need. I'm incredibly flattered you think well of me, but I don't deserve it."

His hand hadn't left her knee, and his fingers had strayed inside the knee slightly.

"Jeff, my feelings are what they are. A friend told me that. It's driving me crazy. If I'm meant to be with you for my life…those other things, well…"

"Anya, this is pretty deep. If you're talking about marriage, I haven't thought about that, with anybody. I wouldn't wish me on any woman as a husband. You don't know me. Believe me when I say I'm not trustworthy when it comes to women. I'm trying to be brutally honest. By now, you should have been frightened away."

"I'm still sitting here, Jeff."

He eyed her deeply. "Okay, Anya, if you still want to go out with me, in spite of what I told you, when do you want to go out?"

"Right away."

"Do you know how difficult this will be for me? You expect me to be a gentleman. I don't know if that's possible."

"All I ask is that you give us a chance to see where it goes. I'm not naïve. I know what you say you are, but how you would be with me, I need to know. Perhaps you might surprise yourself?"

"You haven't seen me in action, darling."

"Am I not appealing to you?"

"You're too appealing. I don't want to mess with your life. Anya, you're brilliant. You've got a chance to make a real mark for good with your life. You don't need my kind of drama."

"Let me be the judge of that."

"Okay. You're making a big mistake, but I can pick you up on Friday. I'll move a few things around and plug you in. Call me if you change your mind. You should change your mind before it's too late."

"I won't. I look forward to this."

She kissed him romantically again before walking out the door. Anya was feeling electric, invigorated, and aflame with excitement. The man of her dreams, at last.

#

When she walked into her room, Christy looked up and stared. "Uh-oh. What did you do?"

"I did it. I went over to see Jeff. We're going out this Friday."

"Anya, is that wise? I know you were stirred up about him, but his track record speaks for itself." Christy looked worried.

"I'll take my chances. It was so stimulating to be there with him…the kisses."

"You kissed him? Where?"

"It was in the lounge of his dorm."

"Oh my, this is worse than I thought. Let me go on record: I strongly advise against this."

"He advised me the same thing, to run away."

"So…why didn't you?"

"I didn't want to, and I don't want to. Having a date again with him, we're going to find out about my feelings. Is he my future husband?"

"If I answer you with the obvious, would you listen? Does he want to be *any* woman's husband? I think he's one of those guys who wants all women."

"We'll see."

"You're okay with running the risk of being another notch on his belt? Do you think you can fix him? Guys like him don't want to be fixed. They're how they are because that's how they want to be."

Anya scowled. "Let's not talk about this any further. You're trying to be obstinate."

"I'm being obstinate—really? Open your eyes."

"My mind is made up. I'm going out with Jeff."

"Okay, but don't say I didn't warn you. That guy could be your kryptonite."

"What is that?"

"An irresistible force…one that destroys you."

"I don't believe it."

"I hope you're right. I care about you. I know we always want to follow our hearts, but sometimes we need to use our heads."

"Christy, I tried every other way, and this is what I'm left with. There's a reason Jeff evokes me. I will find out if we should…be together, and I understand the risk I'm taking."

"I've got a bad feeling about this."

In spite of her stubborn retort to Christy, Anya felt some niggling of doubt about her impulsive act. However, it was too late to take it back. The die was cast.

#

Peter had no inkling of the sea change rolling his way. Hunkering down against the onslaught of bad news, he concentrated on getting back into his school routine, burying himself in his studies. Having no social life with Anya had been the norm for a while, so now, with the cord seemingly cut, he built emotional callousness as a defense mechanism. Seeing her with Christy each morning and evening, he acted aloof to mask his continuing deep pain.

Anya always looked at him sadly. They seldom spoke, other than about the most superficial topics, and even then, in the briefest of terms.

With her having a car, the last connection was severed. She could go to see her mother whenever she chose. Actually, she visited his house far more frequently than he did.

Opting frequently to eat his supper away at the student union to avoid seeing Anya, he also chose to study at the library, until she started to show up there again. It was there Peter got the opportunity to see her with *him*: Jeff Bond. How she was around Jeff starkly varied from how she was with Peter, and not in a good way.

#

His new social life consisted of attending the mixers every Friday night.

Peter wasn't in her dorm room on the Saturday morning after her first date with Jeff. Christy was. "You got back late."

"We talked a great deal, and no, I didn't do anything foolish, if that's what you think. He was very honest, about many things, maybe for the first time with a girl. We talked frankly about what he's done, and what I haven't done, but mostly we talked about careers, life, and even marriage and children. It was his first time talking about it. I got his attention."

"Are you sure? You decided to wear your sexiest outfit. Are you sure that isn't what he noticed?"

"I wanted to look nice for him."

"Duh."

Anya chuckled. "It was kind of exciting."

"It's called sexual tension, and it's called teasing. You're playing with fire, ma'am. I want to ask: how does this solve your problem? Do you honestly imagine you're now in love…because the guy was a gentleman for one night? He *was* a total gentleman, wasn't he?"

Anya frowned. "No. I don't imagine I'm in love. I will say he did nothing to rule out our having options together, and yes, he excites me."

"This does not make me feel better about this mess. Have you talked to your mom?"

"It's not a mess, and my mother told me many helpful things. America is different than home, but men and women are ruled by the same emotions anywhere in the world. She didn't steer me toward or away from anything. Mama told me at some point I'll know what to do."

"So, what's next?"

"We're going to go out again."

"So, Peter is off the board completely?"

"I wouldn't say that."

"What would you say?"

"I'd say Jeff excites me, and I like being excited."

"Be very careful. He's skillful beyond your belief, and that comes from a lot of success in that arena. Things can go crazy in a hurry, and you can end up…compromised."

Anya got an angry look. "I'm a big girl. I decide such things. Thank you for having concerns, but I'll make my own choices, even about that." She muttered something in Russian.

"I won't ask for a translation. You're telling me to butt out. Okay. I'll always love you, no matter what you do or how this goes. I'm your friend."

Anya looked away, but her niggling worries were getting stronger. "I'm going to the library," she said.

#

That was a night Peter was there. Taking Jeff with her, Anya joined Ron and other friends at a table. Peter stayed out of sight. He had no intention of actually meeting with Jeff. He found an out-of-the-way cubbyhole to do his work, away from their sight.

His plan mostly worked, but Anya happened to walk to the stacks and noticed him seated there. She walked over and he pretended not to see her.

"You don't talk to me any longer, Peter?"

"You're busy with your friends, and your boyfriend."

"Is this how you want it between us?"

Peter bristled as his anger simmered to life. "Anya, there is no 'us.' You ended that, remember? Okay. That's your choice. How this is now: what did you expect? I just try to stay out of your way at this point."

"What are you saying? Do you no longer care about me?"

"The fact you even ask that question speaks volumes. My feelings are clear as a bell—they don't change—but it isn't my feelings in question here. You said you're trying to figure out your feelings. Have you done that? You seem really tight with that other dude."

"Jeff."

"Whatever. I don't care about his name." Trying his best to avoid a frosty stare, or an argument, proved too difficult, his rage would not be contained.

"I don't want this bad between us."

"As far as us being 'pals,' I'm not interested. If things change, you know where to find me. Excuse me."

His rage fully reignited for his quick exit and brisk walk back to his dorm.

Anya stood for a time, struggling with hurt feelings, before she could return to her table. Her own angst simmered to life.

"Are you okay?" Ron asked. Jeff didn't notice her unease. Oblivious to her distress, he was chatting with a pretty coed.

"I'm fine," she whispered.

#

Peter's punishment was far from over. By chance the following class day, he walked out of class to see Anya and Jeff down the hall. She was backed up against the wall, with Jeff very close, like they were on the verge of a kiss. Both stared avidly at each other as they were talking. Peter was too far away to hear the conversation and, at that point, he didn't want to.

At the last moment, Anya looked over and saw him. He glowered as she grabbed Jeff's hand and pulled him forward. Peter pondered a quick escape, but they were too close.

"Peter, this is Jeff Bond, remember from that movie night?"

Jeff smiled magnanimously. "Hey, Peter. It's nice to see you again. I want to meet all of Anya's friends. I feel like I know you. Anya's told me about all that you, and your family, have done for her and her mom. You're an inspiration."

Peter's eyes glazed over with dark emotions and Anya got an alarmed look.

Jeff extended his hand. Anya feared an outburst, but Peter merely shook briefly.

"Well, kids, I'd love to chat, but I've got another class. Goodbye. You guys take care."

Jeff smiled. "We will." He read the situation in an instant: jilted lover who couldn't let go.

Anya could say nothing. Seeing the painful look on Peter's face bothered her greatly. Peter walked away provoked.

"So, were you guys a thing? Was he the good guy you were talking about?"

Anya still couldn't speak.

"It will be okay, honey. I'm here for you."

#

The remainder of classes that day was difficult for Peter, and also for Anya. When Peter walked into his room, depressed, Bob looked up.

"Well, I saw Anya's guy again today. She actually brought him over to meet me. I guess she had a pathological need to rub my nose in it. Anyway, he looked like a Greek god; you know the type: chiseled physique, cool confidence, dressed like he's right out of *GQ*, in control of everything around him. If I wasn't toast before, I certainly am now. I had this feeling for quite a while that I was in her rearview mirror, but I was too stubborn to admit it. It's time for me to get a clue and move on."

"That's terrible. Are you sure she's *with* him? Maybe they're just friends?"

"You didn't see them together, and trust me, they are together. She looked at him and I finally saw what having true love in her eyes looks like."

"I would say let's go tie one on, but we're not drinking age yet."

"That wouldn't solve anything. I think I'll go over to the track for a hard run. Maybe I can cause a heart attack and end my misery."

"That's some plan, Peter."

"Sorry if I can't be rational. I'm mad. I'll see you later." Peter had dinner at the union again, alone.

#

When Bob saw Anya at the cafeteria, he wouldn't look at her.

"Peter?" she asked. Bob hadn't volunteered why Peter wasn't present.

Grudgingly, he looked up at her. "Yeah, he told me about meeting your new boyfriend. Did you really think he'd show up here after that?"

Christy objected. "Bob, what are you doing? This is difficult for her."

"And it's not for him?" He had an uncharacteristic grim expression.

The girls glared at him, but he stood his ground. He added, frostily, "Anya, it's none of my business what you do, and with whom. Peter's my roommate and dear friend. If I seem defensive, I guess you'll just need to cope. Decisions have consequences, and that applies to girls too."

Christy bristled, jumping to Anya's defense. "That works both ways, and Anya is my dear friend. You and I need to stay out of this. Anya is dealing with some real trials in her life. Peter and Anya are both our friends, no matter how this goes. We need to be supportive of both, not critical. Do you agree?"

Bob eyed them a moment. Rather than continue the fight, he stood up. "I'll leave now so we can all cool down. Yes, Anya, you're my friend, but I don't have to like your choices."

Anya's face reddened. Bob walked away.

Anya looked at Christy. "Why does my being with Jeff make me feel I should be ashamed?"

#

That weekend, Anya made another impulsive decision. Continuing to struggle with her mixed emotions, rather than seeking compromise with Peter, she doubled down on her choice of Jeff. Anya decided to drive home, but this time she took Jeff to meet her mother.

Peter's parents were surprised: first that they got no warning of the sudden visit; secondly, that they would be meeting Jeff. The supremely awkward situation bothered Jeff not at all. He charmed the bewildered moms and glad-handed Peter's grim-faced father.

Mariska and Edith felt his allure, but they were mature women and not subject to youthful giddiness, like Anya. The mothers acted polite and marginally welcoming; however, George was incensed. He was barely able to restrain an outburst at Anya. Her driving a stake into the heart of his son was intolerable for him.

Jeff handled George's "discomfort" seamlessly, like he was working a room of potential clients.

Anya tried to ignore George's grim stares. She'd brought Jeff to meet her mom.

George excused himself and went to his bedroom to call Peter.

"Hi, Dad. What's up?"

"Anya just got here. She brought some guy with her."

"Jeff Bond. Yeah. I met him. Now you can see what I was saying before. That's what she wants. As I look back, I think it was inevitable this was going to happen, sooner or later. So, with getting it over with, now I move on. As a matter of fact, as strange as it sounds, Allison has been after me for a date. I figure at this point, why not? I'll do my best to shift gears and treat Anya decently, but from now on I'm just her acquaintance."

"I'm so sorry, son. I didn't see this coming. I thought she was a different kind of person."

"I'm not going to judge her for not wanting me. She decided I'm not the one she wants, and honestly, look at him compared to me. I understand where's she's at with it. So be it. I'll start looking for my Plan B girl."

"I honestly thought you'd have the same happy ending I did."

"I guess it wasn't meant to be."

"This kid with his annoying smugness, I feel kind of like smacking him in the face. Of course, all of the women are agog, like he's a celebrity. I remember going through dismal stages when I was chasing your mother, but this takes the cake. It ain't fun."

Peter laughed. "Dad, I'd pass on the fisticuffs. He's a buff dude."

"I was just sharing my feelings."

"I appreciate the heads up. I feel the same way, but this is my reality now. I'll deal with it."

"I'm thinking I might vacate the premises for the evening and leave the women to their own company. I seem to remember a prior commitment at the little local bar in town."

"Be careful, Dad, and don't drive drunk. I don't need any car accidents to add to my woes."

"You be careful too, son. This is a dicey time for all of us. Let's get through it the best we can."

"Amen to that, Dad. Bye, and thanks for the call."

"Bye, Peter. You're still our all-star."

Leaving the bedroom, George informed the others of his decision.

"What? You're going out?" Edith was aghast.

Never flustered, Jeff displayed his best Cheshire cat smile. "It's been so nice to meet you, Mr. Brown."

Edith looked at her husband in alarm. Abandoning her in this awkward situation was the last thing she expected. Peter was her son too. Mariska and Anya looked on sadly. Anya stood aside. George refused to look at her.

George left abruptly. His own memories and demons had been resurrected.

#

Meanwhile, at bedtime, Edith ushered Jeff upstairs to a guest bedroom. George's absence was intended to make a statement, and it did. She pondered if she should move him to another bedroom, away from Anya's room, but if they intended nocturnal mischief, several extra steps would mean nothing and certainly wouldn't stop them.

"I hope this room is suitable for you?"

"Of course it is. Your house is a marvel. You've given me a goal for my own future, and for my family-to-be. Thank you for your kind hospitality."

Anya edged up to them, staring avidly at Jeff. "Good night, Jeff."

He kissed her cheek. "I'll see all of you in the morning." He winked at Anya. Her warm smile and the look in her eyes set off warning bells in Mariska, who started a pointed discussion with Anya in Russian. Anya's face reddened and her smoldering looks disappeared quickly. She dropped her gaze from Jeff. Jeff looked amused at the scene. Nobody needed a translation.

"Good night, everyone," Anya said, turning meekly and going into her bedroom.

"I'll say good night also, ladies. Sleep well."

Jeff closed the door on his room, smiling. A mild impulse to bring their fears to fruition passed through his mind, but it was fleeting. Such a move wasn't necessary. His plans were advancing nicely.

Edith looked at Mariska and pondered telling Anya to lock her door, but realized it was possible Mariska had already told her that.

George managed to get home without mishap. He stumbled through the dark house. Sleeping in the following morning, his antic didn't surprise Edith, though she was irked at his rudeness.

Mariska spoke a great deal with Anya, but always in Russian. Her English was far from conversant, but she could have exchanged a few sentences with Jeff.

Anya didn't miss any of the rampant negative signs from the significant people in her life. Beforehand, she'd felt trepidation at this idea of bringing Jeff to meet her mother. Now that she'd done it, there was nothing reassuring for her here. Rather than feel chastised, she felt childishly defensive, and hardened her stance.

Watching Jeff act oblivious to the glaring undercurrents, smiling blithely, she tried to imagine a life as his wife, inexorably tied to this household. It was a nightmarish idea.

There had been no nocturnal indiscretions, though the thought had crossed her mind. It chafed that the parents acted as if she had succumbed to temptation. It further fueled her ire.

#

When everyone came down for breakfast, Anya acted particularly solicitous toward Jeff, like she was getting revenge against the judgmental parents. The mothers eyed her in grim silence. George grimaced in thinly veiled distaste, though he had his hands full dealing with a rare hangover.

"I think we will leave after breakfast," Anya explained. "We have things to take care of back at school. Thank you for the hospitality."

"Surely," George said. "And you have a safe drive."

Mariska spoke at length in Russian. It had the feel of a diatribe.

Anya's face hardened at whatever was said. She gave no translation to Jeff. Again, it wasn't necessary.

Suddenly, Jeff spoke. "I want to thank you once again for your patience with our sudden visit. You've been more than gracious to a stranger, and I appreciate it so much. I know this was difficult for you, with Peter and all. However, Anya and I have strong feelings for each other we want to explore. I'm sure this is the last thing you want to hear, but our feelings are real. I know you probably won't believe me when I say how I feel about Anya: I haven't felt this before with other girls. She can verify I tried to warn her away from me, but she convinced me to give us a try. With her, I may have a chance at being a better person than I could have ever hoped for. That's certainly no solace for you, for Peter's hurt feelings. I'm truly sorry about that, but, well, there it is."

George was incensed. "Thank you so much for that speech. It's true we care about our son and how much this has hurt him. Thank you also for your honesty, so let me share my honesty. We prefer that you two conduct your activities elsewhere. When Anya wishes to see her mom, we'll make arrangements for her to travel to Anya, rather than you coming here. Any questions?"

Tears formed in Anya's eyes and she started to speak, but George held up his hand. "Don't bother, Anya. You do whatever you think you must. Our priorities in this household will be our family. We'll treat Mariska as one of us, for as long as she wishes to stay."

Anya felt nauseated, and the desired to fall into a deep hole. She stood up and went immediately to get her suitcase. Jeff followed. This wasn't something he could gloss over.

They made their way toward her car. Passing through the kitchen, the cook eyed her sadly.

"I'm sorry, honey. Keep your chin up."

Anya couldn't stop the tears from flowing, and hugged the matronly cook. She heard footsteps and left before the parents saw her crying.

As the car pulled away from the house, Jeff spoke. "Are you okay, honey?"

"No. I've ruined my relationship with the Brown family. I brought you home too soon."

"Anya, it wouldn't have mattered when I came. Their son had his sights set on you. There was no way to sugarcoat the fact that's not what you wanted. It isn't a crime that we want each other. If they want to act mean, I say we don't need them."

Anya sat in silence.

"Whatever you decide, I'll support you, Anya. I'm sure you know how much I care for you."

Strangely, his statement struck her, the same thing Peter would say. Her stress didn't decrease with his assertion; her angst increased. She experienced a pervasive feeling of wrongness about the situation.

He looked at her closely. "Are you having second thoughts, Anya? Do you want me to back off?"

"No, I'm not saying that. I will say you handled that visit very well. I put you in a very difficult situation. I'm sorry."

"There's nothing to apologize for. I surprised myself. Maybe for the first time I'm thinking seriously about my future, our future. To me, it means you've reached a place no other girl has. This is new ground for me. You're changing me for the better. I've developed very strong feelings for you, yet still I sometimes think it would be best for you to turn back."

"I'm not afraid of that. It's gratifying what you're saying, and honestly, I've thought about marriage with you too."

"Eh…marriage…that's a loaded word. Be very careful because once you start that train rolling, it will be very difficult to stop."

"Perhaps I don't want it to stop. I don't know the answer."

"When I graduate and leave the area to go to a job, what then: Would you be willing to follow me to wherever I go?"

"Do you mean transfer to another school to finish my degree?"

"Yes. If I'm out of this area, there would be no other choice."

"I could consider it. I don't know what I want right now. We still have considerable ground to cover before we get to that point."

Chapter Thirteen

Peter was not first contact for Anya when she got back to school. She went straight to her room to explain the difficult weekend to Christy, in detail.

"Going there with Jeff, it infuriated Peter's father. It's the first time I've seen him angry. He left to go to a bar one evening. I was an emotional mess. Mrs. Brown tried to be polite, but she was equally stirred up. My mother berated me the entire time. I'm still a mess."

"Their reaction was predictable, Anya." She stood to comfort Anya with a hug.

"I know, but if Jeff is now my boyfriend, he needed to meet Mama."

"Have you made that decision? Jeff, as your boyfriend: are you ready to get serious with a guy?"

"I like him, but honestly, I still have Peter in my heart too."

"With romance, it's either/or. You can't have them both."

"I know. It's killing me. Peter will hate me so much. I'm sure he's talked to his father about the weekend."

"I wish I had some magic answer, but you already know it's you that must make your choices."

"It may be too late anyway. Mr. Brown told me basically not to come back there."

"Do *you* think you burned your bridges?"

"He was so angry, as I said. My life with them may be over. Jeff may be my only option at this point."

"Where did you leave it with Jeff?"

"We talked about our future. He asked if I would follow him to his job."

"What was he talking about: marriage, a live-in arrangement, or a friendship with benefits? What did you say?"

"I wouldn't live that way, as a mistress. I don't think he meant that."

"Anya, this is Jeff we're talking about. Don't get caught up in just his good looks and charm. The same thing we talked about with Peter could happen with Jeff. Going down that road and having the marriage fail later—I'd worry that he could stay faithful to a wife."

Anya scowled.

"Anya, use your head. He's not a guy to do without, if you get what I'm saying. He will always have options in that area. Girls hit on him and I doubt a wedding ring will stop that from continuing. Don't get talked into going against your principles. I know you don't want to hear this." Christy took Anya's face in her hands affectionately, to express her point.

"Christy, I do want to hear it. I appreciate your concern. This is why I love you and need you. I can't get my mind straight about this."

"I love you too, and I just want what's best for you. Are you going to talk to Peter?"

Anya returned Christy's hug with a firm embrace. "I doubt he'd talk to me now. I truly wanted to feel about him like I feel about Jeff. I can't explain what happened. It just didn't go that way."

"That being said, I think it's better to tell him."

"I know how unfair this is to him, but honestly, the thought of releasing him into the arms of other girls turns my stomach. I'd be so jealous."

"You're right—that would be unfair. You know what you've got to do."

"What would *you* do?"

"No, no, no. I can't make that life-altering choice for you. I think you need some private time to think seriously. Do you want a man who you know will be a good person and a good husband, or do you want to pick the dazzler, knowing he'll always have his eyes on other women? He's lifted too many skirts, so now it's in his blood: conquering as many women as he can as fast as he can."

"I feel stirred up, worried, out of sorts all the time now. It never rests."

"Maybe there's a message in there, Anya. Your subconscious might be fighting your impulsive side. Maybe it knows better. Do you see what I'm saying?"

Anya frowned again.

"You've got this image built up in your mind. That perfect wedding, the image of walking out of the church wearing his ring to the idyllic life. Is that possible with Jeff? The hot-couple fantasy is an illusion, darling."

"You think Jeff is the mistake?"

"I do, but…"

"I know all these things you're saying. Christy, you're like the sister I never had."

They hugged, but…

#

Peter made his own decision—he called Allison.

"Hi. Am I interrupting something?"

"Peter. What a surprise. I didn't expect a call from you. What's going on?"

"You…well…"

"Oh…I heard about Anya hooking up with that stud, Jeff. Now I understand. I'm sure that knocked you out."

"Hooked up?"

"My words, probably not the best description, but you get the idea."

"You said you wanted to go out. I guess I no longer have a reason not to."

"Wow, that was romantic, Peter."

"If you've heard the story about Anya, you should understand my bitterness. I'd apologize, but I'm not sorry."

"What a way for us to start. You're setting a pretty low bar. Did you forget I have plenty of options?"

"I did not, and those options are still available, ma'am. Feel free to indulge." He spoke tersely, his underlying anger simmering to life easily these days.

Allison paused before she spoke. "Listen, Peter, I understand this mood of yours. You thought Anya was the one, your future wife, but the truth is ultimately she kicked you to the curb. However, taking out your anger on me—that's not going to work, for either of us. Count it as free advice."

"Okay, Allison."

"I still want to try us out as a couple, but I'm not going to spin my wheels. If I continue to get attitude and the back of your hand, I'll let you go back to your corner to mope and pout all by yourself. Got it? Anya is going to be enjoying herself with the man of her dreams."

"We're off to a great start, dearest." He made no attempt to mask the sarcasm in his voice.

"Oh boy, this is going to be a bumpy ride."

"You've still got your other options. It's your choice if you want to put up with me. So, did you have something in mind for our date?"

"Peter, you're the guy, so woo me."

Peter chuckled. "Okay, Allison, but if you're leaving it up to me, you can't complain about whatever I choose."

"You've got a deal, but it better not be something stupid. 'Disney on Ice' won't do; no tractor-pulls, or such. This will be romantic, or else. I'm going to dress to kill, so no mud-wrestling tournaments."

Peter laughed heartily. "Mud-wrestling, that's a good one, Allison. I'll come up with something decent."

"You'd better, Peter Brown. I know where you live. My wrath has no bounds if you provoke me. You would truly regret it."

"So, are we talking the weekend or sooner?"

"Either way—you make your arrangements and let me know. I'm giving you a pass on the rude remarks and snarky attitude, but just this one time. I might bring my can of mace in case you fumble this opportunity. You will feel the pain."

"Thanks for the warning, and the kind remarks. I'll get back with you when I have something lined up."

"I'll be waiting with baited breath."

"Sure you will. By the way, if I were you, I wouldn't put your army of other suitors aside. My best efforts might be a pale shade compared to what you usually get from your dates."

"I think we should hang up at this time. Your stupid remarks are starting to pile up, and they're getting on my nerves. Before you completely put your foot in your mouth, I'll bid you *adieu*."

"Bless you, too."

"That means goodbye, lame-brain."

"Sorry. I thought you said achoo."

"Goodbye." She hung up the receiver, forcefully.

Bob eyed him sadly. "So, you're switching horses?"

"My horse already did the switching."

"I get the feeling you don't really want to date Allison. You were pretty rough on her."

"She asked for it."

"I don't think she asked for what you just did. I'm surprised she'd even go out with you now."

"What if your warning was true? She looks at me and sees dollar signs?"

"That could still be the case, but do you want to sink down to that level? You're a quality person who's been dealt a terrible blow. What comes out the other end of this test is who you will be."

"I know that. If I end up alone for a time while I try to get my feet under me again, I'm fine with it."

"Maybe you should tell that to Allison? She's still really beautiful. Would dating her be such an odious task? You might have fun, if you tried. You told me the time you spent in her company before wasn't bad at all."

"I did say that—you're right. I think hanging out with a pretty girl isn't the same as believing there is a future with her, or at least a future I want. I'll try this. I've got nothing to lose."

"It didn't sound to me like you're trying. It sounds like you're just going through the motions. So why do it? My opinion, I don't think Allison's the girl to make you happy."

"You might be right. However, she might surprise me."

"This is so messed up. I'm mad at Anya too."

"I'm mad about her, but honestly, she's got the right to choose whomever she wants. I should have known better than to pin all of my hopes on her, so I take my share of the blame for this fiasco."

"Christy has become so protective of Anya; it's an argument waiting to happen. It makes it difficult between us. I try not to talk about Anya, ever, but the topic comes up frequently. I just listen. Jeff has knocked her for a loop, seemingly."

"That's great news. You can see why I'm going to try Allison. Going to the mixers isn't enough anymore. One other thing, though: I've found I'm really drawn to smart girls. Anya has a brain in her head. Allison doesn't measure up in that department. I'm not saying she's stupid, but the level of discourse I have with Anya just isn't there with Allison. She's not a total airhead, but she has those abilities."

The boys laughed.

Bob opined, "Imagine this: you and I critiquing beauty-queen babes. A couple of toads like us…who woulda thunk it!"

"Well said, my friend. Toads of the world, arise!"

"Power to the people, or the amphibians, or whatever…"

"It's funny you say that. When I first met Anya and was trying to get on her radar, I made the comment my goal was to get out of the lower life-form category and into the mammal class. Obviously, I failed in that goal."

Bob shrugged. "Life goes on. For me, I choose to be an optimist. In the end, I truly believe we'll both be okay. I will say that if Christy and I end up together, and that's my goal, being pals with Anya and this Jeff dude would be really difficult. The type of guy he is I despise. Why would Anya see any merit in a guy like that? I don't get it."

"He floats her boat. That's simple enough to understand. I guess she's more interested in feeling the thrill than in any substance in her man. As I've said before, so be it—time to move on."

"Still, I thought she was different, Peter. I know walking with an exceptionally attractive person is gratifying for your ego, but…"

"Seeing how people react to power couples, it seems that's appealing to some."

"I know that lures some people, but because I'm not one of them, it's hard to understand it. I'm still surprised Anya would be one of them."

"I wish her well. In spite of my personal pain, I don't wish harm on her. As far as him, if he fell into a bottomless pit, I'd be fine with it."

They boys laughed and bumped fists.

#

The sad saga continued. With Anya continuing to date Jeff, soon they were in an intense relationship. Peter started to date Allison, although that relationship didn't ignite in the same way. Peter's natural caution, his suspicion about her true motives, tempered his responses into tepid enthusiasm, in spite of Allison's best efforts to snare him.

In a supremely bad decision, Peter got talked into a joint date, going to dinner and a movie with Bob and Christy, and Jeff and Anya. It was misery from the first instant he saw them together. Seeing Anya excited and exuberant over her "stud" boyfriend sickened Peter to the point he nearly exited the awkward evening before it started. Succumbing to pressure from Allison never seemed to work out well. Seeing Anya initiate her connection taking Jeff's hand struck Peter like a bullet to the chest.

He muttered to Bob as they stepped inside the building, "I'm sure this whole thing is Allison's idea. She's not happy I won't get on board with cozying up to her and forgetting Anya. I guess she decided to take her revenge by rubbing my nose in it by having to be around Jeff. Anya's head over heels in love with a total jerk. I feel like slugging somebody."

"Don't slug him, Peter. I think he could take us both out pretty easily."

Peter snickered. "Thanks for having my back, weenie."

"You're welcome. I want to survive this."

"Okay. Watch me do my best trying to imitate a doting boyfriend."

All of the girls noticed immediately when Peter changed his approach and pretended sudden fascination for Allison, fawning all over her in a ridiculous display.

"Oh, Allison, you're such a vision tonight. I'm so lucky. I could drink your bathwater."

Allison was not amused. Bob cringed, Christy scowled, and Jeff smirked contemptuously.

Anya's exuberance evaporated in an instant, which pleased Peter a great deal in a perverse way. She frowned at him and he smiled in return, but his glee was short lived. This was not a move that helped him, and he was quick to realize it.

As always, Jeff remained above the fray, like the actions of mere peasants couldn't possibly impact him in any way. Believing he had Anya sewed up; nothing else mattered.

Peter struggled to keep from making any further foolish actions in this crucible of misery. Standing in front of him was the woman he loved. That would never change. However, it was too late. He'd drawn female notice, and not in a positive way.

Jeff looked at him, acknowledging the roiling undercurrent at last. His amused look grated on Peter. Anya did not have an amused look. She glared at Peter. Jeff's contemptuous look at Peter came across to him as *You're pathetic, dude*. It provoked Peter toward a worse outburst. Anya saw it percolating and spoke up. "Well, we should go to the restaurant now." Exiting the mall concourse, going into a restaurant, the embarrassment didn't lessen for Peter.

Sitting at the dinner table, Peter decided to salvage his dignity and take a calculated step. He started an intellectual conversation intended to draw in Anya. "Anya, did you read that book on existentialism you mentioned? After you told me about it, I read a copy. It got my mind working, and I read some Jean Paul Sartre. *I am, therefore I exist*. Does that ring a bell?"

She couldn't resist the bait and answered the call to her mind. It was a ploy by Peter that would go over the heads of Allison and Jeff. Anya realized this after a time and looked closely at Peter before turning to her date.

Thereafter, the level of discourse went sharply downhill, so the entire table could be included in the conversation. The latest episodes of *The Bachelor* and *The Bachelorette* made Peter smirk. Anya had a wry smile.

Peter had achieved his goal, and Anya got the message. Allison and Jeff had momentarily been relegated to the sidelines, for perhaps the first time in their lives.

Anya spoke to Jeff. "I'm sorry, honey. Is this boring you?"

"No. Hearing you guys talk is interesting. I didn't want to butt in."

"That's not necessary, darling. You're a part of the group too."

Peter did not fail to notice her heavy use of terms of endearment, her return message to him. It irked him and again he pondered simply getting up to leave.

Allison stared at him in thinly veiled anger. The group date she'd concocted wasn't going as she'd hoped. Rather than a *coup de grace*, symbolically burying Anya and Peter's relationship, instead their underlying feelings for each other remained.

Moving from the restaurant into the cinema, Peter waited until the others sat down before he opted to sit on the far end. Bob and Christy were in the middle, with Anya and Jeff on the other side of them.

Once the lights went down, Allison reached over to take Peter's hand in hers, and pulled it over onto her lap. He didn't respond, not squeezing her hand—he simply left it limp, an unspoken message to her.

She leaned over to whisper in his ear, "Big mistake, dude." Allison placed his hand back on his own lap. She bristled, but he didn't care.

The movie was a love story, running over two hours. Peter was bored out of his mind. At the end, the group stood. Anya led Jeff down the row by the hand, toward the aisle. Christy also led Bob by the hand. Allison didn't bother reaching for Peter's hand. He'd put both hands in his pockets.

Suddenly, she looked back at him. "Stop acting like an ass, little boy. Anya is with Jeff by her own choice, remember?"

The salvo struck home, punishing Peter. He scowled, replying sarcastically, "Okay, dearest, off we go."

"Save your sarcasm. I don't need it. I'm not the bad guy here."

"You're right. I'm sorry."

Reaching out, he took her hand, but she eyed him suspiciously.

Jeff ushered Anya to his car, rubbing his hand possessively on her back. Bob and Christy had ridden with Peter. Jeff smirked at Peter, who then looked grimly at Anya. She glowered defensively. The cars were parked side by side, so Peter saw Jeff's moves.

Jeff spoke. "This was so much fun. Good night all. Anya and I must leave."

It was like a hammer blow to his head for Peter, the implication from Jeff. The thought Anya's evening wasn't over was intolerable.

"Peter, get in the damn car," Allison hissed.

Bob added. "Come on. Let's go." He also scowled at Anya.

It was a quiet ride back to campus. Allison was provoked, but Peter paid no attention. His thoughts were on Anya.

Peter pulled up to the girls' side of the dorm. Bob and Christy got out. Allison did not. "I'll walk back from the lot with you, Peter."

They drove away.

"Are you proud of your performance tonight, Peter?"

"Are you happy with your plan? What did you expect, Allison? Do you think I'd just stop loving Anya? Rubbing my nose in it, what the…"

"You can make me the bad guy if you want. Look at how you treat me, but I keep coming back for more. No guy treats me this way, but I put up with it from you. Why do you suppose that is? Maybe I care about you? Oh, that's right. You're convinced I'm conniving for your folks' money."

"I didn't say that."

"You didn't need to. Do you think Anya's going to be impressed by that sorry performance you put on? Why do you think she's with a smooth operator like Jeff? She endured your clumsy miscues as long as she could but finally got fed up. She wants a secure guy, not a childish and emotional basket case."

"I can accept your dismal description of me, but if that's the case, why are you here? If I'm so addled, what's the lure for you, other than the money angle?"

"You really want to insult me. Why? Why is it so hard for you to give us a chance? Am I not pretty enough? What is it I must do?"

"Okay. I realize a lot of guys want to date many different girls at this stage, I guess to figure out what they want. I'm not one of them. I'm a one-horse type of guy. I found who I want."

"And she found who she wants. You haven't been in Christy's room when we talk. She is pondering some big steps with him, steps she wasn't going to take with any other guys, including you. Do I need to spell it out?"

It was like Peter had been dropped into a frying pan at high heat. He couldn't manage to say anything as the thought and the implication punished him.

"She's looking at him as a future husband. Does it make sense for you to continue ignoring the inevitable? Maybe this will be her night to pull the trigger?"

"Shut up, Allison. How does twisting the knife help your cause? Why did I choose Anya? I want a woman who can go to church with me without being struck by lightning, a good mother to our children, somebody I want to grow old with. I want a woman who makes me feel the way I do about her. If you want to date me, it's just passing the time. You'd be much better off going back to your numerous other troll options. You can get your own 'Jeff,' and then you can try to rub my nose in that."

"Peter," she whispered, shaking her head. "I've had all of those types. I don't want them. Apparently, Anya does. I really want for there to be an 'us.' You found your Anya, but maybe I've found what I want."

"Me? You can't be serious."

"Yes, I can."

They parked the car. Peter turned off the engine. When he started to get out, she grabbed his arm.

"Stay with me, please?"

As she kissed him, he went along with it a certain amount, but when she wanted to go to another level, unbuttoning her blouse, he spoke. "No, Allison. That's not what I want. I'll think about what you've said. Let's go back to the dorm."

"Okay," she whispered sadly.

#

Returning to his room meant the inevitable: facing Bob's questions.

Bob eyed him, like an accusation.

"What now, Bob?"

"What do you think? What was that tonight?"

"I feel no need to defend myself."

"Rudeness is now okay somehow? I guess I didn't get that memo. Everybody in the universe understands how you feel, including Anya. Taking out your frustrations on Allison the way you did is not acceptable. Treat her right or send her on her way. Peter, you disappoint me."

He bristled, mostly because Bob was right. "I'm not in the mood to talk about it."

"You never are. This is a problem that will just get worse."

"Good night. I'm going to crash."

#

Accompanying Bob to breakfast the next morning, Peter surprised himself. Rather than sneak away to hide from the problem, he went to the table where the girls were already seated. Every one of them looked directly at him. However, he only had eyes for Anya. She looked back sullenly.

"Good morning," he said brightly. "How is everybody?"

"We're fine, Peter," Christy replied. "How are you this morning?"

"Just peachy, thank you very much. So, Anya, did you enjoy the movie? Was it all that you hoped for?"

Anya eyed him darkly.

Allison spoke, "Peter, hello. I'm sitting right here."

"Oh, Allison, I'm sorry. Yes, hello to you."

Peter now had three grim stares from across the table. He continued down the tenuous path toward self-destruction. "Anya, that's a new hairstyle? The curls on the side are very sexy. I'm sure Jeff likes that."

"He does, as a matter of fact," she replied in a terse tone. "I aim to please."

It was another blow in a verbal contest he was doomed to lose. Her jab cut him to the core. The implications of her reply were troubling.

"Peter," Christy said. "Please spare us your stupidity."

"Yes. ma'am." He stood and left the table, seething internally. Again, fatalistic thoughts went through his mind. Impulsive ideas, such as moving to a different dorm across campus, transferring to a new school, out of state, driving off a cliff—he punished himself again within the confines of his mind. It was coming to be a very bad habit, getting to this state of distress.

Muttering as he collected his books, he hustled out of the room before Bob got back. His prior distressed thoughts and resulting angst were constant companions these days.

It was Allison who surprised him, hurrying to catch him before he left the dorm.

"Peter, wait. I'll walk with you."

"Why, Allison? Why? You're wasting your time. Isn't that clear to you?"

"I don't agree. You treat me like garbage, and yet here I am. Doesn't that mean something to you? I'm still trying."

Peter shook his head. "I wanted to apologize anyway for how I've acted toward you. It's not your fault, what Anya is choosing to do. Don't take that to mean I've changed my position."

"I can't believe what you put me through, and I take it! I could never imagine being in this situation. If this is love, it sure is a lot more painful than I thought it would be."

"Love? Allison, listen to yourself. Saying that to me, I think you might need therapy."

She laughed heartily and it caused Peter to laugh.

"You might be right, Peter. I probably need counseling for a lot of reasons."

"I just don't get it. Why *do* you put up with it? I really don't want to be mean to you. My feelings for Anya just come out and I can't control them."

"It's funny, how hard you try to drive me away. In talking with Anya, Jeff is still trying to warn her away. Maybe for both of us the element of a goal beyond our grasp is what is so compelling. In both our cases, we acknowledge we have plenty of other options. You say you only want Anya. I could say the same thing about you."

Peter frowned as they walked. "Have you two considered perhaps why Jeff and I say that is because we know we're the wrong guys for you girls?"

"You can't know that. You can have an opinion, but I'm willing to get down in the trenches and do the heavy lifting for us as a couple."

"The fact I only have eyes for Anya doesn't change your mind?"

"No."

"Wow. That's pretty heavy."

"Heavy enough for you to get out of the way of *us* giving it a go?"

He shrugged.

"She's determined, and so am I."

"He's a senior. Graduation isn't far away."

"They're talking about her following him to wherever he goes for his job. I've already told you that. You need to face the facts."

He had no response, only a sad face.

"Can you understand it: the reality of Mrs. Jeffrey Bond?"

Peter scowled at the disturbing thought. "Allison, there's no need to twist the knife."

"I want what I want just as badly as she does. Tonight, you and I, we get together. You can call it a study date, but we talk, in-depth. You're going to make some big choices and some meaningful decisions."

"By that you mean make the decisions you want?"

"I didn't say that."

"Right, Allison. This is a heavy-handed tactic."

"I don't care. Deal with it."

He chuckled. "Okay. I guess it's a date."

His tacit agreement didn't mean he was on board with her coercion. Actually, he thought about having the same kind of meeting, but with Anya.

#

His mind percolated all day during his classes, like he was fitting in puzzle pieces to find a solution. By the time he ambled back to the dorm, deep in thought, he was the last to arrive for dinner.

Allison was talking pointedly with Anya, who was mostly listening. Christy eyed Peter, though he couldn't tell if that was good or bad.

Allison turned her face to Peter, smiling warmly. "Hello, dear."

Peter looked at Anya. She had a look of curiosity. "Hello, Allison. Hello, Anya."

"Hello."

"So, finals week is coming fast. I would guess Allison told you she wants a study date to get ready?"

"She did say you were getting together."

"As far as I'm concerned, that can be an open invitation to us all. Everybody needs to study for finals, even Jeff."

Anya's curious look was quickly replaced by a glare. Allison was incensed, but Peter ignored her.

Turning his head, he spoke to Bob. "How 'bout it, partner: you and Christy joining us for the fun?"

He looked uncomfortable. "It's up to Christy."

"Sure, Peter—we'll join you." Her answer sounded more like a snarl. "I love watching self-immolations."

Peter laughed. "I always suspected that I'm combustible. Good. This will be a nice time for all of us getting together. What do you say: maybe in an hour?"

After that, the meal was consumed in relative silence, like they were on the verge of a battle.

"Peter, what are you doing?" Bob asked when they went up to the room. "This idea of yours has disaster written all over it."

"Desperate times call for desperate measures."

"Ill-conceived plans are never a good idea."

#

Down in the lobby, the girls hadn't arrived yet. To Peter's surprise, Jeff walked over to sit down.

"Hey, guys. Anya called me to join this study session. How are you?"

"Great, Jeff. You must be excited to graduate?"

"What I'm more excited about is my last job interview went really well. I was invited to fly out to their home office, and it was strongly hinted it's just a formality. I've got the job."

"Where is it?"

"Out west, in Seattle. It will be my first trip to the West Coast."

"That's so nice for you." Jeff missed Peter's condescending tone, but Bob didn't, eyeing Peter ruefully.

"Anya seemed excited, so that makes me happy. She's talking about transferring out to Washington, or Washington State. She needs to get the details on her scholarship situation, though."

"Understandable." Peter could barely contain his anxiety.

"She's been such a boon in my life. Now I have purpose and direction. She's so good for me. I shudder to think about where I'd be going with my life without her."

"That's nice, Jeff," Bob said, but he stared at Peter, who was struggling visibly to tamp down his anxiety.

At that moment, the ladies arrived. Anya went straight over to Jeff, giving him a sensuous kiss, after which she eyed Peter. Allison stepped over to give Peter a romantic kiss. Taking his face in her hands, she tried to make a statement to the others showing her ownership. He barely reacted, but she smiled anyway. Christy kissed Bob and the couples sat down to start work.

Instantly, Peter began to read his text. Allison whispered in his ear, "You're not going to dodge our little talk. Look at Anya's short skirt. Can you grasp the message she's sending to you?"

Peter bristled. Anya was draped all over Jeff, and she did glance toward Peter in their ongoing chess match. It was an overt move he ached to answer with a salvo of his own. However, doing something to irk Anya was the last thing he wanted to do.

Jeff was smiling at him, the winner again. He put a hand to Anya's bare knee, owning her, his own version of twisting the knife. Smirking in triumph, staring at Peter the entire time, his fingers glided onto her thigh. His intent was obviously to put it in Peter's mind, *Look what I can do right in front of you; what do you think I've I already done to her?* Peter saw the reaction in Anya, her eyes glazing over. However, things didn't work out as he imagined.

Peter muttered, "*Deus auxilium mecum.*"

"What did you say?" Allison asked, drawing notice. Everybody looked at Peter.

Christy interpreted softly, "God help me." Everybody then turned their faces to Anya. She took it as an indictment from the group, like she was allowing Jeff liberties, and in public.

Peter remained stationary, staring daggers at Jeff, but Anya reacted, scowling and firmly pushing Jeff's hand off. He never saw it coming, and it changed Anya's mood completely. She muttered in Russian and then took out her book to study, adjusting her posture, transforming in an instant from doting infatuated girl to consummate and aloof scholar. Peter smiled at Jeff's look of astonishment. Jeff had never been "dismissed" before.

Allison whispered, "You think you just won a battle?"

"Yeah, I'm sure he never gets the word 'no.' Nonverbally, Anya just informed him she's not his average 'airhead' conquest."

"Do you honestly think he won't win in the end?"

Anya glanced at them and their whispered exchanges. Peter smiled at her and though she tried to resist, she smiled back.

From that point on, this session went the route of actual test preparation rather than Jeff's usual hook-up routines.

After several hours, Anya closed her book. "I'm done for now," she announced. The others followed her lead and stood up also. She gave Jeff a peck on the cheek rather than a full kiss on the lips. It pleased Peter immensely. In turn, he also gave Allison a perfunctory peck on the cheek. It pleased him that Anya noticed; making him feel all hope was not yet dead.

Peter parted with a feeling of excitement. "Good night, ladies. This was nice."

Allison answered, "Good night, Peter. We must do this again. We *will* do this again."

"Goodbye, Jeff. Keep us informed about your Seattle job."

"Sure thing, fellas." He'd regained his composure seamlessly. His self-assured air was back, along with the spring in his step.

#

Returning to their room, Bob questioned Peter. "Did I miss something? Christy and I were reading."

"I think Anya gave me a subtle sign. I'm not giving up."

"Good, I think. It is good, right? I'd be very glad if basket-case Peter comes to an end and we get back to normal."

"You've got it, bro."

Chapter Fourteen

Anya acted somewhat the same for the next week when Peter saw her, but with Jeff's imminent departure looming, there were going to be ramifications. Those, Peter worried about. It was still possible Anya might decide to pack up and leave with Jeff, and it bothered Peter greatly. He was accustomed to feeling helpless regarding Anya, but this time there was greater foreboding.

Ironically, that decision occurred outside of his knowledge, at a time and place he wasn't aware of. On Friday, before finals week, he was sitting downstairs studying. In theory, it was a study date with Allison, although she mostly talked. She showed more flesh than usual.

"Peter, how about we go out tonight after we get done studying? We can take in a late movie and then see where the evening takes us?"

"What?" he muttered, continuing to read the text material?

"You heard me." She pulled down his book to get his full attention. "I'm ready to have a fun night."

"What does that mean?"

"You're a big boy…I'm sure you can figure it out." She started to embrace him, but noticed him look up, behind her. Allison turned her head to see Anya approaching.

"Peter, can we talk?"

"Sure."

"No, no, no," Allison objected. "Anya, we talked about this. You agreed this is my time to get my shot."

"I know I said I would back away, Allison, but…"

Peter spoke. "Back away—what? What's that about? What happened, Anya? What did he do to you?"

"Nothing, Peter."

The look on her reddening face wasn't reassuring. He stood up.

"Peter, no," Allison pleaded.

Pulling out of her grasp, he put his arm around Anya, leading her away, and leaving Allison behind without a reply. Guiding Anya out the dorm door, they went to his car in the lot for privacy to talk there.

Anya was still embarrassed and distraught.

"Anya, tell me. I'm here for you."

"I…we had a serious talk, about next week. He has that job in Seattle and wants me to go with him."

"Do you mean…as his wife?" Peter grimaced, his face showing concern.

"No."

"My God. I should march over and slug that son of a bitch." Now his face was angry.

"Peter, no. I said I wouldn't do that. Can I be honest with you?"

"Please do."

"I have strong feelings for Jeff. That hasn't changed, but his ideas about living that way—I can't abide it."

"Do you think perhaps it's his way of saying he's the wrong guy for you, Anya?"

"I don't know, maybe that is so."

"What do you want to do now?"

"There is a second thing I want to say. I woke up and realized how strong my feelings are for you, Peter. I've been so unfair, and yet you've been a gentleman and a man of good character through it all. If you still want me…well…here I am."

"Of course I want you. That's no secret." He held his breath.

"I will marry you. I will be the wife you want me to be." She looked in his eyes, but then glanced away.

"Eh…wow. I'm happy, but this is a heck of a sea change. So, this is you coming to a realization?" He tried to keep from sounding skeptical, but was only partially successful.

"Yes."

The nebulous tone in her voice didn't reassure him. He thought for a moment before continuing. "Let me go on record: if he did something—if *you* did something—all I care about is you and me. I don't need an explanation. If you choose to share, I'm all ears. Otherwise, it's water under the bridge."

"Nothing happened, Peter. There's nothing to explain."

"Okay, Anya."

"I will marry you, right away, if you're agreeable."

"Now? I…eh…"

"If you don't wish…"

"I do wish…I'll call home and talk to Mom. Maybe she can put together something quick at our church?"

"Good. I would like that. I already called Mama to tell her my decision. She was very happy. She didn't like Jeff much, but she loves you, Peter."

"I love her too. I'll see about getting rings right away. Anya, you've made me happy beyond words."

Anya smiled placidly. It made him feel like a rambunctious puppy she merely tolerated. Rather than looking agog at the prospect of marriage, she still looked to be dealing with whatever had caused this.

She stared out the windshield a moment before turning to kiss him. Peter enjoyed her affectionate act, but suspicion is difficult to dismiss. *Is this contrived or genuine?* he mused.

"Anya, are you sure about this? You know this is my dream, but I know you were moved by Jeff. Do you really want to leave him behind to become my wife?"

"I told you that," she replied defensively. At that point, she turned her face away. Again, it was disconcerting, but he wasn't going to let this chance slip away to get Anya at last.

"So be it. What do you want to do now?"

"I need to go back and study."

"I do also. Do you want to study with me?"

"Maybe that's a good idea. If I go to the lounge, or back to my room, Allison will chase me down to argue. She might punch me."

Peter snickered at the remark.

"So, she got you to agree to back off me?"

"I know that doesn't sound very nice."

"It doesn't surprise me, that she would have an agenda."

"I'm not giving you a good impression. I'm sorry. I do want to be your wife. It's just very difficult dealing with these complicated emotions."

"I'll try to help un-complicate them. We can go to the library."

"I like that idea."

Peter started his car to drive back to the dorm, and then they drove to the library.

Ron was there, like it was his permanent residence.

"Hi, Anya. It's always nice to see you."

"Hi, Ron. How are you? I'm sorry I've been busy. I should be freer now."

"I'm busy too getting ready for next week. Please join us, guys?"

"Okay." She sat down beside Ron. Peter shook his head and sat down on her other side. He couldn't escape the feeling Anya was as happy to be with Ron as with him.

Peter opened his book to concentrate. Anya chatted pleasantly with Ron before she opened her book.

Peter took out a notebook to jot down items from the text. It always helped him to retain data by physically writing it down and helped put his emotional questions aside, focusing on the work. *Is this my actual fiancée?* It was a bothersome question, seeing how she acted.

#

Going back to the dorm much later, Anya took his hand. It was a warm spring evening. Her gesture helped Peter feel perhaps things weren't so bad after all. Maybe it was just his fertile mind concocting nonexistent issues.

"I'll call Mom tonight."

"Okay."

"Anya, I can't wait."

She chuckled. "I'm sorry. You have no choice."

"I didn't mean that. I meant I can't wait for us to be husband and wife."

"That will be a happy day."

"I'll do my best to be a good husband. I want you to be the happiest bride in history."

"Thank you, Peter."

"I meant what I said. Everything before this minute doesn't matter. We start fresh right now."

"Okay. That's a good idea."

"Good."

When he dropped her off at the elevator, she kissed him. Although always nice, he still couldn't escape the sense Anya was trying too hard.

He walked quickly back to his room.

"I heard," Bob said. "Congrats. Christy was as surprised as me."

"Thanks. I've got to call Mom. All of a sudden, Anya wants to get married instantly." He looked at Bob. "I know what you're thinking. She said nothing happened. I'm sure Jeff couldn't force that with her. Whether Anya succumbed by her choice, I don't know that I really want to know. He wanted her to follow him to be his mistress. That was stupid on his part. It shows he didn't bother to get to know Anya."

"There is the other possibility. Maybe he really did love her but realized he would still be a womanizer if they got married. Maybe this was a magnanimous act on his part."

"I never got the impression he is a noble guy."

"You never know, Peter. Don't assume the worst: you could be wrong. Perhaps he intended for Anya to end up with you, in spite of her feelings for him."

"I, eh. You sure know how to put this in the worst possible light."

"That's what friends are for."

Peter took out his cell to call home. He was actually nervous, calling his parents.

"Hi, Mom."

"Hi, Peter. Mariska told me and I'm already working on it."

"How do you feel about it, Mom?"

"How do *you* feel? That's what's important."

"I was shocked, to say the least. The suddenness, how she looked and acted—I do wonder what happened on her end."

"You think she took a serious step with Jeff. I know you and how you think."

"It is a possibility. I hope not, but if she did, I want to marry her anyway. College girls making that choice are hardly rare. On the plus side, Anya has always been adamant about waiting until she gets married. I'm banking on that. Do you think she did it?"

"I'd say it's best we don't go into it. As you say, what's important is looking ahead, not behind."

"I hope this isn't some bad reaction. If she doesn't really love me, what will a marriage be like?"

"For a woman, deciding to marry is a huge thing. She wouldn't choose to wed if she didn't feel it was the right choice."

"I guess we'll see."

"I'll let you know the details, but it's looking like a fairly small ceremony at the church on the Saturday the first week you're home."

"That works for me."

"Dad and I are trying to arrange a nice honeymoon too. It's awfully late notice, but we'll come up with something."

"Thank you, Mom. Can you tell Mariska I look forward to calling her Mom too?"

She chuckled. "I will, Peter. Good night."

"Good night, Mom."

He turned to Bob. "Will you be my best man? I imagine Anya has asked Christy to be the maid of honor."

"Of course."

"I'll see if Anya wants to have more girls in her wedding party."

"That won't be a problem?"

"I've got some friends from high school who can step in on short notice. I'm going to call her now."

"Hello, Peter." Anya's voice was friendly.

"Bob is going to be my best man. Do you want more women in the wedding party?"

"Yes. I know this will bother you, but I asked Allison, and Megan, and three other girls you don't know."

"No problem. I'll get more of my friends to fill out the wedding party. Megan and Allison: are you sure that's a good idea?"

"I want to do this. They are significant girls in my life. I'll take the chance."

"Okay, babe. Mom said they're trying to work out a nice honeymoon. Are you okay with whatever they come up with?"

"I am. I have no doubt it will be lovely. I want to say thank you for doing this. How I acted, and how I treated you—I wasn't sure you'd let me back in. Allison would have been a beautiful wife for you."

"No, thanks, I got the girl I wanted."

"I do love you, Peter. Maybe you'll come to believe it."

"I believe it." Even as he said it, he wondered if it was true.

"Good night, Peter."

"Good night. Dream about me."

Anya snickered. "You're a nut."

#

Finals week was the usual non-issue. Packing his car to drive home, Bob packed up with Peter, with the wedding so close. Christy loaded her things into Anya's car. The guys followed the girls on the long drive to Peter's house. It was perfect weather for the trip.

"I hope this is a good omen."

"It is, Peter. Are you anxious to get this show on the road?"

"Obviously. What about you and Christy?"

"I'd love to, but it's financial. We need to graduate and start getting paychecks before we can tie the knot. I think she'd be agreeable to getting engaged, if I could afford a ring."

"Maybe I can help out. I can pull some money from my account."

"That would be so cool, Peter. I'll pay you back."

"That's not necessary."

"It is, from my point of view. I realize you can afford all of these gifts you give people, but for my self-respect, I need to pull my own weight."

"Whatever you say, Bob. I just think it's wise to get Christy off the market."

"I agree."

"My folks made arrangements about tuxedos, and dresses for the girls. Anya's mom picked out her wedding dress."

"Amazing all of this could come together so fast. I think probably your folks pulled in some major favors."

"That's a very strong possibility."

"Peter, did I mention I love wedding cakes?"

The boys laughed.

#

After Peter pulled into the driveway at his parents' home, George, Edith, and Mariska hurried out to greet them. Starting with the girls, Anya and Christy, they hugged their way on to the boys.

"Welcome home, son," George said. He whispered. "Is everything okay with this?"

"It is, Dad."

They trooped into the house. The men carried the suitcases up to the bedrooms and then came back downstairs to chat until mealtime. Anya stayed in her mother's bedroom.

The scent of food cooking in the kitchen permeated the house and, in particular, the distinct smell of baked bread and apple pie sent their mouths to watering.

"I'm hungry," Bob said.

"Surprise, surprise," Peter retorted.

#

After the sumptuous feast, the women went upstairs to try on their dresses. Peter heard them exclaim loudly over the first sight of them.

"It sounds like so far so good upstairs."

George replied, "Women can get crazy about things, but we're talking about a wedding—that's about the top of the line for them. Peter, I'm so glad this has worked out for you."

"I was stunned when all of a sudden she's there, asking for us to get married. I don't know if there was something between her and Jeff. I haven't asked her for any details, and I won't. As long as she walks down the aisle to me, that's all that I need."

"It was a strange turn of events. She seemed pretty combative when she brought him here."

"I'm sure you were very welcoming, Dad."

The guys laughed. "Hey, it was a dumb move, and I let her know it. I hope I haven't opened a can of worms between her and me."

"I'm going to try to be upbeat and positive about things from now on."

"Good luck with that," Bob chimed in skeptically.

"Shut up, Bob."

"I call it like I see it."

#

That evening, all of the women went to spend the night in a motel in town. The other bridesmaids were gathered there. Imagining Megan and Allison in the mix was mind-boggling for Peter. His groomsmen would meet them at the church.

Standing in the den, Peter shared his feelings. "Dad, I'm feeling rattled."

"That's normal, son. Don't worry about it. Everything will be fine, believe me. Just try to enjoy the experience. It's your wedding too."

"I've longed for this for so long; now that it's going to be reality, it's kind of scary. What if Jeff shows up and she runs away with him?"

"Duh," Bob said.

George answered, "We get all kinds of crazy thoughts and feelings before a wedding. Like I said, you'll look back on this day and not remember any of the silliness."

"I'll take your word for that. Do you think Anya is going through this too?"

"Girls have their share of emotional wobbles too."

"I hate to speak for Anya, but from what your mother told me, women are just as nervous, if not more so. Staying apart adds to the anticipation, but also builds some angst."

#

The following morning, the guys were up early. Dressing in the tuxes, they drove to the church midmorning. The other guys were there waiting: Peter's high school friends.

The minister came out of his office to greet them.

"Hi, Peter. Please come in. Normally I have a series of marriage-counseling sessions for couples I marry, but obviously I've made an exception here."

Peter followed him into the office for a talk.

"I guess I'll try to condense my spiel down to the essence of things. I've met Anya a few times and her mother has been coming regularly with your folks. Marriage is not something to take lightly. I know there is a thrill of getting your very own bride, but making a life with her takes work, and compromise. I've known you all of your life, so I'm comfortable with your fine character. Anya seems like a good person so, on the surface, everything would appear to be copasetic. Reality isn't impressions, however."

"I realize that, sir."

"Do you? Having some dates isn't the same as twenty-four seven. When you dropped her off at the door, she could go to her room to relax and let her hair down, so to speak. Now you're in her grill constantly. When I say compromise, you can't win every argument, and you shouldn't; you've got to think ahead to what she wants. Do you understand?"

"I think so."

"Having a sexual relationship with a wife isn't something to take for granted. She doesn't owe you sex. She wants to be cherished in other ways too. You might be surprised how division of labor in a household can be an issue. If she's doing the housework, cooking, taking care of the children, for example, and doing a job, she's going to look for you to pull your weight."

"That's understandable."

"It's easy to say, but you grew up with wait staff. In your new home, it will be you and Anya."

"I believe I will handle it. I do my own stuff at school."

"I won't go into the philosophical and moral aspects of marriage—we just don't have time. It will be something we can cover later, if you're so inclined."

"Are you going to talk to Anya?"

"Yes."

They eyed each other.

"Is there something, Peter? You seem like there is something bothering you?"

"Well, Anya dated another guy she really liked. We kind of broke up. Actually, she broke up with me. The guy was a senior and about to graduate. I thought she was going to go off with him. Suddenly she does a complete reversal and wants to get married?"

"You wonder what happened, and what they did?"

"It has crossed my mind."

"Let me ask you this. In your worst-case scenario, if they made some choices and took some steps, does that influence whether you still want to marry her?"

"No. Anya has been my dream since day one."

"Then, do you really want to get into it? I'm not saying people should lie, but in this case perhaps you should let sleeping dogs lie?"

"It isn't I would hold it against her, doing that; it's her feelings that worry me. If she loves him, what are my long-term chances in this marriage?"

"Peter, she's putting on a wedding dress to marry you…not him."

"I've been so accustomed to living with romantic issues; eh…it's hard to imagine a happy ending."

"You need to get past that. If you carry secrets and jealousy in your heart, it will come back to bite you. Can you trust your future wife? Don't give me an expedient answer. That's a question for you to think about."

"I will, pastor."

"I hate to rush this, but I need to have my session with Anya."

"Thank you. I'll head out."

"Relax, Peter. This will be a good day for you."

He was tempted to try to sneak a peek at Anya in her wedding dress, but Bob would have no part of it.

"That would be bad luck. You're coming with us."

The guys went downstairs into the church basement to wait. Peter heard female voices as the women arrived. His heart began to thump.

"Mrs. Anya Brown. Dude," Bob said.

All the guys chuckled.

"Do you know what to do?" Shawn, one of his married friends, asked. He smirked, along with the other guys.

"Of course, you idiot."

"It's pretty simple, Tab A into slot B. It ain't rocket science."

They laughed hilariously, even George.

"Son, I'm sure the pastor told you a marriage is more than just the fun stuff. Women can be emotional at the drop of a hat. You've got to cope."

Shawn added, "Amen to that, brother. Wait until they go through pregnancy. You've got a big target on your back for nine months. It's your fault they're carrying around a beach ball in their belly."

Peter looked worried.

Shawn laughed but said, "Don't worry. When you hold your little baby for the first time, it's all worth it. It's amazing you can feel that much love."

#

As time passed, Peter's jitters escalated. Soon, the guys were heading up the stairs for their duties ushering in the visitors. George stayed, along with Bob.

When they heard the organ music begin, Peter felt a moment of panic.

"No, Peter. You're not going to trip and fall," George said.

"I hope not. That would make a great first impression."

"These are your friends and acquaintances out there. No worries. I'm going up to meet your mom. Wait for your musical cue."

Bob and Peter went up the stairs to the waiting room. It seemed like just an instant before they walked out into the sanctuary. He was shocked at the huge crowd in the full room.

When the wedding party started filing down the aisle, seeing Megan and Allison was another shock to his system. Megan had her usual smirk, Allison more of a glare. They were still incredibly beautiful women. The bridesmaids wore bare-shouldered light purple dresses: sexy, form-fitting—and they all had great forms. Peter couldn't avoid silly thoughts, like this was his personal beauty pageant. The girls smiled warmly at him, which was gratifying.

At last, Christy took her place and Anya appeared in the doorway, walking with her mom.

Peter's heart nearly exploded out of his chest at the sight of her. Her white wedding dress was bare shouldered, perfectly fitting to her physique, and sexy. The sight of her evoked him.

"Easy, Peter," Bob whispered. "You're almost there."

Mariska smiled when she put Anya's hand into Peter's. Peter's heart thumped in his chest.

Although Peter worried constantly he would screw up, the ceremony went off without a hitch.

It was difficult for him to gauge Anya's emotions. His own turbulent feelings took everything for him to handle. Anya appeared cool and collected to his glances and as he took her hand, she gave him a smile.

"You may kiss the bride." Finally, the miracle happened for Peter. Lifting her veil, he could barely contain his feelings. The gentle kiss caused a huge cheer from the gathered. Anya eyed him shyly.

At last, the minister said, "Ladies and gentlemen, I'd like to introduce Mr. and Mrs. Peter Brown."

The crowd cheered and applauded wildly.

There was subsequent obligatory time spent at the church as the wedding photos were taken, and then they piled into the limos for the drive across town to the reception hall. It was arduous for Peter, waiting it out. The reception was in his mind, but the wedding night called strongly to him. Anya and the bridesmaids were giddy the whole time before getting into the limo.

#

It was a festive occasion, and Peter was glad he'd learned to dance properly. The crowd milled about, talked, and laughed. Peter was swamped with high school and college friends, all anxious to meet his beautiful new bride. The meal was catered by personal friends of his parents, so it was superb. The throng had choices for entrées. Roast beef, chicken, or ham for the carnivores, and for the vegans, Chef's Surprise, a special concoction without meat.

For the father-daughter dance, it had been agreed George would fill in for that role, and then it was Peter dancing with his mom. Anya had picked the Bette Midler rendition of "The Wind beneath My Wings."

Edith smiled warmly. "I'm so happy for you, Peter. You'll have a wonderful life with Anya. She was so excited; I have no doubt she's all in for this marriage."

"Good. I hope I can make her happy."

"You will. You're a good person."

When the formal dances were over, Peter got an initial dance with his bride. It felt surreal, holding this gorgeous woman at last as the song refrained, "You light up my life."

Right afterward, she was swept up by an endless line of other guys, the first of whom was Bob. Meanwhile, Peter found Megan boldly seeking him out.

"Well, Peter, I must say you surprised me. I didn't think you could win her in the end. I thought Jeff had her on his plane heading west, guaranteed. To my knowledge, it's the first time he's ever lost in the romantic arena."

"I thought so too. Does this mean we have a truce? I never wanted to be your enemy."

"I guess I'll let you live. How do you like me in my dress?"

"You're gorgeous, but you know that."

She laughed. "I just wanted to hear it from you. This wedding was nice. I might need to change my plans to do this too."

"Getting married to the right person is about the best thing possible."

"I can see how you turned out so well. Your mother is a delight. She made me feel welcome, in spite of our checkered history. I'm not accustomed to being welcomed. It's my own fault, but that's who I am."

"I'm not going to make suggestions. You're smart enough to figure out the connection between what you do and the reactions it causes. I just try to keep a low profile and roll with the punches."

"Well, I certainly wanted to punch you plenty of times. But that's over now. Consider me your friend."

"Thank you. I will."

When the dance ended, she gave Peter a kiss on his cheek.

Next up, it was Allison's turn. "I wanted this to be my wedding, but in spite of things not working out, I want to wish you and Anya the best, Peter."

"Thank you, Allison. I don't want bad feelings between us. I was amazed at how nice Megan acted. She told me she's my friend now. I think I'll wait to see how things play out before I fully accept that proposition."

"Well, I'm your friend too. If there is anything I can ever do, please let me know. This was such a great wedding."

"Thanks. I've got my mom to thank for that. She did so much in so little time. It tickles me seeing how happy Mariska is. She's trying to dance with every male at the party. I'll need to give her a whirl too."

Allison laughed. "I like her a lot. She's picked up quite a few English words. The women had so much fun last night. It was an impromptu bachelorette party, but a tame one. I was happy to be a part of it."

"I'm not surprised."

"Has it dawned on you yet that you're a husband?"

"Probably not, but I'm optimistic."

"You got the right girl for you. She loves you, in spite of that other stuff. It took her a little time to realize it and get her bearings."

"I'll never be Jeff."

"So what? If she wanted Jeff, she'd be traveling out west with him."

"Honestly, that was a trauma for me to go through. At this point, I'm not going to look a gift horse in the mouth."

"Put it behind you. Don't let those worries come back to haunt you. She's your wife."

"Yeah, baby." Peter raised his fist in triumph.

Allison laughed and hugged him. She also gave him a kiss on his cheek.

As he danced next with Mariska, she was enthralled. "I have son now," she managed to utter.

"I have two moms now."

Mariska hugged him. "You are a good boy."

"I try."

It was a festive gala and fun was had by all. Peter limited his alcohol to just the champagne toast. He didn't want to be trashed for his wedding night, knowing he didn't do well with alcohol.

His first night with his bride was in a motel room before an early departure for the airport for a flight to Hawaii for the two-week honeymoon. In the room alone with his new wife, Peter stood awkwardly at how to start the intimate moment. Anya looked at him, eyes wide open, for this smoldering emotional event.

"Come, Peter," she whispered. She dropped her wedding dress, after he helped unfasten her back hooks. For Peter, it was a miracle: a goddess was all his. Like she had read his mind, he was further surprised she wore robin's egg blue undergarments, his favorite. Like most young men, he'd perused magazine ads.

Consummating the marital union was beyond his wildest dreams. Continuing the reverie on the islands, the entire two weeks was his dream-come-true. It passed too fast, and soon the honeymoon was over.

Before they boarded the plane to fly back home, Anya already sensed she was pregnant.

Several weeks later, back at home, when she took the test kit into the bathroom and Peter heard her gasp, he rushed in.

"Anya, what's wrong? Are you okay?"

"I'm pregnant." She had a look of distress.

"I'm going to be a dad!" he exclaimed. "Yes!" He pumped his fists in the air.

"You're happy?"

"Of course I'm happy."

Her distressed look gradually melted away. "I thought you would not like this."

"Anya, having kids is one of my biggest dreams."

"Okay." She smiled. "Then I can be happy too."

#

Their married life started out residing in his parents' house for the summer, except now Anya stayed in his bedroom with him. The moms were ecstatic at the news of an impending grandchild.

George took Peter aside. "Son, your life will change forever. It's too bad you didn't have a year or so to ease into the marriage and get your bearings, but having a child is okay. Obviously, we'll help however we can."

"Thanks, Dad. We didn't really talk about it. I guess I should have. It was kind of…overwhelming, being with her. I got lost in the wave of passion."

"Women will do that to us. They're treasures without measure."

"I see that. Now I wonder how I could have lived without this love before."

"At any rate, I'll tell you things from my experiences, but each couple is unique. To an extent, you'll need to forge your own way."

"I can't be around Anya without wanting to grab her in a hug."

"I know that feeling. I still want to grab your mom in my arms. You realize you'll need to do a lot of the heavy lifting. She'll be due late March or early April, so obviously it's in the middle of the semester."

"I've thought about that. I can take care of the baby while she studies. We won't skip a beat."

"It's good to be optimistic, but things don't always go as planned."

"I'll be ready."

"Okay, Peter. We'll see."

#

During the summer, Peter felt much better. Anya's feelings seemed to be genuine, and she treated him like he'd dreamed of. It was an idyllic time, doubly so because the parents could share in the joy. It was the proverbial honeymoon period. Anya was receptive and hands-on with him, a rarity in Peter's experiences with her.

Peter contacted the school about moving into married housing, and was fortunate an apartment came open. They got furniture, including a crib, and started moving things in at the first possible moment after the cleaning crew left.

It was bittersweet when summer recess ended and they returned to school to start fall semester. For Anya, to take on the role of wife was an adjustment. Making breakfast in the morning, domestic chores, sandwiched around studying, hit her as cold reality.

Peter saw it and tried to cope, doing plenty of the chores, including the cooking. This helped ease Anya's angst somewhat, but she still craved her own "me" time, often going to visit girlfriends back at the dorm. Giving up her old life completely was more of a challenge for her than for him.

#

Going to classes in the fall, Anya started to show. She acted somewhat self-conscious, like her looks were now reprehensible. In spite of the fact she was one of those women who carried a child effortlessly, and from the rear didn't even look to be pregnant, her feelings were the same.

Peter did his best to go with the flow, doing more and more of the mundane chores. Her moods remained, however. Finally, he called his mother.

She chuckled. "You don't need to explain, Peter. I already know. I went through it. When a woman is pregnant, her hormones go crazy. I'm sure you've seen it in a lot of different areas."

"That's true. Some of it is really good, but this other side—wow. I'm at a loss most of the time as to what to do."

"That's not a problem, son."

"I'm sorry if I sound wimpy. I don't want to do the wrong thing."

"You're doing just fine, Peter."

"Thanks, Mom."

Chapter Fifteen

They took a drive home for the holidays, first for Thanksgiving and later for Christmas. With her moods, Anya did better in the presence of the moms.

Peter left them talking in the kitchen, heading for the den, where George was watching sports.

"Hey, Peter. How are you?"

"Basically, I'm tapped out, sleep-deprived; however, you want to say it, Dad. I thought I was on an emotional roller coaster before. Anya is all over the map. This is crazy."

George smiled. "I remember. Women become these strange creatures for nine months. It's a wild ride. It gets better after the birth."

"I hope so. I try to do every possible chore in the house, but it doesn't seem to matter to her. She heads out the door a lot to visit her girlfriends back at the dorm. Is it that possible pregnant wives actually come to hate their husbands?"

"I know, Peter. It's a helpless feeling: like they'll criticize us, no matter what we do."

"I know that feeling very well."

"All that you can do is to hang in there and keep an even keel."

"That's easier said than done. I half expect her to hold a pillow over my face in the night."

"I don't think you're in any danger."

"We'll see. If you call and I no longer answer my cell, you'll know she pulled the trigger."

George laughed.

The women came to the door. Edith spoke. "Let me guess: you're commiserating over your terrible trials. We women would be happy to let you carry the babies and see how you do."

Anya smiled smugly at Peter. He returned a rueful smile. She walked over to sit down beside her husband. With that simple gesture, it was the nicest she'd been to him in a while.

Edith spoke, "One more trimester, Peter. Are you ready to be a dad?"

"I am, actually. I look forward to it."

"There is a lot involved in caring for a baby."

"No doubt, but I've got Anya to tell me what to do right. I won't pretend I have a clue."

Mariska chuckled, and then Edith laughed. Anya gave him a playful punch.

Mother and daughter exchanged words in Russian, and then Anya hugged Peter.

"We will have a child, husband."

"I can't wait."

#

The tone of the vacation gave Peter hope for better days. When the families gathered to open presents under the Christmas tree, Peter gave his wife a spoof gift, a T-shirt featuring the words *Baby Enclosed*, with arrows pointing inward on all four sides. It tickled Anya.

It generated a laugh from the family and servants. It was a long-standing Brown family practice to include gifts for the staff. Anya was showered with lavish gifts, as was Mariska. It was amazing for Peter to look at this vibrant, healthy version of that emaciated, sickly woman he first met back in Russia. She was recovered both in body and in spirit, a happy addition to the family, her fatal fate averted. It was a miracle of modern science.

#

After the wonderful family time, while riding back to school, Anya announced, "I've decided to take full courses this summer and next summer, so I can graduate early. Is that okay with you?"

"Whatever you want is fine with me, darling. Is there a reason to speed things up?"

"I'm anxious to start a career and earn money of my own. I've been beholden all of my life. Do you understand?"

"Not exactly. We're going to be set financially."

"I know that. It isn't my point that we won't have enough money. What I'm saying is for my own sense of worth and achievement, I want to make my own mark."

"I think I see what you're saying."

"It's a strong motivation for me, Peter."

"I believe you."

"If I can build up my own money, I can start to do some things for the people who have done so much for me. Your parents are wealthy, but that doesn't mean I can't gift them."

"True."

"One other thing: I have a new friend. I will bring her over to meet you. Her name is Kiala Amiguay, and she's from Jamaica. We hit it off because we're both foreign to this country. I like her very much and she likes me. I can tell her things unique to us and she understands. She goes through it too, being the eternal foreigner."

"Okay. You don't need my permission when it comes to having friends. You don't need my permission about anything. We're equals in all things."

Anya smiled and hugged him. "You're too good to me."

"That's true."

"Hey!" She slugged him playfully.

#

The winter semester was another tester for Peter, however. In spite of the good feelings from the holiday, Anya's moodiness returned quickly, and again frequently she liked to visit away.

She followed through in bringing Kiala for her introduction right away. Kiala had the expected Jamaican accent, and her light skin accurately implied her mixed-race heritage in Peter's mind, which was a nonfactor for a man with liberal beliefs.

"Hello, Peter. Anya has told me so much about you and your lovely family. I'm so happy to have this chance to meet you."

"I'm happy to meet you too, Kiala. You're very pretty, if you don't mind my saying. Elegant is the word that comes to mind."

"My father is Jamaican and my mother is from England. I think she was a beauty contestant back there."

"You definitely got good genes."

Kiala chuckled. "I want to say congratulations on your coming child."

"Thank you; it will be a great event."

Anya added, "It's so refreshing to have a friend who knows and lives my difficult path, not being from America. I love Christy, but some things she doesn't get, Kiala knows. It's very gratifying to be with her. She's taught me so much in the little time we've known each other. Maybe she's a kindred spirit. We're very close."

"I can see that. I'm happy you have nice girls like her in your life, Anya."

"She's a year ahead of us. If I go both summers to graduate early, we might be able to go to work at the same company."

"Oh…well, I guess you've got a plan."

"We've been exploring opportunities as marketing reps."

"I didn't know you were interested in that. It's a job dealing with the public."

"I know. I'm not afraid—I'm gaining in self-confidence. As I said, I want to make my mark."

"What is your career goal, Peter?" Kiala asked.

"Accounting. After I graduate, I must do a year working for a CPA before I can take the CPA exam. I'll probably look around this city for an office to fulfill that process. After I get my CPA, I can look at where I want to go. Dad suggested I think about opening my own office."

Kiala smiled, glancing at Anya. "Peter, Anya and I talk about travel and adventure, at least in the beginning. Marketing jobs can be lucrative with the right companies."

"I've heard that, Kiala," Anya added, turning her smiling face from Kiala back to Peter. "I know we haven't talked about this, Peter. Is the idea of me traveling for work a problem for you?"

"If that's what you want, I'll cope."

"You see, Kiala. He's a perfect husband."

"He is. I agree. You make me jealous."

"Well, honey, we're going to go back to her dorm. I'll see you later."

"Okay."

He was in bed, asleep, by the time Anya returned.

In the mornings, Peter had taken on making breakfast. Anya tended to be slower to get out of bed. Additionally, soon he was cleaning the apartment, doing laundry, and the other mundane chores to spare her. She acceded to his kindnesses and soon it was their routine for him to do the bulk of the household work and laundry, as well as grocery shopping and the other errands. It was the polar opposite of his former favored life at the Brown estate.

Halfway through the semester, on April Fool's Day, sitting in class, Anya's water broke and she was rushed to the hospital. Receiving notice from Kiala, after calling his parents to make the long drive, he hurried to the hospital in town. By the time he walked into the lobby, it was over. They sent him upstairs to the nursing station.

"Congratulations, Mr. Brown. You have a new baby daughter."

"Wow. That was fast."

"Some women pop them out really quickly. Come this way."

Anya was asleep in her room. The nurse led him a little farther down the hall and pointed out his child through the viewing window. Peter could only see tiny hands and feet flailing in the air.

"My God, I'm a dad."

"You are."

"Can I wait in Anya's room?"

"Of course. Do you have a name for the baby?"

"I'll need to ask my wife."

When he sat down in a chair, Anya opened her eyes. "Did you see her?"

"Just through the window, but only her hands and feet."

"Are you happy?"

He got up to embrace her. "Thank you so much, honey. I couldn't be happier."

"I must say, it's so good to have it over with. I can lie on my belly finally."

"They asked about a name. Did you have one in mind?"

"My grandmother's name was Elsa, my mother's mother. Could you live with that?"

"Sure. What about a middle name?"

"You choose."

"Okay. Elsa Magellan."

It made her chuckle. "Oh, Peter, don't make me laugh; it still hurts."

"Sorry. How about Elsa Marie?"

"That's fine."

He went to the nursing station to tell them there.

"We'll get the paperwork taken care of right away. Elsa Marie Brown."

#

Hours later, the parents arrived. Mariska rushed over to embrace her daughter, and a lengthy Russian conversation ensued. Next, they all went to the window to view Elsa.

"Mama would be happy," Mariska said.

"We're grandmothers," Edith said. "Can you believe it?"

"It seems like yesterday when I carried my baby Anya home."

"I feel the same way." She gave Peter a hug.

George stood by, smiling at the baby.

"What do you think, Dad?"

"I think your life has changed forever, but that's not a bad thing."

Next, the nurses advised Anya's friends were showing up.

"What would you like to do?" the head nurse asked.

"If Anya says she's up to it, I have no problem."

Seeing Megan again, Allison, and also Ron troop into the room to hug Anya, it was a strange twist after so much prior drama with them. Kiala was particularly affectionate, which pleased Anya. Kiala spoke at length with her and then with the parents. Christy and Bob were next to appear, adding their congratulations. For Peter, Bob was still like a brother.

Peter led the succession of visitors down to the nursery window to view Elsa. By now the nurses had moved her so they could get a better view. Peter saw her face for the first time.

When they brought her into the room for the first time, Peter understood what his dad had told him about true love. This tiny being was the dearest thing in the universe to Peter at that moment.

The nurse spoke to Anya. "If you're going to breastfeed, she needs her first meal."

"Yes, I am. Eh..."

"We'll go." The parents left, taking the visitors with them.

Peter looked at the nurse. "Am I supposed to leave too?"

The nurse chuckled. "It's up to your wife. Ask her."

Anya was enchanted, holding her child for the first time.

"I can go if you want, Anya."

She looked at him like he was an idiot. "Peter, you can stay. You're her dad."

"I didn't want to come across as a perv."

Anya and the nurse laughed. "Peter, you're always a nut."

"I'll be back later to get Elsa."

"Thank you, ma'am."

Peter sat on the side of the bed. Elsa made little baby sounds, and it warmed his heart.

"I'll help with everything, Anya."

She opened her eyes. "I know you will. Everything will be fine."

#

Taking mother and baby home from the hospital to their tiny on-campus apartment, Elsa got her first experience testing out the crib. The grandparents got rooms at a nearby motel and came over every day to help out. They stayed while Peter and Anya returned to their classes during the day. Anya filled bottles to leave in the fridge during the day for Elsa's feedings.

They stayed for over a month, until Anya advised, "I feel Elsa has grown enough we can use the day care next door."

"Are you sure?" Edith asked. "We don't mind staying."

"We're going to need to get into our routine sooner or later."

"I understand. Don't be strangers with coming to visit us. You've got precious cargo now."

"We will."

For the remainder of the semester, Anya received considerable traffic coming to visit her and the baby. Kiala was the most frequent visitor, although Bob and Christy came a great deal too.

Peter noticed it first: the ring on Christy's finger. "Hey. Congrats, you guys."

"I decided to stop being a chicken and I pulled the trigger," Bob explained. "As I see Elsa, I can't wait to start our own family."

"That will be after we graduate, are married, and have jobs," Christy added.

"Of course, dear."

"Hi, Kiala," Christy said.

"Hello, Christy."

Peter noted the direct looks. He wondered, *Is Christy jealous, like Kiala has stolen her friend?*

Kiala continued to dominate Anya's time. Peter was the one who dropped off Elsa in the morning and picked her up at night. He also took on many of the baby chores, the bottle, diapers, and bathing.

Anya told him, "I must go to the library to study. I need quiet to retain the knowledge. I can't learn when Elsa is fussing."

"Okay. I'll handle it here."

Subsequently, he learned to read his text and hold Elsa at the same time.

#

The week before finals, he came home with Elsa one evening to find Anya sitting with a stern look on her face.

"What's wrong?"

"I'm pregnant again."

"I…eh…you don't seem very happy about it."

"I just got done with this and now I'm back in that way? You don't understand, but you never do."

"Anya, it won't be a problem. I'll take care of them, our kids."

"That's not the point. Pregnancy is no fun, walking around all swollen and in discomfort."

"I'm sorry."

"After this baby, I'm going to take birth control pills."

"Okay."

To avoid an argument, he went to the fridge to get a bottle for Elsa. Anya said nothing and was in a dismal mood the rest of the evening.

Before bedtime, still in a sour mood, she commented, "I'm still going to follow my plans. I'm going to school both summers to graduate early and then Kiala and I are going to get jobs together."

"I never said otherwise. I told you, I'll handle it here."

#

The second trip down this path of heading for a sibling for Elsa was more challenging than the first. Anya didn't seem disposed to "forgive" him for knocking her up a second time.

When she was home, usually it meant Kiala was there too, if they weren't away at the library, or wherever else they chose to go. Peter's life was consumed with handling the chores and then fitting in his own studies. A social life with his wife gradually went to the back burner, seemingly by her choice.

Going straight into her summer school courses, her focus was there. Peter was left with his proverbial rolling with the punches.

His only respite all summer was when Anya agreed to a weekend visit home. Again, back at the Brown estate, her behavior changed completely, like they were star-crossed lovers. Suddenly, she couldn't put Elsa down.

Peter opted to say nothing and let her portray her ruse.

However, George pulled him aside. "Peter, I get the strong impression all is not well."

"Please don't say anything. Anya has been angry I got her pregnant again so soon. If there's more to it than that, I'm not sure. She announced she's staying on track to graduate early and head off into the world, to a career with Kiala."

"Maybe there are issues from her past that drive her."

"She wants to be her own person, and I guess that means not being saddled down as a housewife pushing out kids. I never meant for her to be that, but she doesn't seem to care to hear what I have to say. Mostly she makes pronouncements, with no discussion."

George shook his head.

"Dad, this Anya you see here now, it's like she has dual personalities. I sure don't see this version at home. I've researched post-partum issues in women, but Anya takes it to a new level, like she despises us."

"Don't worry; I'll keep this private, son. I can play the game too. We're here for you."

"I'll handle this. This marriage isn't going the way I anticipated, but at least I'll have gotten a couple of kids out of her."

As he anticipated, the women spent most of their time together, fawning over the baby and talking. The men mostly stayed in the den.

On the drive back home, Anya dozed off to sleep while Elsa was safe, resting in the baby seat in the back. Peter pondered many things, including implementing his own career plans, regardless of the childcare challenge.

It was a quiet ride, as neither of them awoke until he parked in front of the apartment.

Once they unpacked, Peter sat down on the sofa holding Elsa. She stared into his eyes, like she was deep in thought also.

"Hi, baby girl. I'm your daddy."

She smiled slightly and made some cooing sounds, moving her arms and legs. Meanwhile, Anya got on her phone in the bedroom, talking with Kiala. She closed the door.

#

Fall term was more of the same. When Anya left in the morning, Peter didn't see her until evening, and sometimes very late.

"I'm sorry, but I just can't study here."

He always shrugged, as there was nothing else he could do anyway. Having an argument with his wife was the last thing he wanted. Meanwhile, another baby grew in Anya's belly, and she never came to terms with it. Peter tried to compensate, taking on virtually every chore. He got up in the night if Elsa woke up and cried. Anya didn't fight his decisions, ceding all of the menial tasks to him. However, her moods and behaviors remained difficult for Peter, no matter what he did. Walking around in a trance, sleep-deprived, Peter coped as best he could, but it was very difficult for him. Giving up even attempting to hug his wife, he couldn't be sure she noticed.

#

It happened Peter varied his routine one noontime and went to the student union for lunch. This was where he'd first talked to Anya, so the place had some warm memories. She was there having her lunch with Kiala, Ron, and several other students he didn't know.

Her table was full. Quickly dismissing the idea of going over, just as he started to turn away, she spotted him. He waved, gave a perfunctory forced smile, and then went to the farthest possible table away from them he could find. Facing away from them, he never looked back to see her reaction.

If she took it as a proverbial line drawn in the sand, he wasn't sure he cared at this point. His old feelings of unfairness had resurrected.

Ironically, Allison showed up at that moment. "Is this seat taken?"

"Yes. All of my friends are here—can't you see them?"

She smiled and sat down. "So, she's there; you're here. What does that mean: a fight at home?"

"Hardly, I'm a lover; not a fighter."

"Knowing you like I do; I suspect you've got an axe to grind. Jeff is long gone, so what now?"

"I don't want to talk about it."

"You need to talk about it. Don't let these things fester."

"At this point, it seems my presence isn't required in her life. She can't wait to hustle out the door every day to her real life."

"Do you understand you've made her pregnant for much of her college years? That's not the norm for girls, Peter."

"I realize that. She's going to take care of that problem after this next birth with pills. Meanwhile, apparently I need to pay a price for my part in her life."

"Are you upset she expects you to help out?"

"Not at all, I love my daughter more than life itself. I really don't mind doing things at home."

"So, what's really the problem for you?"

"Do you have a week to listen?"

"I think you've never bought into that she loves you. That jealousy thing of yours has just taken a different form."

"It does seem Kiala is surgically attached to Anya, but if she has friends, that's not a problem. I like Kiala."

"Really? Because it seems like it's a problem. I heard Christy kind of got her nose out of joint, with Kiala taking her place. I think you're feeling the same thing."

"If I am, so what?"

"Christy isn't married to Anya like you are. They're just friends. You're so much more in her life, though you don't seem to realize it. It's just my opinion, but are you sure it's a good idea for you to be so passive? Whatever she says, you just buy into it."

"Allison, I don't need more drama. I couldn't convince Anya to take me in the first place. She had to decide that on her own. That's how I approach this. She's focused on this career idea and that seems to include just Kiala. So…well, whatever."

Allison shook her head. "You're treading on a bumpy road. Do whatever you want, but remember: I'm here for you."

He eyed her pensively. It caused Allison to smile.

"Allison, I never get you."

"I realize that." Allison chuckled.

He held up his finger to display his wedding ring. Allison laughed. "I know, Peter. I was there. Things don't always work out as you expect though, do they?"

"Let's change the subject."

"It won't solve itself." She looked over. Anya was staring at them from across the room. Peter gave her a thumbs-up signal. Anya wasn't amused.

A little later, she walked over, along with Kiala and Ron.

"Hello, Allison."

"Hi, Anya. We saw you had a full table over there."

"Did you enjoy your lunch, Peter?" she remarked coolly.

"I did, actually. Allison was a pleasant lunch partner. How was your lunch with your friends?"

"It was very nice also."

"Well, that's a good thing."

Kiala eyed him coolly, while Ron had an amused smile. She patted Anya's back like she was aggrieved.

"So…I guess I'll see you tonight, ma'am?"

"You will, sir."

They walked away. Just like the first time, Anya was showing, but from the back a person couldn't tell it. She was still beautiful, and still his wife. It evoked his warm feelings for an instant.

"So, are you ready to hit it, Allison? I've got to get to class."

"Thanks, Peter, it's always entertaining spending time with you."

#

Anya came home early, for her. Peter had taken care of feeding Elsa, as he always did, and had eaten his own brief meal. They seldom ate supper together these days.

"I'll give Elsa her bath tonight. Thank you for all of the things you do."

"You're welcome. I don't mind doing them. You're the one stuck carrying the babies."

"I think I'm not what you expected."

"I don't believe I had expectations."

They both looked over. Elsa was trying to color, muttering little sounds, like it was work. It made them smile.

Anya continued, "I know you're not happy with me."

"You're wrong. However, I will say I suspect you have all of these flaws you hold against me. Perhaps you need to take a look at your own shortcomings too. I'm trying my best here." It didn't come out well but his frustration emerged.

"Are you sorry about getting married?"

"Of course not. The question is, are *you* sorry?"

"I think waiting to have babies might have been a good idea."

"I'm fine with it. I'll make this work. So what if I like our sex life? So sue me."

Anya smirked. "I'm not saying we shouldn't be together like that. I like it too."

"That's good news."

"I'll take care of Elsa tonight, so you can study."

Peter shrugged passively. His feelings were roiling his gut, so he changed topic. "By the way, since we haven't been able to jog together for quite a while, I've been pushing Elsa in her stroller while I run. I assume you have no problem with that."

"Oh…no. That's fine. The girls, we all go together to the women's IM building for daily workouts."

"Great."

She eyed him, curious if there was a complaint in there somewhere. He felt his defensive juices start to flow and spoke to head off a poor remark.

"Anya, do your thing with your girls. Elsa and I have things covered back here."

She muttered something in Russian, picked up Elsa, and headed for the baby bath.

#

The summer passed quickly enough, and soon it was time for him to return to classes also. The first time dropping off Elsa at the daycare was murder. Up to that time, she was in his presence nearly every minute. If he had errands around town, Elsa went with him. She was six months old now, and aware of many more things.

When she cried, he wavered, but there was no other choice. He rushed home that evening and found her playing happily with the other children. The attendant commented, "They make a big show, but the minute the door closes, they grab some toys and off they go. She'll be fine."

Anya got home much later, after her workout.

"What are you cooking? It smells good."

"I had a roast simmering in the Crock-Pot all day, along with potatoes and carrots. It's ready, so we can sit down to eat if you're hungry."

Anya went over to embrace Elsa. "Hi, baby. How is Mama's little girl?"

Peter tried to hide his chuckle when Anya was rewarded by a burp and an "urp" on her blouse.

"Sorry. I just fed her. I should have warned you. Put your blouse in the laundry. I'm doing a load tonight anyway."

"I'm not helpless, Peter."

She went into the bedroom. Peter placed the meal on the table.

Coming back out, she was in jeans and a sweatshirt. Peter spoke his prayer and they spooned food onto their plates.

"You look pretty, Anya."

"Not tonight."

"I didn't mean that."

"You always mean that."

He started a retort, but thought better of it.

"Peter, I want to say, Kiala and I have been recommended for positions. The end of next summer isn't that far away. We're supposed to fly out for interviews in two weeks."

"Fly out where?"

250

"Don't get angry."

"About what?"

"We're flying to Seattle."

"As in…Jeff's company?" Peter got a glazed-eyed look, like his fears were just proven true, bubbling up and knocking on his door.

"He's doing very well there and said we would do well too. Don't start. We're just going to listen. If things aren't doable, we just fly back home."

"How did…well, whatever."

"See—this is why I have trouble telling you things. You get upset at nothing."

"Did you think Elsa and I would migrate to Washington State?"

"It's something we can talk about. If I understand it correctly, there would be travel in the job, so I'd usually be other places anyway. I'll know more after the interview."

"Okay. It's your choice. It sounds like your mind is made up."

"Peter, it's such a perfect opportunity for a career where we can flourish. I can accomplish so many personal goals. Do you understand how it is for me? My life has been dependent on your money and your family. I want to have my own money to be able to do things. I want to go to different new places and see the sights."

It was a difficult moment for him on so many levels. Her travel goals seemingly didn't include her family.

She smiled playfully. "We can be together tonight."

"You think you can buy me off with sex?"

"Yes."

"Well, that's true, but, in spite of it, this is a tough one to swallow."

"I know it's hard for you. I'm sure we can adjust to make things work out."

There was no answer for him, so he opened his textbook. Anya left him there to go take care of their daughter.

#

Ongoing for the remainder of the time before her trip, Anya was agog at the idea, the lure of a new job in her future, and seemingly undeterred by any geographic consequences. She drove her car with Kiala to the airport for their flight west.

"I'll call you to let you know we got there safely."

"Have a good trip." He waited for her to hug him and then to receive his perfunctory kiss on the cheek. From his viewpoint, it had the feel of a huge omen in his life. Her exuberance further irked him, though he remained quiet about it.

Depression set in for Peter. Even though Anya tended to be away frequently, she was always at home at night. Going to bed alone was distressing. When he got into bed, he'd patted her pillow, but that accomplished nothing in assuaging his lonely feelings.

He was reading a book in bed when she called.

"I'm sorry it's so late, Peter. With the time difference, I forgot. We had a nice dinner; Jeff treated us to the meal. We talked, and it's staggering the amount of money he makes. The bonus part of the compensation package is astounding. There will be a high probability I make as much as ten thousand a month to start. He said the selling piece has been very easy. Getting the job seems to be just a formality. Kiala and I are 'fired up,' as you say."

"Great."

She didn't miss his unenthusiastic tone. "Okay, Peter. I'll let you go. We'll see you in a few days. Remember, our Sunday flight is very late. It isn't necessary for you to wait up."

"Bye."

#

Saturday morning, he got Elsa up for her bath and her breakfast.

"It's you and me, baby girl. We're going to have a great day today. We drive home to see the grandparents for the day and then drive back home after church tomorrow. How 'bout dem apples?"

Cooing, Elsa smiled at him, kicking her feet and waving her hands.

Having no reason to wait around, he loaded her into the car seat and departed right away. During the long drive, Elsa dozed off, so Peter had plenty of time to think. That wasn't always a good thing, with his propensity to look at his life negatively. There were so many possibilities he could see as troubling. *Anya is my wife, but do I 'get' her?* he mused. Forever it seemed he was scratching his head, trying to figure out one issue after another.

Inevitably, the thought of Jeff popped in his mind. Peter scowled. He seemed to be the eternal threat looming on the horizon. "Dammit," he muttered.

#

Arriving home was a balm, as the grandmas hugged him and took custody of Elsa. Peter followed them into the kitchen briefly before going with his father to the den.

"No Anya?"

"She's away this weekend. She and Kiala have a job interview."

"What aren't you saying?"

"It's an interview in Seattle."

"Oh, that's where Jeff went to work."

"Apparently he recommended them to his bosses and they pretty much have the jobs out there."

"So, are you going to relocate?"

"That's a remote possibility, but her job involves a great deal of travel. I'm thinking I open an accounting office, but somewhere around here."

"She's okay with living apart?" George frowned.

"That would seem to be the case. I'll take care of Elsa, no problem."

"I thought there might be some bumps in the road for you, but I didn't see this coming."

"Nor did I. As I told Bob, at least I've gotten some kids out of her. That's something."

"This stirs up all of your old fears."

"Of course it does. Whatever suddenly drove her to me, I'll never know, but apparently, it's no longer an issue. I suspect there's a great deal going on with my wife that I don't know and not in a positive way for me."

"There are innocent explanations for all of it. Maybe she really does want to establish her own footprint. She's lived in our long shadow since day one. I can understand to an extent. Do you trust your wife?"

Before he could answer, the women appeared, Edith carrying Elsa.

Edith said, "Somebody misses her daddy!"

Peter smiled at his daughter. "Hi, pumpkin, are you being a good girl?"

Smiling back at him, she put out her arms and he took her for an embrace. The men dropped the discussion at that point, as involving the moms didn't seem a good idea.

The following day, Elsa was a hit at church, with numerous women fawning over her.

"Peter, she's an angel," he heard frequently.

"Sometimes," he replied. "She has her moments."

His drive home was similar to the drive in. He had time to think, though this time rather than conjuring up the boogeyman, he went into his problem-solving mode. "Okay, Anya," he muttered. "I'm not moving out west. Neither is our daughter. I will cope. You're not going to crush me with this."

He made a point of going to bed early. He made her suggestion he not wait up into a reality. Waking the next morning to find her asleep in bed beside him, cautiously getting out of bed, he crept out of the bedroom to take care of Elsa. He was feeding her when Anya came out, sleepy-eyed and yawning.

When Peter didn't immediately look at her, she felt the need to explain.

"Our flight was delayed, so I didn't get much sleep. Peter, we got job offers. As long as we maintain our grades and graduate on schedule, we go to work. I get a generous base salary and then bonuses based on what we sell. Also, there is a nice signing bonus. Jeff is incredibly successful and will train us how to prosper. I didn't expect such a favorable weekend."

"That's great." He gave her his best crocodile smile.

"You're angry at me."

"No. I fully support you and your career goals. When have I ever stood in the way of any of your choices, career or otherwise?"

She frowned. "I thought you would have a big argument."

"Sorry to disappoint you. I'll handle it, like I always have. One thing, though. I've decided I'm not migrating out west. I like this area and I'm going to stick around here. Our children will have their grandparents in their lives."

Anya looked sad at his announcement and decision.

"Don't take that wrong. I'm not judging your choices, but I have the right to my own choices." He tried to sound conciliatory, not wanting to start an argument and play into her hands. If she wanted to paint him as unfair and arbitrary, he wasn't going to cooperate. In truth, he was perturbed, but he refused to give her fuel for discord.

Chapter Sixteen

After the conversation, Anya acted even more schizophrenic in that some days she was home doting over Elsa and other days she was gone until late with no real explanation.

For Peter, it was more of the same. She was plugged into her social circle during the day, and often in the evenings. If he wanted to see her, he could go for lunch at the union and she would be there with the usual suspects. Ron was always on one side of her and Kiala on the other. Peter never opted to eat with them. The best he would do was a walk-by out in public, greeting her like she was a neighbor or a casual acquaintance.

Meanwhile time marched on, and Anya swelled with baby number two. Thanksgiving and Christmas at home were nearly identical to the prior year, except this time Peter had Elsa to cherish.

As Elsa's first birthday approached, so did Anya's delivery date. She headed for the hospital just days before the planned birthday party. This time the grandparents were in town for the birth.

Peter stood at the nursery window again, holding Elsa in his arms. "There's your little sister."

The baby looked just like Elsa had, flailing her tiny arms and legs. Edith hugged them both: her son and granddaughter, glancing through the viewing glass with them.

"Anya does make pretty babies," Peter muttered. Edith chuckled.

Eventually, he went back to Anya's room. Mariska was talking with her, and the two were smiling.

"You've got another beauty queen on your hands, madam."

"Are you happy?"

"Is that a trick question?"

Everybody laughed.

"Mama," Elsa said.

Peter huffed in mock anger. "Hey, I bust my butt for Elsa and she says mama? What's that about?"

"Poor baby," Edith replied.

"Did you have a name in mind, Anya?"

"You can choose this time."

"Okay. I'll go with Emily Jane."

"I like it."

#

This time when Anya came out of the hospital with Emily, the grandparents opted to stay longer to help. They got rooms at the same nearby motel and spent entire days at the apartment. It was very helpful to Peter. Anya made an effort to be around far more with the parents in town. Still, Kiala was present virtually every day, coming to the apartment and exclaiming over Emily. Later, when the parents finally returned home, Kiala graduated at the end of spring semester and went out to Seattle to start her job. Per their plans, Anya would join her after summer semester.

With Kiala gone during the summer semester, surprisingly Allison stepped in to fill the void, joining Anya and Ron for their lunches. Peter went seldom, as he had two children to care for now. Regardless, Anya kept in contact, talking on the phone with Kiala nearly every day. When she seamlessly ceded all of the childcare and household chores to Peter, he never objected. Again, his benevolent acts didn't change Anya's behavior.

The summer seemed to fly past and soon Anya took her last final exam. She didn't wait for the test scores to come in. She boarded a plane westward the very next day.

"I'm sorry, Peter. They want me to start training right away to catch up to Kiala. She has a big head start."

"Sure. That's understandable."

"Are you okay with this?"

"It's a little late to ask. Go—this is what you want. I'll take care of the girls. We'll be fine."

"Thank you, Peter. I love you."

"Goodbye, Anya." She didn't miss the finality in his tone, or the lack of his return "I love you." Her eyes started to tear up, but she had a flight to catch.

He turned away to go to his daughters without a hug or parting kiss for his wife. In his mind, these precious babies were his life now.

When she called later to let him know she'd arrived, he let it go to voicemail. It was childish on his part, but he felt angry and provoked. "Have a nice life, and say hi to Jeff for me," he groused petulantly. His wife was gone, and there was nothing he could do about it.

#

Settling in to make new routines going forward, he struggled initially with childcare for two little ones while trying simultaneously to handle his senior-level college courses.

In the middle of fall term, he was getting dinner ready for the girls when he heard a rap on his door.

When he opened it, Allison smiled. "Hi, Peter. Can I come in?"

"Okay. I was trying to get some food into my two little monsters."

"Oh, can I help?"

"I guess. I'm working on Em; she can be stubborn. If you want to tackle Elsa, have at it. You might need a shower curtain and a garden hose, though."

Allison laughed heartily.

He continued, "It always amazes me how she can get food in her hair."

"Peter, your daughters are wonderful."

At that moment, Elsa tried to operate a knife and fork simultaneously. Both utensils flipped onto the floor, along with her plate and the remnants of her meal.

"Uh-oh," she said, looking down at the spill.

"Uh-oh is right, madam. I told you Daddy will help you cut your food."

"Dada," she replied.

"That's me."

"You're a perfect father," Allison said. "You're so patient and loving. It shows up in your girls."

"I don't know about that."

"I do. So how are you holding up with Anya gone?"

"You do what you must. There's no other choice. I don't like it, but she has her focus elsewhere. I've got my girls. We're doing fine."

"Peter, listen. I want you to allow me to be your friend. You can't wall off an entire side of your life. You're a young man, a good man, and you deserve better. Christy and I are appalled at how selfish Anya is acting. That's not even talking about the other background issues."

"What are you talking about?"

"All of a sudden she's got to have Kiala in her grill constantly, and then there is Jeff, lurking nearby and sniffing around."

"Don't start. I don't want to hear it. I'm not going to assume the worst."

"I'm not saying she's making bad choices, but just in case, you need to have a Plan B ready."

"Do I? Is this your Plan B, Allison? I have no problem with your friendship, but if it means you constantly stirring the pot, I don't need it. I can manage."

"Does she even call you now?"

"I said enough."

"Okay, but I'm going to look out for you, since you don't seem to be willing to do it."

She started to clean up Elsa's spill, and then Elsa.

After dinner, Allison stayed. "I brought books so we can have a study date."

"Okay, but you stay over there."

Allison laughed. "What are you afraid of?"

"What do you think?"

"What do you think Anya is doing this very minute?"

"Allison, I warned you."

"I'll be good." She didn't act repentant; rather, she smirked, seemingly pleased with herself.

"Somehow I doubt that, ma'am."

She laughed again.

After taking the girls to their beds, it felt odd to Peter, seeing Allison standing in for Anya. Allison was taken with the moment, kissing the girls on their foreheads. Both girls looked at their father. He kissed them too.

They studied for several hours before Peter closed his book and put down his calculator. "I need to crash, Allison. Mornings come early in this house."

She stood and ambled over. Her expression was playful, or perhaps more; Peter wasn't sure.

"Whatever you've got in mind, ma'am, the answer is no."

"You're such a coward."

"Good night, Allison." He ushered her to the door.

"I'll see you again, Peter."

"I have no doubts about that, Allison."

Her question still lingered in his mind. What was Anya doing this very moment? Her calls home had evolved to occasional calls in her morning and leaving a message, since he was in class at the time. Most of those messages extolled her sales exploits and the huge checks she was pulling in and saving. Kiala and Jeff were the main topics, along with various experiences with clients. He didn't return any of the calls as he evolved with the new norm—some might say devolved rather than evolved. He took it as a subtle message from Anya, one of many.

He mused. *Your new life seems to be much better than your old one.*

Elsa was mobile, crawling and taking toddling first steps, while Emily was far more vocal and animated than Elsa had been. However, whatever tests they posed, Peter didn't care. He remained incredibly patient and showered them with his love. His jogs now involved a double child stroller with his little darlings sitting side by side. Em loved to sing out, and she could be loud, like a warning siren the Brown family was coming to any pedestrians in their path.

His daughters' female family was the grandmas. Peter programmed more frequent drives home, and they came to visit him and stayed in the motel.

They received notice from Anya that she and Kiara were flying home for Christmas for a brief visit. Peter had mixed feelings about it. It wasn't that he no longer loved his wife, but there was something in her tone during the call that set off warning bells.

#

Anya walked into the baggage-claim area at the airport, along with Kiala, and went straight to her mom, and then to her daughters.

"Oh, you've grown so much, girls."

Although Elsa was excited, Emily wasn't quite sure who this person was. She had no memory of a mom. She stayed back with her father.

Finally, Anya came over to hug Peter. She looked much changed, dressed glamorously in a pricey sexy dress, an expensive hairstyle, and acting sophisticated. The simple Russian girl seemed long gone, replaced by this new incarnation.

Turning her cheek and leaning in rather than accepting a full hug and kiss, her 'warm' greeting felt more like she was working him, like one of her clients. In response, he made no attempt to embrace her, and he decided to ride with his father and let the women ride together. The girls' car seats were in the men's backseat, as the women's car was full.

"Are you okay, son?"

"I'm not sure what I expected, but I don't know if I'm ready for this. I keep low expectations, but…she seems like a total stranger. Whatever we had, as little as it might have been for her, I seriously think she's moved on."

"I wouldn't draw that conclusion. Don't act badly and make her feel uncomfortable and unwelcome."

"I plan to let her take the lead, Dad. I'll give her all of the rope she needs. We'll see where this goes because this doesn't feel like a family holiday visit to me."

Arriving back at the Brown estate, Peter encountered an unexpected awkward moment when they carried the luggage up to the bedrooms. Anya and Kiala went into the same bedroom before turning to look back at him. He didn't react, instead eyeing them passively.

Standing close together, Anya glanced at Kiala, their eyes locking with some whispered words. After a brief time, she explained to Peter, "Sorry—it's just habit. We share our apartment and travel together."

Peter gave no response as they all stood, at an impasse.

"I'll go next door," Kiala said finally. Anya's hand had been on her side.

Anya glanced at Peter unrepentantly. Overtly he shrugged it off, turned quickly and carried her suitcase into his room. However, his emotions were provoked. Turning, he said, "I know you're not accustomed to having the girls in here to disturb your sleep. If you prefer to sleep over next door with Kiala, it's not a problem for me."

"No, Peter. It's been a long time apart for us." What he noticed wasn't what she said—it was that she wouldn't look at him.

"If you change your mind, just let me know. It's really not a problem." His feelings were not assuaged.

Anya went over to hug her daughters. They both looked at their father like they needed his permission.

Muttering to himself, Peter shook his head and then turned to go back down the stairs. The fact she seemed reluctant around him led him to believe his first impression was right. Seemingly, trouble of some sort was on the horizon.

He happened to notice Anya's purse lying on the bed, open. Edging over to glance in, next to her Russian passport she had an American passport, since she was a citizen after marrying him. It didn't strike him as significant, at that moment.

Anya opted to air her "news" a little later. Sitting down in the formal living room, Peter felt queasy. He decided to seat a daughter on each side of him, in his embrace, like little buffers, leaving Anya to take the floor with Kiala. The parents took various other seats, with all eyes on Anya.

Looking at Peter and then Kiala, she took a deep breath before she began. "I've explained what success we've had in the business. Jeff's expertise in training us has made for a high-competence unit. When we go into an office, we walk out with sales every time. The amount of money we've accumulated is incredible. By the way, Peter, if you need some cash, I've got plenty."

"No. I've got ample money. If you want to send money, I can invest it in funds for you."

"At any rate, the company has been so impressed with our early results they've decided to offer us an opportunity: a big one. They want to send us to Berlin to expand the company footprint into Europe. With my command of Russian, we could be unrivaled there, traveling around the continent."

The pronouncement cast a pall over the room.

"I know this is a difficult idea. Peter, I think I can earn enough money in a short amount of time to be able to leave the field work before too long a time. I know it means we'd be apart again, but as you said, you plan on starting in your job back here."

Everybody turned to face him. With no forewarning, it was another low blow from his perspective, but rather than make a scene in front of his daughters, the two little people he most cared about, he chose a different approach. Now he understood that American passport. Her decision was made long ago, and he had no choice about it. She didn't come here to ask his permission but to put him on notice. His emotions roiled dangerously.

"If you're asking my opinion, it sounds like a fabulous career opportunity, and of course you should advance that career. There's no other choice about it."

She eyed him, his grim expression and terse tone. "I think the company would spring for you to fly over to see me with the girls."

Peter didn't hesitate in his response. "I'm not interested in flying to Europe, and I don't think it would be good for the girls at their young ages. You go ahead and do what you must. We'll hunker down back here, like we always do. They've got their grandmas looking out for them." He kissed the tops of their little heads and hugged them, like drawing a battle line in the sand.

Though understandable for him, it was not what anybody expected from mild-mannered Peter, least of all Anya.

"You don't want to fight this?" She seemed hurt, like she wanted him to demand she come home. Kiala hugged her and looked at Peter like he was suddenly a villain, regardless of her part in engineering this. Now he was irked.

"So, who wants some ice cream?" He ignored his upset wife with the ploy.

The girls squealed, "Me!"

Busying himself with the treat for the girls, he wouldn't allow Anya or Kiala to pin him down for a private "talk."

The grandparents acted subdued and uncomfortable with the tense moment. They also concentrated on the little girls. Anya and Kiala stayed back, watching the proceedings like they weren't a part of them. Their decision had consequences.

Peter and George went into the den later and each decided the occasion called for holiday "cheer." Not much of a drinker, Peter indulged in a bottle of wine. It was a really nice vintage from his father's expensive private collection. The women took care of getting the girls into bed and then came down to join them later. When Peter stayed seated in a single lounge chair, Anya came over to sit down on the floor in front of him. Kiala stayed apart. The grandmas waved her over to sit with them on the sofa. Anya drank wine, as did Peter, which also had a running conversation with his Dad. Anya listened while Kiala and the grandmas chatted.

After Anya arrived, Peter limited his consumption to two more glasses of alcohol.

Standing up later, he advised, "Well, good night all. I'm going to crash. The girls are early risers."

"I'll come too," Anya said.

"Stay, if you want. You don't see your mom often enough."

She eyed him darkly.

"You can come; I was just thinking about your mom."

Anya did go up the steps with him, and into the bedroom.

Peter went over to check on the girls, peaceful and deep in sleep. Anya had started to change clothes when he turned back around. Mostly undressed at that moment, at first she covered herself, looking away like he was a seamy threat.

Peter simmered with growing ire. "I'm not going to accost you, madam. Next door is still an option for you. Feel free to…" He couldn't keep the anger out of his voice, responding tersely.

"I'm sorry. I didn't mean to upset you. It's been a long time for us, away from those things."

"No argument here."

He quickly undressed and climbed into bed, turning away from her, lying on his side. She meekly climbed in. "Peter, I'm sorry," she whispered.

"Accepted…good night." He was in no mood to be conciliatory.

#

He awoke first in the morning and quietly whisked the girls out of the room and down the stairs. The only other people up that early were the wait staff.

"Hi, you little urchins," the head cook said. "What if I bake you into some muffins?"

Elsa laughed. "Noooo."

Peter set about feeding the girls and drinking ample coffee and chatted with the staff. George came out next, claiming a cup of coffee, and then later the grandmas.

"Kiala and Anya slept in." he muttered to his father's glance.

Sitting down at the table, they talked. Mariska was able to converse in English now.

While Edith and George occupied the girls, Mariska turned to Peter. "I know my daughter has upset you, Peter. Thank you for being the big person. My husband was mean, so for Anya to have a wonderful husband, to me, is a marvel. I apologize. I don't know where this thinking of hers comes from."

"It's fine. I'm accustomed to just me and the girls. We'll be okay; I'll make sure of that."

"I worry she will lose you with her silly actions. I'm embarrassed about this."

"Honestly, I don't think I've ever fully understood her. There was history I'm not privy to before she suddenly changed her tune and we got married. There could be ongoing history now. It's her choice. It has nothing to do with you."

"She is walking on your dignity." The look of dismay on her face affected Peter, but he was irked.

"I can't disagree, but my concern is those two little angels. I'm a big person, so I can take it. I won't stand for them getting caught in the middle of something."

"Do you think it's anything more than her career gone wild?" Edith asked.

"That would be the best-case scenario. I can say I trust her, but that could be a very naïve position. I choose not to address it. I would and I will never question her about that sort of thing. If you do such things, I believe it's like a boomerang that will eventually come back on you. I'll worry about giving the best possible life for my daughters."

They talked for a considerable time before they heard a toilet flushed upstairs.

"Let me go," Mariska said.

When she didn't return promptly, Peter decided to follow her. The door to Kiala's bedroom was closed, and he heard them all talking. Turning around, he went back downstairs to rejoin his parents.

"Mariska's having a confab in Kiala's room. I stayed away from that. I'll let her deal with it."

"I thought my tormented trek through the stormy seas of romance was difficult. I'd say you've got me beat, son."

"A distinction I'd gladly forgo. I'm going to bundle up the girls and go outside into the snow."

"We'll come with you."

"They need to learn how to make snow angels."

With his daughters bundled up like Pillsbury dough girls, they plodded out back. Edith held Em while Elsa stood holding George's hand, watching Peter.

"Okay, girls, here we go." Peter fell backward into the snow. He proceeded to wave his arms and legs. Elsa screamed and laughed hilariously, "Daddy fall down."

Peter stood up to show them the angel. Elsa jumped and yelled again. Peter led her over to the snow, and she fell back into it.

"Now wave your arms and legs," he directed.

Emily yelled too, watching her father and sister play in the snow.

Next grandma and grandpa added their snow angels, much to the delight of the girls. They stayed outside for half an hour before going in. The cook had already set out cups of hot cocoa, except for Emily.

Still with no sign of the trio from upstairs, Peter tried to put it out of his mind.

Peter chatted with his parents and daughters. Emily mostly tried to get her little hands on anything close to pop into her mouth. In that she failed because Peter was always vigilant.

Finally, they heard footsteps on the staircase. Anya's face was thoughtful, Mariska looked fatigued, and Kiala smiled meekly.

"Is there more hot cocoa?"

"I believe so, Kiala," Peter answered. The cook was already bringing three more mugs.

Anya looked at Peter. "What was the shouting outside?"

"Our daughters learned how to make snow angels."

That made her smile warmly. She walked over and kissed him on the forehead. Peter gave a small smile in return.

"Mama," Elsa said. "Daddy fall down."

"He did, did he?"

"Yes, Mama."

"It's nice she gets to say Mama," Peter whispered.

"I already got an earful from my mom. I don't need more from you."

"I figured. I'll pay her the ten bucks later."

She slugged him playfully. "Shut up, Peter."

Is this rapport again? he pondered? As little as it was at that moment, it was the best he'd felt since, forever, it seemed.

The brief vacation was saved, but the issue remained. Anya and Kiala would be heading to Germany with Jeff to establish a new office to start operations in Europe. That was never a question.

Starting that evening, Anya acted as his wife again; however, the respite had a limited duration, and soon they were driving to the airport. This time Kiala rode with George, Edith, and Mariska, while Anya rode with Peter and the girls. She seemed truly sad, becoming emotional with her daughters. When they hugged, she kissed both girls with an extended hug. Finally, she gave

Peter an impassioned kiss before she went, with Kiala, to her gate in the international terminal. They would meet Jeff in Berlin. He'd gone ahead and made advanced arrangements. The company had procured a building lease, but Jeff needed to start hiring local staff.

Peter parted with the parents and drove back to school with his precious ones.

Walking in the door and unloading the suitcases, getting the girls fed and bathed and into their beds, just as he was about to settle back to watch a little television, his phone rang.

"Hi, Peter. How did it go?"

"Hello, Allison. Are you ever going to stop stalking me?"

"No—you need me too badly. This time I hear Anya's gone for the long haul."

"Everything was great, to answer your question. What are you trying to accomplish this time?"

"Nothing, I'm just giving you compassionate human contact so you remember somebody out here cares. Without me, what social life do you have, minus a wife?"

"I'm not really up to this verbal dance tonight. I'm going to let you go."

"To sit there alone and mope? Get used to it, dude. This is your life now, unless you want to do a little fine-tuning?"

"I won't ask what you mean by that. I'll give you my blanket answer—no thanks."

"The idea will gain appeal when enough time passes. As I keep telling you, you're a young man missing out on…"

"Good night, Allison." He hung up on her, scowling.

She'd managed to provoke him, again. She was very skilled in provoking him. In fact, his wife was gone and what that would ultimately lead to he really didn't know. For as many positive things he could find, it seemed there were far more negative things to weigh him down.

#

The next class day, Peter went back into his old routine, delving into his studies, caring for his daughters, and blotting out all thoughts about Anya from his mind rather than worrying.

Allison was relentless, magically appearing at his side frequently. When he went shopping for groceries, she came with him to help watch the girls. Often, she came over at suppertime to eat with them. Months into this process, he sat down with her after the girls were in bed.

"Allison, if this was just innocent help from you, thanks, but if you have some idea I'll ditch Anya and then we…well…it's not going to happen. Why aren't you working on a relationship with a guy to be your husband? You can have anybody you want."

"Not anybody…obviously. If I'd asked you why don't you work on a relationship before Anya did her reversal, what would you have said? What *did* you say? Anya was the one and that's the only girl you wanted. Is it so hard for you to understand that's where I am?"

"This is not a good situation. I don't want to say we can't be friends, but that other stuff, these constant come-ons and innuendos, it's got to stop."

"You don't want to think about reality. Anya went off, away from her husband and daughters, awfully easily. Why is that? Making a few cameo appearances on a holiday or two: Is that true love? Why was she agog over Jeff and suddenly…?"

"Allison, I know all of that. You want for me to think she's…unfaithful. That doesn't make it true. Granted, this isn't the ideal situation, but life isn't always fair."

"It doesn't make it untrue either. As I've told you, I was in the dorm room for those many talks we had about guys and romance. What she said about you was like you were a brother or a neighbor. She couldn't say enough superlatives about Jeff. Even Kiala moved past you in her esteem in an amazingly short amount of time."

"Does this lead to your goals: punishing me with these spurious accusations? Do you think it makes me kick her aside? Even if any of these things have any basis in reality, it's my choice if I choose to deal with it. She's the mother of my babies, and I don't want any replacements."

Allison eyed him with a calculating look. "Okay, Peter, but you better look at this with both eyes open. You like to say you prepare for the absolute worst to happen, so you're always ready. Well, the absolute worst has a better chance of being reality than some noble quest on her part. She's conquering Europe all right, but not in the ways you think. Anya has a lot of options and she's young too, long without her husband. You don't think she starts to percolate?"

"Well, I've had enough for tonight. I'll let you go."

He walked to the front door to open it. Staring at each other for a moment, Allison finally stood up and went to leave. She made a point of brushing against him as she passed by.

She whispered breathily, "Good night, darling."

He said nothing in return.

After he closed the door, Peter muttered and shook his head. "What a mess."

Again, she'd managed to pique his underlying worries with the same blazing question. *What is Anya doing this minute?*

#

Peter's trip home for birthday time at the end of March gave him a pleasant time with family. The girls' birthdays were so close together, the family combined them into one party. Elsa at two and Emily at one, they were agog with the celebration, as were their grandparents.

Anya called home to speak by phone. She started her excuse, so Peter cut her off and had her talk to the moms before he talked to her. Eventually they talked.

"Describe them, so I can see in my mind's eye."

"Well, Elsa loves pink, so she's in a little pink dress your mom got for her. Em is in a light purple dress that my mom got. She absolutely slaughtered that defenseless baby cake; I mean, she got it everywhere, including her hair. Her face looked like she was applying a mud pack, but with cake. What a mess."

Anya laughed heartily. "I can see it. I wish I could be there."

"Well, there's good and bad with any decision. You can't be in two places at once. So how are things going?"

"It's incredible. Not only have we gotten off to a flying start, we've scored with virtually every contact, Peter. The amount of money I'm bringing in, I'm stunned."

"That being the case, I'd say we go with my idea to file taxes separately."

"If you think that's best."

"I do. Bringing foreign taxes into my domestic tax situation is not a good idea. Do you have a tax person over there?"

"Yes. Jeff met a woman who's handling him, Kiala, and me."

"It sounds like he's got you covered. I'm going to let you go. I hear your daughters having a territorial dispute over a toy."

"Okay, Peter. I love you."

"Bye." He couldn't manage to reply with an "I love you too." Allison's constant attack to conjure the boogeyman in his mind had its effect.

Plastering on a smile, he returned to the birthday party.

#

After getting back home, he hunkered down for his stretch run, three more months until graduation.

Allison corralled him in the student union for lunch about a week before finals. "Peter, so you've got a job lined up at an accounting firm?"

"I do. They're only fifteen minutes from the apartment, although I'll need to find a new place off campus. Why do you ask?"

"I graduate too. Maybe I can go to work at that firm too? We could find a house to rent and share expenses?"

"You want to move in with me and the girls? Allison, we've talked about this."

"I'm not implying something seamy. Haven't I been a good girl? When you open your new CPA firm next year, I want to apply to be your first employee."

"Uh…I don't know what to say."

"I'll take what I can get to be a part of your life."

"I don't know if that's wise. You're closing the door on your own husband and children."

"I'm content as is. If I'm ever not content, I can look later. Do you see?"

"No, but that doesn't matter to you."

"Maybe we can compromise and I find another girl or two to move in with us. We'd need to find a bigger house."

Peter shook his head. "Somehow, I think you've already looked and have places all lined up."

Allison smiled smugly. "Both things: houses and girls are ready to go when you pull the trigger."

"Do I get a say in it?"

"No. I choose what's best, so get on board, dude."

"You mean what's best for you."

"It's one and the same, me or us."

Riding with her to see the house she picked out; Peter couldn't believe he let her talk him into it. Graduation, moving day, meeting two of Allison's girlfriends, it was a blur. They weren't the airhead types he expected. Actually, they were smart and pleasant girls to be around.

Sitting down at their first supper together, Allison smirked. "So, how do you like your harem?" The ladies were greatly entertained by her joke. Peter, not so much.

Chapter Seventeen

Starting his job was a consuming process as the firm loaded his plate quickly with work.

"Right into the frying pan," the owner said. "It's the best way to get your sea legs. We'll help you, but in your case, I doubt you'll need much help."

Amazingly to Peter, Allison managed to finagle a job too. She wasn't an accountant, having graduated in marketing also, but she'd convinced the firm she could expand their "footprint."

Bringing in new business pleased the owner and put more work on Peter's overcrowded plate.

When they went home in the evenings, Peter was fatigued. However, he never gave up jogging, and that still meant Elsa and Emily got a ride. What was new was now he had three hot female companions: Allison, Susan, and Mary.

It was a strange feeling for him, the reactions when he walked into restaurants and stores, for being in the company of beauty-queen-caliber women, like he was a celebrity.

Getting paychecks was another first. Peter had his own version of pride in building up money he'd earned. Though he dumped it into his existing accounts, it was still gratifying he was making a mark of his own.

Opening college funds for his daughters, he expanded the scope of his finances.

As busy as he was, the end of the year meant the beginning of tax season, and they were swamped with clients. Even the owner had to jump back in to share in the workload, as Allison was highly successful bringing in new customers. It was fortuitous with the female boarders in his house, he had free childcare during the times he had to stay late at the office working. Mary and Susan loved the opportunity to mother little girls.

Christmas and New Year at the firm made for the most lucrative year in their history, by far, and led to sizable bonuses.

The grandparents came down for the holidays, as Peter didn't feel he could get away.

Mary and Susan, along with Allison, stayed to join in the holiday cheer. Allison had no interest in going to her family, and the other two had lost parents to early deaths from illnesses.

Allison was gracious in welcoming George, Edith, and Mariska into the pandemonium that was the group household. For Peter, it was a little grating that she assumed the role of hostess and pseudo-mom, mistress of the household. Her "ownership" role with Peter and the girls irked him, but she smiled her way through it, pleased with herself. He noted Mariska assessing the environment dourly.

Peter pulled her aside later. "I hope you know there's nothing going on. She pretends how she would like it to be. That will never happen; I wouldn't do that."

"I know. You're a good man, Peter. I'm still angry at Anya for doing this. Trying to be Ms. High Society…it's not right."

"She feels compelled to follow her career. Expensive clothes, cocktail parties, a lifestyle rubbing elbows with the elite, that's what floats her boat. There's nothing I can do about it."

"I talk to her and she said she can't fly home for Christmas. They're too busy over there."

"I heard. Oh, well. We've still got each other, Mom."

Mariska chuckled and hugged him. "I feel I need to apologize to you all of the time."

"No need."

"She avoids my calls because we argue."

"Call me, Mom. I won't argue with you."

Allison walked over. "What are you guys talking about: Anya, the missing?"

Mariska eyed her darkly and then looked at Peter, who smiled. "We were having a little private chitchat," he replied. "It's nothing to concern yourself with. It was family talk."

Allison's eyes narrowed for a moment before she smiled again. "No problem. I'll go see if the girls want a treat."

"I think I would like to slap that Allison."

Peter snickered. "Maybe you should hold off on that plan, Mariska. We don't need an assault charge for the holidays."

"The other women seem very nice, though."

"Susan and Mary are perfect cohabitants. Allison knew them and introduced me. They're a huge help with the girls. In this job, I need to work late during this season."

"If you ever need me to come down to help, I will. Seeing my granddaughters is a blessing. I worry that the cancer will come back someday and my days are numbered."

They heard two high-pitched voices squealing as his daughters tangled again. Mariska chuckled. "They're little darlings."

Walking over to the argument, Edith had just gotten down to her knees to extract the toy in question from two little sets of hands.

"Ladies, please," Peter said. "You're supposed to be on your best behavior. We have company."

"Daddy, Em is grabby. She tries to take whatever I have."

"You're never grabby, right, Elsa?"

"Why do you always take her side? It's not fair."

"There are no sides. You both need to be good citizens. That includes sharing."

Elsa muttered something.

Mariska started to laugh hilariously.

"What?" he asked.

"I didn't know she listened in when I talk on the phone to Anya. She's picked up some Russian words I didn't teach her. I'm sorry."

"Oh my."

Edith started to chuckle also.

Allison added, "She's got Anya's brains. You're going to have your hands full, Peter."

"Ah yes, the legendary 'terrible twos.' In a few months, it will be Emily's turn, so I can go through it again. She might be more of a handful than her big sister."

While Edith picked up Elsa, Allison picked up Emily. Watching the scene, Peter pondered the possible long-term effects of their mother not being physically present in their lives. These were the critical formative years, after all.

"Anya…" he muttered, shaking his head ruefully. "Enjoy your cocktails. We're no longer even a blip on your radar?"

#

Her call came on Christmas Day. She was chipper and ebullient. It struck Peter badly, though it was his hurt feelings causing it. Again, he put each mom on the phone and then the girls before he would talk to her.

"Peter, tell me about the holiday for the girls."

"Well, they opened their presents, although there were far too many, so it was kind of a blur. They liked your German dolls, although the clothes you sent went onto the pile pretty quickly."

"What are they wearing?"

"Allison picked out dresses, gifts she gave them."

"Oh."

"Sorry. I didn't think about it bothering you."

"It bothers me I'm not there, not Allison. So, you have two other women in the house?"

"Yes, Susan and Mary."

"Oh, I know them. They're very nice girls."

"They're a big help when I work late."

"Allison works with you?"

"Sort of, I'm in the office and she's out on the road. She does bring in a lot of business, which is a real hit with the owner."

"We're swamped here, but it's been a challenge. Jeff hired local women for the office. They like having the jobs, but I'm not sure they like Kiala and me. Maybe they don't like Americans, or Russians?"

"It happens."

"Would you reconsider flying over for a visit? I miss you and the girls terribly."

"Ah, I can't really fly until after tax season ends, in April. I'll think about it. I figured you've got a full plate with your work, and you have Jeff and Kiala."

"Peter…" she whispered. "You don't think this is hard for me? Your worries are wrong. I know you don't trust me."

"I never said that."

"I'm…"

"So, what are you guys doing for the holiday?"

"We're going to have a little meal later and exchange gifts. Please reconsider. I'll buy the plane tickets. Just give me the word."

"Okay. I'll see what I can do."

"Peter, I need you."

He paused. "I hear you. Goodbye."

"I love you."

Allison was staring at him, trying to read his emotions from his facial expressions. George walked over. "Want to talk?"

They went into the living room.

"What now?"

"She's pushing for me to fly over there to visit, with the girls."

"Why is that a problem?"

"I can say the girls are too young, the flights are too long for them, I don't want to go to Europe, and so forth, but honestly, it struck me like her prior 'turnaround' moment. Back then, she's enamored with Jeff, and suddenly she wants to marry me? That didn't happen in a vacuum. Something occurred, and now—what's changed this time? She chose to follow the man of her dreams out west and leave her babies behind pretty easily, meanwhile adding Kiala into the mix, and then she chooses to go to Europe in this open-ended assignment. There's really no end date in sight. For her, making it a permanent home offshore doesn't seem to be a problem. Apparently, all her current needs are being met, and she's too busy to keep in touch."

He paused as his wrath began to smolder and then flicker to life.

"Son, let me say it this way. Thinking the worst is easy to do. Granted, there are plenty of troubling signs, in a lot of areas, but as I've said, do you want to go there? Before, you wanted her no matter what. Has that changed?"

"It's starting to chafe. Allison's incessant diatribe doesn't help. Anya made a big point of saying I don't trust her and that I'm wrong about that."

"Well, she's right: you don't trust her."

"Regardless, my qualms I keep it to myself. The evidence is circumstantial, so I don't press it."

"And not particularly successful in keeping it to yourself, I might add. Do you doubt what she just told you?"

"What she said was what she would say, no matter what the truth is. Do you see? If she came clean about…choices, there is virtually no good that could come from it. Her egging me into an argument, and accusations, I won't fall for it. If she wants to rationalize what she does over there and a fight with me enables her, do you see? She's made our marriage a long-term blame fest, where I'm eternally the convenient fall guy. Meanwhile, she's alone with Jeff and Kiala, living her life, whatever it might be, seamy or otherwise."

George thought for a moment. "Look at it the other way. She could also accuse you."

"Of what?"

"You live with three beautiful women. Some might conclude a young husband long without a wife, and pent up, could cave in, and might choose to dabble."

"I would not!"

"It helps you to see what I'm saying. What if Anya is innocent and doesn't make those kinds of mistakes? I think you should make that trip over to see her. If she did…stumble, and I'm not saying she did, her saying she needs you, are you going to 'spit the bit' over hurt feelings? Don't conclude you're the only one with moral fortitude."

Peter shrugged, struggling to rein in his cascading emotions.

"I…get tired of this. The last time she was home, it was so awkward at first. She didn't warm up to me until after Mariska tied into her. Down deep, if I'm brutally honest, I believe she cares about me on some level, but she's never been in love. I'm safe, secure, and convenient to raise the girls, and pay the bills, but with my proper place in her world sitting on the back burner. I make a show of indifference to the snubs, but it bothers me, Dad. Whether she's involved outside the marriage, yeah, it's a problem, but distilling everything down to the essence, it's her feelings, or lack thereof, that's the crux of the problem for me. If I start on that tirade…well, I won't. It does make me very angry, under the surface."

"If you think about this deeply, what is it, really? I realize you worry what she feels."

"Am I completely addled and naïve? When my wife talks, or any woman for that matter, are we just getting played? How can I judge if anything is the truth? They could say anything and hide the real facts every time, like we're Plan B, or worse. The *what if*s drive me crazy."

George patted Peter on the shoulder. "I hear you. Let's take a break."

When they walked out of the room, Allison was standing beside the doorway, eyeing Peter intensely.

Peter grimaced. "You had better not say anything."

"Whatever, Peter. You have your hand in this, shooting yourself in the foot. What choices are you making? Can you say the word 'enabling'?"

"Shut up."

They walked over to join the others with his daughters.

"Daddy, look," Elsa said, holding up a gift.

"Grandma sure is nice to you, honey."

"Thank you, Grandma."

"You're welcome, darling," Edith said.

#

The vacation visit ended, but Peter pondered his father's suggestion, for the next three months. After April 15 passed, with the birthdays out of the way, he finally pulled the trigger, making a rare call to Anya. Rather than call her cell, he called the office number she'd given him, knowing she wouldn't be in the office.

The receptionist answered in German.

Peter took a minute to respond. "Yes, hello. Do you speak English?"

"Yes."

"I'd like to leave a message for Anya Brown."

"Yes."

"I've decided to honor her request, about coming over to Europe. Can you have her call me when she gets in?"

"I will; however, she's out of the office for about two weeks traveling in Poland and Russia. Would you like to speak to Jeff, our leader?"

"No, thank you. There's no rush; just whenever she gets around to it."

"I'll pass on the message. Who are you?"

"Oh, I'm sorry. My name is Peter."

The return call came the following evening.

"Peter, it's so good to hear from you. I'm happy you've decided to fly over here. I've got a week and a half left on this road trip, but I'll buy plane tickets for you guys when I get back. I can't wait to see you all. Thank you for doing this for me."

"Sure, no problem—what are friends for?"

Anya paused, trying to digest his questionable comment, if it was meant as a slam.

"I'll let you go, Anya. I'm sure you've got plenty to do."

"Okay, Peter." Through the phone, he heard the sadness in her voice. He regretted his ill-conceived comment, but the words were already spoken and couldn't be unsaid.

"Goodbye."

#

Packing his luggage and the suitcases for the girls later, Allison, Susan, and Mary were all depressed when it was time for him to drive to the airport.

"Okay, ladies, we're off. We'll see you in a couple of weeks."

"Goodbye, Peter." Each of them hugged him and the girls.

"Be good for your dad," Allison said, kneeling down to each daughter, like they were hers.

Peter led them to the car and strapped them into their car seats in the back. When he drove away, Elsa and Emily had their version of a conversation. Elsa at three could speak very well for her age. Even Emily at two was far advanced with her speech. It made Peter smile, listening to them, the lights of his life.

In the busy airport, each girl grasped one of his hands for security, eyeing the legions of people fawning over them.

Sitting in the boarding area, each girl worked on a juice box: Elsa picked orange, and Emily apple juice. A blonde woman sitting across from them asked, "How old are they?"

"Three and two."

"I've got a son who's in first grade. I'm lucky I've got a husband that's patient with my job, with so much travel. He's able to work from home, thank God."

"My wife works in Europe."

"That's got to be tough."

"It's not my first choice, but she has definite career goals."

"Are you okay with that?"

"Yeah. I've got these monsters to keep me busy."

"We're not monsters," Elsa said.

"Okay, then: sort of monsters."

Emily laughed.

"You're a monster," Elsa retorted.

"Daddy," Emily objected. "Elsa called me a name."

"Keep it together, girls. We've got a long way to go."

The woman chuckled.

The boarding process started for their first leg, this time flying via Reagan International in Washington, DC.

On both flights, going first to Washington and then connecting for the flight to Berlin, Peter had three seats together. He took the aisle, putting Elsa in the window seat and Emily between them. The girls did fairly well, thanks in part to coloring books. Managing to color on the books rather than on the airplane seats, or each other, Peter considered that to be success.

#

When they arrived in Berlin, Anya had sent a car to pick them up. Her office was located half an hour's drive from the airport. It was the girls' first-time riding in a limo.

Going into the office, Peter carried the luggage into the lobby.

The receptionist smiled. "You must be Peter?"

"Yes, ma'am, that would be me."

"Please take a seat." She smiled at the little girls.

Moments later, a young woman came out to meet them. "Come, please."

Leading them down a hallway and into a large office, they passed about ten women working there. They looked to be between their twenties and forties. Uniformly, every one of them was attractive. They were typing diligently on their computer terminals.

Peter smiled, stepping up to the nearest desk. *"Guten naben."*

They all laughed.

A brown-haired woman replied. "We speak English, and you just told us good night. It's daytime."

"Oh, I'm sorry."

"You are Peter?"

"I am."

"These are Anya's daughters?"

"Yes. Elsa and Emily."

The women all came over to exclaim over the girls, who backed up against Peter's legs with wide eyes, acting shy.

"It's okay, girls. These are friends of Mama. I'm sorry, ladies. Usually they're talking their heads off."

"Anya is in a meeting with Jeff."

"Of course she is."

They didn't catch his snarky intent.

"Can you follow me to the break room?"

"Sure. The girls could use some coffee."

The women laughed again.

It was half an hour before Anya came to the room, accompanied by Jeff and Kiala.

"Here's Mama," he muttered to the girls. He remained seated, letting the girls have first contact with their mother.

Elsa jumped up to run to Anya's waiting embrace. Emily held back, leaning against Peter. Anya came over, kneeling down to hug her also. After she stood back up, she turned to her husband.

Hugging him while he remained seated, she whispered, "Thank you for doing this, Peter." He shrugged, placing only one arm loosely around his wife. She ignored his tepid action.

Kiala hugged Elsa, and then came over. "Hi, Peter."

"Hi, Kiala. It's nice to see you again." She smiled pleasantly. He got up and hugged her warmly, like they were the spouses.

Jeff stepped up, extending his hand. "Welcome to Germany." He smiled, though Peter read it as condescending rather than friendly. Still standing he exchanged the handshake.

"Thank you, Jeff. I hear you're setting Europe on fire." Giving his best crocodile smile, Peter feigned interest in Jeff and his operations.

"Pretty much; we cut a wide swath."

"Judging by the bevy of beautiful women I saw on the way in, you made the selections in the hiring phase."

Jeff laughed. "Hey, dude, haven't you heard: sex sells. I want a certain impression when clients come into this office."

"I definitely got an impression, so I guess you succeeded with that."

"Peter," Anya said, eyeing him reproachfully.

"Thanks. It's okay, Anya," Jeff responded, unfazed. "I'm not embarrassed about what we've built here. My bosses are happy, our paychecks and investment accounts are bulging, and we're all happy working together. What could be better?"

"I can't disagree. You've certainly got the ideal lives going on. It doesn't get better than this."

Kiala and Anya looked at each other and then at Jeff. He responded, "Listen, Peter, it's great to have you here for this visit, but we've still got an office to run."

"Sure. We'll get out of your way."

Anya spoke. "I'll have a car take you and the girls to the hotel, and I'll see you tonight."

"Great." He simply turned to his daughters.

She hugged him again before they walked away; back to continue their business meeting. He sat back down to sip on his coffee. Peter didn't fail to notice the "dress code," which seemed to be all the ladies in tight skirts or dresses designed to highlight their attractive physiques, like they were going straight to dates after work. He'd seen no other males working in the office.

"Jeff, you've created a world of your own choosing," he commented to no one at all.

"What, Daddy?" Elsa asked.

"Nothing, honey."

"What do we do now?"

"Mama is sending us to the hotel in a few minutes. We can't stay here and disrupt their office."

"Okay. I'm ready to go. This is boring here."

Peter chuckled. "I couldn't agree more, honey. Let's blow this popsicle stand."

"I'll take a popsicle."

"It's a phrase for leaving."

"Oh."

Even the limo driver was a female. Peter loaded the luggage, as the office women came to say goodbye, fawning over the girls again.

Once at the hotel, Peter was ushered into a spacious luxury suite. He had a separate bedroom from the girls. Turning on the television, the girls watched cartoons, though they laughed because the dialogue was in German.

"What's wrong with those people?" Elsa asked.

"We're in Germany, so people speak German here. They would ask what's wrong with you for speaking English."

Emily laughed. Elsa looked at her like she was an idiot.

Anya came in the afternoon. She had an overnight bag with toiletries and some clothing changes. Walking in the door, she chuckled as her daughters were rolling on the floor laughing, as was her husband.

"What are you doing?" she asked them, amused.

"I'm teaching the girls to stop, drop, and roll, in case they're ever on fire."

Anya laughed. "You're so crazy, Peter."

"Guilty."

"Jeff is treating us all to dinner tonight."

"I'm sure he can afford it. Do we go pick him up?"

"No. We'll all meet at the restaurant."

"So, we don't go to your place?"

"I'll stay here. I live in a house; nothing special." She didn't look into his eyes when she said it.

"Anya, I live with Allison and two other women. You don't think I can figure out you live with Jeff and Kiala?"

"I wasn't sure you'd understand. You can be difficult with some issues."

"Listen—that's your life. I'm not a part of it. I accepted that fact a long time ago."

She turned her face in anger. "I know you will never trust me. I don't know why I think it could be otherwise."

"It's funny—my dad made the comment you could accuse me of inappropriate behavior too. I never said anything about your life."

"It comes through like a tornado, Peter. I don't want to start out our visit this way. As far as bad behavior, I know you would never do it. Why can't you believe the same thing about me? Do you think I'm weak, or jaded?"

"My trust issues are with Jeff—not you. Look at that display in your office. It's a heck of a leg show, but in the workplace?"

"He has his way of doing things. It works: clients like seeing pretty women. We never fail to get the new business."

"He knows what he's doing. No argument there."

"So, you think I'll falter, or I've been faltering all along?"

"Truly, I don't think about it. It would have driven me crazy. I stopped a long time ago."

"Are you saying you no longer care about me? Allison wants you badly, and now she's living with you? As you said, I could say the same thing."

"You could, but you already answered that question. I'm not interested in Allison. She gets on my nerves as often as not and yes I care about you."

"I'm not interested in Jeff in that way."

"Fine, whatever you say. Let's table this discussion for now. Little ears." He nodded toward the door.

Anya turned her face. Elsa was at the bedroom door, listening.

"We're coming out, honey," Peter said. "Give us a minute."

"We're not done talking about this, Peter. After we get back tonight, okay?"

"Sure, Anya."

"Did you bring anything nice for the girls to wear? This is a swanky restaurant we're going to."

"Allison picked the clothes, so probably yes."

"I'll go get them dressed and ready. You get changed into a suit."

"Yes, ma'am."

Anya was the last to get dressed. Her choice was a slinky, very expensive red dress, form-fitting and very sexy. Low-cut for ample cleavage, there was a slit in the front so much of her legs showed when she walked or sat down. It was an evocative choice. When she came out, she eyed Peter ruefully.

Frowning with an exasperated look, she spoke tersely, "Can you get it into your brain: this dress is for you, not for Jeff? You say Allison can get on your nerves. It works that way for me also. Jeff will always be Jeff, but his charm wore off long ago for me. I'm not an immature girl any longer. I'm a woman, and your wife."

"I've got it, Anya."

#

Kiala had arrived with Jeff and they were seated by the time the Brown family arrived at the eatery. It was a swanky restaurant, but when two darling little girls came in the door, they drew happy smiles and murmurs from wait staff and patrons alike. Luckily, the girls acted on their best behavior.

"Your daughters are little angels," the hostess said.

"Stay tuned," Peter muttered.

She snickered. "I have three of my own. I know what you mean."

Jeff reserved a smoldering look for Anya, which she tried to ignore. Her face reddened at his antic in front of her husband.

"My dear, you look lovely, as always."

Peter didn't rise to the bait. "Hello, Jeff. Thanks for this free meal."

"My pleasure."

Peter turned his head. "Kiala, you look very nice too."

"Thank you, Peter. Wow, Anya. That is some dress. I wondered when we'd finally see it. You put every other woman here to shame."

Anya chuckled. "Stop that silly talk. I wore this because I had a good reason tonight. My husband is with us finally."

Ignoring her compliment, Peter sat down beside Kiala, with Emily on his other side. Elsa was beside Emily, with Anya between her and Jeff.

Elsa's head was on a swivel, looking at all of the people looking at her. She whispered, "Mama, why don't those people mind their own business?"

"It's because you are so cute, darling."

"Well…I am cute, but I don't like them staring."

They all chuckled.

"You're cute, like your mom," Jeff said. "You're going to grow up to be a heartbreaker too."

"What does that mean?"

"Nothing, honey," Anya said. "He was just trying to make a joke."

Anya glared at Jeff, who was unfazed. He smirked and then spoke. "This is so nice, all of us together again. Peter, life in Europe has been so much better than I anticipated. I'm very content here. I'd say we all are. All of our needs are met."

Kiala looked at Anya. Neither woman responded to Jeff's loaded comment. They looked at Peter, who ignored the barb from Jeff. Instead, he smiled placidly and turned to Emily.

"What do you want to eat, Em?"

"Peanut butter and jelly."

Again, the adults chuckled.

Anya answered, "I don't think they have sandwiches like that here. Why don't you have a nice cheeseburger?"

"I want a sandwich," she complained.

"You're a baby," Elsa said.

"I'm not a baby. You're a baby."

"Girls," Peter said. "We need to be good citizens, or else the Germans might throw us in jail."

"No," Emily whimpered.

"He didn't mean that," Anya clarified. Now she glared at Peter. He smiled playfully.

"Not funny, Peter."

Elsa snickered. "Daddy, Mama is going to put you in timeout."

"It could happen."

Peter was pleased, as it changed the mood at the table. Jeff's idea to charm the ladies in front of him to irk Peter went out the window in a hurry. Kiala and Anya were totally taken with the little ones and with Peter, for that matter. Jeff's intended "romantic ambience" turned into a family-friendly outing that also entertained the other nearby patrons. The bulk of the women in attendance in the restaurant wore wedding rings. The little girls and their appealing behavior resonated. They had children or grandchildren of their own.

Peter turned to Jeff. "So, your company is doing very well?"

"Yes, incredibly so, actually. The management team back at home office in the States had an idea there was money to be made over here in Europe, but success on this scale has blown their doors off. I've accumulated over seven digits of investments, as have Anya and Kiala. We have an ocean of money rolling in. It's mind-boggling and I'm an optimist."

"Congratulations."

"I take my share of the credit, but when those two young women walk into a business, it's no contest. They walk out with new contracts every time. It's a matter of smarts, great looks, the excellent services our company offers, charisma…the list of superlatives has no end really. It's gratifying to have success in your career. Wouldn't you agree, ladies? We percolate as a team out there on the road. It never gets old."

Peter turned to Anya. She looked at him pensively. "That's true, but in both our cases, Kiala and I, we don't look to do this forever. It is highly gratifying to have this stellar success, but the thought of my family back home is never out of my mind. My daily emotions include sadness at being apart."

Kiala piped in, "I agree. As I sit here watching Anya's fabulous husband, the love he has for her and the girls, it makes me so envious. Why am I waiting to get married? I don't have a good reason. I know this is how you would have our lives go on eternally, Jeff. We don't agree."

Jeff looked shocked.

"Going to endless cocktail parties, playing the role, getting propositioned constantly, it gets very old," Anya added. "Why some clients think part of the business model includes us making seamy concessions for their gratification, I don't understand, and I don't like it."

Peter put a sympathetic hand on her hand. "You can come back home, honey."

"Believe me, I think about that every single day."

Jeff eyed her critically. "Anya, are you serious? We're doing very well, but this is a fledgling operation we're still building over here. To the new clients you sold, you and Kiala, you're the face of the company. If you pull out, what are the consequences for the company? They want to continue doing business with you two. Yes, you've each got enough money to retire in your twenties, but is that fair? Our ladies back at the office, their livelihood is dependent on you and Kiala continuing to do your jobs."

"Jeff, we've both told you it's time to bring in new reps we can train. We aren't the only people who can have great success. There are plenty of other beautiful women in the world."

"I'm sorry," Peter said. "I guess there is an ongoing dialogue between you three. We didn't mean for our visit to set off a firestorm."

"It's nothing you've done," Anya said. "We don't mean to put you in this position, but it's good you understand the truth rather than going on the erroneous impressions you've had about us."

"It is eye-opening."

Anya looked at her daughters. They were quiet, listening to the exchange. Though they didn't know the issues being discussed, they understood the display of feelings from the discord in how the adults looked and acted.

"It's okay, girls. We're going to stop talking and have a nice meal." Lovingly, she kissed each of them on the top of their head. The girls relaxed noticeably. However, their lives revolved around dad at that point. The constant in their daily lives, he was their barometer. Both girls eyed their father to gauge if what "part-time Mom" said was true.

Afterward, the balance of the dinner gathering went off reasonably well, though Jeff didn't bounce back as easily as Peter expected, seemingly knocked off his game.

When they parted, Peter was gracious after the unanticipated positive direction of the "fest." When he got back to the hotel with a wife at his side, they went into the room to relax. She looked at his smile.

"You enjoyed that, didn't you?"

"What?"

"Don't play dumb. You think Jeff was humbled, and that pleases you."

"Yeah." He laughed heartily.

"You're incorrigible."

"I am."

Peter wrapped her up in a tight embrace, his first on this trip. Finally, he felt like doing so.

"Daddy, you're going to crush Mama," Elsa yelled.

"I'm okay, honey," Anya replied, pulling out of Peter's arms. She went over to spend some rare time with her daughters.

"Daddy mashes us too, sometimes."

"That's what daddies do," Peter retorted, grabbing Elsa and Emily both in a bear hug. They squealed in delight.

Later, in their separate bedroom after the girls were in bed, Anya turned her face to Peter.

"Go ahead. I know what you want to say."

"That's funny because I don't know. Perhaps you should tell me."

"You want to ask if I was serious."

"I don't doubt your words. My long-term interpretation, you had personal reasons for this path, making your way and taking your own power. I get that. It isn't hard to figure out I prefer you living with us, but it isn't my decision. If you've reached a point you can rethink your career path, there are plenty of other viable options that would have you back at home. Regardless, you decide what you do. Is that clear enough?"

"Deep down, I think you honestly feel I'm a slave to lust and seamy passions—that if Jeff pulls some strings, I'm defenseless. I can tell you we're not intimate partners, and never have been, but to you, these are just expedient words, not the truth. That makes me want to smash your face."

He chuckled. "Smash away, darling. I admit how you handled tonight was a pleasant surprise. If you still want to be my wife, that's what's important to me."

She seemed unsure of his answer, but finally she shrugged it off. Now, for this moment, they could be husband and wife again, at last after such a lengthy gap. Anya got up to carefully close the bedroom door.

"Hey, baby," Peter whispered playfully.

"Shut up," she whispered, and they both chuckled.

"Woo-hoo," he continued.

She gave him a smack, causing him to laugh further.

Chapter Eighteen

The visit was a quantum shift in Peter's universe. For perhaps the first time, he could banish his angst and nearly accept that Anya might truly love him. Ceding her back to Jeff was a noisome prospect, but finally he didn't fully assume the worst.

He pondered, *is it possible Jeff isn't her default choice as a lover*—a concept that was at the basis of his painful fears? In the hotel room as the time to depart approached, they talked.

"Peter, Jeff was right. I can't simply get on a plane right now and come home. Kiala and I will push him to find replacements for us. How soon that can happen and how soon they'd be properly trained, I can't say. Do you understand?"

"Yes."

"Do you accept it?"

"What choice do I have?"

"At least I think you know I don't like this either."

"We, in our relationship, took a huge step; I agree with that."

"I've missed so much with my girls; it gives me real urgency to fix this and get back home."

"Good. I'd say from now on, why don't we start to Skype for face-to-face talks?"

"I'd like that. I can see the girls."

"My thought exactly."

"I want to also say, with your jealousies about my situation, I feel the same way about Allison living with you and my girls. She was driven in the past, and I'm sure nothing has changed for her. I might start to practice some boxing."

Peter laughed hilariously. "Wow. A chick-fight? I never saw that coming."

"Just be careful, Peter. I don't trust her when it comes to you."

"I've got it covered, honey. If you're coming home, I'm going to look into a new house just for us. Of course, that's after June, when I finish my year and can take the CPA exam. I might start some market tests to find the best place to go for my own office. My boss tells me daily I can't take any customers with me and away from him. Getting out of the area is the obvious choice."

"I'll think about my job too. If I go back to doing US contacts, it will still be like before with the travel. I'll consider what alternatives I can find."

They looked at each other for a moment.

"What is it?" she asked.

"This is optional to answer, but you can put my mind at rest. When you seemed really into Jeff, what happened: Why did you suddenly turn to me to marry on the spur of the moment? Yes, I thought you guys did something back then, and maybe you regretted it."

Her face reddened. She sat down and pondered the question for a time. Finally, turning her head, she replied, "That relationship got to a point of making choices. What you thought, of course it's what Jeff wanted. I admit I was lured. I had never made love with a man before and it was an exciting thought. It wasn't so much any bad things he did that stopped me; it was in my mind. I could only see you as my future husband. We never did the deed, Peter."

"I always thought it was the fact I came up short in your mind. For a long while, I felt like I got nothing but the back of your hand. It was tough sledding."

"I know that. I was young and my feelings were…confusing. That's no longer the case. Do you have any other questions?"

"No."

"Do you see, I've never asked if you turned to another woman? I know who you are."

"Thank you, and you're right: I never would have."

"Then you can see how frustrating it is for me. My behaviors have never been in question, except in your mind. There are no words I could say to change that. Only you can decide to trust me."

"Okay, I accept your premise, but can you see the other side of that coin? I did and I do look at your behaviors. Can you see how frustrating that was for me? Even with factoring in my natural bias toward negative conclusions, look at it with impartial eyes. You never made me feel the love. After we started out, when you jumped into dating other people—wholeheartedly—I was an afterthought. I was trying to win you over, even when you were agog over Jeff and, well, I truly thought you would end up with him. Regardless of your sudden reversal and marrying me, graduating and quickly leaving our home and family to work away, doing that didn't come across as any problem for you. I don't mind raising the girls—they're my life now, but all of these years of our youth are gone, with me alone in bed every night. We can't get them back. Your decisions have consequences for our whole family."

She frowned. "I know that, Peter, and my regret grows on a daily basis. I didn't seek companionship elsewhere either."

"Well, I'd say we table the matter. You do whatever you need to do, and I will also. If you choose to come home, I would like that very much. Got it?"

"I've got it." She hugged him firmly.

"Are you able to swing some time off, so we can take the girls to see a few of the sights?"

"I'll try. I would love to do it, and Kiala offered to cover the extra work for me, but I can't impose on her too much. Maybe a day or two?"

"I'll take whatever I can get."

"There are a few places we can go to the girls would like."

"For the days where you need to work, is there somebody else who can take us around to interpret the language and help pick destinations?"

"I think Jeff would allow one of our ladies to take off. Greta is the woman in her early forties that you met. She had her children young, so they're all in college. She would be perfect as a guide. Would that be acceptable?"

"Of course. Tell her I'll use extra mouthwash."

Anya snickered. "Will you ever grow up?"

"No way; not never."

"Another double negative, Peter?"

"It's another endearing facet to my charm."

"Not!"

"You've got American jargon down pretty good, little lady. It's much better than my Russian."

"Your Russian will always be terrible. My mother laughs every time you try to utter something. You're worse than an infant."

They heard the girls exchanging heated words.

"Let me take care of it," Anya said. "I've missed out on mothering them too much."

"Okay, have at it, babe. I'll jump in the shower."

#

Traveling for the day, the girls were enthralled at the sights and sounds. Having their mother with them was a new pleasure, and even little Emily came around to this semi-stranger she'd barely known. For Anya, it was a taste of the life she could have had, being the mom. It whetted her appetite for more. Husband and wife resumed rapport and that was a very good thing. Having Anya in his bed at night was a thrill all over again, and she acted loving during the days, another quantum shift.

Lunch time at a restaurant drew friendly looks and words from other patrons. The girls always evoked that in strangers.

"They're little angels, and so well-behaved." Peter and Anya heard similar words numerous times during the outing.

"See what you've done, Peter," Anya mentioned, as they returned to the hotel. "Our daughters are as you've molded them. What an accomplishment. Maybe it was good I wasn't there to get in your way. You have so much patience, it amazes me."

Peter shrugged and then smirked, "I accept cash donations."

Anya chuckled and slugged him. "Shut up and stop trying to spoil the good mood."

Dinner in the hotel was like a repeat of lunch in drawing the notice of other patrons to the girls.

In this case, there were other Americans staying there.

One woman came over to speak to them. "I travel a lot in my business. Seeing your daughters makes me think of my own children. I wish they were so well-behaved. I've got a daughter and a younger son. They fight all of the time."

Peter replied. "Don't think we don't experience the dark side too."

The woman laughed and then looked at Anya. "You're a lucky woman."

"Thank you, and I do know how lucky I am."

After she left, Peter leaned over to whisper to Anya. "Speaking of lucky, baby? Tonight: you and me?"

Anya smiled and whispered, "Shut up with that at dinner, you fool."

"I was just checking. I always like to get my ducks in a row."

#

The following day it was Anya's other day off to go around her with family, and then it was Greta's turn to plug into the equation.

"Thank you so much for doing this, Greta. My German is very limited," Peter explained.

"That's fine. What can you say?"

"*Auf weidersehen.*"

She chuckled. "That means goodbye."

"Oh. How about *Qué pasa*?"

"That's Spanish, Peter."

"Duh. I have yet to get a clue about much of anything. Sorry."

She laughed and turned to the little ones. "Let's go and have a fun day." She smiled at the girls, who smiled back.

"Let's go have some fun, Daddy-O," Elsa said.

"Daddy-O? Where do you learn those things?"

"I don't know—around. I'm gifted."

"Some gift, Elsa."

Greta laughed and hugged Elsa and kissed her forehead.

He muttered, "What kind of day care is that?"

"Peter, it's charming. She's a love."

It was another pleasant day, though Emily chose that day to demand to be carried frequently at the zoo. For Peter, it was like carrying a heavy stone after a while. Greta eyed him sympathetically. "I can help you some," she offered.

It got them through the rest of the day.

Anya was late getting home from work, so they had to dine fashionably late.

"I'm so sorry. Kiala did a great deal, but work piled up. It's not a one-person job."

"Well, you're here now, so relax, honey."

"I will, thank you, Peter. Greta said she had such a good time today. I'm not surprised. She marvels at how you deal with the girls. Her husband wasn't as hands-on as you are. Unfortunately for her, the marriage didn't work out and they're divorced."

"That's too bad. The guy must have been an idiot, letting her get away."

"She hasn't explained the details or the issues, and we don't ask. I agree: she's a very neat lady. I like her very much, as does Kiala."

"It's an imperfect world. Bad things happen out there."

"Why are men such dolts?"

They both laughed. It was nice Peter could laugh and not take her joke as casting an aspersion at him. She was trying to be funny, and he could finally "get" her.

"You couldn't live without us, babe."

She kissed him warmly.

He continued. "I came, I saw, I conquered."

"So, you think you've conquered me?" she asked playfully.

"Yeah."

"You're pretty confident, sir."

He eyed her for a moment before saying, "I know we're joking around, but I can honestly say, maybe for the first time, I believe that, and I believe you, honey."

"That's a very good thing. Have we turned a corner?"

"I think so, and it was a corner that needed to be turned."

"I love you, Peter Brown. You're the man in my life and I would want no other."

At that point, the girls wandered over. "Mama, Emily stinks."

"Girls, please. Elsa, you shouldn't say mean things about your sister."

"Well, it's true."

"Life in the fast lane," Peter muttered. "See what you've been missing."

Anya frowned at him reproachfully.

#

The remainder of the visit seemed to fly past, and soon they packed the suitcases for the trip to the airport. Anya was genuinely affected, fussing over her girls, checking their suitcases, and talking with them as much as possible. At the end, when vacation time was done and they had to leave, she hugged each girl, and then her husband.

"I meant what I said, Anya. You can come home right now if you'd like. We've got plenty of money."

"I can't. Kiala and I have committed to getting replacements ready, but it will be at the soonest possible moment."

"Okay, honey. I'll leave it up to you. If you need anything from me, just call, or tell me when we Skype."

"I will miss you. Please don't go back into that funk and act like you couldn't care less about me. That has always hurt me."

"I'll do better. I'll pretend to get excited about your Jeff stories."

She glowered.

He kissed her deeply and went out the door with the girls. Anya accompanied them to the limo to go to the Berlin airport.

"Mama, can't you come with us?" Elsa asked.

"I'm sorry honey, I can't. I'll come home as soon as I can."

"I'll go back and check out of your room at the hotel desk."

Peter hugged her again.

"Take care of my little girls, Peter."

"I always do."

Getting into the limo, the girls were strapped into their car seats, eyeing him soberly.

"It's okay. We know how to take care of ourselves. Mama is going to switch back home to work as soon as she can."

Neither girl uttered a sound. The limo drove away and their long journey home began.

#

On the return flight, Peter took the center seat with a daughter on each side. They both lay against him and fell asleep quickly, covered by blankets. It was cool in the aircraft cabin.

A full meal was served as they flew over the Atlantic Ocean and the girls awakened for that. Elsa did a good job eating good portions, Emily somewhat less. Peter finished off the remainder.

With full bellies, they fell back to sleep after trips to the restroom for each girl.

It was a long day of travel, negotiating the crowds at the airport, picking up their luggage, and trudging out to the car parked in the long-term lot. Strapping them into their seats in the back, Peter drove home. All three women rushed out to meet them. Allison grabbed the girls in a hug, after which Mary and then Susan took their turn.

"Peter, we missed you guys so much. The house wasn't the same. Welcome home."

"Thanks."

"Are you hungry? Can we make something?"

"Thank you, Susan. Yeah, we could eat."

Sitting down a little later at the table to grilled cheese and soup, he could relax.

"So, how are Anya, and Kiala?" Allison asked.

"They're doing very well. Jeff said the success they've had has floored their bosses back in the States. Anya has piled up a big number in her bank."

"So, what's next for them: more of the same? Didn't you say they're a perfect team?"

"Allison, I know what you're trying to do. As a matter of fact, Anya and Kiala both are working on getting new hires they can train as replacements. Anya's goal is to come back home at the earliest possible moment."

"Is that right—has Jeff signed off on that? Somehow, I don't think so. I'll guarantee he's still got some bullets in his gun. He isn't suddenly incompetent with women. Can you say categorically that you're getting the whole story?"

Realizing she was trying to provoke him, he replied, "You do realize in three months after the CPA exam, I'm probably moving on to wherever I choose to set up my new office."

"I'm happy to be your first new employee. You saw what I did at our current employer. I can guarantee your new business will survive and prosper."

"I'll think about it. Regardless, cohabitating has an expiration date."

"That's understandable," Mary said quickly, before the moment escalated to turn dire. "Susan and I have talked about making our own moves. This taste of family life with these precious little girls has made us hungry for our own children."

"That path is one you should look into, Allison," he said, pointedly.

She eyed him darkly for a moment. Turning her head, she smiled at the little ones. "More soup, girls?"

"No thank you," Elsa replied. Emily shook her head. She was busy gnawing a grilled cheese sandwich; her cheeks needed a wipe of crumbs and butter. Allison reached over to handle the task.

Turning her head back to Peter, and smiling sweetly, she added, "We can talk later."

Peter shrugged his shoulders at the thought of a "talk" he didn't want to have. "Sure, Allison, whatever you want."

She held him up when everybody else was in bed. "Peter, why do you treat me this way?"

"What are you talking about?"

"Have I been anything but your friend?"

"No."

"You think I still have some dark motives after all this time? Believe me, if I wanted to seduce you, it would have happened long before now, and it *would* have happened. My point is your naïveté, which never seems to end. I won't lie that I love you, but I've accepted you want a life with her. What does she want? Do a few glib words mean your fears were never valid? When I say I was in the room at the dorm talking with her and Christy, I got that look behind the curtain. Jeff really knocked her loopy. How is it you think that just went away? What she told you is what she would say: something to smooth your ruffled feathers. All that time away, with him: Are you so sure it was harmless, innocent, and appropriate for a married woman?"

Peter scowled.

"Jeff is a stallion; he doesn't change. Do you think he simply does without? Does that make sense to you, regardless of whatever she says?"

"Is there a point to this?"

"I don't want you or the girls to get hurt. You deserve better than that from your wife."

"Duly noted, but Allison, I'm tired. It was a long day of travel so, good night."

After he got into bed, he muttered, "This has got to end. I don't need any more stress."

#

The end of his work year at the CPA office was much anticipated for Peter.

"Thank you, Paul. I appreciate all that you've done for me."

"Peter, you're going to do great. Anything I've done for you has been repaid many times over with the new business you and Allison have generated.

I hate to lose you, and her. Good luck with starting your own office. Have you decided where you want to go?"

"I've decided to move near my folks' place. I know people in my hometown and in the area, so I think it will be an easier sell than total strangers in the beginning. Hopefully my good work will build a reputation Allison can sell to outsiders."

"That sounds like a plan, son. I knew you'd pass the CPA exam the first time—congrats for that. Take care, and don't be a stranger."

"Thanks again."

The bittersweet crossroads continued as they said tearful goodbyes to Mary and Susan.

"Peter, I can't tell you how fantastic this has been—sharing your life," Susan explained. "Mary and I both have decided to move in with our boyfriends, and I think you guys will be getting wedding invitations before too long."

They both hugged him firmly and hugged the girls.

"Where are you going?" Elsa asked.

"We're all moving on to different phases in our lives," Mary explained gently.

"I don't want you to go."

"Thank you, Elsa, but everything will be fine. You're going to live close to your grandparents now. We can all still come to visit from time to time."

Allison stood by, stoic. The raw emotions of parting from dear friends affected her more than Peter had ever seen before.

Piling into his car, they left the house for the final time. Allison followed in her car. Peter had conceded to Elsa riding with Allison, so she wasn't alone for the long drive, while Emily rode with him. All of the personal effects were bulk-shipped separately to the new house.

Again, Peter made a concession, permitting Allison to move in with them temporarily until she found her own place.

George, Edith, and Mariska were all waiting when they arrived. It was a nice house in an upscale subdivision.

"Hi, Mom." He hugged his mother, and then he hugged Mariska. George shook his hand.

"I found the perfect office space. A friend had some plans for it that never came to fruition, so he agreed to let you take over."

"Thanks, Dad. I need to get on that right away. Did you hear that, Allison?"

"I did. I'm ready when you are."

"I'm thinking of getting some ladies to answer the phones, starting out hiring an experienced CPA, and maybe hiring a new one just coming out of college. With three of us, we can cover the initial startup process and get things rolling. I'd have help in training the newbie."

"I know you want to do this on your own, but I've got friends happy to send business your way."

"Thanks. I'm not too proud to accept help. Establishing cash flow is essential, obviously."

"I'll even let you take over doing our taxes."

"Are you sure Arnold won't balk at that."

"Arnold's getting ready to retire anyway."

"Maybe he'd be a good candidate to work for me in the short term."

"I can talk to him."

"What's the word from Anya?"

"Well, the last I heard, Jeff finally hired a couple of new women. Anya and Kiala have been training the hell out of them."

George laughed.

"I think Anya is serious about coming home."

"After all of the turmoil and stress, it's about time you got a break."

"I can't disagree."

"Allison?"

"She's like a bulldog with a bone. She won't let it go, but I'll admit she hasn't stepped over the line. As much as I try to get her to date other guys, she still focuses on mothering the girls."

"It's her choice, but I agree with you. Anya is going to plug back in, and Allison is going to be the odd woman out. That could be an emotional powder keg."

"I really don't want to see Allison get hurt."

His father shrugged at Peter's statement. Even though he believed his son's assurances, imagining all of those wifeless years living apart, never falling for Allison's come-ons was hard to believe.

"Well, let's get you moved in. I see the moving van coming down the street."

#

They went to dinner at a restaurant later. Neither Mariska nor Edith had any problem with Allison being there. She had been a part of the group for so long it was simply accepted.

The next day, the girls went to the estate for a day with the grandmas, while George joined Allison and Peter at the new office. The furniture was delivered early in the morning, and the phone system was installed.

"By the way, I talked to Arnold and he prefers to retire."

"Okay. Maybe it's good I find another person I don't know to fill that slot. Also, I called the college and set up slots for appointments with graduating seniors to pick one of them. I'll hire some office staff right away too. This is kind of exciting."

"I'll hit the pavement as soon as you're ready, Peter," Allison said. "We'll get our phones ringing soon enough."

"I have no doubt."

Peter's first hire was a married woman in her forties coming back into the work force after taking time off to raise her children, who were now in college.

"Martha, I see you were an office manager previously?"

"I was. I can give you references."

"Actually, based on what I see, that's not necessary. What I like is the instant rapport we have. I think you're exactly what I want. How soon can you start?"

"Right now, consider me working for you."

They both chuckled. "What do you say, Allison?"

"Welcome to the company, Martha."

Martha was involved in the subsequent job interviews for office girls. Peter hired Melanie, Rachel, and Latrice.

Sitting down later for their first meeting, he explained, "Obviously we're not running yet, but my hope is that will change rapidly. I'm going to hire two accountants to start. One of them will be experienced, and the other will be a new grad. That person will need to work a year here before they can take the CPA exam. Does anyone have questions?"

No one replied.

"So, settle in and set up your work stations. We'll try to have work for you to do as soon as possible. Also, I'm going to train you in doing simple taxes.

Obviously, don't ever guess. If you have questions, ask me or the other accountants. We'll be handling other types of things too. Always be pleasant and friendly. That makes a good impression. If you get difficult phone calls, don't fight with customers: let Martha or me handle it. I'll try to start with some training tomorrow. Once again, welcome to the family, ladies. By the way, I'm springing for the pizzas and cola for lunch."

That evening, back at their new house, Elsa answered the doorbell before either Peter or Allison could get there. He heard her loud voice. "Hello."

"Hi, dear, are your mom and dad home?"

Peter stepped up. "Hi, I'm Peter Brown."

"We're your neighbors, Bill and Barbara Bigby." They were probably a decade older than Peter. Relatively attractive physically but their worldly lifestyle showed in their garb. His Hawaii shirt wasn't fully buttoned. With her short skirt; her blouse displaying plenty of cleavage, and the look on her face, Peter took a step back as she invaded his space.

"Nice to meet you, neighbors. Please come in. I hope you'll excuse the mess."

Allison walked in from the kitchen. "I'm Allison."

Elsa and Emily stood beside her, eyeing the strangers.

Barbara spoke. "Your children are beautiful. Our kids are a little older, a daughter in fourth grade, a son in eighth, and a son who's a sophomore in high school. I can see the resemblance in your kids."

Allison smiled at Peter and snickered.

"Ah...Allison isn't my wife. She's a boarder at this point, until she finds her own place. My wife is Anya, and she works in Europe currently. She's expecting to be able to come home soon."

"Oh...sorry, I guess I just assumed."

"There's nothing to apologize about. We shared a house before with two other women, so this family has adjusted with my wife gone."

He felt embarrassed. The Bigbys both smiled, but Peter felt judged nonetheless.

"Would you care for some coffee?" Allison asked. "One thing that is unpacked is the coffee maker."

"Sure," Bill said. When they went to the kitchen table, the girls drew chairs up to join them.

"Do you guys want coffee?" Peter asked facetiously.

His daughters laughed, as well as everyone else. Elsa spoke. "We don't drink coffee, Daddy."

"Oh, I forgot."

Barbara eyed Peter warmly. "You have a nice manner with your children. It's easy to see they're loved. I like that."

"What do you do?" Bill asked.

"I just opened an accounting office. I'm in the process of hiring and training staff. Allison is my marketing rep. That is a job she is very good at."

"I believe you." He eyed Allison appreciatively. Allison smirked, looking at Peter like it was another coup. He rolled his eyes.

"Perhaps we can talk later. It may be you offer better services than my current accountant. I'm willing to consider other options."

"Sure. We can have a sit-down at my office fairly soon. I'm still hiring, but we should be functional possibly as soon as next week."

Peter wrote down the office phone number and handed it to Bill.

Later, after the Bigbys went back home, Allison laughed.

"Allison," he chided. "Don't start."

"You have to admit, men are predictable, and pretty lame. I'm not sure he realizes I have eyes in my head from where his eyes were focused."

"If he's a prospective client, that's the extent of our involvement. Any other issues he might or might not have, I'm not going to waste time on."

"Barbara seemed to like what she saw in you too. Hubba-hubba, big guy."

"Shut up, Allison; not funny."

Allison laughed anyway.

"I'll be down at school tomorrow for those interviews. I hope to come back with an accountant in the fold."

"Good—the sooner the better so we can get this show on the road. By the way, we got a message from your dad. He's recommending a senior accountant named Cliff Platte. Apparently he's relocating to this area from the Southwest."

"When is he arriving?"

"He's here now. As a matter of fact, he was planning on swinging by tomorrow for a look-see."

"You and Martha can chat with him to get a feel if he'd fit into the family. You know the type of office atmosphere we want. I can discuss the particulars with him later, if he seems to fit."

"Will do, boss." She did a mock salute.

"One of these days…" Peter muttered, brandishing a fist. All of the women laughed at his mock threat.

#

The following day, Peter had three interviews before he met a young woman who jumped out at him, Myleka Hayes. Her knowledge, grades, and other measurables were at the top of the heap, but what was particularly appealing was her bubbly personality. She was instantly endearing with a total stranger.

"Listen, Myleka, would you allow me to cut to the chase?"

"Okay."

"You've sold me in the thirty minutes we've talked. I'm opening a new office, so you have a chance to get in on the ground floor. To start out, we'd have me, you, and another accountant: somebody with plenty of experience. I have somebody to handle marketing who will bring in plenty of work. How does that sound to you?"

"Very nice, so…where is your office?"

Giving her the site of his new office, Peter told her the financial offer and then noticed the look on her face. "Is something wrong?"

"Eh…"

"Please be honest. Is it something I said?"

"No, of course not. This hard to say, but if a person of my race goes to a rural area, I've got to take that into consideration. There can be perils for me, like racial prejudice."

"One of my office girls is black and she's doing fine. I happen to think there will be no problem, but I understand what you're worried about. I hope you're willing to take my word we'll take care of you. In the unlikely event something comes up, I'll handle it. What do you say? You've graduated, so I'd like to get you moved right away."

She paused for a moment before deciding. "Okay, I'll trust you. You're sure this is what you want?"

"It is, and thanks for the trust. I'll make sure you don't regret it. I want to have a diverse workplace."

Chapter Nineteen

Peter stayed the following day to help Myleka make moving arrangements.

"Do you have a problem riding with me?"

"No, of course not."

"It will give us a chance to get to know each other. Also, I can get you a room at a motel until you get a place, but would you be agreeable to my parents' offer to stay at their estate in the meantime?"

"They would do that? I...don't want to impose."

"Yes, to answer your question. I can take you there and you can decide."

"Okay. That's very generous. Do they know I'm..."

"Black? Myleka, you can ditch those racial concerns because it won't be a factor. You'll understand when you meet them. Also, are you in a romantic relationship? Will it be a problem for you, moving right away to take this job?"

"I date, but I haven't gotten to that point with anybody. Maybe I'm too particular. I do seem to have my own unique tastes in that area."

"You're an attractive young woman; you've got your whole life ahead of you. Things will work out in that department."

"I hope so."

"Also, I've decided to look into a full-service office where we'll not only do accounting but also offer finance and investing services; and insurance services too. I know it sounds like I'm taking on too much too soon, but we'll work our way into it."

"I like challenges."

"I picked up on that in the interview, and it's part of why I hired you. Taxes are going to be our initial focus, but the rest will be coming down the pipe as quickly as I can manage it."

"I don't want to seem like I'm prying, but the paychecks?"

"Cash flow will come into the office sooner than you think. In the meantime, my dad is a wealthy man, and he's staked us with ample funds to grow into a thriving business. You won't have any paychecks bouncing."

"That's very good news. I'm just starting out, so I've got nothing in the bank and a bunch of student loans to pay."

"I understand. It won't be a problem. We'll take care of you. I'm thinking we get securities licenses, in addition to our accounting work. Are you agreeable?"

"Yes. I'll try it."

"As I understand it, we must pass a state exam and also a national exam for securities licenses."

"That's fine."

"I've done a lot of reading in the area. I think we can do some real good for people. It's funny: two of the most important aspects of life aren't taught in school—how to parent and how to handle money. I see that as a problem."

"I don't disagree."

"In our infancy as an office, we knock out the license tests, and I'm thinking we also get licensed for mortgages and insurance. As the business grows, we can hire and develop people to specialize in each area."

"You do have big dreams."

"Am I a megalomaniac? Probably so."

Myleka laughed. "I didn't say that."

"I'm just thinking out loud. I realize things don't always go well, but I'm diligent in pursuing my goals. I'll take care of everybody, so we won't go belly-up."

"I believe you. I'm anxious to get into this and see where it goes."

"I know you just graduated, so I'm willing to float an advance of some cash. You'll need money to get started. There's no hurry to move out of my parents' estate, but when you're ready, you'll have the wherewithal to make your move. Getting a car…there are a lot of reasons you need money in the till."

"You're incredibly generous, Peter."

"I just put myself in your shoes and think of what I'd need."

By the time they completed the drive, Myleka and Peter had established great rapport. She was comfortable with him and his promises. They even successfully discussed topics like religion and politics.

Meeting the parents, the Browns and Mariska, again Myleka was enthralled with genuine, decent, and generous people. "I so appreciate you taking me into your house. Your home is dazzling."

Edith replied, "You're welcome here as long as you like, dear."

"I've lost my parents and I am an only child, so this welcoming atmosphere means more to me than you can imagine."

"I'll leave you to settle in," Peter explained. "Tomorrow, we hit the ground running at the office. Dad will drive you over. We can go car shopping, so you have your own transportation."

"I look forward to it."

Peter drove straight to the office to meet Cliff. He was talking with Allison and Martha still.

"Hi, I'm Peter Brown. Thank you for coming in. Have the ladies explained my grandiose ideas?"

"Yes, and I have no issues with anything. Most of my experience is in accounting. As I told them, I like variety, so expanding into securities, insurance, and mortgages is an intriguing challenge I'm happy to tackle. I did a stint in my earlier years working with law enforcement in forensic accounting, trying to ferret out criminal schemes with their dirty money. It was exciting, in a way, as they always thought they were smarter than the law. That was never the case. We busted them every time and unraveled their schemes."

"Wow—that's almost like going off to war."

"Not really. I was in the background and never in danger. The big guys did the physical take-downs."

"My closest experience with danger was when I went to Russia with my wife to get her mother and bring her back here to America. She lived in a criminal-controlled small town. My dad hired these former *Spetsnaz* soldiers to protect us. They were the personification of *badass*. We were outnumbered, but they faced down the criminal boss and his thugs without blinking an eye. They could definitely do some damage."

"I'm sure that got your blood pumping."

"It did, and I managed to hold my water."

They laughed, along with the women.

"Anyway, I hired a woman who just graduated in accounting, so the three of us will handle the initial workload. I'll ask that you help me with training the office girls on doing simple taxes, helping answer any complex questions on the phone, and so forth. We'll get our various licenses right away and then open the flood gates. Allison is very good at marketing."

"I believe you." He eyed her admiringly.

"Myleka will be here tomorrow. You guys will all like her. She's good people. In the morning we'll be out getting her a car, but that shouldn't take long."

Martha spoke. "Peter, we had a first: our phone rang. It was a friend of your father calling to sit down with you."

"Fantastic. We'll celebrate tomorrow."

#

The following day, Myleka followed Peter, parking her newly acquired two-year-old Chevrolet Malibu beside his Mustang in the office lot. After the greetings, Peter stood up to address his new crew.

"This is exciting, getting us all together for the first time. I want to explain: the first 'sale' I'm going to make once I get securities licensed is to write a 401K for this business, so you guys have a retirement plan in play. I'll look into if I can swing including a doable pension plan too. I may need to work my way into that, depending on future cash flow. Obviously, if you want additional personal IRAs also, we'll offer those too. There are plenty of other plans for the future, like Coverdell ESAs for college funds for your children once they come along. When I say IRAs, that will include Roths. The distinction is pretax accounts reduce your taxable income each tax year, but when you take it out later, it's all taxable. Roths are post-tax, so it's free money when it comes out later. All retirement funds become available after age fifty-nine and a half. If you take it out early, there is a 10% penalty and it's all taxable income in that year. There are some hardship exceptions, but we can discuss the specifics later. I'll make contributions to your retirement plans. Any questions?"

Nobody said anything.

"Okay, so today Allison is heading out to start making contacts. The rest of us get busy. Cliff and I will start the tax training, and Cliff, Myleka, and I will start our own courses to get licensed. Today's lunch will be sliders from White Castle. In this office, we only go for fine cuisine."

Everybody laughed.

Meanwhile, half a world away, Anya talked softly with Kiala. Jeff was already gone to work; like always, he was first out the door of their joint house.

"Jeff is not happy…he keeps putting up barriers to impede our plans. Sonja and Marta are more than capable right now. There's really nothing more to teach them. They just need a little seasoning and they can plug in seamlessly."

"Did you expect otherwise, Anya? Jeff is in love with you. It's a condition he never thought he would experience. You're that unattainable prize he never got—do you see?"

"Why would I be different from the multitude of other beautiful women he knows?"

"You're the one who said no. He thought there was no woman he couldn't conquer."

"Well, he can't stop us from leaving. Do you agree?"

"Yes, it's frightening, though. We've all been together for so long, splitting up is unfortunate, if you grasp what I'm saying."

"Kiala, you know why I'm going home. I've missed out on too much time with my husband and daughters. If you want to stay with Jeff, you can certainly do that."

"Anya, you know why I would follow you anywhere and not stay with him. I love Jeff, but you're the center of my universe. Do you see? You matter to me."

"That's a nice thing to say. You're dear to me also."

"So, do you have a time frame in mind?"

"I see no reason to continue waiting. I'll talk to him today about the work transition and us leaving for home."

"I don't envy that conversation."

"It must be done. We're not his chattel."

Kiala chuckled. "What a way to put it. Chattel: where did that come from?"

"I read it in a romance novel."

"Would you like more coffee, Anya?"

"Yes, please. I've become so dependent on caffeine to get charged up in the morning."

"I also."

"Peter is a coffee drinker too. The smell of coffee is a part of mornings for me."

"I think everybody feels that way. The girls are three and two?"

"Yes, but their birthdays aren't that far away now. I want to be an at-home Mom when Elsa goes to school, so we've got a couple of years to work out our future careers. I've got enough money, but initially I anticipate being on the road traveling in the USA. Peter says I can work out of his new office, marketing like Allison. They've really expanded into many areas."

"Would Peter hire me too?"

"I wouldn't think it would be a problem."

Kiala handed a cup of coffee to Anya.

Anya replied, "Thanks. I've developed a taste for flavored coffee. Peter will only drink his coffee without flavorings."

"His loss, we know you need to expand your horizons, and tastes."

"He wouldn't agree. I think I might be too liberal for him now. I've evolved from the timid girl I was."

"Men are silly creatures. I'm not surprised. We women make sense."

"We make sense to us—not them. They believe women can't be explained or comprehended."

"There's undoubtedly some truth in that; however, we can say the same about them."

"He's called me fickle so many times. Am I fickle, Kiala?"

"That's a difficult question. I'd have to say define fickle."

They laughed and hugged.

Anya whispered, "You're so good for me, darling. You understand me."

"Likewise, you're good for me too. I can't imagine where I would have ended up if I'd never met you, and I can't imagine a life without you in it."

"Thank you, Kiala. That's so sweet. I feel the same way."

They hugged warmly before Kiala spoke. "Well, I guess we should hit the shower and get ready for work."

"You go ahead first, while I finish my coffee."

Anya sat at the table thinking about home rather than worrying about pulling the plug with Jeff.

"Allison…" she muttered. "Are you ever going to leave Peter alone?"

In the secrecy of her mind, Anya felt her own version of jealousy, though she'd never told Peter how she felt. For her, the fact he was completely trustworthy mitigated her level of angst, unlike what Peter always felt, worrying about her straying.

She smiled, remembering times she spent with the girls: her girls.

"My babies," she whispered. "I'm coming home."

There was no greater incentive to face down Jeff than that.

Kiala came out in her robe, toweling her wet hair. "All yours, darling."

"Thanks. I'll be out shortly."

Shortly a little later, dressed to the hilt, like always, the women looked at each other.

"You are such a beautiful woman, Anya."

"No more so than you. Let's go knock 'em dead."

#

Driving to the office, Jeff was always early to arrive. He was high energy when it came to the business.

He came out of his office to greet them. "Ladies, you look lovely."

Anya jumped in. "Jeff, Kiala and I agree it's time for Marta and Sonja to take over. They've been ready."

His eyes narrowed. "What are you saying?"

"We want to go home. I miss my girls, and I miss my husband. We've done everything you asked to get this operation on solid footing. Please don't make this difficult."

He glanced away. "Okay. If that's what you want. I thought we had a good thing."

"We do, but careers are only a part of life. I want my family life back."

He looked back at her with a haunted expression.

"Jeff, please. This is no rejection of you. I don't want you to feel badly."

"Too late."

"What is it you think should happen: I never go home? You must understand, I never wanted that."

"You know you caused me to think about things, like marriage and children. I can't imagine any other woman in that role for me."

"I could only see Peter as my husband, and that will not change. I'm sorry, but that's final. There was never going to be an 'us' in the romantic sense. Jeff, you can have any woman you want."

"Obviously not. You're the woman I want."

"Eh…" She looked at Kiala, who was highly provoked. Whether that was at the thought of her being cherished by Jeff or in defense of Anya's virtue, she wasn't sure.

"Anya, I can't stop you. If you want to go back to him, have at it." Jeff acted provoked.

"We're transferring back to USA operations; are you going to cause us trouble with that?"

"Of course not, I'm not some vindictive ass. Am I allowed to continue contacts with you?"

"Jeff, we're not severing ties; we're just changing our career paths."

"That being the case, we'll tell Marta and Sonja today about the change."

The women watched Jeff acting distraught for the first time they'd ever seen. At a loss for words, suddenly he seemed just another guy.

Anya continued. "We're very grateful for everything you've done for us. Don't think we're not. It's time for us to move to the next phase in our life journeys. I don't want to leave you feeling badly, but I don't know what else to say or do."

"Anya, I've held my tongue all these years, including back in college, in deference to you and your fine character. In this situation, what I would want is for you take off that wedding ring and choose me. It's selfish, not the best for you, but that's what I want. I don't expect it, obviously, but I wanted to say it so there are no questions in your mind."

Anya was affected by the statement and the proposition. Jeff, a man any woman would covet, did occupy a place in her heart, and now at the key moment, the time for them to part, she felt the lure and the draw. For a time, she battled her feelings and her mind as thoughts flitted to life about some questionable steps. The fact it could gain any traction frightened her.

Shaking her head at her feelings of lust she whispered, "No, no. I can't do that."

She walked away while she still could, against the escalating desires. Such lurid impulses she'd held at bay from the start…suddenly a young woman long without her husband struggled with them. Jeff had always been a strong lure for intimacy, and now, with the prospect of parting, her reacting body became her enemy.

"Hold it together one last time," she muttered, going into her office. Still, her heart was thumping at the near miss. Her mind punished with impure thoughts. *Going into his office and closing the door, who would know back home? Sneaking into his bedroom in the middle of the night?* It was too easy a rationalization for either scenario.

Immediately, she got on her phone to make flight arrangements back to the USA and hired a moving company to pack and ship her personal property. Making those same arrangements for Kiala, Anya walked over to her office to give her the data.

"Are you okay, Anya? You look flushed."

"My answer is yes and no. I'm not sure what's wrong with me, but suddenly I'm feeling crazy, like Jeff is…well…"

"Irresistible? I know the feeling. I'm going through it too. He's put out romantic feelers forever, and we've dodged the bullet. Why it's different now…I don't know. I'm in the same boat."

"Thanks, I feel better knowing it's not just me. It's good we don't have a long wait before we fly back home."

"Agreed."

#

The few remaining days passed routinely. Their temptations averted. Virtue intact, the women focused on going home.

"So, is it going to be a problem if I hang around?"

"No, of course not. Remember, Peter is still dealing with Allison in his grill, as you say."

"Well, if she doesn't back off your husband, now you can clean her clock."

Anya snickered at Kiala's joke.

"Anyway, I'm afraid we'll start out back in Seattle until we can work out some alternatives. Peter still says I can market his business. I don't see why you couldn't also."

"So we work with Allison?"

"I don't have a problem with it."

"You really trust Peter. That's very commendable."

"It's isn't me—it's a reflection on him. He's a moral titan and that's why I never worried about Allison. She could probably conquer nearly any man with her wiles, but Peter is strong in his choices. Jeff had a much better chance of his seamy victory than Allison did. I'm confident of that."

"Hypothetically, if Peter stumbled at some point in time, what would you say, and do?"

"I…eh…"

"See what I mean? That's difficult, isn't it? As strong as it was, the lure to stray before we left, almost stumbling to a love god, I always wonder when I hear people say they're immune to temptation. I don't believe it, but maybe it's just me that's weak."

"No, Kiala, you're not alone with weaknesses. I don't look at Peter the way I look at my own shortcomings. Everybody in the world copes with their temptations in their own unique way. Is there anybody alive who doesn't look back and say, 'I wish I hadn't said that,' or 'I wish I hadn't done that'? We all struggle at times and we don't always make good decisions. One thing all humans have in common is we're all fallible."

"We are that."

"Some secrets are best kept as secrets. No good can come from bringing them into the light. You know what I'm saying."

"You're right, Anya. Talking about that problem, I got some very explicit come-ons from clients. I just don't get that. They're married and still looking to score?"

"That is how some people are structured. They don't seem to have the moral compass that they should have."

"At any rate, it's over now. I'm anxious to get going and move to our next phase."

"I can't wait to hug my family again."

#

Peter felt like events were conspiring against him that day: the day they picked up Anya at the airport. He needed gas in the car, the girls seemed to pick up on the excitement in the air and acted out, calls were flooding into the office, with most callers wanting to talk to him…it was a zoo, so to speak.

"Cliff, you're going to need to take care of things for a day."

"Are you comfortable with me making command decisions?"

"I'll have to be, and I trust you. This isn't your first rodeo."

"Okay, as long as I get a pass. Essentially I know your plans, but I'm not you, and I wouldn't necessarily see some answers the way you do."

"I'll live with it."

At long last, Peter climbed into his car, with his daughters secured in the backseat. He was serenaded on the trip by Emily, although what the song was, he couldn't identify.

Elsa had enough before long. "Dad, tell Em to shut up."

"Elsa, don't say 'shut up'."

"How else do I get her to shut up?"

"You shut up," Emily retorted. She was well-versed in child speak by that time.

"You shut up, brat."

"Dad, Elsa called me a brat."

"Ladies, please. Let's enjoy our drive to the airport. Remember, Mom is home from Europe now."

"Is Mama coming back home to live?"

"I don't know, Elsa. She still has her job, so we need to make some decisions."

"Do I get to decide?"

"Mom has to make that decision, honey."

"That's not fair. She always goes away. I don't think she likes us."

"Of course she likes you. She's your mom and she loves you."

"Right."

Pulling into the airport lot, he parked the car and led his daughters by their hands into the international terminal. On the arrivals display, Anya's flight was listed as 'on time.'

"See, Elsa: Mom's flight is right on schedule."

"I'll believe it when I see it."

"What's with all the skepticism today, Elsa?"

"Just because we're kids doesn't mean we're stupid, Dad."

"Who says you're stupid? You're light years ahead of other children your age, and so is your sister."

Elsa looked at Emily.

"See how cute she is."

Elsa didn't reply. Peter took them into a terminal restaurant, where they were treated to small ice cream cones.

"Don't get vanilla, Dad. That's too plain."

"What do you want?"

Emily pointed to rocky road. Elsa pointed to orange sherbet.

The ice cream mollified the girls until they went down to baggage claim. As they glanced up at the board, it showed Anya's flight had landed.

"They're on the ground, girls."

Elsa finally started to get excited. When they saw their mother coming down the escalator, along with Kiala, the girls started to jump with excitement. Anya spotted them, smiled broadly, and hustled over, kneeling to embrace her daughters. Kiala came over to hug Peter.

"Hi. Did you have good flights?"

"We had a few bumps, but not too bad. It's good to be on the ground again."

Anya came over to hug and kiss Peter.

"I missed you so much," she whispered. "I'm done with living away. We're going to go to Seattle in the short term, but just to give notice and work out the details here."

"You can start at my office as soon as you like. Allison is already drumming up business, so the work is humming. I could see hiring a lot more staff in a short amount of time and expanding our footprint for as far as we find new business. You can still take business trips out of state as you desire, and you can stay around as often as you wish. I'm flexible."

"The idea of sticking around is very appealing right now. I want to be the mom in my own home finally."

"Did you hear that, Elsa?" Peter asked.

Elsa grinned and rushed over to wrap her arms around her mother again. Anya kissed the top of her head.

Peter picked up the suitcases off the conveyor and they headed for the lot. Both girls hugged their mom the entire way.

Sitting in his car with a wife beside him was a strange feeling after so long as the only parent in the car. Having Allison ride in that seat wasn't the same.

Anya was smiling, listening to her daughters' chatter at Kiala in the backseat.

"They speak so well."

"Anya, they got your brains. What do you expect? You better be ready for 'the' question."

"What's that?"

"Why?"

Anya chuckled.

"They ask 'why' about everything. I'm just giving you fair warning."

As if on cue, they heard Emily ask Kiala "Why?"

After driving first to the house to drop off the suitcases, they continued over to Grandpa and Grandma's place.

"By the way, one of my accountant hires is staying here. Myleka, you'll like her. She's fresh out of school, wide-eyed and gullible to my jokes."

"That poor girl," Anya replied with a snicker.

"Hey, she gets a paycheck from me, so she has to laugh at my humor."

"I repeat, poor girl."

Once Peter pulled into the driveway and opened the garage door, the family came outside to greet them. Mariska hugged her daughter and they talked in Russian for a time. Myleka waited inside to meet them.

Myleka smiled warmly at Kiala, like they had a separate wavelength. "Hello."

"Hi. I'm Kiala."

"It's nice that I'm not alone. I'm glad to see you."

"Hello," Anya said, stepping up to her. "Welcome to this family because now you are a part of it."

"I've come to realize that in a short amount of time. This is how everybody in the world should be to one another."

The household staff came out to hug Anya and welcome her back to the US.

After a sumptuous meal, they went outside as a group to walk about the grounds. Predictably, the little girls started running around, screaming like banshees.

Peter smiled at Anya. "They're all yours."

"I don't mind."

"Stay tuned, honey. The magic wears off pretty quickly."

"They've grown so much."

"Well, I kept feeding them, so I think that's why."

Anya chuckled. "You will always be a silly man. I love you so much, Peter. I'm sorry for what I've put you through since, well, forever."

"You're here now."

She took his hand as they walked.

"Mama, watch," Elsa yelled. She executed a cartwheel of sorts, though she ended up seated on the ground after an awkward landing. Emily laughed at her sister.

Peter clapped and cheered. "Way to go, Elsa." Anya clapped too, as did all the others.

She stood up and came over to hug him. "Thanks, Dad, but I know I stink at flips."

"You looked fine to me."

"You have to say that. You're my dad."

"Oh, I didn't realize that. I thought I was being honest. You're too smart for your own good, little missy."

Emily came over to hug him too. "Daddy," she said.

Kiala and Myleka stood by, smiling appreciatively at the loving display of family.

Kiala stayed behind, taking another of the guest bedrooms in the estate, when Anya drove home with her husband and daughters. Having his wife all to himself was a pleasant development for Peter. "Wow, Anya. I could get accustomed to this."

She smiled. "It's very nice."

"I look at you now, this glamorous, stunning woman you are, confident and in control, compared to that hesitant girl I met in the beginning. It's an amazing transformation."

"Is that a good thing?"

"It is. I'm not a man to be intimidated by the success of women—quite the opposite. I relish your success. It's given you the feeling of validation I think you were always looking for. You've proven to yourself what you can do. There's really nothing you can't accomplish. If you're ready, we can work together from now on to make our mark with our own business."

"I am ready."

"Allison gets back tomorrow. What are your feelings there?"

"Am I jealous of her? No. I never have been."

"She's been a big help all of these years you've been gone, but at the same time, I had my hands full dealing with her goals, if you get what I'm saying."

"I do. Do you want me to…how do you say…kick her ass?"

Peter laughed heartily. "That's not necessary, darling, but thanks for the offer. I'm wondering if you guys can mesh and work together without any problems."

"I have no doubts we'll be fine. She was our friend back in school. We'll simply pick up where we left off. I like your new girl, Myleka."

"She seemed perfect. All the candidates were great, but Myleka had a little something extra. It's hard to explain."

"I understand. I think we will be very close friends. In some ways, she reminds me of Kiala."

"That's good, honey."

Chapter Twenty

For Peter, what had started out as such a complex puzzle in meeting Anya, finally those puzzle pieces were falling into place. At last, he could foresee a happy outcome, although there were still steps to be taken.

He worried about mixing Allison into the new paradigm, hooking up Anya and Kiala with the marketing and advertising piece. Her unchallenged ownership of that aspect was about to change.

As the entire "family" of his business gathered at the office for their first combined meeting, Allison smiled and hugged Anya warmly, and then hugged Kiala. For Peter, he had his opinion as he watched the greetings that Allison was pretending graciousness.

"Good morning, everybody, this is a new day and the start of a new era for our little enterprise. I feel we've assembled the perfect staff to pull this off. I realize I'm asking a lot from all of you, but this won't be a job in which you'll be sitting bored and watching the clock. What we all have in common, I think, is we love challenges. Soon you'll be asked to help train even more new employees as we expand. I'm confident in our road team and once they bring the business to our door, we have the best people available to bring home our promises to our client base. Already our phones are ringing steadily, and once Anya and Kiala get to work out there…we will be jammed, and that's just what I want. I doubt there are any questions, but if anybody has one, raise your hand."

There were no hands.

"Okay, so let's saddle up and knock 'em dead."

Anya, Kiala, and Allison followed him into his office.

"I hired a woman to handle our corporate travel. It won't be like what you have with your current company, but she's experienced and I think she'll do a nice job."

"We fly to Seattle tomorrow, but I don't anticipate a long stay," Anya explained. "We've made our decision."

"Do you have anything, Allison?"

"No, not really. Did you have a plan for how we coordinate? Is someone in charge to make decisions?"

He looked at the three. There was no doubt of the "who" Allison imagined in that role.

"I guess we decide that when you ladies get back from Seattle."

"Okay. I'll take Anya and Kiala with me for my stops today so they see what's involved."

"Good idea."

Anya smirked at Peter as she walked out of the office. These three incredibly beautiful young women were now the faces of his company.

The instant they turned on the phones at nine, calls started. True to his vision, the busy workday passed rapidly.

Myleka was forced to learn on the fly, as there were more inquiries than Cliff and Peter could handle alone. By the end of the day, they were tapped out.

"Are you okay, Myleka?"

"I survived. It's invigorating, but scary too."

"You did great," Cliff said. "Each day it gets easier."

"I hope so. I don't want to let you down."

"No worries," Peter answered.

His three "reps" walked in the door at six. Nearly everybody was still at their desks, wrapping up the work from the day.

"So, I don't see any black eyes. I assume everything is copacetic."

Allison smirked, "What did you think: that we'd have some territorial throw down?"

"Pretty much."

She chuckled, along with Anya and Kiala. "Chick fights: why are men such blockheads?"

"We'll never know," Anya replied. "It must be some male thing."

"So, ladies, have safe flights out west, and I'll see you when you get back."

"Goodbye, Allison, and thank you. It was a great day, traveling with you."

"I think we all see the possibilities. I'm excited for so much more. You've expanded my horizons."

"Likewise, I think this will be fun."

"I can see why you two clicked so well. Now we're a threesome and I can't wait to get after it."

After she left, Kiala went to the Brown estate, and Peter drove his wife home. "Really, was it okay out there?"

"Certainly, what Allison does isn't so different from what we do."

"I meant between you guys."

"Peter, don't worry. We're fine."

"I hope so. Allison really liked pretending to be the mom. She got a lot of personal satisfaction mothering our daughters. I wonder if she can relinquish that role without a fight."

"I'll deal with it if she does. It was me who went away to pursue my selfish goals. If I have a price to pay, so be it. I'll be patient with her feelings. Allison is an asset for our business I would never squander. If she needs an adjustment period, I have no problems with it."

"That's an optimistic approach. I hope you're right."

#

Dinner at home, cooked by the actual mom for the first time, was its own kind of adjustment.

"I like grilled cheese," Emily said.

"You can't have grilled cheese every night," Peter answered.

"You're a baby," Elsa whispered.

"Dad," she complained. "She called me a name."

"I heard. Be nice, girls. Eat your food."

Anya sat down and the four grasped hands for Peter to say grace. "Dear Lord, bless this food for our bodies and nourish our spirits with the bread of life. Show us your way and guide us down your path so that our lives can be pleasing to you. We ask this in your precious name, amen."

"Amen," said the others.

Anya eyed Peter warmly. "You're a good man, Peter."

He shrugged but smiled in return.

In the morning, it was sad to see Anya leave to go pick up Kiala to go to the airport.

"Mama, you said you were staying," Emily said.

"I'll be back soon, darling." Anya knelt down to hug her little daughter.

"Promise?"

"I promise."

Elsa stood back, eyeing her skeptically.

Elsa then hugged her dad for a feeling of security.

Parting ways, Peter and the girls returned to their usual routine, coping without Anya.

#

Meanwhile, Anya and Kiala departed for what they planned to be their final trip to the company headquarters in Seattle.

To their great surprise, they were greeted by Jeff, who'd flown in from Berlin.

"Jeff, what are you doing here?" Anya asked.

"Senior management wanted to include me since we all know one another so well. I suspect they can see what's coming from you."

"Jeff, it was a very difficult decision, but we've made our choice."

"Well, you can try to explain it to them. I'm here as your friend. I've missed you guys."

"We miss you also, but all of these years Peter and my girls missed me. Do you see?"

He eyed her thoughtfully for a moment. "At any rate, let's go. You're first up on their agenda this morning. Are you up for dinner with me tonight?"

"Okay."

Anya was shocked when they filed into the conference room. Seated before her was the senior leadership in the corporation.

"Hello, ladies," said the CEO, Michael Marstan. "Thank you for joining us. Before you address us, I'd like to say we're impressed with what you've done here for us in your spectacular careers. You're remarkable young women in your own right, and as a team you were perfect complements for each other. Although we suspect you've decided to move on in your careers, we want to discuss that choice with you. Perhaps there is a way we can all come out of this well."

"What are you saying, sir?"

"What would you say to spear-heading an office back in your home state? We would offer a ridiculous salary because we know you'd make it back for us many times over. You could live at home with your family and still continue your career with us. I do want to mention that in your current contract, if you leave, you're required to give two weeks' notice, so you'd need to stay here to work out those weeks."

Anya looked at Kiala. "I don't know what to say."

"Well, at the very least, you've got two weeks to think about it. If you give notice today, you'll have that time to ponder if you want to change your mind."

"That's a generous offer. Neither of us thought about such an idea. We would like to give notice. My husband's new business, we're looking to work there."

"We can look his way with our considerable business, which will guarantee his smashing success."

"I'll call him tonight to talk about it and see what he thinks. If I stay here working for this company, even though I live at home, I'd still be on the road traveling all of the time. I wanted to be a part of the daily lives of my children."

"Life is decisions, Anya. No matter what direction you go, you'll always have choices to make at inevitable forks in the road."

"That's true, sir, but I wasn't ready for this fork in the road."

"Kiala, what do you say?"

"Obviously Anya and I are close. We've chosen to remain a working team. Whatever she chooses, that is where I go."

"So be it. Let us know whatever you decide. I'll let you spend the day with Jeff."

They left the meeting in a different temperament than when they entered. It was a twist of the plot neither woman saw coming. Suddenly the decision wasn't so certain.

"Did you have a hand in this, Jeff?" Anya asked.

"I received a call and was asked to share my thoughts and opinions."

"You led them to believe we could be swayed."

"Only you know what's in your heart and mind. Listen, I don't discount your husband and children, but there was always something else percolating, and there still is to this day. That day you showed up at my dorm back in school, the rapid escalation in mutual feelings when we dated, your strong impulses when you left Europe, and, oh yes, I knew you were strongly considering…"

"Jeff, please don't make this difficult, and don't make it about that."

"I'm not doing anything other than stating the obvious, Anya. I saw it in your eyes and how hard it was for you to fight it. That's means something. Because your husband is a wonderful mate, does that mean no one else is also? You know better than that. We were very close to…going in a new way in your life."

Her face reddened. Kiala eyed him frostily.

Jeff was nonplussed, smiling with confidence. "It's no secret you captured my heart long ago, and if you're honest, I think I captured yours too. What you felt was I couldn't be a husband and father, like Peter. Are you sure about that? Perhaps, you failed to factor in the life we would have had, and I guarantee it would be beyond your wildest dreams. I've got plenty of satisfied partners who can verify I'm not just blowing smoke up your skirt. You know literally I can rock your world—I would rock your world, baby."

"Jeff, I…eh…why are you doing this to me?"

Kiala chimed in, "Excellent question, Jeff. Why are you doing this to her. You had your shot and she chose Peter. He's the father of her daughters and she couldn't ask for a better person."

"Thank you for your opinion, Kiala, but why don't you butt out. You can see by the look on Anya's face this is a decision she's rethinking. Don't think I don't understand your feelings and the stake you have in it."

Kiala bristled, but Anya replied, "Not a smart move in attacking Kiala, Jeff. We three have been close for many years, but you've put that relationship in real jeopardy with this approach. When you say 'it,' I don't know what the 'it' is you're referring to, regarding Kiala."

"Life is choices and risks. If I want the best outcomes for both you and me, now is the time for me to lay it out there. I'll leave it the same way Michael left it. You've got two weeks here to think about it. You have the option of staying here, with me."

"That's not going to happen," Kiala said ruefully.

"Are you sure?" he asked with a smug smile. Anya's face was red again. "Anya, you've given him more than his due. He's got two children out of the deal, but now it's time to think about the best life for you. I can be a great dad too. If you want those daughters, I'll help raise them, and of course, our own birth children would be superior. Look at our genetics. Say the word and we replace that ring you're wearing with a better one. I'd go with you right now to file for divorce, and then we marry the instant you're free. We can have our wedding night as soon as you'd like. I don't need to wait. No-fault divorces can be done in less than a month, sometimes a couple of weeks. It would be a wedding night for the ages you would never forget, so much better than your first one."

Kiala looked at Anya, shocked she didn't instantly dismiss the proposition out of hand. Anya seemed frozen in stasis. Could Jeff be right?

Kiala grabbed her hand and literally dragged her away. That seemed to snap her out of the funk.

"Anya, what was that? You can't seriously be considering going with Jeff. Do I need to state the millions of reasons why?"

"I…don't know what happened…why it got to me this time. I mean, it really got to me. What if he's right? He does appeal…in that way. What did he mean, what he said about you and your feelings?"

"It's not hard to figure out. He's implying I want you…for myself."

"Huh? What does that mean?"

"It's how he looks at things, Anya. Maybe it's his fantasy…girls together like that?"

"Do you mean…oh—oh my."

"Don't waste time on his silly barbs. He was trying to rattle you."

"He succeeded."

"And he was tossing bombs at me because I stand in his way too. We just left your real life, that wonderful man and those two little angels. Lock onto that. Maybe this is some cosmic final test for you to pass. You can do what's right. Can you envision sitting with Jeff in a church, doing wholesome things? You know what he would do to you; it would be like stringing together eternal one-night stands. You don't need that kind of life."

"I'm sorry for being so weak."

"He's a supreme seducer; it's mostly on him. You're not alone. I'll help you."

Anya remained feeling out of sorts nonetheless. She called home that evening to advise Peter.

"I'm sorry. We're stuck here for the two weeks. I didn't see that coming. I'm going to be honest with you. Jeff has made a proposition, for me to go with him and be his wife. I can't believe it, but there it is. Of course I rejected it. The one thing that might be of interest in this situation is that the company CEO made an offer for Kiala and me to open a new branch back home, so I could live with my family. Is that something you want to consider? Obviously, they're talking considerable money and complete control of the operation."

"I think that decision is yours to make, Anya. I suspect it would involve far more travel than you'd have working at my company. Of course, I'm sure you'd have periodic meetings at home office, and that means more exposure to Jeff. This proposition he's made—do you finally see why I was worried all of those years? He has you in his sights, and I think he will never let it go. Yes, you can say I'm in the same position with Allison, but I don't have the feelings for her that you have for Jeff. Please be honest because I'm not naïve or stupid. The truth is his come-on was a strong lure for you, and difficult to dismiss."

"My feeling is it's a reflection on the difference in our characters. You're so much stronger as a moral person than I. I shouldn't be tempted."

"Anya, that's wrong. Anybody can be tempted. Allison is beautiful, and very alluring. It's nice for my ego that she values and cherishes me. I've had impure thoughts too, but neither of us acted on those impulses. You're all that I need in my life."

"Kiala said maybe this is some final cosmic test."

"Well, I know my choice."

"That's my choice too, husband. I love you and I'm sorry he could affect me."

"As I said, I want you, so no matter what happens, I'll be here waiting. Just remember that verse in the Bible, *Get thee behind me, Satan*."

"You deserve a wife as perfect as you."

"I'm not perfect: a long way from it."

"I'll be home when this couple of weeks is over, honey. Hug my little girls for me."

"I will. I love you too."

Anya felt better after hearing his voice and the supportive things he said. It helped her immensely and she resolved to end this, once and for all.

When she went to talk privately with Jeff, he had an amused smile.

"You don't need to bother, Anya. I already knew what you'd decide. I just had to make the effort. Will you forgive me?"

"You don't look repentant."

"What can I say? It was true what I said about loving you. I suspect it's my one and only trip down that path. Going back to who I was, that's probably the path I was destined for."

"Oh, Jeff, that's not a good idea. There are other wonderful women to be your wife and the mother of your children."

"I've never lost in romance before. It's a shock to my system."

"I'm sorry. I made my choice, and I don't want to change. I need to make up for all those years I took away from my family. I was selfish."

"I know. Don't worry—I'll cope with this and get through it. You do what you've got to do."

He embraced her, but this time in a friendship way. At last, Anya had been freed. Her face was filled with relief. How close she'd come to accepting his pitch still shocked her. She still had to blank her fantasy, surrendering to him for the best sex of her life.

#

Flying home later, Anya met her family feeling like a new person.

Peter saw it. "You seem at peace, honey."

"It's like I've shed a heavy burden that's weighed me down all this time. I didn't realize the subtle ways Jeff had a hold on me. For the first time, I can honestly say I've put it behind me. I decided to work with Kiala to open a new branch here for the company. You don't really need us. Allison can train others to help her. We're familiar with our work, and there are a lot of rewards waiting for us."

"Okay. We can make it work."

"Thank you, Peter."

"Mama," Emily said, wrapping her arms around Anya's legs.

"Hi, darling, I'm glad to be home."

"Can we get ice cream?"

Her parents both chuckled.

"We don't want to spoil your dinner, baby girl."

Peter added, "We don't need a sugar buzz and a little girl climbing the walls."

"Oh, Dad," she complained.

#

Life in the Brown household settled into the new routine. Having a mom when the girls went to school later, just like the other kids, helped immensely.

For Anya, the glitzy life with Jeff on the road, the cocktail parties, the come-ons from clients, she didn't miss. In her new office, she opted to train other reps to do the road work. Initially, Kiala went out to guide and train them, but as they got up to speed, she too spent her time in the office.

Her operation was the success everybody anticipated, and her ample accumulations of money continued to grow. As a surprise to her, Peter insisted she amass her earnings in her own name, and they were eye-popping.

His business success was no less impressive, as his plans panned out perfectly. Peter and Anya were well on their way to duplicating George and Edith's prodigious financial success.

Anya birthed two more children, two sons for Peter: Robert and David, and then finally another little girl, Bethany, whom they called Beth.

Peter loved all of his children, but Beth had that special "something" that made her his favorite.

Once her personality developed, he told Anya, "She's just like you: brassy, sassy, too smart for her own good, and lovable beyond words."

"Is that good?"

"Of course it's good, honey."

"I never thought I'd have so many children."

"Is that a bad thing?"

"No, it's just surprising. I'm happy, Peter."

"You're my dream come true."

"Of course, when we go to do anything, it takes me forever to pack up for this mob. No fancy sports car for Anya. We drive this big clunky suburban."

"Sorry, honey. I just can't stay away from you."

"You know I'm joking, Peter. Russia seems so long ago. I shudder to think what would have become of me and my mother, if I'd never met you."

"Things worked out as they were supposed to."

#

Allison and Jeff finally gave up their quests to break up the Browns, and once that happened, they both got married rapidly. Birthing children also came quickly in both cases. Kiala met a man, as did Myleka, and later they also got married.

For Peter, his life of trials and tribulations seemed to be over, at long last. Fighting the good fight, so to speak, had paid off in the end. It was soothing with Jeff married; he could feel that threat was over. Anya seemed truly happy now, and content. It helped Peter feel the worst was over. Reconnecting with college friends, they could enjoy companionship with Bob and Christy, and their children. Mariska was happily entrenched with Edith and George. Even Megan reappeared, with a husband and kids, a totally changed person. She and Allison became friends, along with those two families.

#

As years passed, their children were the focus in their lives, and in the center of it, Anya and Peter were particularly taken with little Beth. She battled for her place in the big family. The youngest, she showed great tenacity coping with older siblings and the predictable jibes she got from them.

Later, on a visit to the Brown estate, when the children were inside with the grandparents, Peter went outside on the back patio to sit and sip coffee with his wife.

"Anya, all of those difficult years, I worried I wasn't good enough. When you would tell me things, I couldn't seem to get past the feeling you were saying expedient platitudes to mollify me and that down deep, your sights were set elsewhere. Do you understand?"

"I do. You dwelt on that feeling, and it was clear to me. It was never you. In me, there was immaturity, curiosity, and yes, I was lured by…"

"The 'Jeffs' of the world."

"Of course, but as I grew up into a woman, and after spending time in their world, yes they knocked on that door of intimacy—that's no secret. Was I interested in letting them in, I think is what you're getting at?"

"It wasn't that I didn't trust you; I didn't trust them. With Jeff, he was a master in working a woman. I thought he would find a way, no matter how long it took him."

"He could never force me to do seamy things, Peter."

"You miss the point. He isn't a man who needed to force anything from a woman. He had plenty of them working to rope him. Do you get the distinction? It's like all those past women who dreamed about a George Clooney, for example. He was a fantasy in their minds instead of a real person. They ascribed all the positive attributes to him in their fantasies, and he wasn't around to disprove them—do you see? There's no such thing as a perfect man."

Anya chuckled. "Are you saying women are unrealistic?"

Now it was Peter who chuckled. "What I was trying to get at is now I can honestly say those issues are gone. Finally, I can say I know in my heart how you feel. I no longer fear some hidden agenda, a worrisome business trip with hanky-panky. I'm being honest. I worried about that a lot during all that time you were away."

"Well, thank you so much." She spoke sarcastically.

"I didn't mean it as a slam, honey. I'm trying to say, your contentment, it's my contentment too. I never would have had another woman, but I finally realize that as my wife, you'd never have been with another man. That's a game-changer for me."

"Peter, I'd never pretend I didn't make mistakes, but crossing that line was not going to happen. When I married you, I made a promise for life, and I've never regretted it."

"Of course, the consequence for both of us is we're the parents of those five hooligans. God help the world when Beth comes of age. We thought Elsa and Emily were testers, but Beth will wreak havoc."

Anya laughed. "Oh Peter, you will always be the silly man—my silly man."

The End